W9-BJN-227

IMAGES

IMAGES

IMAGES

a novel by

Cara Saylor Polk

❖

ST. MARTIN'S PRESS / *New York*

IMAGES. Copyright © 1986 by Cara Saylor Polk. All rights reserved. Printed in the United States of America. No part of this book may be used or reproduced in any manner whatsoever without written permission except in the case of brief quotations embodied in critical articles or reviews. For information, address St. Martin's Press, 175 Fifth Avenue, New York, N.Y. 10010.

Design by Laura Hough

Library of Congress Cataloging in Publication Data

Polk, Cara Saylor.
    Images.

    I. Title.
PS3566.O475I5 1986   813'.54   85-25170
ISBN 0-312-40916-8

Grateful acknowledgment is made to the Paramount Music Corporation for permission to quote from the song "Silver Bells" by Jay Livingston and Ray Evans. Copyright © 1950 by Paramount Music Corporation. Copyright renewed 1977 by Paramount Music Corporation.

First Edition

10 9 8 7 6 5 4 3 2 1

To my newsman husband
and all our IRE (Investigative Reporters and Editors) friends
and bloodhounds,
with special thanks to Marion Goldin
whose encouragement and enthusiasm
let me keep the faith in my own images.

IMAGES

. . . and then the mirror trembled so terribly . . . shattered into a hundred million million and more fragments . . . and these flew about in the world and whenever they flew into anyone's eye they stuck there and . . . saw everything wrongly. And the demon laughed till his paunch shook, for it tickled him so.

—Hans Christian Anderson
"The Snow Queen"

One

❖

THE COLD WINTER SUN filtered through the frosted window. Marlena lifted her hand from the white table linen and held it up against the light. Opaque. Slender enough for her eyes to trace the long, narrow bones extending from the fingers to the wrists. But she couldn't see through it.

At six years of age she had spent long hours beside her great-grandmother's rocker, begging the frail lady with the dim eyes and sweet smile to raise her ancient hands to the light. Grandma Emma's hands were soft and dry and fragile. The skin was so thin that Marlena's small fingers could follow the veins up to the lace at Grandma Emma's wrists.

Grandma's hands were magically translucent. How six-year-old Marlena had wished for hands she could see through in the light. At forty-one she was in less of a hurry.

"Grading your manicure?"

Marlena swirled her pale curls. "Roger. Roger Marley!"

"Do that again," he said, smiling. "You look like a shampoo ad."

"Silly to the end." She shook her head as she surveyed

1

him. She'd have recognized him anywhere. In a crowd or alone. He looked older, but after over twenty years, less changed than she'd expected.

His sandy hair, now brushed with gray, fought to curl above the large, pale gray eyes. It's still a shame to waste those lashes on a man, she thought. As tall as she remembered, but thicker in the middle, fuller, filling more space in an attractive way.

He stood, hesitant.

She smiled, half in greeting and half in amusement, at his obvious indecision about what came next. "Please, Roger. Sit down." She extended her hand.

He sat opposite her and allowed her hand to hang in midair a moment too long before he reached across the table, narrowly missing toppling the single red rose.

Coolly, she avoided his hand as she lifted her wineglass to her lips. "Traffic problems?"

He glanced at his watch. It looked very gold and very real, she noticed as he said, "Three minutes after one. I call that amazingly punctual."

"In my TV world it's called disaster." She laughed easily.

That broke the ice as Roger relaxed and joined her laughter. "If it weren't for that subway construction outside, I'd have been early, but the side door's boarded shut."

"That's the price we must pay for sitting so close to my historic spot. The first story I covered when I got here from Chicago last year was the indictments involving the company drilling away over there. That was the case that toppled the labor secretary. Remember?"

"Of course I remember. I'm not that forgetful. In fact, I'm not a bit forgetful."

She tensed, on guard. She'd arrived determined to keep this lunch date light and easy. Her eyes slid from his face to the expensive fabric of his well-tailored tweed suit and the monogram on his left shirt cuff. "It looks like you're doing well as always."

"I'm doing all right. Staying off the dole, anyway. No," he answered the unspoken question, "I wasn't disinherited. It simply occurred to me one day that it was time to cut myself loose from Father's purse strings."

"Really?" That was out of character for the Roger she remembered.

He nodded. "Now it's come full circle and I've turned into Alison's doting, coddling parent."

"And that's why you asked me to lunch? To see if I could find Alison a nice, protected summer job at IBS?" When Roger's call came through, like a buried memory from her emotional grave, he'd mentioned his daughter was interested in TV reporting.

"She's not quite eighteen. She's so young."

She could be my daughter, Marlena thought, not wanting to feel old enough for that. As she turned back the wheels of memory to when she and Roger had been a campus "item," it felt like a hundred years ago, but it was as clear in her mind as the glass in her hand.

"She claims she wants to commit herself body and soul to TV."

There was the echo again.

"I think," Roger continued, "that she should sample it first. Even you started out as a part-time gofer, right?"

"Right. In the pits." She nodded thanks to the waiter and accepted the menu, which felt too weighty for a light lunch, and stared sightlessly at the French calligraphy, listening to the origin of the echo.

New York

"I think you've sold your soul to IBS," Roger stormed. "All you do at the station is pour coffee and answer phones. What difference will it make if you call in sick?"

Static electricity crackled as she diverted her emotion into brushing her fine hair.

Roger fiddled with a moth hole in his heather Shetland. "And I thought you promised to sew this thing."

She swung around from the mirror to inspect. "Sorry. I simply forgot. It's been a crazy week. And I do more than pour coffee and answer phones. Research. You know as well as I do that I am doing real research on rent control." She pulled a rubber band around her long sandy hair and snapped it with decision.

"Of course I do, since I'm the one who told you where to find the relevant cases."

"Your help was only a tiny part of it. I'm the one who spent hours and hours poring through the city directories."

"Let's not argue about it. Tonight's important to me. The Law Review awards are a big deal, and Professor Mendel's invited us to go out afterward."

She noticed without comment that he hadn't mentioned her help in editing and typing his award-winning articles. "Roger, I'm really sorry, but Dave needs my research tonight. He starts taping interviews tomorrow."

"Lena . . ." Roger reached for her, grabbing her around the soft waist, kneading a moment, out of habit.

"Stop. I hate that. It reminds me I have to diet. You lured me off on too many fattening picnics this fall."

"Glorious, sunny afternoons untouched by restraint." He pulled her into a bear hug, whispering in her ear, "I love you. You're as important to me as any law award could ever be. And I want you both tonight."

She fought the physical attraction that always weakened her resolve. "My not going along to the Law Review dinner won't make any difference. You'll still get the award. Hey, Rog . . ." She hugged him hard before stepping away from his arms. "I'm proud of you, really. And if I could get out of work tonight, I would."

"Would you? Ever since you started working for that stupid little TV network, you've been off in your own little world. If you're going to make it into law school the year after next, you better pay more attention to your own studies, too."

She hurled a pillow across the room, knocking down a Kennedy campaign poster. The carefully framed souvenir shattered on the floor.

"Damn!" Marlena stomped across the parquet to look. "Ow!" She backed away from the broken glass and plopped down on the bed to examine her foot.

"Let me see." Roger knelt beside her. He pushed against the side of her foot. "Does that hurt?"

"So now you're a doctor, too?"

"That's how we started," Roger said, laughing, giving her ankle a tug. "How quickly they forget."

Marlena's reciprocal chuckle acknowledged the soft memory. As a freshman volunteer, she had tripped, dashing into the campus Kennedy headquarters, twisting her ankle. Roger, fair and handsome in his slender, angular fashion, had come to the rescue, posing as a medical student. With his handkerchief and masking tape, he had bandaged the offending ankle, neatly printing CRIPPLES FOR KENNEDY on the makeshift cast.

"We started with bullshit." She accepted his handkerchief to daub at the blood trickling from the ball of her foot. "God, my feet are filthy."

"They wouldn't be if you wore shoes . . . and you wouldn't have cut yourself."

"Thank you, Doctor Fraud." Gingerly, she took a test step.

"But you have to get any glass out. It could infect."

"I don't have time and it's just a little sliver. It'll work itself out." She frowned and limped past the glass, leaving a tiny trail of blood spots to the bathroom. "At least this way you can keep track of me," she tossed over her shoulder.

Roger used a *New York* magazine to push the fragments into a glittering pile.

Three minutes later Marlena reappeared, dressed in a red tweed skirt and red sweater. "I decided to match my blood."

"Yeah?" Roger dropped the magazine atop the broken glass. "I'd say you're acting pretty cold-blooded."

"I'm being responsible."

"No. You're being stupid. Your part-time job for extra money we don't even need always gets in the way of our plans."

"*Your* plans." She sighed. "And about the money, how many times do I have to tell you that I need my own money?"

"I don't see why it bothers you where the money comes from. It doesn't bother me," he said laughing, "as long as it keeps coming."

"It should," she snapped. "Are you planning to let your father support you forever?"

"Why not? He can afford it." Roger grinned. "After we've both passed our bar exams, we'll be able to scrape by with just a nice subsidy."

For the past year she'd floated along without plans of her own, listening to his plans for their life together, granting them no more reality than shared daydreams.

With his prodding, she'd taken the preliminary LSAT and was delighted that her high score made him happy. It meant she could probably get into Columbia Law School. Law was interesting, but not her passion.

Roger was both, despite the ups and downs they'd had since she'd taken the part-time IBS job over his protests. Coming home to him and the three-bedroom Riverside Drive penthouse still held the excitement she'd felt during the fall of her sophomore year when he'd announced he was turning her into his "three-fer" by kicking out his three roommates, all for her. How could she have refused such a flattering offer?

"Lena, you're turning into a real bitch," he said as he tossed the magazine in a corner.

She felt bad. She didn't want Roger to be in a dour mood for the awards banquet. She wanted him to enjoy his honors. She thought quickly, went into the kitchen, grabbed a hunk of salami and cheese, plopped them on a plate, and carried it into the living room, bowing. "Fair maiden make atonement to god of love. Beg forgiveness."

"Fair maiden will have to do great penance before moon crosses sky," he growled, "and get our poster reframed tomorrow."

"I will. I promise."

"And quit that stupid job before it destroys everything."

She didn't reply as she rushed out to the old metal elevator with the ornate wrought-iron doors and descended twelve floors into the November rain. She shivered and tightened the belt on her old tweed coat.

There was no point in going upstairs for an umbrella. She'd lost both of theirs.

She ran five blocks to the subway, the memory of the scene she'd left behind sour in her mind. Roger deserved better. But he wanted so much of her, she was losing room for herself. Nausea fluttered through her, reminding her that she hadn't eaten. Maybe her body was telling her it couldn't stand conflict.

Dripping into the IBS studio, she plopped the disintegrating manila folder on the desk she shared with the other student assistants; she peeled away the soggy cover to inspect her precious pages of research.

Special Reports Producer Dave Winslow peered over her shoulder. "Marlena, you didn't have to sweat over the stuff that much."

She groaned at the pun. "That's my ninety percent perspiration you say must accompany my ten percent inspiration."

"Thanks for all of it." Dave lifted the sodden report page by page, noting the names, addresses, and phone numbers of landlords and tenants. "This is good stuff, kid."

"Do I get a bonus?"

"I think you've already gotten it."

"How?"

Dave handed her a carbon of a letter he had written to WWKB-TV, a small IBS affiliate in Wilkes-Barre, Pennsylvania.

Marlena skimmed the copy, smiling at the adjectives—"industrious," "bright," "eager." "That's nice, Dave, but I don't think anything will come of it. They'll probably laugh at my demo tape."

"Don't knock the demo tape. I personally directed it for you."

"But I've never been on the air."

"Tom Wells doesn't know that. With the news set and outdoor locations, it looked like the real thing. Hey, you better make a good impression at your interview. I went out on a limb for you with that tape. I think you could be a good reporter and you have to start somewhere—even if it's Wilkes-Barre."

"What interview?"

"See? I told you you'd make a great reporter. You don't miss a thing. Tom Wells, the general manager of WWKB-TV, called me this afternoon. He wants to see you in Wilkes-Barre on the twenty-second, the Friday before Thanksgiving."

"Dave, that's fantastic! I sent the demo tape to the address you gave me, but I felt about as hopeful as when I buy a lottery ticket." She hugged him. "I can't believe it. Thanks, Dave!"

He smiled at her enthusiasm. "Tell you what. Take that Friday off, with pay. Tom will reimburse your bus fare. It's only a couple of hours' ride. Your interview is at noon."

"Oh, no."

"What's wrong?" Dave's gray brows knitted.

"I have that day off. Roger is taking me to Palm Beach." She didn't add that it was the weekend Roger wanted to announce their engagement to his parents. "Do you think I could change the appointment until after Thanksgiving?"

"Tom sounds like he wants to make a fast decision. He's down to three applicants. If you're serious about it, you'd better do it now."

"Roger will kill me if I don't go with him. And I'll kill myself if I don't try for the job." She looked sodden and woebegone.

"Welcome to the grown-up world." Dave patted her shoulder. "There will always be watershed moments. Think about it overnight. I told him you'd call to confirm tomorrow afternoon."

"Thanks, Dave," she said, still more depressed than elated. "I think this is what I really want. I just wish I were sure."

Dave picked up Marlena's report and tossed her a dime. "Now, go earn your keep and get me some black coffee so I can stay awake to digest all this stuff."

"Any news tonight?"

"Nothing earthshaking. The Soviets have arrested a visiting Yale professor for espionage, but I don't think that will affect the rent-control debates."

Marlena watched her stocky mentor disappear into his small office. She glanced at the TO DO list on the interns' desk. But she had a bigger decision she could not avoid: Palm Beach and Roger, or Wilkes-Barre and a shot at a reporting job. Her stomach lurched. She rushed for the ladies' room, gagging.

Maybe she was catching the flu. More likely she was reacting to the inevitability of a decision. God, she hated personal confrontations. She felt cold at the thought of life without Roger. To prod, amuse, spoil. And demand. And mold her into his image. "My thirteenth rib," he once called her. Only a little funny.

Roger. She didn't want to jinx her chances by telling him about the interview, not unless she got the job. In her mind she could hear him argue that it was dumb to drop out in her junior year of college, dumb to go to Wilkes-Barre for anything, a fool's decision. She knew all that. But the brass ring was too close. Not to ride the wooden horse for one spin, one grab at it, was to deny all the potential she believed she had.

She rinsed her mouth and hurried to the coffee machine. She swallowed hard as the thin brown liquid filled the cardboard cup. It smelled terrible.

Dave glanced up from her report as she placed the coffee on his desk. "This is good work, Marlena." His dark eyes rested on her pasty face. "But you look terrible. Are you catching a bug?"

"I'll be okay," she muttered.

"At $1.90 an hour you don't have to play Saint Joan. Go home. You have enough to worry about tonight."

"I'll go lie down in the conference room for a while. If I don't feel better, I'll leave."

Dave looked concerned. "Stick your head in before you go. And take a taxi. It's nasty out there."

"Thanks, but I'll be fine."

In the dark of the conference room Marlena collapsed on the fake leather couch, shivering against the chill of it. She should have brought along her coat. Should have, should not have. It seemed she spent half her mental energy second-guessing herself. She should never have moved in with Roger, should never have filled the spot she hadn't known was empty. She should have shared the good moments, but stayed less involved.

So many good moments. Tap dancing together on the library steps. Becoming the amateur theatrical couple—her Eliza to his Henry Higgins. His sense of the dramatic and whimsical matched that side of her so well. But on his terms. His love was on his terms. She was the one expected to mold and curve. It was never articulated, simply assumed.

She felt bloated, mentally and physically. Dave was right. She went home to bed and pretended to be asleep when Roger got in. She forced her body to be still while her mind whirled, trying to figure out how to tell Roger that Palm Beach was out for her.

The next morning Roger forced gaiety, parodying the dean's remarks and Professor Mendel's pompous "atta-boys." She pushed herself for lighthearted replies, which rang false to her ears. Roger didn't seem to notice as he dashed out for his nine A.M. class. She could breathe again.

She needed space to sort out her thoughts. Her stomach fought the Cheerios she'd forced down in her attempt to keep the morning normal.

She couldn't sit through class today. No way. She dug behind the spaghetti boxes in the white wood cupboard and pulled out the antacid. She'd poked fun at Roger for his morning-after swigs. Now she was grateful for his leavings. She gagged on a mouthful, but held it down. Nothing was easy this morning. Not even relief.

She let the phone ring. She wasn't in the mood for Emily's endless cheer or her mother's curiosity. She wondered if her mother would be as happy about the Wilkes-Barre job as she was about the part-time IBS one. Marlena laughed at herself. She didn't have the job yet and she was already worrying about Maggie's reaction.

The phone stopped ringing. She washed and dried the breakfast dishes quickly and turned to the living room. She wanted to put physical order in her life; perhaps mental order would follow.

In the bedroom she pulled open Roger's top drawer and felt for the small, blue velvet box. The diamond. It was huge, over two carats. He'd wanted her to wear it when he grandly presented it on her birthday, November 1, but she'd insisted they wait until their families were told. He had balked, but finally agreed. She'd been relieved, but she'd also felt flattered and thrilled and warmed. She blushed to recall the long, unrestrained night of making love.

How many places had they made love in the past two years? In the science lab, stealthily, hilariously. In a service elevator, standing up while Roger held the CLOSE button. Hundreds of times on their patchwork-quilted bed, laughing to think what her Aunt Louise, the quilt-maker, would have thought. Under blankets on picnics. At the beach. In Roger's vintage MG. Tongues, hands, bodies meeting and merging wherever imagination and lust kindled.

She made the bed mechanically, her mind turning to the slip of paper in her wallet. She reached for the phone.

The voice of Tom Wells was deep, warm, welcoming. He looked forward to meeting her. The tape showed promise. He gave her specific directions from the bus station. "Any problems?"

"Could I possibly come earlier in the week, say Wednesday the twentieth?"

"Let's see . . . No, I'm in Philadelphia for meetings through Thursday."

"Late the next week.?"

"I want to fill the job by the weekend. If you're seriously interested, Friday's the day."

She assured him she was more than interested and promised to be there on schedule. She held on to the phone as if it were a talisman. He'd said the tape showed promise. Her mind swarmed with images of herself covering everything from political campaigns to mob murders in the Poconos. What else was there around Wilkes-Barre?

Suddenly the job seemed more possible. And Roger more impossible. He'd have a fit, but he could come to Wilkes-Barre weekends for the next year and she could look for a job in New York TV after he finished law school. She'd have real experience by then.

Her daydreams of compromise felt unreal. She knew Roger too well. He'd consider her moving away and not going to law school a personal betrayal. He'd paint it black-and-white, either-or.

The phone interrupted her uneasy conjectures.

"Where were you?" Emily's voice demanded. "You weren't in Theater History this morning!"

"Just beat. And I feel a little queasy."

"Too bad. *Breakfast at Tiffany's* is playing at the cheapie matinee and I thought you might like to catch it."

"We saw it last week," Marlena said giggling. "Great fluff. We bought doughnuts afterward and ate them in front of Tiffany's."

"Rog should buy diamonds, not doughnuts, at Tiffany's."

"You're the most mercenary romantic I know." She almost told Emily that Roger had already given her a diamond, but stopped. Telling Emily was the same as a public announcement.

"Well, if you won't play truant with me, I guess we'll have to go to Poli Sci after all."

"I'm not going to make it. I'm going to lie low. My stomach still feels god-awful."

"Hope you're not pregnant," Emily chirped. "Did you hear Maryanne Snyder is? She and Andy are getting married next week. I didn't think they were a serious item, but I guess they are now." She rattled on about the love lives of other classmates while Marlena listened with half an ear.

Emily took life so lightly, Marlena thought with envy. Nothing disturbed her endless cheer. Certainly not social issues. Emily's solution for the ghetto problem would be interior decorators. At least Emily had the sense to pick a career that fit her personality—display design. Marlena thought that Emily and the windows at Bloomingdale's would be very happy together.

"Well," Emily concluded, "I'll check with you after class to see how you're feeling."

"Remember to take notes for me and my stomach."

A lot of good having a doctor for a father and a nurse for a mother does me when I don't even know what pregnant feels like, she rued, suddenly wondering if Emily's joke could be real.

She had to know. If she were, it could ruin everything. Even without Wilkes-Barre.

She called the friendly neighborhood gynecologist. No emergency. Regular check-up. She tried not to admit panic. Next week. Fine.

La monde c'est bleu comme un orange. Her paper on Gide was due Friday. She might as well get some work done. Was the world blue *as* an orange or *like* an orange? The interpretation of the preposition *comme* made a world of difference—a nonblue world or an orange world.

She couldn't concentrate; she needed a plan. Soften him up first and get him in a good mood. Maybe make him duck with the orange sauce he loved so much. Gide's blue oranges would have to wait, she decided.

Savory aromas and candlelight greeted Roger as he came in from his five o'clock Contract Law class.

"Hey, what's the occasion? Was Poli Sci called off?" Roger kept better track of her schedule that she did.

"I'm celebrating not getting the flu." She laughed. "I felt rotten so I stayed home, nice and dry. We both benefit."

Roger was delighted with the duck, and she kept postponing broaching her changing plans. When he began talking about the trip, singing "Nine days 'til sunshine, Nellie," she couldn't bring herself to burst his bubble.

"Are you sure you're ready to have your mother meet me in person? Have you forgotten about the tantrum you said she threw when your sister told her we were living together?"

"Hey, that was a year ago. And we're going down to tell her we're going to get married, that I'm making an honest woman out of you. Don't be so uptight. She'll love you."

"What should I talk to her about?"

"Anything. Just be yourself. There's only one taboo," he cautioned. "Don't make your own bed. Mother says that's a sure sign of people who aren't accustomed to servants. They make their own beds."

Marlena sighed. Pediatricians' families in Des Moines didn't starve, but they hardly had servants who made beds. Not that the beds in the relaxed Williams house were always made. "I'm sure I can remember not to make a bed," she said laughing. "And I can always discuss recipes."

"Bad idea. Mother doesn't cook. Clothes are a better topic. Or talk about me. She loves to talk about me."

"Am I supposed to look forward to all this?"

"You and my father will hit it off. He'll love you. Just don't tell him I do dishes. You'll ruin my image."

"You do scrub a mean kettle."

"Only because you burn them so well. I keep telling you, we're a great team." He snapped a damp towel at her.

"Who can remember every little burner every minute?"

"I've no complaints." He looped the towel around her waist and pulled her close. "I'll never throw in the towel."

"You're silly. Maybe you should go into politics. It's a perfect place for comedians."

"Who knows? I could if I wanted to. Would you like to be a senator's wife?"

"Maybe I should ask you if you'd like to be a senator's husband?" she retorted.

"You'd better stay away from those women's rights folks. They don't like men."

"Don't worry, I'll never have that problem." On that note, her problems all unresolved, she proved the point in their bedroom.

"Let's not go to Palm Beach," she whispered before they went to sleep. "Let's stay here, catch the shows we haven't had time for, go to museums."

"You're being female and silly. There's nothing to be nervous about. Mother's not a complete dragon. We'll have a great time, you'll see. Besides, you need the tan."

"Mmmm . . ."

"Lena . . . it doesn't matter what she thinks. I love you. That's all that matters."

"I hope so."

"Now cuddle up and go to sleep."

That was easier said than done. She watched Roger peacefully sleeping long into the night.

On Wednesday, two days before the scheduled departure, Marlena saw the doctor. Far from discounting the possibility of pregnancy, he insisted on tests, promising a report by Monday.

On Thursday night, one day before departure, Roger came home with champagne and an armful of roses, oblivious to her allergy to the flowers. "I'm getting you in the mood for my mother," he announced.

Marlena chewed on her antihistamines and said nothing. "We scream inside when we whisper to the world," she wrote in her diary, but she wasn't even whispering her darkest fears. And long before Monday, she had to face the Palm Beach dilemma.

The worst thing was that she was fully aware she was

compounding all her problems by not confronting them. "Up front with it," was her father's favorite phrase. "Most mistakes aren't tragic unless you run away from them."

She pictured her balding father with the twenty extra pounds and the twinkling blue eyes behind gold-rimmed glasses. If it turned out she was pregnant, he'd berate her for primal stupidity—*urdummheit* was his Teutonic phrase—but he'd help if she hollered. Her mother would rally too. But how could she tell them? She wanted them to stay proud of her.

After the champagne bottle was emptied Roger began packing. He was only taking a small carryon for books to read at the beach. He had piles of summer things in Palm Beach and had instructed her not to bring much. They could buy what she needed down there.

Then he noticed she wasn't packing at all. "Dammit, Marlena. We have an early plane to catch. Get cracking."

She answered by bursting into tears.

"Hey? What's this?" He sat beside her on the bed and put a tentative arm around her. "Lena?"

"I can't go with you," she said sobbing.

He withdrew the arm. "That's nonsense. They're expecting us . . . expecting you."

At the sound of the word *expecting,* she cried harder. What if I'm really expecting? she screamed in her mind. They wouldn't be expecting that.

"Get hold of yourself, Marlena," Roger ordered.

She struggled for control. "It's this job interview . . . for next semester. It just came up. I tried to change the appointment, but the only day they can see me is tomorrow."

Roger turned, incredulous. "A job interview! You want to muck up our vacation because of a stupid job interview! What does it take to get it through your thick skull? You don't need to work, not now, not ever. I can support both of us through law school."

"I'm not sure I want to go to law school."

"You know what the problem is? You can't stick to any decision or make up your mind about anything!"

"All I know is that I don't like you making up my mind for me without giving me a chance to think it out for myself."

"You're acting like a three-year-old."

"At least that's my choice." She watched Roger stamp out of the room. Curled up, she welcomed the sleep of emotional exhaustion.

Morning dawned with a chill. Roger was still seething at breakfast and she was too tired to think about how to appease him.

"Well?" He was glaring. "You still aren't coming?"

"I'm sorry you won't understand," she whispered.

"You know you're just being stubborn, don't you?" In exasperation, Roger threw her airline ticket on the table. "Lena, I want you to come along. I don't understand the big deal. If the job's right for you, if it's meant to be, it'll still be there later."

"That's not always true and you know it. It's always a question of timing . . . and luck."

"Well, your timing stinks," he snapped.

She didn't answer, her irritation rising to realization that he'd never even bothered to ask anything about the prospective job. All he cared about what she did was whether it fit into his plans.

Roger tried another tack. "You act as though I'm asking you to do something terrible. Sun, relaxation, a few laughs. Tell you what, fly down Monday morning, all right?"

"I still haven't finished my Gide paper," she said, hedging.

"You never did intend to come along, did you?" He stared at her. "You can be a real bitch, Lena."

"That's not true. I was planning to come with you until the interview came up and then I put off working on Gide and . . ."

"Forget the excuses. They don't wash." He grabbed the airline ticket and stuck it in his pocket. "I'll get Randy to come along. At least I can always count on *him*."

"Sure, as long as you pick up the tab," she snapped, piqued. Randy the leech, one of the many who swarmed around Roger. Like the others, Randy was a more dedicated friend when his pockets were empty. Roger couldn't see it. He thought of himself as a leader of young liberals, while they saw him as a free lunch.

She cleared the table, mocked by the pink roses she'd carefully arranged in the old cut-crystal glass, a reminder that Roger was so self-centered he couldn't even remember she was allergic to flowers.

She left the dishes in the sink unwashed and the bed unmade, then ran a hot bath in the deep old tub. The steamy bathroom felt claustrophobic as her unhappiness closed in around her. She sank into the warm water and turned on the hot-water tap full-blast, letting the temperature rise. She had a flash of a body lying in fluids, the first long soak of the mummification process. Maybe she craved some final solution.

Refusing to dwell on such morbid matters, she concentrated on preparing her body for the process of living, trimming her toenails and shaving away the fine, light hairs disclaimed by society. She was a liberal, but could never join the hairy-legged set. Mother Maggie, old cleanliness-next-to-godliness, had gotten there first.

Next problem: what to wear. Warm, bright colors might help. The pink cashmere with the soft pink and gray plaid skirt. Knee socks? Not for this. Nylons and the gray suede heels Maggie had bought for her under protest. "Gray suede looks too old," she grumbled. Now she was glad she had them.

If she landed the job, she'd tell Maggie the shoes had clinched it.

She brushed her hair, thinking the way she wore it was all wrong. It made her look too young, long and fine, streaming down her back like Alice in Wonderland. But this was no time for second-guessing. Tom Wells had the demonstration tape. She couldn't go looking like a different person.

The bus to Wilkes-Barre, shabby, with a pervasive aroma of stale smoke, left on time. Her attempts to read on the bus were futile.

She kept rehearsing answers to unknown questions. Yes, she was dedicated to becoming a TV journalist. She had been working for IBS for three years—a lie Dave had promised to back. Or had they agreed upon two years? Yes, she could take the job right away. She had enough credits to graduate early, at the end of the fall term. She need not mention that was fall term *next year*. She could finish them up later, anywhere.

What did Tom Wells look like? She had forgotten to ask Dave. She knew Dave had worked under Tom when Tom was IBS's bureau chief in Chicago ten years before.

Dave said Tom was one of the best in the business, that Tom would be running IBS's network news if he hadn't let booze and women interfere. "Three ex-wives, or maybe it's four," Dave had said with a laugh, "but Tom says he likes the Wilkes-Barre operation. He's getting a kick out of working with young reporters and he's proud of the ones he trained who have moved on to major markets. The old video gunslinger. He probably puts notches in his belt." Marlena loved the image. Someday, a notch for her.

The trip seemed interminable. The old bus rattled into Wilkes-Barre at 11:49, twenty minutes late. WWKB was only three blocks from the bus station, according to Tom's directions. She had plenty of time.

The place was easy to spot. "Factorylike building. Takes up half a block. You can't miss it," Tom had said. Factorylike was kind. There was the feel of a warehouse to the crumbled corners of brick and the old metal stairs leading to a second-floor entrance. The ground floor was fronted by three steel garage doors with loading docks.

Inside things were more encouraging. An effort had been made to modernize the wide old hallways and cavernous rooms. Bright graphics in primary colors swirled on the walls, integrating photos of the WWKB news team. Marlena caught herself visualizing her own photo there, and fought back the image, not wanting to push her luck.

The gray-haired receptionist, glasses resting on the tip of her nose as she leaned three inches above an old typewriter, didn't notice when Marlena entered.

"Hello," Marlena croaked. Thank God the lady didn't look up. Her heart was pounding. What if Tom Wells had already given the job to someone interviewed earlier in the day?

The slender woman looked up. A warm smile softened her pointed features. "Hello, dear, I didn't hear you come in."

Marlena returned the smile and explained her mission. "I know I'm a little early. I can wait."

"I don't think you'll have to." Her tone dropped to become conspiratorial. "I'm afraid the last interview didn't go well at all. The poor boy left after five minutes."

"That's great! I mean, that's nice, because perhaps Mr. Wells can see me early." She stumbled over her words.

The woman chuckled. "I understand. My name is Anna, Anna Feinman. My husband is Dr. Feinman at the college. I'm the mother hen around here."

"My father is a doctor, too, a pediatrician in Des Moines."

Anna's laugh was merry. "My Arnold is a Ph.D. in history. But he should have been a pediatrician. We have five children."

"You're in great shape for that." The comment slipped out.

"Thanks, but the youngest is twelve. I've had time to recover."

Marlena fidgeted. If Anna prattled on, Marlena would be late instead of early.

Mother Anna picked up the body language. "I'll ring Tom."

The place seemed informal. Anna and Tom, not Mrs. Feinman and Mr. Wells.

Tom came out to usher her into his office. His stride was rapid. Emitting a nervous energy and a faded charm, Tom was in his late forties. The contrast between the friendly dissipation of his face and his dark, wavy hair made him look older than if he had grayed on schedule.

He sat her in the sole armchair in his large office and studied her silently. Remembering Dave's briefing, she perceived him as a sculptor studying a new lump of clay.

Then he spoke. "Your delivery isn't bad, but it needs work. We can tighten it. You photograph well enough, but after you lose fifteen pounds you'll be dynamite. How are you on records?"

She looked blank.

"Researching. Records," he said impatiently.

"I've been plowing through rent-control papers and leases at the courthouse for a series we're doing at IBS." She tried to sound professional.

"That's a start." His smile was engaging. "I like to think of myself as a good mentor."

"Dave said there's nobody better at teaching young reporters."

"Dave said that? That's nice to hear. Dave and I go back

a long way. He was best man at my second wedding. Or was it my third?" He laughed at himself. "I do better with young reporters than wives."

"That's nice, since I'm looking for a job as a reporter, not a wife."

Tom laughed and made a check mark in the air. "You don't smoke?" He lit a cigarette from the burning ash of another one.

"No." According to her mother, smoking made allergies worse. "Only when I'm mad," she added.

"I'll remember that." He glanced down at the papers on his desk. "I've seen them all, all the 'eager, fine young applicants.'" He mocked the terms. "And I've about made up my mind."

"When do I start?"

"That sounds pretty cocky."

"Hopeful." She smiled, realizing she wanted to reassure and please him. "I really want the job."

"Let's go to lunch. It's twelve-thirty and I need a break. You have time?"

"My bus doesn't leave until four."

"Great. We can walk."

Tom led the way through streets of fine Victorian mansions grown shabby to a large brick Georgian building housing the University Club.

"Wilkes-Barre has more poor than rich," Tom said. "It never recovered from the advent of oil. It began as a mining town, and when people stopped using coal for home heating and the market fell out, not much came in to take its place. You have the usual doctor, dentist, lawyer, county seat stuff, but no major industry. The college helps. And the congressman got some lung benefits through for the old mining people, but sometimes I feel like there's more a-dying than a-borning here."

"The Chamber of Commerce must love you!" She laughed.

"I only want you to know this ain't New York City. You will be underpaid and overworked; and starved for entertainment the few hours I'll give you off. We only have three reporters on staff—you'll make it four. Two are just out of school like you, Fred Riggens and Larry Goldman; and Clarence Argotti is a retired navy intelligence guy on a nice pension so he doesn't notice the starvation wages. Clarence does all the sports stuff.

"We have two regular anchors—Michael Brandt, the old pro come home to retire, and Ed Puchalski, the local kid working to get away. Millie Meyers, cheerleader-turned-weather girl. A few cameramen, engineers. Anna, you've met. A couple of secretaries. That's about it . . . except for my right-hand man, Alan Cameron, news director. You'll report to him."

It seemed to Marlena that Tom controlled the news operation. What was left for Alan Cameron?

"We have two film cameras," Tom continued. "One works at a time, if we're lucky. Most of the stuff is done in the studio while the reporter reads the story."

"Dave says low-budget operations make a reporter creative."

"And frustrated." Tom chuckled, motioning to the middle-aged waitress. "Help, Sadie. A double martini," he ordered. "Marlena?"

She almost said "Tea," but quickly replaced it with "A Bloody Mary." She didn't want to come across limp.

"Fear not, Sadie. She'll be drinking double Scotches before the month is out."

Sadie didn't look worried; she didn't look as though she had time to care, being the only waitress for all twenty tables.

Tom gave a casual, unwelcoming nod to an enthusiastic "Hello, Tom" from a small, watery-eyed, phlegmatic type two tables away.

"The college's PR assistant," Tom explained softly. "He's pushing us to run a series on the school—on the news, no less," He sipped and studied his martini. "Everyone wants free promotion. Small markets don't have fewer headaches, just smaller, more persistent ones."

Tom's hand trembled as he lighted a cigarette.

Sadie skidded to a stop beside them. "Ready to order?"

"Special of the day?" He asked Marlena. "Feel courageous?"

"Fine. You know the food here."

Sadie sped away.

"This place is my main kitchen. The cook is better than any wife I ever had." As Sadie approached, balancing their platters, he added, "Faster, too." Then he frowned at the broiled fish Sadie plopped in front of him. "Cook on a diet again?"

"He's lost five pounds this week," Sadie said.

"Bring us a double order of fries." Tom patted his rounded stomach. "Let him suffer alone."

"What kind of stories do you do?" Marlena munched on the bland fish, perfect for her nervous stomach.

Tom poured catsup on his. "Anything will help," he muttered as Marlena grimaced. "The usual small-town stuff. City Council meetings. Water commissions. Zoning stuff. Visiting politicians. High school awards. Murders, mostly domestic. Proclamations from the mayor. We're big on weather. There are still a lot of farmers around. Farm shows."

"Is the police beat open? Or the courts? I'm interested in law."

His answer was a huge guffaw. "With five reporters— two of them anchors—there ain't no such thing as a beat. You'll do it all—*if* you can do it at all."

"If?"

"I'm giving you the job on a six-week trial. Tell Dave I agree you have potential, but also tell him his dummy demo tape wouldn't fool a mud hen in heat. This is your first time out, kiddo, and you'll have to work your tail off."

"I know." She hoped her nod looked mature. He had no idea how much she would sacrifice for that six-week trial. She would make it. "When do I start?"

"I need you a week ago. We've been stretched since our former lady reporter had to go have herself a baby. And she's not coming back on the news. I will not juggle baby-sitters with the news. She can go write for the paper if she insists on working full-time." He was obviously continuing an ongoing argument. "Maybe an afternoon talk show. We'll see."

"I can't start a week ago."

"How soon can you? Mrs. Shannahan's rooming house is a block from the station, clean, cheap. My secretary can check if there's space for you. If not, we'll book you in the old hotel, but the rooming house is better. Trust me. They say the hotel is ready for renovation. Demolition is closer to the truth."

She hated to talk about money, but Tom had not and she needed to know if she could afford the job. "How . . . how much will I make?"

"A hundred a week to start with and one twenty-five if I sign you on after six weeks. It may not sound like much in New York, but it's damn good for starting in Wilkes-Barre."

She did some fast mental multiplying. Six thousand a year. That was decent.

"Mrs. Shannahan's costs about twenty dollars a week for a room—forty dollars if you eat there. She has good food and nice people for tenants. You can't beat it."

The money was no problem if she could make it through the next week.

A crash from the kitchen sent their heads swiveling in time to see Sadie run into the dining room, arms flailing in awkward directions.

"The President has been shot," she wailed. "It's on the radio. He's been shot in Dallas."

Tom snapped to attention. "Where's the radio?"

Dazed, Sadie turned from the startled diners and ran back into the kitchen, her Irish heart breaking.

"I've got to phone." Tom raced off into the kitchen. He was back within minutes. "I'm off. All hell's breaking loose. Sounds bad. Call if you have problems. Otherwise, December second. Nine sharp." He was gone.

She restrained the urge to race after him; she would only get in his way. But how would he handle it on the local level? Would he send out reporters for reactions?

Sadie burst from the kitchen, choked with tears. "They think he's dead."

Then the emotional reality struck Marlena. It was more than a big story, it was her President, dead. A shudder of horror chilled her.

She felt isolated. Like Sadie, she wanted to scream at the wrongness, but Marlena didn't want to be with strangers. Did Roger know that his hero, their hero, had been gunned down?

Suddenly starved for details, she joined the small crowd of customers huddled, frozen, by the kitchen radio. "As the President's motorcade turned into the Plaza, shots rang out. Texas Governor John Connolly has been wounded. The President, sitting bareheaded in the back of his limousine beside the first lady, is believed to have been shot in the head. Reports coming from the hospital give little hope. It is believed the shots were fatal. We switch you now to the Plaza where . . ."

The room felt too small, the people too strange. She wanted to go home, back to New York. She hurried out, needing air.

On the street she felt too alone. She turned a corner

and saw a general variety store, went inside, and emerged with the cheapest portable radio she could find.

She huddled on a dark wooden bench at the bus station, clutching the radio, letting the tragedy fill her mind. By the time she boarded the bus Lyndon B. Johnson had been sworn in as President. A day of changes, she thought, and her decision felt small in comparison.

On the bus, grief and shock gave way to remorse. They'd hoped so hard during the campaign three years before. The poster. She'd never replaced the glass. Too much had broken.

The phone was ringing insistently as she entered the apartment, dusty and weary from the high and low of the day. She flicked on the TV before she answered, knowing the phone would keep ringing, knowing it would be Roger.

It was. "Where have you been all day? I've been calling and calling ever since I heard."

"Out. Wandering. It's terrible. It's hard to believe."

"Where were you when you heard?"

"On a bus," she lied. "With strangers. A kid had a radio blaring music and they broke in with the special bulletin."

"I can't believe it. And I can't believe Johnson's the President now. It happened in Texas. Do you think he had anything to do with it? Isn't Connolly one of his good-old-boys?"

"I don't know." She didn't care at the moment.

"My organized-crime professor told an anecdote last week about a mobster getting shot while he was walking down the middle of a street with another guy. The professor said the worst thing that happened to the other guy is that he wasn't touched. It doesn't look good. Watch. There'll be a cover-up."

"Roger, you read too many thrillers. They have the assassin in custody."

"I need you here, Lena, now. You could take the morning plane and be down here before noon."

She could if there wasn't the other major question still to be answered: Would the rabbit live or die? "I still have the Gide paper, Rog. And I'm glued to the TV."

"It's too unreal on TV. We should meet in Washington for the funeral, so we can say our farewells in person."

"I don't want to stare at some casket. I'd rather remember him the way he was when he visited campus. So alive. He seemed surrounded by such energy."

"Charisma. I felt it too. It's like a Greek tragedy. The death of a king . . ." Roger rambled on, mixing his allusions.

"Rog, don't you want to hear about my interview?"

"No. The only thing I want to hear is when you'll arrive."

Personal frustration overshadowed the national tragedy for her. She fought back tears. She needed comfort too. The plastic phone felt cold and distant.

"Marlena . . . Lena . . . are you there?"

"Mmm." She sniffled.

"I'm broken up too," he said. "We need each other. Promise you'll take the morning plane."

Her tears froze. "You always think things are so simple, Roger. It never occurs to you that other people can't do things as easily as you. In case you forgot, you gave my ticket to Randy and I don't happen to have money sitting around in an egg jar to buy one."

"No problem. My father's secretary in New York can buy one for you. You can pick it up at his office. Problem solved."

Letting him solve the problems his way was easier, but she didn't like feeling bullied. She paused, forming her response.

"Marlena . . . Marlena . . . are you there?"

"I'm here."

"You'll take the plane tomorrow, okay?"

The spoiled little boy wanted his own way. "I'll see. The earliest I can come is Monday. I still have work to do."

"You'd think that Gide paper was the Holy Grail," he complained. "But all right, you can take the first plane Monday. I'll arrange it and call you in the morning."

First thing next morning, Saturday, she took a chance and found that the doctor's office was open. If all was well, she thought, she could fly down Sunday and surprise him, but the rabbit had died, along with her hopes that things might turn out to be easy.

She packed her things quickly and retreated to the empty dorm room she let her father finance rather than face his disapproval of her living with Roger.

The room felt cold, a cell in which to contemplate the cost of carelessness. She forced herself to face and check the alternatives.

A long-distance call to the clinic suggested by the kind nurse in her doctor's office found the clinic open and available. It was also expensive. Five hundred dollars worth. How could she afford it without asking Roger for help?

Her head swarmed with different images of his reaction. He might be furious at the thought of a shotgun wedding, hardly the kind his parents would like. But then he'd help her pay for the clinic. She hated to used the words *abortion clinic*, even in her mind. But he might insist they get married immediately and that would close off all her options, especially Wilkes-Barre.

Then she thought of the ring.

On the way downtown to the West 40s, Marlena couldn't pull her eyes away from the three toddlers in the subway car. Their bright, round faces brought a new chill of reality to her day.

Worth thousands, the ring brought $875 at the pawnshop. It would be tight, with plane fare and food, but possible. She could make it to Puerto Rico for a Tuesday morning "procedure," as they called it. Everything had fallen into place so easily. She told her conscience, it was an omen; the choice was fated.

Monday night she entered the unmarked clinic, hidden in adobe sameness on a side street of Old San Juan. Somewhere in the air she'd passed over Roger and his parents' beach house. She didn't like to think about it.

The clinic, with its pervasive antiseptic odor seemed professional, impersonal. But the rooms were clean and private. And the nurse who discussed the procedure made it sound like having a wart removed. Her thoughts were sinister, but the place wasn't.

Early Tuesday, unconscious of the beach-bright skies, she was handed a white robe and led into Dr. Cordez's office. She steadied herself, exhibiting a calm belying her tension.

There was no general anesthesia, only a local painkiller, no chance to wake up and call it all a dream, no sleep for self-delusion.

"Roger," she whispered in her mind as the first numbing needle entered, "why didn't you notice anything?"

Everything felt messy.

The silver probe was a cold intruder. She felt shamed and invaded.

Twelve minutes later she was wheeled to the recovery room to rest, alone and empty, oblivious to three other girls on cots. Each was staring at her own corner of the green walls. Marlena had no small talk in her either.

Past and done, she thought. She had made her bed, or unmade it, she thought wryly. Now she was free to become the best goddamn reporter Wilkes-Barre had ever seen.

By midafternoon she felt well enough to explore Old San Juan and browse through the small colorful shops in the narrow back streets, replete with marble steps and rusty iron railings.

She heard herself humming "Roses are Red," Roger's favorite. Unwillingly, she recalled a romantic night in a cozy, family-run Spanish place on the Upper East Side. There had been roses on the tables. But she was allergic to roses and she'd turned her back on Roger's gardens.

She idly entered a shop that sold hand-embroidered blouses. Food or adornment, take your choice, she thought, noting the twenty-dollar tags. Without warning, she doubled over as a sudden severe cramp hit her, followed by a wrenching pressure and then a release, as though a wall had ruptured inside her. She felt liquid pouring out and looked down to see blood drip beside her open sandal. A flash of shame greater than the pain sent her running from the shop, fighting vertigo as she ran the long two blocks to the clinic and inside to the nurses' station. "Help. I'm hemorrhaging."

The young nurse quickly examined Marlena and assured her it was natural. "Only the afterbirth, the placenta and unformed fetus. You should have been told not to go out—to expect it." She made it sound clinical, acceptable.

"You'll be fine." She gave Marlena a sisterly pat. "You can have many more children later. When it is better for you to have them, yes?"

Marlena stared at the dark massy clots. There was no personality to it. But she wished the girl nurse, with the soft Latin accent, had not said more *children*.

It could have been a child. Hard truth. She had an irrational urge to try to put it all back inside her and make it right. She loved Roger; she would have loved their baby. The word, even as a thought, sent her into tears.

"Is there something I can do for you?" asked the young nurse.

She shook her head. There was nothing the nurse could

do. It was done. Dead. And Roger was dead to her too. She'd given up more than she had thought.

Conscientiously, she would keep her commitment to redeem the diamond, putting aside money from each small paycheck. The ring was her symbol of guilt.

When she reclaimed it in late summer of 1965 she felt a sort of atonement, as though she were also redeeming her integrity. But she never sent it to him.

Two

MARLENA'S HAND STRAYED from the large menu to her Mark Cross purse, a world apart from the patchwork satchel that had borne the diamond from the pawnshop.

Almost whimsically, she'd tossed the worn blue box in her purse that morning. The box had felt light, uncharged by adolescent follies. It was time to return it. Marlena Williams, network star of "Later . . . on IBS," should be big enough to let bygones be just that.

But the ring and the memories attached to it gained substance in Roger's presence. She felt Roger's attention on her hand and she opened her purse, feigning a search. "Oops." She looked up at him. "My lighter is on the table." She reached for a cigarette. "Dumb me."

"Is that the price you pay for turning blonde?" He smiled and offered his Dunhill's flame. "I'm amazed at the way you've reversed the effects of time. Blondes turn brown; you went from sandy to blonde."

"Have you gotten caustic with old age?"

"No, only gray. I'm just jealous because you're not."

"I wouldn't know if I were." She laughed.

"You are far too young anyway." There was twinkle in his eye. "I read the *TV Guide* article all about the thirty-five-year-old anchor . . ."

"If I weren't a grown-up, I would throw my wine at you." But she was smiling.

"Hey, I love it. I can tell people I was in school with you and get away with calling myself prematurely gray. I'll back you up anytime."

Her tension was ebbing. Marlena felt Roger's warmth and good humor reach across the table. "You liked the article, aside from the few minor discrepancies?"

"Put me off a little. Made you sound like hell on wheels, doing your own writing, going out on location, creating story ideas. I was prepared for a three-minute interview with some bruiser holding a stopwatch."

"It wasn't that bad." She paused. "Well. Have you caught the show yet?"

"Wouldn't miss it for the world. But you had to ask." He spoke with delight. "You're still you."

"Seriously, what did you expect?"

"More gloss; more shield. It's the hair that makes the big difference. I still have the Alice-in-Wonderland image of your long, fine hair, pulled back from a smooth, pure forehead with a tortoiseshell barrette, leaning against the balcony, the Hudson in the background, a book in hand . . ."

Words had always come easily to the Roger she had known. She had no trouble dashing off scripts or pouring it out to her journal, but in talking to people she was better at one-liners than personal paragraphs.

"Alison wears her hair like that now," he went on. "Long and straight. She doesn't have a drop of affectation in her soul."

"I hope my soul hasn't become affected, just my hair."

"You take yourself a lot less seriously."

"Please God. If I didn't laugh at myself half the time, I'd have gone crazy years ago. It took me longer than I like to admit to learn that."

The waiter returned. Marlena ordered the tournedos well-done, telling Roger she had conquered her fears of appearing foolish in fine restaurants. "It's gotten so I give my dates points for liking well-done. It's easier to order two disasters for a French chef to mutter over."

Roger opted for tournedos, rare.

"That's it. This is the last lunch I will ever have with you," she said, laughing.

"I hope not." His strong, artistic hand reached across the table to rest lightly on her own.

A kinesthetic memory woke up and triggered warm physical images of young bodies. She swallowed and reached for a cigarette with her free hand.

He pulled the lighter from his pocket.

"Thank you," she said lightly, withdrawing her hand, well aware that acceptance of the touch was an implicit invitation. The band on his finger was not a cub scout ring. She had sworn off married men.

"Alison." Roger gave her hand a light pat before lifting his for a cigarette. "I think you'll like her. She's bright and nosy. She could make a good reporter."

"TV reporting has a lot of levels. There are a lot of reporting jobs in TV, more variety than in print. Local reporting, national, anchoring, producing, researching, directing . . . I could go on for hours."

"Alison could listen for hours." He laughed. "Or talk. Just push the button."

"She's seventeen?"

He nodded.

"They're so fresh at that age."

"And surprisingly mature. I'm amazed at some of her insights. But she always was a wise little thing, even as a toddler."

Marlena didn't like picturing Roger with his baby daughter, a child that could have been hers, theirs. She recognized her envy of his family.

The scuffed knees she never had to bandage, the sniffles she never helped cure, the first school days, the first dance—romanticized images of motherhood flashed by. She tried not to dwell on the lack or loss. It always seemed there would be time later, when her career was secure, when the right man came along. When she wasn't alone. She had other friends who'd raced past relationships that might have borne fruit.

On her forty-first birthday, a month ago, she'd resolved to stop discussing it. Forty had seemed the cutoff point, although the medical evidence indicated there was still hope. But a woman still couldn't do it by herself.

She stared down at the endive salad, rejecting the bitter taste as she considered the genetic time clock. The moments had gone by so unwittingly.

Roger broke the silence. "You never had children?"

"No."

"Pity. I always thought you'd make a great mother."

Her laugh was defensive. "I'm better at creating ex-relationships than children."

"Amazing." Roger looked at her with increased interest. "You're still vulnerable. You always were the softest, most open and vulnerable girl I'd ever known. Maybe it's still all there."

"I'm a lot tougher than I seem right now." She smiled. "You knew me in my most vulnerable stage." She could still remember the qualms and questions of those years.

Roger's commitment, as she remembered it, had been to his image of her role in his future. His tick, her tock.

Had her own goals been defined when they first met instead of crystallizing under pressure, she might have stayed and battled for balance. But she'd chosen to abandon a battle before it had to be fought. Had it been running away—or running to?

"Marlena, I cared for you a lot back then. Maybe it wasn't in a real grown-up way, but I cared and I've never stopped caring. Have you been happy?"

"Have you? Did you find your Galatea?"

"Is that what you thought I wanted? To play Pygmalion?"

"Wasn't it? You had it all laid out. A two-lawyer family. The beach house. Eighteen months in the Peace Corps. Ten years of practice before you entered politics with your perfect family. All nice and neat. How did it turn out?"

He ignored the question and addressed the statements. "But you never argued with me about it."

"Because you never listened to objections. I'm not a shouter or a fighter."

His eyes were serious. "True. You didn't fight. You disappeared."

"A coward, but a doer." Her quip fell flat.

"I guess you did what you had to. We all do, one way or the other."

She stubbed out her cigarette and crossed her arms over her solar plexus, as if seeking protection from the memories.

"But can you explain why you never answered my letters or phone calls?"

How could she offer accusations as explanations? He'd been too controlling and she'd been afraid of that. And there'd been her personal guilt about the abortion; she knew that to see Roger was to stir that up in her conscience.

"When we're young and insecure we avoid things because of the fearful images we build up in our own minds, pictures of accusations or anger or hurt we don't want to face."

"You could have called and said 'drop dead' directly."

"Roger, back then you'd have fought me tooth and nail about Wilkes-Barre." She had loved the job and the people and even Wilkes-Barre, and she knew Roger couldn't have understood or been part of that world.

"I've sometimes wondered how life would have turned out if you'd stayed." His lips twisted in a half smile. "We had all the possibilities."

"It's all kind of pointless at this point, don't you think? 'If' is such a useless word."

"If something's bothered you for nearly twenty years, if it's been holed up in a dark corner of your mind, sad and unresolved, it would be nice to put it to rest. I've a confession to make."

She looked puzzled.

"I was too proud to admit you'd left me high and dry just for a job. I spread a nasty rumor that I'd kicked you out for sleeping around. Like Freud says, men have to turn their madonnas into whores."

"What a strange thing to do," she said softly. "Rejection was that difficult for you?"

"Didn't you ever wonder how I was doing or what I was feeling back then?"

She didn't want to play the analysis game. Deliberately, she lightened the tone. "There wasn't much time for regret, Roger. When I got to Wilkes-Barre I had to work my tail off, plunging headfirst into a job I was totally unprepared for. Sure, I'd been a gofer at IBS and done some research, but I'd never scripted a news story and I knew nothing about camera angles, interviewing people, or anything else technical. Remember, this was a little station in Wilkes-Barre. I didn't even have a producer to help. It was just me and my cameraman, wings, and prayers."

Roger played with his fork, half listening.

"My first assignment was covering a supermarket opening in a two-bit town outside Scranton. I'd been sent to get comments from the mayor, who was slated to officially conduct the ceremonies. I was trying so hard to come off cool and professional. I didn't want to ask dumb questions like 'Who's the mayor?' So I got logical and interviewed the distinguished-looking man standing next to the gray-haired woman who cut the ribbon, obviously his wife. And he was obviously the mayor.

"Back at the station, I learned to my horror that the woman wasn't the mayor's wife, she was the mayor. The man I'd interviewed was her cousin, the town freeloader who'd stood beside her during the ceremony to share in the free buffet afterward." She laughed. "Lesson number one stuck. Since that day, I've never minded asking a dumb question or questioning the obvious."

"I still can't understand why anyone, let alone you, could have left me for that podunk coal town, Wilkes-Barre." Roger was not entirely joking.

Marlena looked down at her salad, still without appetite for it. She could picture Tom, the way he'd been then. She thought about Roger back then. To this day she didn't think the choice had been dumb. This time she allowed herself to look at the memory.

Wilkes-Barre

"Lettuce and parsley are inventions of the devil," Tom Wells growled at the appearance of a spinach salad. "Greens are for rabbits and cows. When fire was invented civilized man learned to cook."

Alan ignored the comment and dug in. Marlena swallowed a giggle. Alan's pale skin and hair, and his overbite, made him a perfect candidate for a rabbit.

Then she made a mental note never to serve Tom salad. Not that she ever cooked for him. Tom had kept her at arm's length, communicating through Alan Cameron, the twenty-eight-year-old news director who also moderated the Sunday talk show. Everyone wore at least two hats in the low-budget operation, except Marlena, who was still struggling with her role of reporter.

"I like to cook," she ventured.

"And eat, too, I'd guess," Tom grumbled.

"What does that mean?" She asked, her hackles rising.

"It means if you want a shot at weekend anchoring, which Alan's been bugging me about, you'd better lose those fifteen pounds. You can get away with your baby fat for short news reports, but I look at the longer ones and want to send you to a fat farm.

"I am not fat." She flared from Tom to Alan. "Alan, am I fat?"

Alan, as lean as he was fair, shrugged.

"How tall are you?" Tom demanded.

"Five-seven."

"What do you weigh?"

"A hundred twenty."

"A hundred fifteen, hundred ten might be better. You're small-boned."

"I've lost five pounds already, working myself to the bone."

Tom's lined face creased in amusement. "You haven't met hard work yet. These first few months you've been learning what you should have known before you were hired." He laughed. "But you get points. You're now ready to be hired."

"She really has made great progress," Alan murmured.

Tom signaled for his third martini and waved for the waitress to remove his untouched salad.

"Yes." Tom leveled his gaze on Marlena. "Step by baby step. But you still have to say 'may I?'"

Marlena squirmed.

"You're a tough man, Tom," Alan said dryly.

"Professional. We have to play by the rules." His smile returned as the waitress presented his thick sirloin, the best the old Hotel Sterling had to offer. "First you have to know the rules," he muttered half to himself, "then you can see how far they can bend." He raised his fork in edict. "Rules are tools."

"Rules are tools," Alan parroted. "That's nice."

It would be on the bulletin board tomorrow, Marlena thought.

Marlena nibbled on a french fry, studying Tom. He was drinking a lot, but he didn't seemed to be affected. Alan had said Tom was on the edge, a barely controlled alcoholic, but still a great newsman. Marlena approved of his plaid wool tie—old but fine, like a worn wool jacket with real leather elbow patches. Tweedy and seedy, she coined silently.

"Tom, could you pass the salt, please?" Alan asked.

Alan's "Tom" sounded more formal than "Mr. Wells" coming from anyone else. Alan could be a real toad, she thought, her eyes moving from Alan to Tom's hand, which was passing the salt. Tom's hands looked old, older than his forty-seven years. The chewed nails, bloody at the corners, confirmed his nervousness. But overall there was charm, with bursts of buoyancy and the unruly dark curl that slipped down to meet his thick, dark brows. She liked his horned-rim glasses too. She cast him as the dedicated, dissipated professor, class and glass in hand. He had an almost academic sex appeal.

Tom took a break from his attack on the sirloin. "There's something I want to talk to you about—and I want Alan to hear. Your arson story."

She smiled, relieved. She had been first on the scene, first to interview both the detective and the family. Alan had called her coverage first-rate.

Tom went on, "You were too emotional. Your questions to the detective were inflammatory. 'How can citizens be protected from this kind of madness? Will there be a harsh sentence when you catch the arsonist?'" He paused dramatically. "Now what was wrong about that?" He looked from Marlena to Alan.

"A reporter is not a prosecutor," Alan tried. "A reporter should only report. And she did get pretty emotional."

"But . . ." She had to come to her own defense. "A reporter is the public's representative, right? And if a situation is outrageous, why shouldn't the reporter share the outrage?"

"If the information creates outrage, that's enough. Emotion is dangerous; it can blind you to the facts."

"But my facts were accurate, even if you think I was too emotional."

"Think about your questions. What did you say that was wrong?" he barked.

She looked at Alan for help. He shrugged.

"The detective told you it was *suspected* arson. Suspected. I know you *said* that at the top of your story, but your overemotional questions created the misleading impression that it was a fact, without any question." Tom's tone turned mocking. "'This kind of madness . . . Will there be a harsh sentence when the arsonist is caught?'"

"The follow-up report confirmed it was arson," she said.

"And you can thank your guardian angel for that. Beginner's luck doesn't last forever. What if it hadn't been?"

She toyed with her cold burger, avoiding Tom's eyes. "But it was."

"If you want to scream about tragedy and injustice, write editorials. If you want to be a reporter, learn to report, dammit."

Marlena sat, silent.

"Ever ask yourself what news is?" Tom answered his own question. "Half of it is gossip—neighborhood gossip about other people—murders, indictments, awards. On network it's national dirt. We get local. The other half is a mixture of optional information—health hazards, disasters, uprisings, politics, and poker. For most poor bastards, it's 'There but for the grace of God go I,' with a few sighs of sympathy. Mostly, it's relief that their own little worlds are untouched."

Marlena had to counter. "News should also make people aware, motivate them to look outside those little worlds, shouldn't it?"

"News is for information, not inspiration. Bottom line. Reporters don't suggest changes . . . or actions."

"But they can report on others' suggested changes?"

"But not their own." Tom was firm.

"He's right." Alan nodded.

"It doesn't seem fair."

"It's tough enough not to slant the news by what you choose to put into—or keep out of—a story. But to allow opinions . . . God, Marlena, no one could ever sort out the facts."

Tom paused, giving Marlena time to digest his advice, before continuing. "And talking about facts, don't confuse what you know with what you *think* you know."

"Like who's mayor," Alan added pointedly.

Marlena kicked Alan's shin under the table. Whose side was he on?

Tom chuckled. "That was basic. And like calling suspected arson, arson. Get a notebook and make lists if you must. What you know. How you know it. What you think. Why you think it. Find your own method, but get it straight. I don't have room for sloppy reporting. We may be a penny-ante operation, but we'll be an accurate penny-ante one."

Tears dripped on the half-eaten hamburger, turning it soggy as well as cold. "I'm sorry," she said miserably. "I really am a fuck-up."

"Come on, kiddo. Cut it out. I can't stand it when

women cry. If I didn't think you had great potential, I wouldn't waste my breath on you. You're a learner. It takes more than being smart. It takes caring about being right. And it may be even more important to want not to be wrong."

"She cares, Tom." Alan handed her his handkerchief.

"I know she does. Kiddo, we've all been there. Everybody who makes it in this business has to pay dues. Learn the hard way, but learn. It will pay off, I promise."

The dessert tray stopped, a succulent array of homemade pies, cakes, and cannolis. Marlena picked up her ice water and drank deeply, determined to resist.

"You'll be all right, kiddo. I'll bet on it." Tom spoke with a certain smugness. "I rarely make mistakes about people."

For a second she wondered how he rationalized his ex-wives, but she didn't dare to ask. The man had finally treated her as a real reporter.

Single-mindedly, she devoted herself to learning her craft. Checking and rechecking her facts, experimenting with Charlie, the crazy cameraman, for more interesting angles, seeking human commentary from people involved in local stories. She worked hard to move beyond the obvious, interviewing merchants along the beat of the wounded cop as well as the cop's wife, spending hours digging out national statistics to compare with local trends, studying agricultural journals before covering the farm show, searching for depth and interest.

Quietly, she dedicated herself to getting better, doing better. No more doughnuts or subs. Each morning she stepped on a cheap C. J. Murphy scale. A step at a time, pound by pound, Tom got his reporter.

By the time August sweltered into the Wyoming Valley Marlena had shed both the fifteen pounds and her fear of failing. Another five-dollar-a-week raise confirmed she was passing Tom's tests. Local campaigns kept her dashing from garden party teas with candidates' wives to polka parties replete with kielbasa and sauerkraut.

She appreciated the ethnic disparities of the Polish, Irish, Welsh, and Italian communities. Generations after they had moved to the valley, following the black gold in the anthracite mines, they had maintained a cultural identity.

The superintendent of schools said things were changing. Originally, the mine owners had created town divisions according to heritage. Divide and control was the philosophy. And each group had its own small schools. The football teams were small, but terrible in their clannish rivalries.

Now there was consolidation and expansion, blurring loyalties among the young. Marlena talked Alan into letting her do a series to air after the elections. She worked assiduously to be objective, allowing the old to display the touch of poignancy and the young show themselves as little touched by their attitudes.

She reported on the election rhetoric by day and researched by night, her own world centered on the four-story building that housed WWKB-TV. The most relevant thing about her twenty-second birthday was that she now shared the WWKB family number, Channel 22.

After the eleven o'clock news that night Alan dragged her back to his first-floor apartment in an old brick colonial on Northampton Street. "I have a bottle of Mateuse. You have to at least get a birthday drink."

The gesture was sweet, but Marlena was beginning to suspect that Alan was getting too interested in her.

"I'm starved," Alan said as he uncorked the dark green bottle.

"Save the bottle," Marlena instructed. "They look great with candle wax dripped over them"

"Maybe in college dorms."

"Don't be snide. You're not that old."

"Have you eaten today?" he asked, pouring the wine.

"No, but I pigged out at the Republican rally yesterday. Roast beef, gorgeous onion rolls, hickory-smoked ham, the best cherry pie I have ever tasted, chocolate brownies—gooey, just like I love . . ."

"Stop it! Now I'm starved."

"I'll fix you something." She looked for the kitchen.

"Don't . . ." Alan stopped as Marlena screamed.

"Disgusting. This is the worst pigsty I've ever seen. I should call the health department. What a great story. 'News Director of WWKB-TV Arrested as Health Hazard.'"

"Very funny."

"You must earn enough as news director to afford a cleaning woman. Even once a month. Some of this stuff looks six months old!" Marlena pushed up the sleeves of her soft beige sweater and attacked the chaos.

"It would feel . . . wrong . . . funny."

"You think this is funny?" Marlena wrinkled her well-shaped nose at dried egg on a plate. She held it up for Alan's inspection.

"Marlena, my mother works in a factory here, sewing blouses. She's worked eight- to ten-hour days as long as I can remember and come home to make dinner for five kids and a shiftless husband, clean up, supervise homework, sit up sewing dresses for my sisters and shirts for me, and somehow figured out how to send all but one sister to college. We're out of the house now, but she's still working at the factory and putting in her off-hours on church projects. Somehow, as long as she's working in that factory and I'm in the same town, I can't hire a maid."

"That's a strange attitude. I guess it would be all right if you got married and had some poor dumb broad do it—and work in a factory too." Marlena scrubbed at something burned and indefinable.

"Look, it's my kitchen and if I can live with it, I don't see why it bothers you."

"Has your sainted mother seen it?"

"Once." He couldn't help smiling. "She closed the door on it and told me to get married."

"Since you're such an old-world character, maybe you should. God, Alan, you'll be thirty before you know it. Your family will start suspecting you're homosexual."

Alan moved close behind her. "That I'm not. And I'll be happy to prove it to you."

Marlena swung around to face him, realizing she had gone too far with her teasing. Her affection for him was sisterly. She wanted him as a friend. Maybe she had to fill the void left by Roger, who'd been playmate as much as lover. She pretended surprise. "Alan! You're my boss. Remember Tom's lecture on conflicts of interest?"

"He was talking about sources, not colleagues."

"Really?" She tossed him a roll of paper towels. "Employees should *work* together. Use these to dry. I wouldn't trust your dishtowels to clean up cat shit."

"You really are terribly earthy."

"Earthy!"

"You just are. Like the way 'cat shit' sounds natural coming from you."

Marlena began to giggle. Alan would never make it as a Casanova.

"And since you lost weight and put on cheekbones, you look great. Earthy, sensual. Wide smile. Do you know you're a total turn-on? It isn't even that you're so gorgeous."

"Thanks a lot."

"Let me finish. I think you're wonderful looking, but there's something else. No matter how hard you try to be cool as Lois Lane, there's something soft and sexy that comes in the door with you." He blushed.

"I suppose I'm destined to inspire men to poetry." She sighed. "Except for Tom. I inspire him to lectures."

"He likes you. He thinks you're getting good."

"For a baby. If he calls me 'kiddo' one more time, I'll start calling him Mr. Methuselah."

"And you could start looking for another job." Alan dropped the empty paper towel roll on the floor beside the heaping wastebasket.

She tossed him an exasperated look. "The rest will have to drain. Honestly, Alan, you're so organized at the station."

"Home is a place to relax and play." He lightly walked his fingers up her back, stopping at the nape of her neck to massage.

"Don't, Alan." She stepped away.

"Why not? We're both single. I know you like me. So why not give it a chance?"

"I don't know. It feels too incestuous. It's creepy. You're my friend. I don't want to mess that up."

"It wouldn't. It could make things . . . friendlier."

"Or complicated."

"It might help get you a shot at weekend anchor."

"I don't believe you said that."

"It was a joke."

"Besides," she said meanly, "that's not your decision. It's Tom's. I'd be sleeping with the wrong man."

"Touché."

"You've gotten me mad enough that now I'm hungry too. What's in the refrigerator?" She opened the door, stared at the moldy chaos, and slammed it shut in the face of the stench. "That I cannot deal with. It's all yours."

A chastened Alan dug past black bananas and emerged, triumphant, with a head of lettuce, only slightly wilted, and a carton of eggs. "Omelet and salad," he announced.

She took charge, assigning Alan the role of *sous* chef.

Under her direction, he ferreted out tins of parsley, onion flakes, and a bottle of fine herbs, the glass opaque with a greasy film.

She didn't comment on the quality of his finds. He was sufficiently embarrassed for the moment. She whipped up five eggs—one for good measure—and deftly added seasoning. "I like to cook. When I get my own apartment I'll give a real dinner party for all the reporters . . . and their wives, of course."

"Be careful, Tom could bring all three. He still talks to all of them."

"I didn't say I'd invite him. I said the reporters."

"You don't like Tom, do you?"

"He plays God, shut up in his holy office most of the time. He acts as though I don't exist—unless I fuck up."

"I should have warned you. He does that with everyone at first, until he feels you're part of the family. I went through the same thing. So did Fred and Larry and Millie. Clarence was here before Tom, so I don't know. Last year Millie got so mad at his cold shoulder, she marched into his office and had it out with him"

"Did it help?"

"They fought for a week. Then they seemed to get pretty chummy. For all I know they might have had an affair. If they did, they got over it. Nothing serious."

"Just your casual office fuck." Marlena shuddered. "If that's what it takes, better he should ignore me."

"What do you think of Millie?"

"I like her. She's funny and seems open enough, even if she doesn't 'tell all' to satisfy the office gossips."

"I wasn't putting her down. If there was anything, she handled it well. And she's a worker. She doesn't just take the weather off the wires. She talks to the weather service and asks questions, dreams of having state-of-the-art equipment. She has a rain measure on the roof, you know."

Marlena sprinkled a dash of dried parsley on each fluffy omelet and led the way into the living room. It was dusty, but in order. "That's all she'll get." Marlena laughed. "She'd better find another station to dream about."

"We're growing. We've been moving in on number two."

"Out of four stations. There ain't much gravy for dreams around here."

"Great omelet. You're amazing."

"What's amazing is that you don't have roaches."

"This isn't New York."

"Any intelligent roach would crawl here from New York just to die happy in your kitchen."

He regarded her solemnly. "Do you miss New York?"

"Who has time to miss anything?" She kept her thoughts away from New York—and Roger—as much as possible. Only on the nights she came home too early did she feel the hollowness and fight the guilt and loneliness. She coped with the empty visions by working late and avoiding her un-manned room until she was too tired to care about anything but sleep.

"Do you have time for dreams?" Alan slipped off his loafers.

Marlena's camera eye recorded the polished contrast of the leather shoe with the dusty red shag rug. A study of tex-ture. She was beginning to think visually.

"I've been having some great ones," Alan continued. "I picture myself in larger and larger markets, Chicago, maybe Los Angeles. Someday soon, I'll be in a position to help bright young talent. We could make a great team, Marlena."

If she'd wanted to be a team, she'd have stayed with Roger. Alan was getting way off base. Time to go home. The last thing she wanted from him was sex. She wanted to keep feeling clean. She had not moved past the emotional grime yet.

He smiled at her as she rose and patted the couch beside him. "Sit here."

"Come on, Brother Alan, take me home." Brother Alan sounded safe.

"Cut the brother shit unless you want to walk home."

Marlena coolly grabbed her coat. "So I'll walk. No big deal."

Alan rubbed his long, narrow nose on his wrist and sniffed. "Okay, kiddo, Tonight you're the boss, but tomorrow . . ."

Marlena hurled a faded print throw pillow that bounced off Alan's shoulder in a burst of dust. "You *are* a health hazard." She giggled. It'd take work to keep things light with Alan, but it would be nice to have a friend moving up the ladder, willing to reach down and give her a hand up. That is, if he got there first.

At eleven the next morning Marlena dashed into the newsroom, breathlessly late.

"How were the campaign headquarters?" Alan called from across the newsroom.

"Gotta write!" she called back before sitting down to attack the old Remington manual, polishing her noon election report.

At precisely eleven-thirty a round-cheeked boy entered the newsroom carrying a small white box balanced on a cardboard carton with HEALTH DEPARTMENT—HANDLE WITH CARE stenciled in bright red letters.

The boy studiously avoided looking at Marlena and stopped at Millie's desk. Marlena bit her cheeks to avoid a smile; Jake, her landlady's son, had been carefully briefed at breakfast.

"Alan! Package for you!" Millie shouted.

Alan sprang up from his desk and hurried to the

chubby messenger, looking first puzzled, then suspicious. "Do I need to sign anything?"

Jake shrugged. "I don't think so."

"Do I owe you anything?"

"Not really." He hesitated long enough for Alan to produce a dollar. Jake grinned and turned his rosy cheeks toward the door, unable to resist a last wink at Marlena.

Millie leaned over the package. "What is it? Props?"

"I don't know," Alan muttered.

The staff swarmed around as if it were package-opening time at a five-year-old's birthday party.

"Hurry up! Open them!" Millie demanded.

Drawn by the commotion, Tom emerged from his office. "What's going on? We do have a noon show today, folks."

Ed Puchalski grabbed the smaller box. "I'll help." He ripped it open and lifted out a cover letter neatly typed on Health Department stationery. "'Dear Mr. Cameron,'" he read aloud. "'The state of your kitchen has been brought to our attention. In light of the foul situation we are sending along something for which we have no further use, but which you may find appropriate.'"

Ed reached back in the box and lifted high a small glass jar filled with roaches. A red-labeled strip of adhesive tape identified them as ROACHES, GENUS CAMERONIA DIRTUS.

Everyone broke up. Alan's kitchen was a news-family joke.

"Yuk!" shrieked Millie, retreating behind her desk.

"*Where* did you get them?" Alan, red-faced, glared at Marlena.

"Ask the Health Department."

"I'll get you for this." He glowered at her.

"Don't forget the big box." Ed ripped open the carton, pulling out dish towels, ammonia, sponges, detergent, and dozens of cleaning products, piling them high on Alan's desk.

"You're making a mess on my desk!" Alan protested.

Everyone laughed harder. Ed grabbed his stomach. "I can't stand it," he gasped.

Even Tom was grinning. "Okay, you clowns. Show time in fifteen minutes. Get moving. And if any of you isn't prepared, I'll wash his or her mouth out with soap."

Alan was the first to move.

Marlena felt as wonderful as if she'd broken a story. A good practical joke took the same skills. Listen hard, think, and be ready to put the right elements together.

"Hurry up," Michael called. "You're at the top of the show."

Marlena raced to catch up with him.

"Nice going, kiddo." He gave her shoulder a friendly pat.

Marlena didn't mind the "kiddo." She knew she had finally stepped inside the WWKB family circle.

After the show Alan admitted her joke was "practical." He did need the supplies. She hugged him for being a good sport. He was all right.

Then the election schedule crunched down on all of them. She made a conscious effort to remain detached on the air. Off the air she waxed partisan. Johnson had to win. Otherwise all the Kennedy initiatives—social programs, civil rights, Peace Corps, everything—would go down the tubes. She was euphoric as Johnson swept in by a landslide.

As they closed down operations in the wee morning hours, Tom stopped by her desk. "Pretty enthusiastic, weren't you?"

"I thought I gave good factual reports all night long."

"Until the concession you were cool as ice."

Marlena silently chafed. The man could ruin anything.

Tom's lips softened in a world-weary smile. "I know. It was bigger than both of us." Then more genuine amusement sparkled in his eyes. "Thank your lucky stars this is Democratic country. You probably boosted our ratings with your youthful enthusiasm."

He can be attractive, Marlena conceded to herself. "Enough to give me a shot at anchoring?"

"When you're ready, kiddo. When *I* say you're ready."

"I weigh in at one-o-nine now!"

"That's a good start." He grinned as Michael joined them. "Come on, anchorman, let's go celebrate!"

Marlena's eyes blazed cold fire.

"Patience, kiddo, you have all the time in the world."

She was furious. She had been driving herself for that man for a year—eleven months and three days, to be exact. And Alan had been wrong. Tom would never warm up to her.

If he didn't give her a chance at weekend anchor by January, she would . . . she would . . . keep on trying. The thought was deflating. She didn't feel secure enough to leave. She knew she was learning all the time.

So she wasn't as polished as a network reporter yet. She couldn't do worse anchoring than the "mumblers," her epithet for Ed and Michael. Michael, the old-timer who had started in radio before she had been born, had a detached bass delivery that sounded disinterested. Ed, the local-boy-made-good, still stuttered nervously after five years.

In the wake of the election, Marlena felt drained and depressed. Her mother's call caught her at a vulnerable moment. Yes, she would come home for Christmas. She missed them all too. Tom had to let her go; she hadn't taken one minute of vacation all year.

But there was no Christmas in Des Moines for Marlena. As junior member of the news team she got last dibs. Larry had scheduled Chicago interviews; everyone knew he was ready to move up and away. Tom was encouraging him. Fred's home was Hartford, Connecticut—not that far—but it would be his first Christmas back there in four years.

"Hey, don't feel down." Millie had caught up with her as she slumped out of the scheduling meeting. "You'll spend the day with my family; I've gotta do the show too. My mom's used to scheduling family dinners around the news."

Millie didn't give Marlena room to object. Not that she wanted to. She liked Millie, and she didn't want Alan pressuring her to be his Christmas date.

Her mother was disappointed but philosophical. She remembered working the Christmas night shift her first few years in nursing. Maggie said she would make the "supreme sacrifice" and mail Marlena's presents. Maggie hated to mail packages.

Her mother sounded good. Busier than ever since she had taken a full-time teaching job at the community college. She gave Marlena progress reports on her favorite students, proudly telling her about the ones who'd landed good jobs, thanks, in part to her recommendations. The tone of pride reminded Marlena of Tom when he talked about Larry's network interview. Tom and her mother were about the same age; no, Tom was a year older. Why did that seem strange?

The snows came the second week in December, and Marlena was in her element. Her mood lifted as the flakes tumbled down. She volunteered for anything that would take her outside. Picking up sandwiches, running over to the newspaper to check obits. No meeting was too far, no errand too small.

The winters of her childhood had been the same. The deep and blowing snows that blanketed Iowa were her winter wonderland. Slides, closeted in carousels in her father's study, documented her many snow sculptures, from her first "snow baby" on through to the sophisticated teenage castles and forts. While others huddled by fires to avoid facing the cold,

Marlena perfected her cross-country skiing and snowshoe racing.

Her clear complexion glowed, rosy as her disposition. With her stockpile of down coats and thermal mittens, she was a child of winter.

The news was filled with snowplows and sand trucks, and a few heart attacks from shoveling snow. In the northwest storms turned California and Oregon into national disaster areas and she noticed that the British Parliament was considering a bill to abolish the death penalty. But in Wilkes-Barre life went on.

The Christmas Eve newscast was as powdery as the new snow of the day. She had gone on location, filming carolers and interviewing shoppers. Millie's weather report was long and picturesque. The sports report was centered on toboggan races, ending with a light piece featuring Clarence sledding down a hill with some neighborhood kids.

They had a good, friendly time doing it. And she had been allowed to anchor. She knew she had begun nervously, rustling her papers too much, tripping over the first sentence. Then she realized it wasn't that different from reading her regular news copy. Just more of it, and she wasn't doing it alone. Michael reacted to her stories, made little comments. And when he tossed it back to her, she could say, "Thanks, Michael." It felt less impersonal; she wasn't a robot reporter. She was a person, talking about the news. She liked that feeling.

The moment they went off the air Alan dashed out of the control room, his hand raised in a V-for-victory sign. "Great, Marlena!"

Michael gave her a paternal hug. "Not bad, kid. Best first time out I've seen."

She basked in their kind words. But where was Tom? Had he watched? She declined Alan's offer to go along to Midnight Mass. He hurried out, not wanting to keep his mother waiting.

Millie, looking like a Christmas confection in a red coat and hat with furry trim, waved good night. "See you tomorrow at eleven."

"Great!" Marlena was glad she'd be at Millie's house for Christmas.

She carefully filed her first anchor script in her bottom drawer and cleared her desk. Time to go.

She heard a radio playing "Silver bells . . . it's Christmas time in the city." She loved New York in the magic of those first few sparkling white hours of new snow. She could picture herself and Roger racing out to the wide old balcony to taste the first cool flakes. Like children. It seemed as long ago to her as her first toddler effort at making a snow baby. ". . . dressed in holiday cheer, soon it will be Chr . . ." The song stopped. Marlena turned, aware that someone else was still there.

Tom walked out of his office, wrapping a scarf around his neck. He frowned at the sight of her. "What are you doing here?"

"I work here, remember?"

Then he softened, joking. "That's right. Now I know where I've seen you before. On the news."

"Night and day."

"Christmas Eve, a thousand miles from home."

She laughed, avoiding the sentiment. "This place has become my home."

He stopped at her desk. "You've done all right, kiddo."

She smiled, waiting for more.

"You're turning into a good little reporter."

"Thanks. Well? What did you think about tonight? My anchoring?"

"You had to ask." He laughed. "I can't fault your accuracy anymore, but you still run short in the patience department. It was so good I'll drive you home."

"I'm still at Mrs. Shannahan's, remember? Two blocks away. Thanks, anyway."

"Then I'll buy you a drink."

He was lonely too. Marlena found the thought startling. Her eyes held his, looking into the edge of sadness.

"It's Christmas Eve. No man should drink alone," he said, acknowledging Marlena's perception.

She followed him silently, waiting for him as he checked locks and turned out lights, making her own mental adjustment to this new, human view of him.

"Look, Tom." She tugged at his sleeve as they stepped outside. She pointed to the ice-coated snow gleaming on the old iron railing of the stairs. "It's beautiful."

Tom followed her finger and looked back at her. "Yes. It is." His hand reached up toward her soft cheek and hesitated. He patted her shoulder. "Watch your step, ice princess. It's slippery out here."

She laughed happily. "I love it! The icier the better!" She ran down the snowy steps to prove her point, tripped on the last one, and threw herself into the snow piled up beside the shoveled walk. "See? All in one piece."

"You're a crazy woman. You're going to kill yourself one of these days." He brushed at the snow covering her from shoulders to toes. "You'll be soaked, too, when you melt."

She laughed. "I'm used to it."

They had to wait for the starter of his old diesel Mercedes to glow before Tom could turn on the ignition. He stared at the button, impatient. "I have an idea. I have to put up my Christmas tree tonight and do something about decorating it. My kid is coming over tomorrow morning. Want to help?"

Her head tilted at him, questioning. She didn't know about any child.

"My ex has him tonight, but I get him tomorrow. He's four—and funny. He'll give me hell if I don't get his tree up."

"A four-year-old gives you hell?"

"He's a tiger. Takes after . . ."

"The old man," she finished with him.

That broke the ice, and they rode across town gossiping about the show and the staff. Marlena realized that Tom kept a better eye on the staff than she realized. He knew his people.

The Christmas decorations were piled in grocery bags, lights and tinsel twisted and tangled. But Marlena noticed with pleasure that Tom's small house was warm, cozy, and clean. The furniture was a comfortable mixture of styles, a wide leather couch facing a fireplace and two high-backed Chippendale wing chairs. A long modern brass-and-glass coffee table seemed oddly right near the cherry end tables and Chinese lamps.

"Approve?" He closed the door behind her.

"It's charming."

"You look surprised."

"After Alan's . . ."

"I should be able to do a little better than Alan." He laughed.

"I know, I just . . ." She felt tongue-tied again, embarrassed.

"Don't worry. I'm taking it as a compliment. And I'm being a poor host. Let me take your coat." He noticed the melting snow dripping on the polished hardwood floor. "I'll hang it in the kitchen to dry."

She walked into the living room, then moved closer to the prints and paintings on the walls. She didn't recognize the artists, but they were all signed. They were as eclectic and compatible as the furniture. Small, beautifully framed modern line drawings mixed with larger oils and watercolors.

"I collect young artists . . . like young reporters. You never know how far they'll go," Tom called from the hall, where he was mopping the melting snow.

"I'm sorry, I should do that." She hurried back to him.

"No." He was amused. "Here, I still do the grunt work. Except Thursday, when the cleaning lady comes."

"Thank God. Your mother never worked in a dress factory."

He straightened and cocked his head at her. "What does that have to do with the price of alfalfa?"

"Not much," she said. "Alan says he can't have a maid because his mother still works here in a factory, sewing."

Tom didn't laugh. "I can understand that. Alan is a sensitive kid. He's got some depth."

"Seems to me that most of the time he's just your yes man."

"He listens. And he thinks. I admit I keep control over who gets hired, but I give him a pretty free hand with the news operation."

"I thought he just delivered your messages."

"That too." Tom chuckled. "Now, let's get down to serious questions. What would you like to drink?"

"Scotch and soda sounds good."

Tom's bar was an antique carved cupboard in the living room, cleverly equipped with a small ice machine.

Tom poured her scotch and mixed himself a martini. Then he raised his glass in a toast. "To Marlena Williams, WWKB's Saturday co-anchor for 1965."

"Every Saturday?" Marlena gasped.

He leaned over and kissed the tip of her nose lightly. "You're ready." He smiled. "I say so."

Merry Christmas, she thought.

"Enough dillydallying. On to the Christmas tree." Tom opened the back door and dragged in a full, well-formed blue spruce, potted. "When I was a kid," he explained, "I hated to see our Christmas trees die. It gave me the feeling that all good things have to end. Then, one day I discovered you can buy them with roots, to plant. I have eight of these little spruces lining the driveway outside. This will make nine. Thank God, it's a long driveway. I kind of like it here."

She never would have suspected that Tom was sentimental. The ornament bags confirmed it. He rambled on about the tiny tin soldiers from his childhood, the carved angels bought in France during the war Marlena had only studied, the silver snowflakes from Chicago, the ceramic snowman his second wife had made. Each ornament had its own history to form a journal for his live tree.

He directed and performed a historic running commentary while she carefully hung each ornament. "Higher, lower . . . to the left. The right."

"All done." She stepped down from the stool.

"Not quite." Tom disappeared into the kitchen for a minute, emerging with a frosted bottle of champagne in one hand and a hollow alabaster angel in the other. "My Italian ice angel. Milano, 1946. The only good vacation I ever had with my first wife."

"It's wonderful." Marlena touched the sparkling, white figurine.

"Hell of a lot better than the plastic light-up things," Tom agreed as he worked on the champagne cork. He grinned when it popped neatly into the towel. "Tradition. I always celebrate the crowning moment."

She watched him fill cut-crystal champagne glasses.

"Waterford," he explained. "Dublin, 1962. A divorce vacation." He lifted his glass.

"What would you have done if I weren't here?" She raised her glass.

"Suffered more in the morning," he said, laughing.

"What time must you get up tomorrow for . . ." She didn't know his son's name.

"Toby. I promised to pick him up at eight. And that was a compromise."

She groaned.

"They live only five blocks away. I can walk if I'm not in shape to drive."

She should go home before it got too late. Home. The small room at Mrs. Shannahan's had little of the comfort of her parents' home nor the old elegance of the New York penthouse. Tom's home had a bit of both. "I should go home," she murmured.

Tom ignored the statement. "This one's mine," he announced as he stepped on the stool to place the angel on top of the tree.

She applauded, then sipped her champagne, glancing at the label. Dom Perignon. Roger's favorite. Did Roger treasure the crystal icicle she had bought for him on their last Christmas?

It made her sad to remember. The letters had stopped months ago. Had he forgotten her? A tear fell, mixing with the champagne.

Tom crawled behind the tree and plugged in the lights. "Well?" He crawled back out, looking at her for approval. "What do you think?"

"It's beautiful. So beautiful it makes me want to cry." She sniffed. She sat down on the couch and saw a blurry tree. It was beautiful. She felt Tom sit beside her and turned to see his face, kind with concern.

"Marlena . . ."

Marlena. Not kiddo. Not little-girl reporter. She was a person to him. Then, without quite knowing how it happened, she was sobbing in his arms.

"Shh, shh," he whispered against her soft hair. "It's okay." He let her cry it out.

She was making a fool of herself, she thought, but she couldn't help it. He had pulled the trigger with his touch of sympathy. The comfort helped. "I'm sorry, Tom. I don't know why I did that. I didn't know I felt so lonely."

"Everyone feels lonely now and then." He handed her the champagne glass, full again.

She sipped thoughtfully, feeling spent but warm beside him.

"I thought you were making friends here. Millie, Alan."

"Work is fine."

"I thought that you and Alan were—what should I say?—seeing each other?"

The statement brought back her smile. "Yes," she said, "but in different lights."

Tom returned the smile and she hugged him and lifted her lips to his spontaneously.

He hesitated. "God, you're so young."

"Is that bad?" she whispered. She wanted him to want her. She wanted him to know she was more than a weepy little girl.

His voice was unsteady. "I have suits older than you."

"But I'm a learner. You said it." A dimple appeared for a moment at the right corner of the soft mouth. "I'm just out of practice. Tom?" His name was a soft plea.

He answered with a sudden long and deep kiss that left her breathless and shaken. She had almost forgotten how strong the achings could be. But he was backing off. "Don't stop. Please."

"Those are supposed to be my lines." He was breathing hard.

"Don't you want me?"

"Of course." He almost sounded angry.

"Then come." She moved against him, her head swimming a delicious bit from the champagne and Scotch.

She felt his body tense, then relax suddenly.

"Tighter," she whispered.

"I'll crack your ribs." His voice was hoarse.

"I'm tough."

"No . . . no, you're not." He stood up, taking her hand and looking down at her. "I'm afraid of this, Marlena. I don't want you to get hurt."

She looked back at him, serious. "I won't unless it all disappears tomorrow."

"You aren't that kind, are you?"

"Not a casual fuck." She rose. "And not a cock-teaser."

"Wash your mouth out with soap, young lady!" He reached behind her playfully and slapped her bottom. "Child-woman."

"Woman." She moved close to him with the whole length of her body.

He stroked her cheek gently. "Soft. Baby soft."

Softly, she rocked her body against him, swelling his hard response. The words came naturally. "Let's go to bed now."

The lovemaking felt natural too. Tom's passion and experience brought her to new levels, building her physical sensations with a knowing control, finding pleasure centers she had never sensed before, readying her until he could hold back no longer.

"God." He lay back, cradling her against his steamy body. "I could be in trouble."

"Why you?" She smiled in her new contentment.

"I think I could fall in love with you."

She was startled silent. She hadn't thought that far.

"What do you think about that?"

She thought she had never felt more completely approved of. She felt wonderful about herself—and him. "I think," she said between tiny kisses on the soft inside of his elbow, "I think 1965 could be a great year for finding a great love."

"Let's not ignore the last five days of December 1964. Hey, I forgot to tell you. I'm running your 'Wilkes-Barre:

Changes' series next week. It's the best thing you've done all year."

She didn't want to think about work at that moment. It reminded her that she was in bed with her boss, a thought that shadowed her feelings. If Alan found out, would he think that was why Tom was letting her anchor?

"Well . . ." Tom pushed the damp hair back from her forehead. "It may not be the best thing you've done for me all year, but it's the best you've done, speaking professionally."

"Let's not. Not tonight."

Three

ROGER REFILLED HER GOBLET, creating an artist's still life beside the single red rose, the grapes, and the cheeses. Her focus widened to include him in the picture.

"Marlena? Are you with me?"

She smiled, coming back to the present. "It's nice seeing you again."

"For a long time"—his speech slowed as he felt for words—"you were like a shadow that stayed with me, like something you've been deprived of as a child that you can't get over."

Like the death of a child. She left the words unsaid as the image flashed in her mind of the awful moment in Puerto Rico when she'd recognized the killing part of it.

"I find it totally disconcerting to discover you're much more than a distant shadow. Not the same as before, exactly, but real. Older, yes, but almost nicer. Those wonderful laugh lines!" He lifted his hand to touch the fine lines beside her eyes. "It's a shame you can't smile on camera more when you do the news."

She leaned back in her chair, away from him, and crossed her arms, clasping her shoulders like a modest nude. "You think news folk should smile on the air?" She stretched her mouth into a wide fixed grin and spoke through her teeth. "Today, 8,357 people were killed as an earthquake devastated Tokyo. The federal deficit is expected to exceed three hundred billion dollars in 1986 and unemployment is projected to rise."

Roger leaned back with a hearty laugh and signaled the waiter. "Coffee?"

"Please." Her instinct to back off had been right.

"Dessert? I saw some great-looking pastry by the door—whipped cream, strawberries, chocolate tortes."

"Don't torture me."

"Tempt is the word, m'dear. You can stand it. You don't look as though you've gained a pound since you left me."

That was unfair, to keep pulling her back to what had and hadn't been. She didn't want to play mind games, to be sucked into old guilt. It had hardly been a perfect match back then. Now they were two people who'd shared a college romance that had had some whimsical and painful moments, but two people with separate lives for a long time. He wanted her to do a favor for him and his daughter, as an old friend. And that was how she must play it.

"If anything," he continued, "you look thinner."

"I should hope." She could be precise too. "I'm actually seven pounds thinner. For years I was sixteen pounds thinner, but I gave up the fight—or at least moderated it. The extra nine pounds helped round out the new wrinkles." Let him be turned off by unattractive trivia. "I hope Alison doesn't have a weight problem. Weight's a dreadful issue with some news directors. I had one once who practically weighed every bite I took for two years. Cameras add ten or fifteen pounds to your image. If you look perfect in person, you'll look plump on camera."

"Am I making you nervous?"

"No. Why?"

"You're chattering. You always used to chatter when you were nervous."

"Dammit, Roger. That was twenty years ago. This isn't a time warp, I hope. I've changed. You've changed. When or why I chattered back then simply isn't relevant."

"Are you saying old feelings aren't relevant to new ones? I can't buy that, Marlena."

Feelings were the last thing they should be talking about, but wasn't that why she had agreed to lunch? To see if there was anything left to feel? She twisted the diamond on her third finger, left hand, and thought about Roger's diamond in her purse and the gold circle on his hand. Too many rings, like an ancient tree. Did the past hold on, circle upon circle in ever-widening barricades between the life inside and present realities? "I have always thought that people who dwell on the past lose the present."

"I love the bons mots that wrap it all up, sound reasonable, and totally miss the point. Great TV writing," Roger concluded.

"It's more than an empty phrase. If you spend your whole life looking back, you'll end up leading with your rear."

Roger laughed and held his palms up in mock surrender. "I'm not lobbying for the impossible, to turn back the clock. But some things in the past can feel unresolved—like an unfinished good-bye you never quite understood."

The coffee was cold. "Surely you haven't spent the last twenty years wondering why I left. It must have been obvious. I had an opportunity I had to take. I knew you would have fought against it. I didn't like fighting so I did what I had to do. It's as you said. People do what they have to do."

"Did you fall in love with your Tom when you went to

that first interview? When you didn't come to Palm Beach with
me?"

She didn't like being pushed. The rings of the past felt
fragile and vulnerable to splintering. "No, I didn't, but what
would it matter if I had? I'm not going to get into a fight we
should have had twenty years ago." She saw a new question in
his eyes. "And I am not going to fight about whether or not we
should have fought about it then. This is ridiculous, Roger. We
were confused selfish kids, running after stars."

"I don't believe you can't remember why, after you ran
off chasing your so-called stars, why you wouldn't even talk to
me. Your memory can't be that bad."

"I'm not an elephant," she joked uncomfortably. It was
the perfect opportunity to be honest, to hand over the ring
and the truth. But she didn't like the way he was trying to
put her on the defensive. She didn't like being emotionally
bullied.

"The good reporter stays above the pain to remain objective?" Roger was relentless.

"It's not always that easy, but we try."

"I'm not concerned with public pain. I'm interested in
how you handle your personal thorns these days."

He was pushing again. "Life isn't very thorny these
days. My main problem is figuring out when to sleep with my
bizarre work hours."

Roger raised his eyebrows in silent query.

"Only crazy, compulsive people get into this business
and stay. You have to be a news junkie. A lot of starry-eyed
kids walk in looking for glamour, but they rarely last long."

"You started as a gofer at IBS, right? Do they still have
jobs for students like Alison?"

"Not like the old days. Now we hire college students
summers and holidays and have official intern programs. But
it's still a good way to see if a kid can handle the real grunt
work behind the illusions."

"Guess loyalty pays off. You've come full circle, ten rungs up the ladder. Have you always worked for IBS affiliates?"

She nodded. "They've always been fair and have made good on promises. ABC was nibbling at me last year before IBS gave me the 'Later . . . on IBS' show, but . . . I guess loyalty's important."

"In your personal life too?"

She laughed. "I'm not perfect, but I try. Do you?"

"Some say I'm trying," he retorted. "Ready to get out of here?"

"Yes, I could use some air." She rose. "Lunch was lovely. Thank you. And please have Alison call me this week. I'd love to meet her."

"And she would more than love to meet you." Roger smiled.

"Roger. The check."

He looked blank for a moment then followed her glance to the waiter patiently standing beside Roger, living up to his profession by waiting.

Roger paid him in cash. "That does it. Ready for some air?"

She nodded. Both mind and memory felt overworked.

"I promised Alison I would pick up a book for her. Want to walk over to Scribner's with me?" He unwadded a wrinkled ball of lined yellow paper. *The World, the Universe and Everything.*"

"That about wraps it all up, doesn't it?"

"Just the beginning." He helped her on with her elegant, full-length silver fox coat.

Outside, Marlena opened her lips to the sky and reached up her hands to meet the snow tumbling down at them. "It's wonderful!"

"Looks serious." Roger analyzed the steady fall of small flakes and the thick, dark sky.

"I hope so. I need my big snow every winter. At least one."

The streets were wet and glistening. The snow was losing the early battle to the traffic, but the sidewalks and roofs were well covered with white, the cracks and graffiti blanketed.

She felt fresh and clear-headed above the wine. Her pulse quickened with an eager, unnamed anticipation. Snow. It always pumped up her blood, giving her back the vibrant feeling of youth, of being on the brink of discovery. "Let's race." She dashed around the corner toward Park Avenue.

Roger skidded after her, narrowly avoiding a head-on crash with a pink designer umbrella and the embarrassed pin-striped man hiding beneath. "Sorry."

Marlena's lizard sling-back pumps were sloshing, but she didn't care. The air was crisp. The snow cascaded from the skies and the avenue was turning postcard charming. She glanced behind to see Roger trailing and swung around, running back to him. "Isn't it wonderf . . ."

His smile and arms were wide as she reached him. She slipped, unable to stop, and he caught her close, swinging her around into a hug with a laugh.

A boy of kindergarten size darted past them, sloshing joyfully, ignoring the "Tommy! Slow down" shouted from behind. The imp picked up speed and plopped bottom-down on the white sidewalk.

"I warned you."

"Oh, Mom." The imp frowned past Marlena, pulling a green knit hat from his blond curls in disgust.

Marlena shared a warm laugh with Roger, but her thoughts reached back to Toby during the good years, the years she hadn't savored properly while they were going on.

Roger held on to her hand. "Come on, snow bunny. Can you handle ten blocks? We'll never find a cab in this stuff."

"Fear not. This is mild where I come from."

Wilkes-Barre

Toby clapped snow-matted gloves together in glee. "We did it!"

The snow fort was a masterpiece, Marlena agreed. It was five feet high, surrounding a seven-foot-square space with snow benches along two sides. The benches also served as surveillance walks for Toby, who peered over the walls, scouting for Indians or other would-be invaders. Marlena hoped they'd made the crawl hole large enough for Tom. They'd soon find out.

"Wait till Daddy sees it. He'll go crazy." Toby's rosy face beamed. "When will he be home?"

"Not until after the news. Good God, Toby! What time is it?" She brushed away the snow covering her watch. "Four o'clock! I'll be late." She dropped the shovel and ran into the house. "Come on inside!"

Toby stomped after her.

She dialed the phone with one hand and mopped the melting snow she and Toby had tracked in with the other. No answer. Shirley, Toby's mother, had promised to pick up Toby by three. Marlena looked at Toby, who was looking at her, waiting for an update. She pulled the tyke into a quick, cold hug and patted his bottom. "We're both freezing. Take off your coat and sit by the radiator while I change. You're going to the station with me."

"Mommy's late?"

"Guess so."

Toby shrugged. "She's always late."

Marlena didn't comment as she sped into the kitchen

and poured milk in a pan for hot chocolate. Then she took two steps at a time up the stairs.

"I can make the cocoa. I can," Toby called after her.

"Just add the chocolate stuff and stir! Carefully!" she called back. "Shout if it boils."

Three minutes later she was downstairs, dressed in a soft red mohair dress. She could do her makeup at the station. "Boiling?" she asked.

"I don't think so." Toby frowned, squeezing his round brown eyes into slits. "But there was one bubble."

Perfect. Marlena poured steaming chocolate into mugs. "Mmm. I needed that."

"Mmm," Toby echoed. "I needed that too."

"Coat on. We have to hurry."

Toby obediently picked up his coat from the floor beside the kitchen radiator.

"Dry?"

"Almost."

She felt. "Almost, my foot. It's wet as a dishrag. You can't put that on." She rummaged in the kitchen coat closet and pulled out an old Irish fisherman's knit of Tom's rolled the sleeves back double, and buttoned it on Toby. It reached his ankles. "At least it's dry," she said chuckling.

"It's okay." Toby's little soul was flexible.

"It's an oversweater, like an overcoat. You look like a pixie, a nice warm pixie. How are your boots?"

"Only one has a hole."

She sighed. With all the money Tom gave Shirley, the woman could keep Toby in rubber boots. She raced upstairs and returned with a pair of Tom's socks, the one-size-fits-all type. All but little boys, Marlena thought as she stripped off Toby's soaking originals and rubbed icy white toes briskly. "You could get frostbite. Your mother will have to get you new boots."

"Those used to be my cousin Lou's."

"Terrific," she muttered as she bunched the socks around his ankles and added the old boots. "You're a mess."

"I am?" He looked like a waif.

"No." she gave him a reassuring hug. "You're not a mess, but your outfit is."

The phone rang.

"Let's get out of here," she said, "it's probably your father calling to tell me what I already know—that I'm late." She started for the door, then swung around to get the phone. It could be Shirley. Toby followed her circles.

"Hello?" she barked. "Alan, I'm on my way out the door. I'd be on the way if I weren't on the phone." She slammed down the phone, irritated that it hadn't been Shirley with a last-minute rescue.

Toby stood silent, put off by her irritated tone.

She took his hand. It wasn't his fault. She gave Toby a warm, reassuring hug. She'd buy him new boots tomorrow, without fail.

The streets were still icy. Toby bounced in the seat beside her, chattering with total trust. For the first time Marlena felt responsibility for this small creature, and she also experienced the accompanying fear. If some fool sideswiped them from the right, sliding on the ice, could she protect him? She slid to a stop at the Main Street light, more cautious than usual, half listening to Toby chirp on about the dog his mother wouldn't let him have.

"Almost every kid in my class has a pet. All I have is the goldfish Daddy won for me at the farm fair. And goldfish can't do nothing."

"Anything," Marlena corrected automatically.

"That too," he agreed cheerfully.

As the old Mercedes eased into the slick but reserved parking space, Marlena slid to a full stop and pulled the emergency brake with relief. "Let's go, tiger." Together, they carefully maneuvered up the treacherous ice of the old stairs.

At the reception desk Anna laughed at the sight of the scraggly duo. "Stop in Tom's office before you go on into the studio."

"Somebody should do something about the stairs," Marlena said. "Salt or sand. They're a hazard."

"You're beginning to sound like a mother," Anna said. "I'll call maintenance."

"Thanks." Marlena followed Toby, who raced ahead to Tom's office.

Tom looked up, startled at the sight of Toby. "Where the hell have you been? Sorry." He looked from Toby back to her. "You're half an hour late. And you're crazy to bring Toby in looking like that. Where's his jacket? You both look like a mess."

"That's what Lena said," Toby agreed cheerfully.

"He was soaked," Marlena said.

"I'll bet you haven't even read over the copy for tonight's show, let alone written your own stuff. If you want to become a full-time anchor, you've got to be professional, Marlena. Every day."

Marlena stared at him a second before bursting into tears of fury. It wasn't her fault. It was Shirley who had screwed things up. She'd bailed out Shirley and now she was getting the grief. It wasn't fair.

She whirled out of Tom's office and ran into the ladies' room, fumbling in her purse for makeup. She still saw a stranger at first glance in a mirror. The image. It had been six months since Tom had convinced her to go short and curly blonde. She'd made the change to please Tom more than herself. She missed the feel of her long, soft hair. Ungrateful wretch. She did everything to please him and what did she get in return? "You look like a mess."

But the mirror confirmed Tom's analysis. Her hair was curling in more directions than a compass had markings. Her face was smudged with something black. She remembered the coal they'd used to decorate the tower of the fort. There was chocolate on the corner of her mouth. She had hurriedly wiped Toby's face, but not her own. She couldn't help laughing.

A fast scrub, brush, a touch of mascara and eye shadow, and she was ready, her color high from the outdoor afternoon. The soft cowl neckline of the red dress made her neck look slender and elegant. Maybe she should start wearing earrings to emphasize her neck. Not without piercing her ears, she thought, or she would spend the rest of her life looking for "the other one."

Alan waited at the door to the studio, copy in hand. "I wrote your copy for you when I saw zero hour approaching. I hope you don't mind."

"Mind? You're a sweetheart."

"Ready to run away with me yet?"

"You missed your chance a year ago. We're coming up on anniversary number one." A short and long year. "Thanks for the copy." She smiled. "Brother Alan, I don't know what I would do without you." She hurried into position in the seat next to Ed's behind the long news desk.

"Car trouble?" Ed asked.

"No. Ex trouble. Tom's ex didn't pick up Toby." She scanned the news copy, making a few word changes. On the whole, Alan had captured her style. Ever faithful. She wondered how long he would continue to moon around. He'd been devastated when he learned she was sleeping with Tom, and downright surly for months after they were married.

"Okay?" Alan called from across the studio floor.

"Great, thanks!" she replied. She made an A-O.K. circle with her thumb and forefinger. She should encourage Alan to go out, she thought, but she liked having Alan available as an emotional backstop, especially on Tom's bastard days, like today.

There was no time for her to fan the irritation into anger. "Alive at Five" was on the air. Marlena looked into the camera and slated the show. She and Ed carried the show until six, when Michael took over for her. Michael and Ed anchored the main six o'clock news and stayed on to do the eleven o'clock while Marlena reappeared, bright-eyed, for the six A.M. report. Most days she covered a story personally as well. Today, she thought, the only news she'd covered was ex news and that was becoming an old story.

Her stomach no longer turned over with violent anxiety when the camera light blinked on. It merely fluttered with a controlled surge of adrenaline. She had come to terms with the camera, calling it "Harvey" after Jimmy Stewart's invisible rabbit. She read her copy to Harvey, transmitting an edge of sadness when the story warranted and a glint of humor for the puff pieces. She'd toned down her enthusiasm and outrage as far as she could for Tom, but she refused to read copy like an unfeeling android.

Tom conceded that she was reaching a nice balance and finally admitted that the subtle undertones of reaction in her voice added interest to the news. She'd taught the old dog at least one new thing, she thought, satisfied for that moment.

"Tell Harvey to cool it with the close-ups," she told the floor manager during a commercial break. "I put my makeup on in two seconds."

"You look fine." Alan's electronic reply boomed in from the control-room mike. "Harvey says so."

"You guys are nuts." Ed barely wiped the smile off his face in time to report on a runaway semi that had lost its brakes on the downhill run into town and smashed into a local pickup before rolling over an embankment.

"The WWKB-TV news family" that the ads touted now felt like a family to her. As in real families there had been hills and valleys in the relationship. The first year she'd been on trial, the new kid on the block, half mascot, half scapegoat. The second year she'd been the hard-working, ever-helpful junior member of the team until her affair with Tom became known. Then she had to work her way past the quiet, snide allegations of brown-nosing and apple-polishing. She'd asked for no favors and gradually had regained the respect of the family.

After she and Tom were married she had kept up the pace, fearful of renewed resentments. She'd insisted they spend their brief honeymoon in a Pocono lodge less than thirty miles away so she could work on her Pocono resort series. Six months later, when Tom assigned her as anchor for the "Alive at Five" report, she'd expected a resurgence of the old resentment. None had come.

She initiated a biweekly buffet for the staff, where they could air ideas and gripes. She wanted to keep the "family" happy. Tom pooh-poohed it as unnecessary, but humored her, discovering that it also humored the staff, and contributed to a smoother operation.

On the domestic front, she cooked with enthusiasm and a growing stack of cookbooks ranging from *LaRousse Gastronomique,* which Tom translated for her, to local church collections of favorite recipes. She made few changes in Tom's house, which she found comfortable. She apologized to him for having little to bring to him but herself. Tom laughed, saying she was plenty for him. "Heiresses don't make good wives. Tried one once, and forget it."

Her own family was another issue. Marlena was aware of Maggie's reservations about the May-September relationship.

When Marlena called to tell Maggie she was marrying

Tom the next day in a civil ceremony in the Luzerne County judge's chambers, Maggie let loose with her objections.

"Lena, he's old enough to be your father. You know I was never thrilled about Roger, but at least he was your own generation."

"Age is a mental state, Mother. Tom thinks young."

"Maybe immature's the word. This is his *third* marriage?"

Marlena didn't have the heart to correct Maggie. It would be Tom's "fourth and last," he'd said.

"When you're forty-two he'll be nearly sixty. How does that sound?"

Better than the seventy Marlena calculated, she thought to herself, but forty-two would be more than twenty years away. A lifetime.

"What about children? Don't you want children?"

"Eventually. I don't see why we can't if we want to. Right now we're too busy working to think about it. I'm just beginning to be halfway decent as a reporter."

"Decent. Do you truly think Tom will be a decent husband?"

"Oh, yes, Mama, I really do."

"Mama," Maggie said softly. "You're still a baby to me. But it's your life and I want you to be happy." Maggie tried to end on an upbeat note. "Just feed him lots of vitamin E and oysters."

"I love you too, Mama."

They flew to Des Moines for a family celebration. Her father, Bill, related to Tom as an equal while he still treated Marlena as a child. It felt strange. Her mother joked her way through the weekend, but Marlena knew she was anxious. Maggie kept burning the heat'n'eat rolls. Burned rolls were a family joke, but three days in a row meant Maggie's mind was nowhere close to food.

Her brothers pulled her aside for their teenage words of wisdom.

"That guy's older than Dad, I swear," Dave said darkly. "You are out of your skull."

"Thanks a lot. I'll remember those kind words next Christmas."

"They're building a nice old-age home out by the lake," Steve added. "He and Dad can play checkers there together in a few years."

"You guys are real sports." She tried to brush it off, but it disturbed her that her brothers didn't approve. But how could they understand? They were only twelve and fourteen, babies. "Tom likes you guys. How can you be so mean?"

"Hey, we like Tom," Dave objected.

"He's a nice guy," Steve nodded.

"For an old guy. I bet he dyes his hair. What do you think, Steve?"

Marlena interrupted the conversation by hurling a pillow at Dave. A merry melee ensued.

"Cool it, kids!" Bill called into the living room from the den. "Some of us are trying to have an adult conversation!"

"Lena started it!" Dave protested.

Marlena refused to defend herself like a little kid. "You boys are silly," she said, straightening her blouse before joining her parents and Tom in the den.

Tom and Bill were deep in conversation about the Battle of the Bulge. They had discovered that they'd fought in different divisions but in the same area of France and Belgium during the war. It was old home week—for them.

From Des Moines Marlena and Tom flew to Chicago for two days so Marlena could meet Tom's mother and sister. Mrs. Wells, in her late seventies, reminded Marlena too much of her own grandmother in Boston. Both were energetic, birdlike ladies who liked lace on the neck and wrists, still carried real handkerchiefs, and kept up on the news. Both lived alone with a day maid cooking and cleaning, and both had spacious apartments in elegant old buildings. Marlena could only relate to the feisty old lady as a granddaughter. "Mother Wells" was hard to say.

Mable, Tom's sister, reminded her of Roger's Aunt Gladys in New York. The comparisons made Tom age before her eyes, but Mable and her husband, a steel manufacturer already considering retirement, made Marlena feel welcome, if not contemporary with their generation.

She was grateful when they landed in the dumpy Wilkes-Barre airport, happy to be back where the generations didn't gap so close to home.

The hour news show went quickly, with few hitches. She concentrated on the content of her copy, trying to remain easy and relaxed. As she relinquished her seat to Michael, she steeled herself for the return to Tom's office.

Tom had been grumpy all week. It wasn't age, he insisted, when he complained about pains in his arm. It was the old war wound, the Nazi shrapnel. Cold always bothered it.

She opened the door to his office, hoping his humor had improved during the broadcast.

"Shut the door!" he shouted.

Tom was squatting on one side of the room behind his desk. Toby, in a mirror pose, hunched near the door.

"Gribbich." Toby hopped toward her. "Dad is teaching me to be a frog."

She burst into laughter. No, Tom was not getting old.

"Shut the door, please," Tom begged.

She shut it, giggling. "If Alan could see his hero now."

"Gribbich," Tom growled, and gave an awkward hop before rising to human stature.

"I can hop better than Daddy." Toby proved the statement.

"Come on, kid. Put your coat on, such as it is. I bet Lena will make bacon cheese dogs for us if we're nice."

"Yeah!" Toby hopped erect.

On the way to the car with Toby-the-frog hopping between them, Marlena said, "Tom, why don't we get Toby an extra set of clothes for days like this? He's over at our house a good bit."

"Winter's a bad time, Lena. Fuel bills, electric, dry cleaning—everything's high just now. We already give Shirley plenty for his clothes."

"Sure. Enough for her to drive to Hess's in Allentown to buy herself a new coat. That's where she was today."

"I know. She called."

"Doesn't it bug you?"

"It rankles. But she's young. She needs her outlets."

"I'm young too," Marlena snapped.

Tom opened the back door for Toby and helped Marlena into the front seat, leaning down to plant a soft kiss on her lips. "I forget. You seem older."

"Thanks, I think."

They waited for the diesel starter to signal ready.

"Do you think we should talk to her about it?" Marlena asked.

"Who? About what?"

"Shirley. About Toby's clothes."

"Things are tough for her, going back to school."

"Not too tough to buy a new coat at Hess's."

"There are better times to discuss this," Tom said tightly. "Too many little ears around."

"My ears!" Toby announced from the back seat. "You always say that when I'm around."

"That's right, froggie." Tom reached in back to tweak his son's ear.

"Lena's going to get me new boots, Dad. My boot has a

bi-i-ig hole in it. The snow comes through. Wait till you see our fort. Will it show in the dark, Lena?"

"When we turn on the porch light."

"It's the *best* fort you ever saw, Dad. Will you be surprised!"

Tom properly admired the fort, calling it a remarkable effort. He even agreed to crawl inside to inspect it with Toby while Marlena went inside to make dinner.

Just as she had finished wrapping bacon around the cheese-filled hot dogs, Toby dashed inside, gasping. "Help. You've got to come out. We're in the middle of a serious problem."

Laughing at his phrasing, she went out to discover she had failed as a snow architect, misjudging Tom's size. The wall above the crawl hole had cracked and caved in after Tom had gotten inside.

"Hand me the shovel!" Tom demanded.

She shook her head. "He's our prisoner, Toby. What shall we make him promise?"

"Make him promise never to make me eat salad!"

"Your father's son. What do you say, Tom?"

"No salad for a week."

She moved the shovel inches away from Tom's reach. "What do you think, Toby?"

"A month!" he insisted.

"Two weeks," Tom bargained.

"Sounds fair." Marlena handed over the shovel, then looked at Tom with panic of her own. "The cheese dogs!" She raced back into the kitchen in time to rescue them from the broiler. The edges were dark, but the bacon was perfect and the cheese only half melted over the sides. The oven bottom was a dark, glutinous mess that she ignored as she heard Tom order Toby to wipe his feet. Quickly, she set the kitchen table. They were all starved.

Three hot dogs later Tom kicked off his hoes. "My feet are frozen."

Marlena picked up his shoes to put them by the radiator and noticed a hole in the sole. "I'll have to buy both my men boots," she joked.

"You will not. I can buy my own shoes, thank you. And I don't want you buying Toby boots either. That's my responsibility."

"But if I want . . ."

"We'll discuss it later."

"When my little ears are not around," Toby added wisely.

"You got it, froggie."

Toby stuck out his tongue at Tom. "Gribbich."

"Same to you. Gribbich."

"Gribbich to both of you," Marlena said, half amused and half irritated because Tom seemed to resent her wanting to help.

After dinner she mended a hole in Toby's mitten and quietly glued foil-covered cardboard inside the hole of his boot with rubber cement while Tom read Toby the story of the little red caboose. Then they walked Toby the five blocks to his mother's house all in a row, Marlena and Tom each holding one of Toby's small hands and lifting him over icy spots with the swing he loved.

"More," Toby demanded.

"That's it. You'll wear out the old man."

Marlena winced at the phrase. "How's your arm?"

"It needed some exercise, but that may have been too much."

"How many more blocks?" asked Toby.

"Two," Tom said.

"It's cold." Toby shivered.

"We can make it," Marlena said encouragingly. "Remember the little red caboose."

As they reached the pavement in from of Toby's house they were laughing and chanting, "I think I can, I think I can." The noise brought Shirley to the door, looking angelic, Marlena thought. Shirley's long blond hair fell in soft curls to below the shoulder of a soft pink lounging dress.

Shirley's cool blue glance brushed past Marlena to rest warmly on Tom. "Hello there! You and Toby look like you're having fun."

Sensitive to Marlena's stiffening back, Tom kissed Toby good night and sent the boy inside, turning him over like a little prisoner of war marching across the neutral territory of the old, gray-painted wood porch.

"She's pretty. Don't you think so?" Marlena asked as they briskly retraced their trail in the snow.

Tom replied with an insouciant air, "She'll fade early. Another ten years and you won't look at her twice."

"Like Kim Novak, right?"

"What does it matter? How can you be jealous?"

"I don't know, but I don't like the way she looks at you. It's territorial."

"That's absurd. You know I only married her to make Toby legitimate. It was a fling. She's a nice kid, but love it was not."

"You're awfully nice to her." Marlena felt mean even as she spoke.

"I'm nice to all my ex-wives, but I don't sleep with them. I may have my faults, but I try to be a loyal bastard, if nothing else."

Marlena's step widened. "How can you be so nice to her when she's just bleeding you? And she's not even spending the money on Toby. If Toby were mine . . ." She stopped. Toby wasn't hers. And she hadn't even given her nameless could-have-been child a chance to be. She did the mental arithmetic. It would be three and a half now. It seemed a lifetime ago.

Tom caught up with her and took her arm, slowing her pace. "But he isn't. I wish he were, but as long as she's being a decent mother to him, she's in control. Except Wednesdays and our weekends."

"Unless she needs a baby-sitter," Marlena grumbled. "Like today."

"Maybe we should have one of our own," Tom said softly.

She stopped short, surprised, letting the statement sink in. A month before he had said he was through with fathering children. Toby was enough for him.

"Don't worry," he joked, perceiving her surprise. "I promise to take out lots of insurance."

"I wouldn't worry. You're too mean to die young. You'll live to be a hundred. You'll probably outlive me *and* Toby."

"Would you like that?"

"Being outlived by you?"

He laughed. "No. Having a child of our own."

"I think so." She made a little skip to get back into step with his strides. It could put to rest the old guilt for the never-was child.

"You could take a couple of years off from the station, until he or she was old enough for kindergarten, at least."

"Whoops." She stopped both of them in their tracks. "Why would I have to stop working? Haven't you ever heard of nursemaids?"

"Not for small children. That is when little minds are formed. I don't want some dodo messing up any child of ours."

"But Shirley is okay for Toby."

"She's a little flighty, but she's no dummy."

"You could always shift me to the eleven P.M. news, and

then you could watch the baby while I worked. And we could get a part-time girl for afternoons while I did stories."

"It would be too much for you."

"It wouldn't be any more of a crunch than going back to school at the same time."

"Shirley only went back to school this fall, after Toby was back in school."

"I'm not Shirley. Plenty of people keep working. You let Charlotte do the Wednesday-afternoon talk show."

"Maybe I'd let you have a talk show. I think Alan's getting fed up with the 'Sunday Seminar Show.' We can work it out." Tom's smile was warm but serious as he held open their door for her. "I want you to be happy."

"Really?"

"Come upstairs and I'll show you."

Their lovemaking had mellowed into comfort as much as passion. But this night Tom's desire swelled quickly. And the thought of having their own baby made her want him inside her, planting new seeds, driving them deeper and deeper within her.

But in the months that followed she didn't stop taking her birth control pills. Her hand would hesitate now and then as she stared at the numbered pink plastic circle before she religiously clicked to the pill of the day. She wasn't ready for semiretirement. Tom would put her out to pasture on "Sunday Seminar" like a milk cow.

By the spring of 1968, she was getting restless. She tried not to show it, but she knew Tom was sensitive to her growing discontent.

When he made a mild criticism of her coverage of a school-board meeting she bit his head off. "It wasn't my fault. Charlie's getting too old. He misses all the good shots."

"That's bullshit. Charlie is as good as anybody in the country. When he's sober." Tom laughed.

"Then maybe he wasn't sober."

"He was sober. Charlie never drinks during the day. Neither did I, even at my worst. That was part of the deal when I brought him with me from Chicago to Wilkes-Barre."

"Here's to WWKB, the northeast branch of AA, where no challenge is ever great enough to send a would-be alcoholic over the edge."

"Cut the crap. What's really bothering you?"

"I don't know. Nothing. That's what's bothering me. Nothing is happening. I'm not going anywhere."

"Where is there to go? I promised you Paris in September. Paris isn't good enough?"

"Paris is fine," she said absently. "But you know what I mean."

"Not really. You do reports all week long, anchor 'Alive at Five,' and drive yourself batty now that you're doing 'Sunday Seminar' too. You're recognized in supermarkets and at the movies. Not bad for a kid of twenty-four."

"Twenty-three," she corrected. "I won't be twenty-four until November. You always try to make me older." Tom had turned fifty-two the week before. More than twice her age.

"You're suffering from a slow news week," Tom said. "You can't stand the change of pace. Worry not. Things will pick up. It's an election year."

"I'm not that interested. Johnson has me disillusioned."

"You and the rest of the world."

"He's out of the race anyway. And I'm not a Bobby Kennedy fan. Humphrey is too much like the Pillsbury dough boy."

"Why don't you go eat worms? You're in that kind of mood. What do you want? More race riots and burned out ghettos like last month?"

"I want a big story to happen here. Another Appalachian meeting or something." Idly, Marlena poked at the grapes and cheese she had centered on the table for dessert.

"Stop that."

She looked at Tom questioningly.

"Stop poking the cheese. Other people might like some too."

"I'm not Toby."

"You're not acting much better."

"I'm buggy. Can't I get buggy sometimes?"

"You pick funny times. Things are going smooth as buttermilk. Our ratings are up. We have money in the bank. Personally. For the first time in years we're out of debt."

"I was never in debt."

The sudden *I* wiped away Tom's smile. "Whose team are you playing on these days?"

"I'm sorry, Tom. That was nasty. I didn't mean it. It just seems like nothing is going anywhere."

"You've already made that clear."

"I think we should think about things. I mean, where do we go from here? I can become main anchor someday and then what?"

"That's a lot, Lena. And it could take you a couple of years to get there. Anyway, then you'd gripe about not having enough time to cover more stories."

"But then what?" She ignored his criticism of her attitude. "We don't have any goals."

"What's wrong with living well and being happy?"

"Nothing, but there should be more."

"You mean you're twenty-four"—He caught himself—"twenty-three, and you haven't reached the stars yet."

"That's not fair. You've been there, you've done network in big cities, and you know what's out there. I don't."

"A jungle, babycakes, a jungle is out there. Stop me if you've heard this joke. Jane was up in the tree house one night smashing bananas for the chimp's dinner when Tarzan came swinging in on a vine. 'Quick, Jane, mix me a triple martini,' he gasped. 'What's wrong, Tarzan?' Jane asked. 'You never drink triple martinis.' 'You don't understand, Jane, it really *is* a jungle out there.'"

Her laugh was polite.

"Cute?"

"Cute."

"You're probably a bit down because you feel as though Alan is moving up by taking that job in Pittsburgh."

"You can't move up in TV unless you go to a larger station," she complained. "That's the way everybody does it, the way you did it."

"Moving from WWKB to PBS isn't such a giant step. The PBS station in Pittsburgh has a lower budget than we do."

"It doesn't matter. It's a larger city, a new place with new stories."

"The stories will all seem the same after a while, even in Pittsburgh," he said, laughing. "Cheer up. Next week I'll take you to a network shindig in Philadelphia. After you meet the brass, the kings of the jungle, you'll be grateful to get back home."

"Sure."

"Come on. Give me a hug."

Obediently, she moved in for the hug. "Tom." She leaned against him. "Why don't we buy WWKB?

He patted her head lightly. "I think your mind is going. I said we were out of debt, but my credit isn't good enough to get back in debt that much. You're talking about a few million dollars."

"Old man Donneker's getting old and he doesn't have any children interested in the place. He might make a deal."

"Not without a hefty down payment. You know that old

Scrooge. And what would we have that would improve our lives? All the headaches instead of only a fair share."

"If we already have the headaches, why not have the profits too? And the power to innovate."

"Innovation is expensive. I can innovate all I want to right now as long as it doesn't cost Donneker a lot of money. Even if, by some act of God, I could put together a local syndicate to buy him out, we wouldn't have the extra money to get creative."

Marlena hugged him. "But it would be fun to own the station, wouldn't it? To really have your own station?"

"It sounds good, but I'm not sure it would be worth the aggravation."

Marlena felt better. She had planted the seed as it had occured to her, and Tom hadn't thrown it away like a weed. It didn't matter if they didn't know anyone who had that kind of money. If she saved every cent of her salary, now up to $14,000 a year, it would take fifteen years to build a nest egg. She pushed aside the fact that Tom would be old enough to retire by then. It was a goal.

By the next week her mood was as sunny as the spring meadows. There was no reason for it other than the daffodils and bleeding hearts beside the kitchen door. She backburnered her new savings plan and took Toby shopping for "summer Ts," the bright, striped T-shirts in vogue for eight-year-olds, spending three times the money Tom had given her for the expedition.

Toby sat quietly, drawing horses in Tom's office as she did Tuesday's "Alive at Five" news. Then the threesome celebrated nothing beyond the pleasure of being together at a small Italian restaurant for Toby's "scetti and balls."

"What do you want for your birthday this year?" Marlena asked. Toby's birthday was August 3, but she liked to plan ahead.

"A horse!"

"Of course," she rhymed. "But you don't have room in your yard for a horse."

"We do." Tom smiled.

"There's where I draw the line. I'll cook for you two, clean up your messes, scratch your backs, and laugh at your silly jokes, but I will not shovel horse manure."

"We don't want her that liberated, do we, Toby? Shoveling horse shit is men's work."

Toby giggled. "Men shovel horse shit," he parroted, proud to use the taboo word.

"Nice talk." Marlena shook her head.

"You say it too." Toby looked her in the eye. "When you're mad."

Tom laughed. "Score one for the kid."

"Will you get me a horse, Daddy?"

"We'll see." Tom winked.

"You wouldn't put a horse in our backyard," Marlena protested.

"You'll see. I can't be entirely predictable or I'd lose my charm." Tom turned to Toby. "Maybe we'll give your mother a horse for a wedding present and then she'll give Lena and me both you and the horse."

"Yeah?" Toby's eyes grew wide.

"Is the wedding for sure?" Marlena asked. "I knew she was getting serious, but I didn't know they'd set the date."

"June thirtieth. She wants to be a June bride."

"How romantic."

"Don't be sarcastic. Valentine's Day is just as sentimental."

"Sweet and romantic," Marlena said as she gave a fast hug to Toby, sitting beside her on the red-padded bench of the booth.

"Like when Daddy kisses you?"

"Like that." Her smile was warm for both of them.

"I'm the catcher for my Little League now. We have a game Saturday. Can you come?"

"I'm sorry, Toby, but Lena and I have to drive to Philadelphia for a business meeting."

Toby's smile dropped away and he rubbed his eyes.

"How about next week? Do you have a game?"

Toby nodded soberly. "It won't be as good because we're playing the littler kids, but it's on Wednesday, when you do the news."

"Tell you what, son. I'll watch your game on Wednesday while Lena does the news and we'll both come watch the next game you play on Saturday. Okay? Okay. Now, we'd better get you home before you fall asleep on the table."

"I am *not* sleepy," he said with a yawn.

On the drive home Toby sat in front on Marlena's lap while Tom drove. She leaned her cheek on Toby's head as he snuggled against her, asleep before they had gone two blocks.

"He's getting so cute," Marlena whispered, giving her sleeping stepson a soft kiss on his softer curls. "Freckled like a cornflakes-box kid."

"Don't tell him that. He'd shoot you. He hates cornflakes."

Then Tom carried him up to the door and turned him over, literally, to Shirley and Mike, her fiancé, who looked far from ecstatic about the turnover.

Tom returned unencumbered. "I had a strange conversation with Shirley this afternoon."

"Yes?"

"You were complaining about life being too dull. What would you think about our having custody of Toby?"

The thought was startling. Since Shirley had met Mike several months before Marlena's relationship with her had improved. Shirley flirted less with Tom and sent fewer hostile glances in Marlena's direction. Marlena realized she had considered Shirley the "other woman," standing threateningly in the shadows. With the engagement ring on Shirley's finger, the imagined threat melted from Marlena's mind.

"Well?" Tom was waiting for a reaction.

"I've never considered the possibility a reality. I didn't think Shirley would ever give Toby up. She's such a strange mixture of a negligent and doting mother."

"She told me that Mike feels Toby cramps his style. He could be tough on newlyweds."

Marlena silently bristled at the attitude that moved them into an "old couple" status.

"Shirley called to ask me what we'd think about a reversal of the current custody. He'd live with us and she'd take him for dinner Wednesday nights, and every other weekend, and when we wanted to go on vacation. She likes you and she likes the way you are with Toby."

"Thanks."

"Without support to pay we could hire a housekeeper or at least someone part-time to be there when Toby gets home from school, someone who could start dinner for you, clean, do the laundry."

"You've been thinking about this, haven't you?"

"Only since this morning. I also was thinking that when we have the household set up, we could work a little harder on giving Toby a brother or sister."

She was silent. Was that the carrot to goad her into taking on Toby?

"You do like the little bugger, don't you?"

"Tom, I love Toby. You know that. I think it would be fun to have him. We could turn your den downstairs into a bedroom for him and make the extra bedroom we use for storage into your den."

"You don't want our style cramped either."

"I wouldn't want him upset by strange bumps in the night."

They were still parked in their own driveway. It was not a conversation easily interrupted. Tom leaned over from behind the steering wheel and kissed her gently. "I love you, you know that?"

"I know that. And maybe having Toby around full-time would be good for us all." Maybe it would alleviate the restlessness.

Tom made love to her that night with a sweet and patient passion, working his way with his finely tuned tongue from pleasure zones to erotic triggers, giving her selfish, shuddering pleasure before coupling in a hard and primal drive that brought them to a mutual climax that left them panting, satisfied.

Marlena didn't take her pill that morning or the rest of the week as she directed her investigative skills toward finding a suitable housekeeper and little-boy bedroom furniture. By Saturday she had a report on everything from the cost of polished pine bunk beds to the median wage for local domestics. The report lasted from the scrambled eggs and sausage at the breakfast table until they pulled up to the canopy in front of the gracious old Barclay Hotel on Rittenhouse Square in Philadelphia at five that evening. She was so full of enthusiasm for her progress on the home front, she had not given Tom space to brief her on the network personalities they would soon meet.

Their suite delighted her. The spacious parlor was tastefully decorated in cream and Williamsburg blue, with fresh fruit on the carved cherry center table and Dom Perignon on ice awaiting their arrival.

"Some jungle." She laughed.

"Wait and see. We're still in the tree house."

Marlena looked out of the deep-silled window at the

square, where a few people were walking dogs in the balmy twilight. The sky above the soft green of the trees was tinged with the subtle gray-pink and lavender tones found only above major cities. The soft, radiant glow came close to making pollution acceptable. Clean sunsets lacked this mystical depth.

She looked down from the sky to the gracious old brick and granite buildings facing in, quietly complementing the square as they had done for generations. She noted the bright flower beds stretching beside the walks and circling the statues. A trim, well-groomed Irish setter bounded into view, leaping over a flower bed to pursue a squirrel that escaped, by a whisker, up an old maple.

"Tom!" Marlena swirled back to her husband, inspired.

"You like?"

"Let's get Toby a dog for his birthday. We need a dog. I don't know why I didn't think of it before. Dad can bring one of the puppies along in August." Her father was an amateur dog breeder. Marlena couldn't remember there ever being fewer than three dogs in the Williams household. At present the Williams kennel included two Samoyeds, one elkhound, and a German shepherd that had gone into heat before Bill Williams noticed. The shepherd was expecting a litter of Samoyed-shepherds or elkhound-shepherds. Only time would tell.

"Toby's heart is set on a horse."

"Do you really want to shovel horse shit?"

"Not really. I get enough around the station—and around the house sometimes too."

"Toby is old enough to handle a dog poop patrol. And a dog would be his friend. It might help him make the adjustment to a new house."

"I wouldn't have to turn the garage into a stable for a dog, would I?"

"Good. It's decided. I'll call Dad and put in an order for

one of Duchess's whelps. Mama will just love driving in from Des Moines with a puppy weeing all over her."

"You're wicked."

She handed Tom the champagne and corkscrew. "Let's drink to that."

She turned on the radio, searching for romantic music, tuning past Bill Haley's "Rock Around the Clock" before settling for the Beatles' "Hey Jude." She peeled off her jacket and slipped out of her shoes. "Mmm. Why can't we stay here and have a quiet evening? Room service. Soft music. I love hotels. They make me feel like a loose woman." She licked her lips, ran her hands through her soft curls and leaned back, seductively on the wide blue couch. "Don't be afraid," she echoed the song. "Come here and I'll show you what I mean."

Tom leaned down to hand her a glass of champagne. "Cool it for a couple of hours, Mrs. Wells. Cocktails begin at six o'clock downstairs and we have to put in an appearance for the honor of WWKB and the network with which it is affiliated."

"Affiliated. Why can't we get affiliated first?" She gave the word new meaning.

"No time. They'd come looking for me because we're at the head table. I'm introducing Read Brewer."

"Read Brewer, boy wonder president of IBS? You didn't tell me that. How come?"

"How come? Because I make great introductions. And I happened to be his first boss at IBS. I'm the man who taught that bastard to be a boy wonder. He came to us cold, an English major fresh out of college. I had to teach him that cutaway does not mean edit out half the script. Like the line? It's true. That's what he thought his first day on the job, but he was a learner."

"That's what you called me too, once."

"You are. It was all true. But if he had your other virtues, I wouldn't have let him get away either." Tom lifted his glass to toast her and he blew her a kiss.

"That doesn't seem fair. Just because I'm a woman, you want to keep me three paces behind."

"My darling wife, in another five years you can take over as general manager and demote me to janitor for all I care. As long as I can stay on top where it counts."

She didn't believe him, but it sounded gallant, so she responded with a very warm kiss.

He backed off with regret. "Change into your fancies. We have to get downstairs."

Marlena glanced down, giggling. "Now who has to cool it?"

"Do not touch or I could lose my job." Tom stepped away with a chuckle. "Your timing on getting sexy sucks."

"So do I," she said softly.

"Enough!" Tom retreated into the bathroom. "Five minutes," he called like a stage manager.

Ten minutes later she had metamorphosed into an elegant creature clad in a sheer ice blue dress with silvery tights and silver sandals. The soft fabric molded to her body as she walked.

"No one will hear a word I say tonight," Tom said. "I think hem lengths are going up just for you and your legs."

"No," she whispered as she moved forward, touching him with the length of her body. "For you."

"The hell with the introduction," he whispered into her ear. "I don't want to share you with the lechers downstairs."

She giggled. "Not when I have my own lecher upstairs." She liked teasing him.

"We won't stay for the after-dinner chitchat. We'll escape as soon as dinner is over. I promise."

"Good. I hate crowds of strangers. I'm terrible at names unless I can write them down."

When they reached the lobby people were already filtering into the banquet room, where the old gilt chandeliers cast the soft dark shadows of the crystal and yellow roses across the white linen tablecloths.

"Oh dear," Marlena murmured at the sight of the dozens of roses.

Tom misinterpreted her concern. "Don't worry." He handed her a name tag. "Everyone will be wearing one."

"It ruins the lines of my dress," she complained.

"Then don't wear one. That is, if you want to remain an unknown."

She carefully pinned the tag to the top of her dress. She could always have the neckline cut lower if it left holes.

Faces turned toward them as she followed Tom to the head table. She straightened, carefully avoiding returning the attention. She realized that they were looking at her. She felt a charge of energy stronger than the surge that always filled her the moment she knew the cameras were live. She felt like a star, and she gave Read Brewer and his wife a dazzling smile as Tom introduced her to them, acutely aware that she had the room's center stage.

"Sit down, please." Read patted the chair beside him.

Her feeling of glamour was shorter-lived than the yellow roses cut in their prime. Within minutes she began sneezing uncontrollably. She had to stand and back away from the table in order to explain that she was allergic to roses. Then she had to suffer the mortification of Read summoning the waiter to remove the roses from the head table. They refused to allow her to have supper alone in the suite.

Her mascara was running. She could feel it. Her eyes felt scratchy and swollen. She stumbled out of the room feeling like a naked emperor. Tom followed, asking her what he could do to help. She sent him in search of nose spray and antihistamines, vowing to see an allergist first thing the next week.

All she wanted to do was hide in their room. She felt miserable and ashamed. They were holding up the entire IBS dinner. She would ruin everything.

Tom wouldn't hear of escape. "It will become folklore, Lena, and we'll laugh about the way you made even the boy wonder wait on your sneezes. Marlena's roses will become an IBS family joke."

"I'm a joke, all right." She sniffled.

"But you're not a quitter. Go upstairs and redo your makeup, take your pills, spray your nose, and be back down here in fifteen minutes. Like a pro."

Tom was good for her. He didn't allow her self-indulgence or self-pity. Gentle and tough. And usually right. That part rankled.

A cold, wet washcloth helped calm the irritation and dry the tears. When she returned to the banquet room everything seemed the same except that there wasn't a rose in sight. Every table had been deflowered for her. She had the power to banish roses and delay dinners, too, she remembered, as contrition quickened her step.

The black ties of the tuxedo-clad waiters flashed by as they carried the prime rib platters protected by silver domes. Marlena toyed with her food, having sneezed away her appetite. She still felt stuffy, and the antihistamine was making her drowsy. She fought to keep her eyes open and pay attention to the repartee bouncing across her from Tom to Read and back. She permitted herself a long blink, just a few seconds to ease the gritty feeling of her eyes. Tom touched her shoulder in warning and her chin snapped up with an automatic smile.

"Wait for Read's speech to fall asleep," Tom joked.

Read signaled a waiter and asked for coffee. "I know how allergy pills are," he said to Marlena.

She was grateful. Read didn't seem to fit the role of king of the jungle.

Then Tom took over and called the crowd to order, then began his good-humored welcome that segued into a kidding introduction of the "ugly duckling who turned corporate swan, your boss and mine.

"Here was this gangly kid I thought was too dumb to tear wire copy out of the machine," Tom said. "What I didn't know when I'd see him staring blankly at the AP wire was that he was figuring out how to develop a TV version of a wire service, the international TV syndicate service that now helps IBS stay profitable and enables us poor folk in the hinterlands to have network programming at a price that leaves us *almost* enough money to pay AP too."

Tom rambled on, swinging his remarks into an impressive recitation of Read's accomplishments, concluding by wondering if the boy wonder, who had just gotten his first pair of reading glasses this year at age thirty-nine, was wondering what ever happened to the boy?

Read stepped up to the mike, put on his reading glasses, and told the crowd he felt, thanks to Tom, that "I learned to take it all on the chin, like a man. But after meeting Tom's wife, I just hope I can grow up to be half the man that Tom has to be."

Marlena blushed, as much from anger as from the crowd's attention. She liked a good off-color remark as much as Tom did, but she was more than his fluff ball or sex symbol. She was a professional too. She looked down at her short silk skirt and her mind cooled. She had dressed sexily. What did she expect?

Enjoying the compliment to his manhood, Tom squeezed her knee under the table and winked. His hand felt warm against her cool leg. She let it be. This was no time to dislodge his good humor. And if Read or the others ever saw her work, they would see that she was more than a pair of legs. The contrast might intensify the impact.

Tom reneged on his promise to escape after dessert

when Read invited them to join a select few in the presidential suite for after-dinner drinks.

"My dear, you are just divine. How do you stay so thin?" DeeDee Biddle Brewer, an angular woman who had never recovered from her debutante ball, gushed at Marlena. Marlena wondered what Tom would say if she told DeeDee Tom weighed her in every morning and shamed her away from food if the scales tipped the wrong way—above a hundred pounds. She accepted this area of tyranny as a given. She had grown up with a father who had his own fetishes about her physical condition. Bill's concern was not weight but regularity. Better to suffer an occasional fast than enemas or chocolate laxatives, she thought, her tongue curling at the acerbic memory.

"My wife is a very disciplined lady," Tom said.

Andy Froelich, news director for WIB-TV, the Philadelphia affiliate of IBS, guffawed. "Sorry, Tom, but she's the most deliciously undisciplined looking thing I've seen in years."

"Don't mind him." Nancy Froelich clapped a well-manicured hand over her husband's ample mouth. "Andy's not very disciplined himself tonight. He more than did justice to your lovely wine at dinner, Read." She smiled at their host.

Read's thin laugh and lean body did credit to his name. He spoke in a tenor that sounded boyish, contrasting with Tom and Andy's full, deep voices. "If Andy weren't such a damn good news director, I'd send him away for a year of finishing school."

"Or bury him in Wilkes-Barre." Nancy laughed wickedly. "No offense, Tom. I hear you like it up there."

"I've always been a country boy at heart."

Nancy was a tall, well-built woman in her early forties with short, carefully curled hair. Aggressive in a darkly humorous way, she was the kind of woman Marlena thought would make a better friend than enemy.

Nancy removed her hand from Andy's steadfast smile and blew him a kiss.

"I don't worry about Andy getting out of line," Read said. "Not as long as Nancy is around."

"Keep them on a short leash and they'll never stray." Nancy winked at Marlena. "It's about time one of Tom's wives learned that."

"You are outrageous, wife." Andy laughed. "Tom, you look great. Whatever you two are doing it's working. Congratulations."

"Read, darling," Nancy said, "do you know you're the only person here who has met all of Tom and Andy's wives?"

Marlena's grip on Tom's hand tightened. She felt out of place, like a high-school girl at a college fraternity.

"This is my *last* and *best* wife," Tom stated. "She's also the best reporter I have ever trained and the nicest woman I know. She can cook too."

"Tell them, Tom. It's refreshing to hear a man speak that way about his wife."

Amen, thought Marlena. Thank you.

"You haven't been married long, that's evident." Nancy remained the cynic.

"You work?" DeeDee's thin, clean-plucked brows rose a millimeter, stopping just before the point where wrinkles would form. "How nice for you."

"Those who can, work. Those who can't, play tennis," Andy cracked.

"Kitty played wonderful tennis. Do you play tennis, dear?"

Kitty had been Tom's first wife, the heiress who'd run him in alcoholic circles. She glanced at Tom. Tom was still, too still. He was fuming.

"Time to put away the fangs, ladies," Read said. "They're on their bad behavior, Marlena. They hate having to listen to my speeches almost as much as they can't cope with a beautiful young woman who doesn't need to spend hours at Elizabeth Arden."

"Touché." Nancy grinned. "Sit down and relax, DeeDee. We have to be nice."

"Maybe I should have a triple martini," Marlena whispered in Tom's ear.

He laughed, and she could feel him relax beside her.

DeeDee and Nancy enmeshed themselves in a private conversation, discussing designer fashions, masseuses, and other parties. Marlena caught enough glittering scraps of conversation to piece together the fact that Nancy and Andy socialized a lot with DeeDee and Read's moneyed set.

The men discussed figures, ratings, and advertising rates. Read was obviously pleased with Tom's operation. She learned that Wilkes-Barre had been IBS's worst affiliate until Tom took over and turned it around. WWKB now had one of the best profit margins and ratings in the network. She felt proud of him and pleased with herself, as though her own choice of a man had been given a corporate seal of approval.

Noticing Marlena's silence, Tom turned the conversation to Marlena's accomplishments. Since she had taken over the "Alive at Five" anchor slot they'd moved up from number two to number one for that hour.

Andy and Read were impressed.

"Sounds like you've got yourself a good team in a couple of ways," Read said.

"Anytime you're ready to move back into the big league, Tom, give me a call," Andy added. "Baumgarten is thinking about retiring, and I'm ripe and ready for general manager."

"You and Andy were a good team, Tom. I'd give my blessing."

Marlena remembered that Andy had been Tom's assistant bureau chief in Chicago, where Read had started out.

Tom didn't even nibble at the bait. "We like Wilkes-Barre. I'm growing a nice little stand of blue spruces there that I'd hate to leave."

"He looks like a happy man to me," Read said. "I can't argue with that."

"The offer's open." Andy shrugged.

Marlena squeezed Tom's leg. He didn't look at her.

On the drive home Marlena broached the subject of moving to Philadelphia. Tom was firm. It would be wrong for them, especially for Toby. They couldn't uproot Toby with so many changes already going on around him.

"It's not Toby, is it? It's you. You're afraid of the fast track."

"Maybe. It got bad last time around."

"But it would be different. We're a team. I'm not a Nancy or a DeeDee or a Kitty."

The car swerved for a second before Tom regained control. "Sorry. You surprised me. I forget what a good listener I've trained you to be. No, you're not a Kitty. But the news director's job isn't open yet. Andy's crazy. Baumgarten can't be more than, let me think, fifty-eight at the most. He's not ready to step down for Andy yet. Andy had a lot to drink. That makes for wishful thinking."

"It sounded like more than that to me."

"It wasn't. Forget it. Besides, network management jobs are like musical chairs. Who knows when the music stops?"

"Then Baumgarten might find another chair anyway."

"And Andy might not get the general manager's job either."

"But if he did?"

"Then we'll see."

"He might *really* offer you the job?"

Tom was noncommittal. "He might."

She tucked the thought in the back of her mind, where it lay glittering like a bright and distant star to wish upon at night.

Four

❖

Wilkes-Barre

WHEN BOBBY KENNEDY lay dying in the hotel kitchen in mid-June she heard in the new pain the empty echoes of earlier deaths. She welcomed her parents in July, shepherd-elkhound puppy in tow. New life for Toby and Tom and her.

Marlena cuddled the small, furry creature while Toby danced his joy beside them. "Do I still get a horse for my birthday?" he asked Tom.

"Oh, why not?" Tom mimed shoveling.

"Men shovel horse shit," Toby told Maggie.

"Don't they just." Maggie laughed.

Her father looked out the kitchen window. "Those are nice trees you have beside the drive. Norwegian blue spruce?"

"Yes, sir," Tom said. "Christmas trees. Come on out. I'll show you."

"And forget the 'sir' stuff. It sounds silly. Just call me Bill." Bill tweaked Toby on the nose. "Coming along, son?"

Toby ran after Bill and Tom. "I can show you the best one."

Marlena kissed the puppy on its tiny nose. "I love her, Mama. What shall we name her?"

The little pink tongue answered with a lick.

"Chewer might be appropriate. The little rascal ate right through my purse strap." Maggie held up the tattered proof. "But she's the prize of the litter. Your brothers picked her out for you. They said she was just like you. A little growly and bossy, but nice. She controlled the rest of the litter."

They shared the laughter. Maggie reported that the boys were doing fine, although they were following in Marlena's footsteps with practical jokes. "I thought I could relax and stop worrying about whether there was salt in the sugar after you left home, but your brothers are worse. Our house is like a mine field. I never know what's going to explode next."

Marlena chopped onions and shredded cheese for a quick quiche while she listened to Maggie.

Maggie was happy. She enjoyed teaching and only regretted that she hadn't gotten into it earlier. "One of these days I'm going to get my Masters degree. Then I'll have so many brains you won't be able to talk to me anymore."

"I'll send you memos."

Marlena felt good about the visit. She and Maggie were friends again. Her mother had accepted Tom; only an occasional remark revealed a residue of disquiet about the long run.

"Mama!" Bill called through the kitchen doorway. "Where did you put my binoculars? Tom and I want to take Toby for a bird walk."

"I didn't put them anywhere. They're where you put them—if you packed them."

"Then they must be in the car, if I didn't take them out at home." Bill's shiny, bald head disappeared.

"He never changes." Marlena giggled.

"He's a nice man. It's been fun growing up with him."

"Ouch. I didn't see that one coming. I know I can't grow up with Tom because he's so far ahead of me. Maybe I'm just growing up to meet him."

Maggie knocked on the wooden table. "I'm happy you're happy now. I'm sorry, but I can't help worrying sometimes about twenty years from now."

"You always told me if you worry about the present the future takes care of itself."

"Guess I did."

"Mama, Tom isn't that old. He doesn't have a gray hair on his head."

Maggie's forehead wrinkled quizzically. "Then his face is getting prematurely old."

"Very funny."

"Have you decided about children of your own?"

"You don't beat around any bushes."

"Well?"

"We've been . . . trying. Nothing yet."

"Maybe Tom should see a fertility expert. They're making a lot of progress in helping . . ."

"Older men?" Marlena shook her head. "Picasso's wife was forty years younger than he was. Look at Justice Douglas."

"It's fine now, but I've seen too many young women nursing sick old men."

Marlena put down the paring knife, picked up the puppy, and sat down at the table beside Maggie. "And I've seen your friend Rodney Davis nursing his twenty-five-year-old wife with cerebral palsy. People can get sick at any age."

"That isn't the norm."

"Mama, we're happy. I like living with a grown-up." She jumped up, holding the puppy away from her. "Damn!"

Maggie laughed. "I would say you're all wet." The

puppy had let go of its small, untrained bladder in a big way, tinting Marlena's white shorts a sunny yellow.

"I'd better change before the men get back. They'd all tease me blind."

Maggie followed her daughter upstairs and poked through her closets while Marlena took a fast shower. The puppy sniffed around the bedroom floor, its looped, furry tail wagging. "I think your friend is proud of herself," Maggie called.

"We should name her *la pisseur* and call her *P* for short."

"It would be one way to make her obedient. Here, P! And she would."

Marlena returned to the bedroom wearing only a smile. As she rummaged in a drawer for fresh underwear, Maggie sat on the edge of the bed. "I can count your ribs," Maggie accused. "Are you eating right?"

"Of course I'm eating, but I have to keep my weight down for the cameras."

"Ten pounds would keep you from looking like a victim of Auschwitz."

"Tom would fire me if I got fat."

"Then how can you think about having a baby?"

"They could shoot me from the shoulders up." It could be a problem on location work, she thought.

"If you do get pregnant, don't diet. I don't want a rickety grandchild. Grandchild. Grandma. That makes me sound too old."

"We'll never call you Grandma, I promise. Mama Maggie." Marlena slipped on a bright blue flowered sundress.

"That's pretty. Is it new?"

"Last year. I should take you to the factory outlets around here. You won't believe the designer clothes manufactured in this area. Forty to fifty percent off. Millie, my friend at the station who does the weather, and I go crazy at those places. We dress better than New York anchors!"

"You always were backward." Maggie smiled. "I stocked up on clothes *before* I got married. Then clothes went to the bottom of the list. First it was things for the house, then for you kids."

"I know, Mama. My real binges came before I got married too. I haven't bought much since. Tom earns good money, but he was paying a lot in child support and alimony. He'd agreed to support Shirley completely while she went back to school to get her degree so she could teach. Then the payments were supposed to go way down.

"It all made sense for the long run, as you like to put it. But Tom was squeezed the last couple of years. And he refused to let me pay for any basics. I had to pay on the sly for extra groceries. He practically audited the receipts. So I would go buy a dress for twelve dollars that retailed for forty-five and spend the difference on the house."

Maggie's laugh was full. "Man's pride is the greatest cause of woman's small deceits. It was probably that way in the stone age. Some poor cavewoman had to pretend she accidentally found the mammoth she'd speared for dinner."

"Come on, Mama. We'd better go downstairs and wash the strawberries you bought for lunch."

"You mean the ones I accidentally found in the back forty."

Toby burst through the kitchen door to greet them. "That was great! We saw lots of starlings. They can be mean birds, can't they, Grandpa Bill?" Toby looked around for his new hero as Bill and Tom entered.

Maggie grinned at her husband and gave his shiny head a fast, loving rub. "Grandpa Bill, huh? Time flies when you're having fun."

Bill's smile was only a little sheepish. He winked at Marlena. "You have full custody now. That gives Grandpa Bill a little custody too." He looked at Maggie. "Show Grandma Maggie the fossil rock we found, Toby."

"Farewell sweet youth." Maggie's smile stretched from Bill to Toby. "Let me see. Yes, that is a real prize fossil. I can count the leaves on the fern."

Tom winked at Marlena, signaling his approval.

"You explorers must be famished," Marlena said. "I'd better get busy."

"No way," Tom said. "We're going to Victorio's to celebrate our find."

Marlena frowned at him. She knew Tom had already blown their budget entertaining her parents. Another expensive lunch wasn't necessary. Her parents were happy just being there.

"On one condition: I treat." Bill rumpled Toby's blond curls. "I helped make the find."

"No way. This is my turf."

Marlena shot Tom a dark look that went unheeded by Tom, if not by Maggie.

The two-week visit was over too quickly for Marlena. With Tom treating her as an equal and her parents as peers, she saw them in a new perspective, more as people than as parents. And she liked them. It was a nice discovery.

Everyone helped name the puppy before Bill and Maggie drove away. The imperious little creature's full name became Madame Beulah Pisseur Shoemaker Wells. Beulah, because Maggie said the puppy looked like Bill's old Aunt Beulah, Pisseur, because Maggie and Tom had both been baptized along with Marlena, Shoemaker, because Marlena had unwittingly contributed two pair of sandals and a precious pair of pumps to the teething process. Everyone called her Madame.

Marlena's summer romped by with the frisky pace of

Madame and Toby. The three of them failed obedience school together, but they persevered in teaching Madame and her bladder that the backyard was the only place to go. On his birthday Toby settled for a racing bike, which didn't need feeding or walking.

Local news was soft, with county fairs vying for attention with minor boating accidents. The national news was harder, but too distant to touch their summer smiles.

August saw a United States with little heart for the renewed fighting in Vietnam. Eisenhower, the beloved general in the last respectable war, suffered his sixth heart attack two days before his protégé, Richard Nixon, won the Republican nomination. The Soviets invaded Czechoslovakia and the world complained publicly while the purge of suspect Czechs went unchecked.

The week before Alan left for Pittsburgh the national news came closest to affecting the local scene. The report on the Yippy arrests in Chicago, when they presented a live pig as a Presidential candidate at the Democratic Convention, was accidentally aired back to back with a local story on the prize-winning pig at the Luzerne County farm show. The sixty-three newsmen attacked by the police seemed far away. Marlena felt envy. Feeling injured would be better than feeling out of touch, unnewsworthy.

Tom was swamped as he interviewed people for news director and did his own and Alan's job too. Marlena hadn't realized how much Alan had handled. She had thought of him as Tom's yes-man, but he had taken care of a myriad of small details that now had Tom bogged down.

Marlena complained that she was too young to feel like a widow with child. They hadn't yet found a full-time housekeeper and the sixteen-year-old mother's helper who allowed Marlena to get away to cover stories afternoons went back to school the second week of September.

Since Toby went back to school at the same time, Marlena temporarily solved the problem by arranging for the girl to come after school and watch Toby until she dashed back from the studio at six forty-five.

As the temperature cooled so did Marlena's enthusiasm for the new domestic arrangements. Toby was as much work as fun. She chafed at the domestic juggling, cooking, cleaning and shopping, monitoring homework, shopping for school supplies, and packing lunches. She knew her reporting was suffering. She was barely covering one story a week beyond the five o'clock anchoring.

Tom was too pressured by his own dual roles to have much sympathy for her. He gave her "atta-girl, you're doing fine" reassurances.

She came up with a new plan. If he would let her anchor the eleven o'clock evening news, she could cover stories during the day when Toby was in school and they could eat at a normal hour, unhurried, and put Toby to bed before she went in for the late news broadcast.

"No way," Tom objected. "You need more sleep than you would get because of your six A.M. report."

"Take me off the morning report. Then you wouldn't have to make Toby's breakfast anymore."

"I don't mind that. It's the only time I get to talk to him these days. The bottom line is that I'm handling too many changes now. Neither Ed nor Michael wants the early show, and I can't break in anyone new. Not now."

"I thought you loved me."

"Love has nothing to do with this."

"I spend half my time taking care of Toby because I love you." She heard herself laying out the guilt for him to pick up. She didn't care. Any weapon was fair if it made him realize the present situation was unfair.

"I'm talking as the general manager of WWKB, not as your husband or Toby's father. No more changes."

"You don't seem to mind putting me through changes," she muttered.

"It's not as bad as all that is it?'

"Tom, I'm the one who has to run around in circles trying to get everything done for all of us. Since you took custody of Toby you've been home less than before. You don't have the slightest idea how much more work there is. The late suppers we have out no longer give me a break. I still have to cook for Toby. Half the time he's asleep before you get home."

"You're right." Tom sighed. "But this won't last forever. I'll find a good news director soon. Then things will change. If you'd make a real effort to find a housekeeper now that we can afford one instead of saving money with that teenager, you wouldn't have to play the martyr." He looked at her as though seeing her for the first time that evening. "You look run-down."

If Toby hadn't come into the kitchen at that moment, she would have burst into tears. She'd placed ads in the paper for weeks and visited every employment agency within forty miles. She'd interviewed a dozen people who were all wrong. Finding someone who could work five days a week from noon to eight at night wasn't easy—not in Wilkes-Barre.

"Dad." Toby was oblivious of the tension. "Want to play some baseball?"

"I have to go to the office. Sorry."

"It's Saturday," Toby objected.

"News happens every day. Sorry about that."

"Yeah," Toby grumbled. "Just like you're sorry we don't have a color TV yet."

"Christmas, Toby. You have to have something special to look forward to. By then all the programs may be in color."

"NBC already has one hundred percent color programming," Marlena said.

"You're a big help," Tom snapped. "JBS won't be there until Christmas, if then."

"It's dumb. Joey Ardino has a color set of his own and his father doesn't even work in TV."

"Maybe that's why he's rich enough to afford one," Marlena quipped.

"Complain, complain, complain. If that's all I hear around this place, I might as well go to work and hear more of the same."

Toby threw his baseball at Madame.

"Don't do that," Marlena ordered as Madame ran under the kitchen table for protection. "If that ball had hit her, you could have hurt her."

"Sorry," Toby muttered, his face pulled into a pout.

Marlena's mood was as dark, but she couldn't stand seeing Toby so unhappy. Somebody had to do something. "I'll come outside and play catch with you as soon as I do the breakfast dishes," she said.

Tom rose from the bleak breakfast table. "And take a nap this afternoon—both of you."

"I don't want a nap. I want freedom to report," she snapped.

"What's Lena mad about?"

Tom picked up the morning paper. "Women get grouchy sometimes. It's probably her time of moon."

Toby frowned. "I'm going outside to get the bat and my catcher's mitt, okay?"

"Okay." Marlena stared out the window, trying to control her irritation. It was not her "time of moon" and Tom knew it. He didn't know that she was back on her birth control pills. Toby was enough for her to handle.

Tom tucked the paper in his briefcase. "Need the car?"

"No. I'm not going anywhere these days."

"Patience, Lena. It'll calm down in a couple of weeks. Patience." Patience was a quality that seemed to come more easily at fifty-two than at twenty-four. He tilted her chin up and leaned down to brush her lips with a kiss. "And I do appreciate all you're doing."

"Thanks."

"I do."

"Lena!" Toby's high-pitched voice carried inside.

"I'll try to get home early. Get a sitter and we'll catch a movie tonight."

She stared after him as he left, realizing she hadn't looked at the paper yet. Tom was forgetting that she was a newsperson too.

That night they went to see *The Thomas Crown Affair,* which only depressed her more as she compared her domestic morass with the glamorous life-style portrayed by Faye Dunaway. She didn't stop to think that the TV viewers who watched her on the air, reporting the news with every curl in place, gave as little thought to the possibility of her mundane responsibilities as she gave to the realities of Faye Dunaway's grocery lists.

Tom tried to make things easier by coming home from the office for a few hours at dinnertime, then dashing back to the studio. The strain began showing on him too. Tempers were shorter than their hours together.

Millie noticed Marlena's blue mood and talked her into a Saturday shopping spree that continued through dinner and Marlena's second movie of the fall, *The Graduate.*

Over dinner Millie admitted that she envied Marlena's situation—a man she loved, a home to run, even Toby to take care of. Millie said she felt like a baby, still living at home at twenty-eight, but her mother was old-fashioned and didn't think it was right for Millie to get her own apartment.

Marlena perceived Millie's meadows as green and free and she told her as much. Millie could stay out as late as she liked, take off for Philadelphia parties, make last-minute trips to New York for plays. Marlena sounded as old as her mother to herself as she advised Millie to enjoy her freedom while she could.

Millie complained that the men she dated were silly little boys, fun but immature. None of them was worth settling down with. She liked a lot of them and loved and respected none. She was beginning to feel bad about getting a reputation as "easy," but she slept with a lot of her boyfriends because she liked them all the same.

Marlena lent Millie a sympathetic ear, but she didn't pour out her own discontent because it was obvious Millie saw no problems in Marlena's situation.

The Graduate was even more depressing. There was less of an age difference between Dustin Hoffman and Anne Bancroft than there was between herself and Tom. In the movie it was obvious to her that the characters were in different time zones. The affair was an exciting interlude for them, but neither could pull the other into the same world.

The difference with her and Tom was only because, as a woman, she was more flexible. Tom was trying to pull her into his world and make her old before her time. He refused to reach into hers, to look for new challenges, new places. The only way things could get better was if she could shake him out of acting old and settled. She would have to try harder.

Toby had spent the afternoon and evening at Millie's house, playing war games with Millie's younger brothers. He was half asleep as Marlena led him home. It was a day of war on all fronts. Internationally the carnage in Southeast Asia was going strong while Marlena battled within her own home.

When Tom got back at midnight after the late news he was too tired to rise to any bait. He poured himself a drink without asking if she wanted anything or inquiring about her day. None of the prospects he had interviewed that day had passed muster.

"What does it matter?" she asked. "We don't get anything newsworthy out here anyway."

"Don't start with me tonight."

"Tonight is perfect. Big news for Wilkes-Barre. It was Mickey Mouse's fortieth birthday."

Tom took his drink upstairs without replying. As she turned off the kitchen light Marlena thought that a man her own age would at least have threatened to throttle her.

Her days ground on into October. Local news seemed prosaic to her as events exploded around the world and in America's power centers.

Johnson bowed to controversy and withdrew Abe Fortas's name from nomination for the Supreme Court. Despite his fast-approaching lame-duck status, Johnson pressed the State Department to sell supersonic bombers to Israel; two weeks later the United Arab Republic took credit for shooting down three Israeli jets the same day Johnson signed into law a bill prohibiting interstate mail order sales of rifles and shotguns. The noise and irony of the news roiled far from her doorstep.

Apollo 7 was successfully launched from Cape Kennedy nine days before Jackie Kennedy launched her second marriage to Onassis on a Greek island. De Gaulle went to Turkey on a historic first visit to that country by a French head of state and the Russians launched a manned spacecraft of their own four days after Apollo 7's astronauts' safe landing. The crew of the *Pueblo* still awaited release in North Korea while negotiations crawled on.

Although the Presidential race heated up in October, Marlena's interest was cool. She was in direct touch only with lackluster local elections where Democrats were calmly waiting to shoe-in again. She found Wallace's bluster and Agnew's outrageous foot-in-mouthing further cause to bewail the news subjects at hand. While Wallace lauded "rednecks and peckerwoods" and castigated "pointy-headed intellectuals," Agnew courted indignation as he called Humphrey and Muskie "squishy on communism" and called for law and order while sinking to "Polack and fat Japs" name-calling. Covering Agnew with his foot in his mouth could be interesting for a reporter on the scene. But Marlena was not on the scene.

Her most pressing issues were where to find a pumpkin for Toby to carve and what to cook for her double-shift dinners. Tom had finally found a news director, but he was working late, training the new man.

And the new man was unsure of himself despite ten years' experience with an NET station in Rochester. Tom had discovered that the guy had done more fund-raising than news-directing soon after he started. Tom persisted in putting in long training hours, although he admitted having an incompetent news director was worse than having to do both jobs unassisted. But Tom was too stubborn to fire the man. The hiring had been Tom's decision and he said he would turn the man into a decent news director if it killed them both.

Marlena grumbled at Tom's stubborn stance, but life improved the last week in October, thanks to Millie and her limitless family. Millie's newly widowed Aunt Bessie came to live with Millie's family and was looking for work. The short, stocky woman with faded red hair worn in crimped nineteen-thirties curls answered Marlena's prayers. Noon until eight was perfect for Bessie, who liked to sleep late.

As the ivy climbing up the clapboard siding of their house turned into a burnt orange trail of glory, Marlena's mood climbed with it. With Bessie taking over the cleaning and laundry and shopping, Marlena could go back on the street again and do her own reporting for the five o'clock news. She felt a youthful anticipation again.

The Wednesday before the elections she returned home from the six A.M. newscast in time to send Toby off to school with his Roy Rogers tin lunch pail, neatly filled by Bessie the night before. "Your pants are getting short," Marlena said as she noticed an extra inch of sock showing above his shoes.

"I'm getting tall. Dad says I'll be taller than him," Toby said happily.

"Not for a while," she said, laughing. "Now run or you'll be late."

She made a mental note to take Toby shopping on Saturday. Maybe the vitamins her mother had sent from Des Moines were too strong. He was the tallest kid in his class, and Tom was only five-ten. Toby had become a boy, a different creature from the round urchin she had first met four years before. Four years. She poured a cup of coffee and picked up the paper with a sigh, feeling old and tame again. Twenty-four this Friday. On her way to thirty.

She skimmed the headlines without excitement. Humphrey was a little boy grown up but not old. Muskie reminded her of Ray Bolger in *The Wizard of Oz*. Nixon's eyes were too close together, a trait Marlena's Grandma Williams said indicated dishonesty. Agnew hadn't said anything quotably outrageous for a change. Boring. Boring.

Her coffee was cold. She dumped it and poured in hot with a smile, thinking about the used-car salesman jokes about Nixon. If the polls were right, he would be getting the next best thing to a used-car lot to manage—a war-weary, used country. She wondered if any of her friends from school had been killed in Vietnam. She'd lost touch with their lives . . . or their deaths. Her own political involvement seemed like a shadow on an old wall that was as crumbly as the ancient bricks of the WWKB ex-warehouse.

Marlena's birthday celebration was short and gay at Victorio's. Both Tom and Marlena were working straight through the preelection weekend. A diamond and sapphire pin matched the pinpoint sparkle of tiny earrings ostensibly from Toby. They glittered with icy fire like winter stars, too far above her Wilkes-Barre world. She loved Tom for splurging on them, but she would have little occasion to wear them.

"You like?" Tom asked, needing the reassurance.

"Love them and you. Next time Burt Samuels and his ramrod wife take us to the country club. I'll dazzle the old bird." She laughed.

"Want to join? Burt's pushing me on it. They're going to add four more tennis courts this summer, he says." Marlena shivered as though someone had walked across her grave. Tennis. Golf. She might as well have stayed in Des Moines and married a young doctor in her father's clinic. Home or away, petrification was the same. "I didn't think we were the country club type," she said with a grimace.

"Just checking. You said you were getting bored with the same old news. Thought you might enjoy the pool."

"I would," Toby chirped.

"The pool I take you to is fine," Marlena said.

After they tucked Toby into bed Tom opened the birthday champagne and apologized for the twentieth time about canceling the Paris vacation.

Marlena hadn't complained about that. Without a housekeeper in September, it would have been too difficult for Madame and Toby.

"If only I could trust John Rawlings, we could fly to the islands over Christmas." Tom continued to have problems with the novice news director. "I may have to let him go and start looking again." He sighed. "I'd hate to have to do it."

"You're a stubborn critter, aren't you?"

"What is stubborn to some is loyal to others." He reached for her hand and leaned his head against the back of the high couch.

"Then I guess I should consider myself lucky." She saw Tom's eyes flutter shut. He was exhausted. "But you better replace Rawlings before it kills you."

He opened his eyes. "About a vacation. I don't see getting away for any length of time soon, but I did accept an

invitation to speak to the Canadian Broadcast Association in
Quebec in February. What do you think about celebrating our
anniversary in old Quebec? Then all those hours you spent
listening to the French records preparing for Paris wouldn't go
to waste. There's a wonderful old hotel . . . almost like a castle . . ."

"Yes, I would like that." She could wear her diamonds
and they could speak French. "There must be some good skiing up there too."

"I'm afraid I'm rusty on skiing, and I'm getting flabby."

Marlena couldn't disagree. She knew by touch his skin
felt like crepe over his untoned muscles. "What you need, Mr.
Wells, is more exercise right before you go to sleep. Get those
muscles working."

Tom tried valiantly, seeking all her erogenous spots, but
his lovemaking felt old that birthday night. His sigh after climax held more relief than satisfaction. "Happy birthday. I love
you." He rolled over on his side, staying in touch if not in
tune.

As she gulped down a vitamin with her orange juice the
next morning, Tom gave her his weekly Monday lecture. "Try
not to get carried away with your election coverage this year. It
looks as though Nixon will win, but don't let yourself sound
too depressed on the air."

"I won't, boss."

"Just give the results."

Nixon won by a margin wider than her interest. Time
dragged on. She had a persistent feeling that she was dying by
days and inches. Nothing changed except that the weather got
colder, Madame got fatter, and Toby got taller. She felt as
though she would wake up one morning and find Toby in
high school and she'd still be doing the five o'clock news and
Tom wouldn't be gray yet and Bessie would still be cooking pot

roast on Thursday and chicken and dumplings on Monday. The thought made her feel cold and old. An ad for cemetery plots beside the river caught her eye. Plan to die.

Then snow glittered down and Christmas lights went up, spanning the lampposts and turning the streets of Wilkes-Barre into lighted bridges between the houses at night. Phone calls back and forth from Des Moines picked up as Marlena planned the family Christmas with her mother. The Wells contingent, including Toby, were flying to Des Moines on Christmas Eve.

Marlena's afternoons were devoted to shopping. She found an old weather vane at a thrift shop and bought a front yard rain measure for Millie to put on the windowsill at the station. "The rusty rooster is a far cry from an ibis," Marlena told Tom as she displayed her finds. "But poor Millie has been waiting so long for sophisticated weather equipment, I had to do something."

"Back to your *practical* jokes, I see." Tom approved of her brighter mood as much as the joke.

She hadn't been in a whimsical or joking mood for months. Although the holidays and snow were helping, her festive mood lay like a lace tablecloth over a dark, unpolished table. She needed to push herself to make merry, make the expected batch of Christmas sand tarts, and make ready for the trip.

The visit to Des Moines was a mixed bag. A cousin had enlisted in the air force, and he chattered endlessly about all the exotic places he was going to see. She saw green. Maggie reported that she'd gotten a Christmas card from Marlena's college friend, Emily Kroll, with a note saying Emily had been made a senior editor at Ambler House Publishers. "Nothing but success for you girls." Maggie beamed.

Success? Marlena didn't feel as though she had moved away from the starting line.

Marlena worked hard keeping up an enthusiastic wall of cheer. She took Toby skiing and skating with her brothers, and shopped and cooked with her mother, sidestepping any questions deeper than her holiday skin.

Tom spent half his time on the phone with John Rawlings, trying to keep things running smoothly under the man's still rocky direction. He appeared to enjoy the Williams' holiday, but he, too, was happy to get back to Wilkes-Barre to hold tighter reins at the station.

A pile of Christmas mail waited for them on the marble hall table. She scanned the postmarks. Mostly local, with a dozen or so from Chicago and Washington—Tom's friends. Her mother had gotten a card from Emily. Marlena had lost all contact with school friends. Now her friends were "their" friends. Had she nothing of her own?

Philadelphia. Who could that be? She ripped open the envelope and read the handwritten note inside the large, formal blue velvet card. "Tom!"

"I'm still unpacking," he called down from the bedroom.

She took two steps at a time to reach him. "It's a card from Andy—in Philadelphia. Listen. 'I wasn't joking about the news director job. Things are in motion. It could be a good year for all of us. Call me when you get back from your vacation. Andy. P.S. Greetings from Nancy.'"

Tom laughed. "Greetings, my eyeball. More like poison arrows."

"But it sounds as though the Philadelphia opening is real."

"Maybe." Tom carefully lined up his shoes in the closet. "But we have a pretty good thing going here. The money keeps going up along with the ratings. Madame wouldn't like the city, Toby wouldn't want to leave his mother and friends, and Bessie wouldn't move away from her family."

"You don't even know what Andy is offering."

"It would have to be fantastic."

"Maybe it is."

"I doubt it. WIB-TV is only third in that market. They can't be that fat."

"At least call him and find out."

"All right, but you'll see."

Marlena plagued Tom about the call all evening. Finally, at bedtime, he agreed peevishly. "All right. I'll call him, but just to get you off my back."

She felt bad that she had pushed him into anger, but glad the call would be made. "Please, promise not to close your mind before you hear what he has to say. Remember, it's like you tell Toby, no guts, no glory."

"I thought it was no glory, no worry."

"Very funny." But she rolled over into his arms, feeling better about the possibilities for their lives.

"I'll call him tomorrow," he whispered into her ear before he began using his tongue for a more sensual purpose than idle talk.

Tom didn't have the chance to make good on his promise. Andy called him first thing the next morning and announced that he'd be in Wilkes-Barre on Thursday.

Tom's before-dinner drink became plural that week. Marlena knew he was tense about the lunch. She didn't know how to ease his disquiet, afraid his negative attitude would become more entrenched if she tried to lobby him.

"I'm getting rid of Rawlings," Tom said on Wednesday night. "I already have two interviews scheduled for possible replacements."

"You went the second mile with him; nobody can fault you for not trying." She agreed that Rawlings should go, but she realized the task of breaking in a new man would be an instant excuse for not being able to consider a move. The thought colored her bright expectations gray.

A salesman. Andy should have been a salesman, Marlena thought happily at lunch on Thursday. For every objection Tom raised Andy had an answer. He used Tom's positive involvement with WWKB as fodder for his offer. If Tom could do this for a low-budget station in the wilds, he would be perfect for WIB-TV's morale. Andy commended Tom's organization as he toured the station, a tour he had insisted upon.

Marlena was delighted to show Andy some of her reports when he asked to see them. She ignored Tom's reluctance and assured Andy that she had plenty of time before her five o'clock broadcast, contradicting Tom's muttered excuse.

Andy didn't hide either his surprise or his enthusiasm for Marlena's product. "That's what we don't have at WIB-TV, brains as well as beauty on our team. An anchor who can go out and report, and help capitalize on all the time and money we spend promoting anchors."

Tom frowned at Marlena. He obviously didn't like Andy's hype.

"And I also need an assistant who knows a story when he sees one. The guy I have now doesn't know a story from his . . . from a hole in the ground." He glanced at Marlena as he rephrased. "And I don't have time to read all the goddamn papers for him."

"Wait a minute, Andy," Tom said. "I thought you were talking about a job as news director, not assistant news director."

"What's in a title? It would be assistant news director, but only for six months, and from day one you would *be* the news director. I'll be spending full-time getting ready to take over as general manager. I still don't know beans about the financial stuff."

"You're asking me to move from general manager of a number-one station here to *assistant* news director of your number-three station down there? You've been eating mushrooms, Andy."

"You can pull our ratings up, Tom. I know it. I have it fixed so you'll take over all the locally produced stuff as well as the news. With your bombshell wife to help, it'd be a cinch."

"And you'll sit back and take the credit so the general manager's job will be a shoe-in?"

Andy laughed easily. "Not necessary. That part is already set. You were right about Baumgarten, by the way. He was far from thinking retirement. He'll become a VP for the network in September and I'm his declared heir. The board is solidly behind me. It's a sure thing. But my feeling is why wait until September to get a good thing going?"

"With network politics, nothing is a sure thing. I still haven't forgotten Chicago."

Marlena watched Andy for the rebuttal. Tom rarely talked about the Chicago incident, but he had told her the story right after they were married.

As the fair-haired boy of the network, bureau chief in Chicago at thirty-eight, Tom was promised the move up to the more prestigious and tougher Washington bureau chief's job. All the details were worked out and hands had been shaken on it. He'd rented his Chicago town house and leased a Washington apartment, feuding with Kitty, whose friends and family were all either in Chicago or on the west coast.

The day he walked into the Washington studios, expecting to do a pro forma signing of the contract and take over the reins of power, Tom had told her, he'd "stepped into a crock of shit." There had been a palace coup over the weekend. The board had ousted the IBS chairman and chief operating officer and brought in an outsider, a whiz kid who had built an advertising empire. The new chairman had put a freeze on everything as of Saturday.

Tom could have kicked himself seven times seventy for not flying in the week before to sign the contract as the old chairman had suggested. He'd wanted the extra time in Chicago to get things perfectly organized for Andy Froelich, his assistant, who was taking over in Chicago.

The new man had done his homework. He came in with a long list of his own people for the key spots, including Washington and Chicago bureau chiefs. Tom was given the choice of number three in Washington or number two in Chicago. A comedown in either place.

His return to Chicago was as bitter and cold as his soon to be ex-wife, Kitty. She was furious. Unlike most of the others being deposed, Tom didn't even have a contract they would have to buy him out of. If he'd signed the new contract, at least they would have had to pay him top bureau chief rates even if they made him number twenty. "It was the last straw for Kitty," Tom had said. "She could barely tolerate my insisting on being a 'poor but noble newsman,' but she couldn't handle my being foolish and poor."

The new regime took away his control of the Chicago news operation, and Kitty flew west. Tom drank, ate crow, and drank some more. He called them "the dark days," that time before he escaped to Wilkes-Barre and crawled back to life.

"Come on, Tom. That was a long time ago, a crazy situation. You can't let it scar you for life. Shit, I was pushed so far down the totem pole during that purge I had to sell vacuum cleaners at night to pay for my car. It's a different ball game now. Read can't be pushed out, and he's solid on the changes. Clyde Yardley is definitely retiring and leaving the VP of finances spot open in September. Yardley and Read both want Baumgarten there and me as general manager in Philly. It's Read's ball game all the way. And he's been encouraging me to go after you ever since dinner last year."

"Burned and learned, Andy. Talk to me about it in September."

"Tom, I need you now. Yesterday, really."

"Impossible. I'm interviewing for news director here, and the man will have to be trained."

"Let the new station manager do it—whoever it will be. It doesn't have to be your problem. What are you making here now?"

Marlena silently rooted for Andy.

"Forty," Tom said smugly.

Marlena knew it was thirty-one but she kept her mouth shut.

"How does forty-eight sound? Plus car and club membership. And twenty for Marlena?"

Her jaw dropped open. That would be twenty-three thousand more than they made now.

"You're a serious man," Tom said.

"I need you and I'll pay to get you. You've buried yourself in this outhouse too long. You're too young for this semi-retirement."

"Amen," Marlena breathed.

Tom tossed her a sharp glance.

"I really need you, Tom," Andy said.

"Lena and I will have to talk about it. We have Toby to consider."

"There are great schools in Philadelphia, not the city ones, but great private schools. My kids are at Friends' Academy and they love it."

"That gets expensive," Tom countered.

"Couple of grand a year. Okay, we'll play hard ball. Fifty-two for you and twenty-two for Marlena."

"The money isn't everything."

"But it can solve the other niggling little problems. And you need to come back to a real news town, Tom"

"It's an interesting offer."

"But are you interested?"

"In September." Tom's face closed. "If it's real."

Marlena looked at him. Was he afraid? She knew he got afraid for her or Toby. He was always worried about them. But could he be afraid of the challenge?

Andy wouldn't let him off that easily. "Here's another scenario. I'll hire Marlena, try her out on our five to five-thirty evening news. She can commute or stay over in the station's suite in the Barclay. Weekends she goes home. I'll put you on as a consultant and you can come down a day or two at a time to begin learning our operations. Get used to the place before September. I'll make it twenty-four for Marlena to put up with the hassle and give you a hundred and fifty a day whenever you can make it. You call the time."

Tom put his arm around Marlena's waist. "I couldn't do that to her. The commute would be brutal. Two hours each way in good weather. When the fog sets in it's more like three. And I don't think the old Mercedes is up to it."

"I'll throw in a station car, a new Ford."

"Tom." She looked at him hopefully.

"It would make life too complicated," he said.

"But interesting."

"Interesting until you fell apart from exhaustion."

"I am . . ." She bit back the phrase "young enough to handle it" and substituted "Willing to give it a try. Tom, you're too good to stay here forever."

"You both are," Andy added. "Look, Tom, if you don't like the way it's working out, you can walk away. Marlena can come back to Wilkes-Barre and everything's fine. I won't hold it against you. But I'd consider you a prize fool for turning it down."

"Tom, how can we say no?"

Tom smiled at her young enthusiasm, cracking his marble jaw for a moment. "We'll talk about it tonight with Toby and Bessie. When do you need an answer, Andy?"

"I'd like one on Monday. I can be flexible about when

you start, but I need the assurance that we're all moving in the same direction. Otherwise, I'll have to come up with a new game plan—and new players."

Marlena was on cloud nine, closer to the stars than the ground. After the five o'clock news Tom drove her home, listening to her chatter only because she didn't give him the space to object.

"Think of it, Tom. I would get almost five hundred dollars a week, and even if it didn't work out after a couple of months we'd have a pile of money stashed away. But I know it'll work. Andy sounded so certain. You said yourself that when there are changes at the network level everything's been worked out behind the scenes before it happens. But this time you're part of it. As news director at IBS's largest affiliate. That's coming back to where you should be."

"Working under Andy," Tom said.

She frowned at him, realizing he disliked the idea. It wasn't as though he were suddenly switching from overlord to underling of the man he had trained. They had gone different directions and places years before. That shouldn't nettle him. "But you'd be the one running the news."

"It's still a couple of rungs below Washington bureau chief for the network, and Philadelphia is at the bottom of the stations the network owns."

"But it's still a major market—one of the largest in the country. And, Tom, Andy's offering us nearly twice the money we're making now."

Tom laughed. Her enthusiasm was contagious. He shook his head. "I don't know about that. Our overhead could double."

"We could be careful."

"We'll have to be careful." He turned into their driveway and switched off the ignition. He stared at the row of blue spruces for a long moment before turning a sober face to her.

"It sounds good, Marlena, almost too good. I'm afraid of this . . . for all of us."

She gave him a hug. "It's not as though we were making a final decision. We have nine months to sample."

"It only took one bite for Snow White," he muttered.

"Huh?"

"Come on. I bet dinner's on the table."

Tom avoided any discussion of the proposal as he kidded Toby about his little girl friend and gossiped with Bessie.

Marlena finally brought up the subject of Philadelphia, telling Toby about the wonderful museums and the baseball stadium, painting the city as a playground for eight-year-olds. She plunged ahead, ignoring Tom's tight silence, and asked Bessie if she'd mind sleeping in on the nights she and Tom had to stay in Philadelphia. When Bessie said it would be no problem Marlena raced on to the possibility of all of them moving to Philadelphia in September so Tom "could become the news director of the great big Philadelphia IBS station."

Objections poured out like gnats and mosquitos from Pandora's box. She'd said too much too soon. Toby wanted to know how he could see his mother on Wednesdays. Bessie didn't want to be that far from her family. Toby insisted that Madame would hate living in a city. Madame reacted to the babble of voices by waking up from her position under the table with a loud bark of objection at being disturbed.

"See?" Toby said. "Madame doesn't want to."

Tom smiled at her, an I-told-you-so written in his eyes.

"Hold it!" She raised both hands for silence. Everyone obeyed except Madame and her bark. Marlena quickly stabbed a piece of pork chop with her fork and held it out to the furry noisemaker. Madame pulled the meat from the fork and gulped it down, delicately licking the fork before sitting down in polite expectation.

Marlena gave Madame another bit and affectionately scratched the dog's head. "Look at that smile."

"If Lena could do it, she'd have Madame sitting up at the table with us." Tom laughed.

"She does eat nicely," Marlena insisted, giving her pet yet another bite.

"Come here, Madame." Toby place his plate on the floor.

"Are you finished with your dinner?" Tom asked.

"He saw the chocolate cake for dessert," Bessie said.

"Madame, come here." Toby watched Madame waiting for him to bring the plate closer to her, barking from her position beside Marlena.

Toby picked up the plate and handed it to Marlena. "Here. You give it to her. She's your dog, anyway."

"Let's not fight, children," Tom said. "Put it on the floor, Toby, and she'll come get it as soon as she sees it's not going to be handed to her."

Bessie chuckled as Madame stretched and padded over to inspect Toby's leftovers. Marlena hoped the platter that Andy was offering Tom would be as much of an incentive for him to move.

Madame took a meaty bone and plopped herself under the table munching loudly.

"You'll see, Toby. Madame will love Philadelphia. You will too, Bessie. We all will."

Tom remained reluctant about the sweetheart deal. Marlena discovered the depth of his resistance when Andy called them at home on Monday night saying that Tom hadn't called him with the promised decision. She wondered, if fate had not placed her closest to the phone that evening, whether she would have made it to Philadelphia at all.

Tom worked out a delayed schedule. She wouldn't begin in Philadelphia until after the Canadian trip. The commute would begin the first of March. More waiting, but now there was something worth waiting for.

Five

HE REACHED FOR HER ungloved hand and squeezed it. She wondered if she were equipped to handle this flirtation that danced around an old flame.

Roger acted casual about holding her hand, warm and friendly. "Now that's our old New York," he said, tilting his head at a Salvation Army coronet trio, caroling in the snow beside the traditional iron pot. A derelict slept blissfully beside them, his scraggly head resting on a pile of sheet music. One of the musicians had blanketed the old man with a navy wool jacket.

"Sweet dreams." That poor old soul wasn't going to waste his time watching the pot, hoping it boiled, she thought. Still smiling, Marlena reached into her coat pocket for the emergency cab money she always kept there and dropped it into the pot.

Roger quickly dug into his pocket and dropped in all his change with a clatter that turned the head of the small gray-haired lady in the bonnet. She beamed a smile Roger's way. "God bless you, sir."

"Merry Christmas," Roger said as he hurried Marlena past the scene, retaking possession of her hand.

"Do you get a wish?" Marlena asked.

"A wish?"

"Like a wishing well. Do you get a wish?"

"Maybe a shot at salvation." Roger laughed. "Or the assurance that there's always a bed waiting for me somewhere if I need it."

Her hand was still warmly held by him, snug and content. It felt homey. "I wonder how many homeless people there are in New York this Christmas." She had done a story on the holiday homeless in Baltimore years before, a sad story because there were no individual answers for each tragic person—just collective shelters and soup kitchens, temporary relief.

"Too many," Roger said, stopping several feet short of Scribner's glass doors to glance back in the direction of the off-key rendition of "Joy To The World." "I wish I could believe that one of the reasons we pay taxes is so the city can provide reasonable places for the displaced."

"The Great Society never quite made it, did it?"

Roger shrugged. "It got lost somewhere between the war and the peanut fields and the tax cuts."

"And now we're in for fewer shelters and 'safety nets' and more who need shelter, whose lives are less secure." She shivered, wondering if she had lost her own idealism along the way. Had what she was reporting become less important to her than how it was received—the accolades, the promotions? She gave Roger's hand a squeeze of her own, grounding herself. If nothing else, Roger was bringing her back to square one on some things.

She broke away from her thoughts and saw him studying her uncritically. She smiled, not minding; her thoughts at that moment didn't need concealing.

"Shall we move on to *The World, the Universe and Everything*?" He held the door open for her.

Roger walked over to a clerk to ask where to find the book in question while she browsed through the holiday gift table. Books traveled well. Maybe she could find something for the Des Moines folks. She already had presents for her brothers' children. She had trouble believing her brothers were over thirty now, although Dave was already losing his hair, like their father.

Her eye was caught by a large book of photographs of European castles. Since Bill's retirement her parents were taking all the trips they had postponed throughout their forty-plus-year marriage. Perhaps the book would give them some ideas for their next trip.

She leafed through the pictures. The closest she had ever been to Europe, she thought, was the long weekend she and Tom had spent in Quebec before she started working at WIB-TV in Philadelphia.

It had been a delightful weekend, their last such. With an exciting new world to anticipate, she had relaxed and drunk in the seventeenth-century charm of the oldest city in North America. The Frontenac, a castle of a hotel atop the St. Lawrence bluffs, had swept both of them into a mood of Old-World elegance. They had been gracious, warm and passionate with each other. She smiled to herself, remembering their amusement at discovering that a Howard Johnson had replaced one of the fine old restaurants and their pleasure in the high tea served each afternoon in the gracious salon of the old hotel, a colonial string quartet, in costume with powdered wigs, playing Mozart.

She vaguely remembered Tom trying to talk her out of the Philadelphia venture. Her ears had been deaf. He might as well have been speaking French to her as well as to the merchants.

She couldn't remember if he'd actually foretold the end

of their relationship in the beginning of her network climb. Instead, she remembered rising above the undercurrent of disquiet to enjoy the old city.

She flipped past the castles of the Rhine, realizing that it was odd she had never made an effort to vacation in Europe. She had found Quebec's centuries-old streets and churches fascinating. Perhaps, in the back of her mind, she'd been waiting for Tom to show her Europe long after he was no longer part of her life.

"Magnificent," She said as Roger peered over her shoulder at a photo of a gilded salon in Versailles. "Ever been there?"

"Only in my feckless youth." Roger's laugh was clean and friendly. "After my father went broke and the dole disappeared I was lucky to keep my beach house."

"You mean you had to get a job after law school?"

"It's a long story."

"I'm curious."

"Too long for Scribner's."

"It's a great place for biographies," she joked.

"What about thrillers?" His eyes brightened with anticipation. "Let me buy you a good mystery thriller. You know, something like that Barnaby series."

"No, I don't have time for thrillers. The news is thrilling enough. Not that I don't love them when I'm at the beach." She didn't follow him as he stepped toward the fiction section. "Don't, Roger. It'd be a waste of money. I don't want you to buy one for me." She'd snapped more than she'd meant to, but she'd been reminded of the old Roger, always buying things. To cajole, convince, bribe.

"All right, all right! If you feel that strongly about it, I won't. We'll get out of here. But why don't we go uptown to my place so I can make my house specialty for you, hot chocolate with miniature marshmallows. Could you ask for anything more during a snow storm?"

Yes, she could. She could ask for Roger to be single. Then the hot chocolate would be a nice warm-up. "Hot chocolate sounds fine, but we're closer to my apartment. I don't have any marshmallows, but we can stop at Gristede's on the way. Besides, I should get back and walk Gerda. She's probably sitting on the white couch right now. It's the only place in the apartment that's off limits."

Marlena's building faced Central Park in the low sixties, a new structure sandwiched between old granite and marble matrons.

"You've gone modern," Roger commented.

"Only for the moment. I'm an old-fashioned girl at heart. I drool with envy at the old high-rises next door. Ten-foot ceilings, inlaid parquet, carved walnut. I'm looking. IBS found this place for me furnished. It'll do until I can sell my co-op in Baltimore and buy something here—if the show continues to do well."

"Nice view." Roger looked out the wide windows facing the park, which was now an impressionistic swirl of branches through the snow. "The fourteenth floor generally has a nice view in New York. High enough and low enough. Just about right." His smile was warm as he turned back to her.

Marlena inspected the white couch, ignoring the significance of the fourteenth floor. "She's been on here, all right."

"Where is she? Some watchdog."

Marlena disappeared down the wide hall and called back, "Taking a nap—on my bed."

Roger followed the sound of Marlena's laughter and stepped inside the bedroom door to see Gerda, eighty pounds of fur, curled in the center of a king-size bed, her paws cradling a large stuffed rabbit.

"Look at that baby."

Gerda's mouth opened and her tongue drooped out across the rabbit's nose in a smile.

"Gerda." Marlena's tone firmed. "Off the bed. Now."

The beast opened her eyes but did not move.

"I'm going to get your bunny." Marlena leaned over and tugged at the one-eyed stuffed rabbit with tattered ears. "My bunny."

Gerda's teeth snapped shut on a stuffed leg. Her growl sounded menacing, although her bushy tail wagged.

"Don't do that," Roger warned.

"She's playing." Marlena tugged harder. Gerda came awake and shook herself, releasing the rabbit. Marlena tossed the toy into the air above the bed. Gerda leaped, neatly caught it in her gleaming teeth, jumped off the bed, and raced into the living room.

"My bunny!" Marlena raced after her.

"*TV Guide* lied," Roger said as he caught up with them playing tug-of-war beside the white couch. "You could not possibly be thirty-five. Five, maybe."

Marlena let Gerda win the tug-of-war and patted her head. The wide, square dog rolled over, begging for a tummy rub. Marlena sat on the beige wall-to-wall carpet and complied looking up at Roger. "I think people should grow up, not old. Age is a state of mind. You can think someone isn't old whether they're twenty-five or fifty-five and then, when you get to know them better, you soon find out they're *old*."

"What does 'old' mean to you?"

"Being afraid of change, progress, wanting to hold on to some little corner of the world. I guess I've been 'old' myself a couple of times in my life, but I try to get over it—and not get too secure."

"There's nothing wrong with security. I've had enough insecurity to last me a lifetime. And I still have bouts of it." Roger's eyes widened like a guileless child's.

"I'm overstating, maybe. We all need some security. In TV we call it contracts. But contracts end—two, three years.

And knowing our 'security' could terminate keeps us on our toes. If you can't take the heat, bury yourself in the snows of West Des Moines or Wilkes-Barre."

"Like your first husband?"

"Like a lot of people."

"What kind of dog is Gerda?"

"My brother calls her a furry brick. She's an elkhound. Ready for your walk?" Marlena clapped her hands.

"Do you really want to go back out again? I'm just drying out."

"I'm talking about a short walk." She smiled as she walked to the terrace door and struggled to pull it open. "Help!"

Roger added his muscle to the frozen door. "Not completely liberated?"

The sliding door lurched open and snow swept in like down billowing from a torn pillow.

"I have never been liberated. I'm always tied to something. Gerda!" She glared at the animal, who flopped down out of the snow's reach.

Finally Gerda stretched into a swaybacked prayer position and moved slowly to test the snows.

"Out!" Marlena demanded. The snow was changing the beige carpet to white. Gerda yawned and stepped out joining Marlena on the narrow terrace. "Hurry," Marlena urged, the snow falling heavily on her shoulders.

Gerda stopped, her stomach only inches above the snow, and looked back at Marlena.

"Go!"

"She'll never make it."

As if to prove him wrong, Gerda suddenly leaped to the left and obediently yellowed a patch of snow.

"Good girl." Marlena smiled proudly. "Back inside."

Gerda hopped fifteen feet to the far end of the terrace,

where she peered through the railing and barked sharply at the pedestrians below, ignoring Marlena's orders to be quiet.

"I'll go get her back," Roger offered.

"No, let her stay out for a while." Marlena struggled to slide the door shut. "She'll stop barking in a minute."

Roger added his muscle. "You have great control of your dog." He laughed as the sliding door banged, cutting off the blowing snow.

"The only thing I have control over is me, and even that can get shaky."

They shared a laugh as they looked at each other.

"You look like an old, white-haired man," she said.

"And you don't have to worry about your roots showing."

"It's crazy what some folks do for a dog," she said. "This dress will never be the same."

"Snow-stained silk for a souvenir," Roger mused. "Almost a title."

"Souvenir? For the next encounter, in another twenty years?"

"I hope not. Souvenir for the 'second time around' sounds better."

She didn't want to touch that line. "You're going to be soaked in a minute. I am already." The melting snow was making the thin, wet silk cling to her like a T-shirt.

"On you it looks good."

"And feels cold. I don't think I can afford to get sick." The clinging silk made her feel undressed, vulnerable. The chemistry Roger seemed to be testing inspired her to beat a cool retreat into her bedroom, grab a plush robe, and instantly reject it as too blatant an invitation. The navy wool blazer and red-and-white pin-striped blouse was hanging on the closet door, ready for her rapid change into the "Later . . . on IBS" anchor person. It was too early to chance wrinkles.

She rummaged through her jumbled sweater drawer, searching for something not overly seductive, but flattering. Soft and tweedy.

She reflected in the mirror for a moment. Her color was high and her eyes sparkled from the day's exercise. She could handle almost any color. Not red or rose, she decided. She was pink enough. She tossed sweaters on the bed in rejection.

Then she reached her decision. The soft blue ribbed cashmere turtleneck and a navy wool jumper. Two-inch navy pumps. Flats or slippers always made her feel young. She could cope better in heels.

Gerda barked imperiously at the bedroom door. Marlena fled the disorder she had created in the bedroom and walked into the hall to find her snow-covered pet. "What is this?" She called to Roger. "The abominable snow dog?"

A chocolate aroma came from the same direction as Roger's voice. "I let her in. She was scratching at the door."

"Thanks." Marlena and her snow-caked guardian trotted into the kitchen.

"Perfect timing." Roger poured steaming hot chocolate into white mugs and topped them with tiny marshmallows.

Gerda barked and Marlena plopped a small marshmallow in the dog's wide mouth.

"My." Roger looked at her. "You're all dressed up again."

"Just grabbed the first dry things I could find." She pulled a terry towel off a rack and briskly rubbed Gerda, returning her to her furry self.

"We should be at my place," Roger said as he carried the mugs into the living room. "It's a great day for a fire."

"Next apartment will have a fireplace," Marlena said as she followed with a plate of Brie and crackers.

"Looks like I didn't feed you well enough at lunch."

"I'm not hungry, but as Maggie always says, the way to a man's heart . . ." She caught herself midcliché.

"Is that the direction you're heading?" Roger's eyes leveled on her.

She deliberately avoided sitting beside him on the soft couch taking a side chair. "Tell me about your life, your wife. You've talked very little about yourself today."

"Just like a reporter." He loosened his tie. "Gets you alone and starts the interrogation."

"Right. When did you get married and what ever happened to the Peace Corps?"

"Boom. Twenty-five words or less."

"Or more."

"I got married right after graduation. The Peace Corps disappeared under piles of diapers when Alison was born. I went with the state prosecutor's office, figuring I could do some good for the world. The first couple of years were fine. Life was easy. Father picked up the tab for nurses, and for my wife's law school and the apartment. My toughest problem at the time was pretending to feel empathy with the other guys at the bottom of the legal totem pole who kept complaining about the lousy money."

"Perfect young liberal couple."

"Don't be snide. The yellow brick road didn't last forever."

"You always did want a two-lawyer household." She scratched Gerda's ruff as the dog relaxed at her feet.

"Yes." Roger chuckled. "I was great at game plans. I thought I could control the world."

"Is control still so important?"

"Control of Roger is still important. Alison might disagree and say I want to control the world, but I like to think I've learned to suggest, guide, and counsel only when I see a real need for it and then leave the control of other lives to the other people. More an educator than a dictator."

"But by qualifying information you control actions—by what you don't say, as much as what you do."

"Spoken like a true newslady," he said. "But what about you? You seem to have controlled your own destiny. You wanted to become a star and you are."

She found that funny. "TV reporters never control their own destinies. It's all work and luck. All you can do is pay your dues and get into a position so luck can happen. You have to be willing to work for peanuts and forget about a social life in the beginning, be willing to make the sacrifices."

"That includes sacrificing other people too?" Roger asked, obviously referring to himself. He paused for her comment. She acknowledged him silently, so he made it stronger. "Or stabbing them in the back?"

"No, Roger." She avoided his inference by addressing the question. "I don't like backstabbing. If I've ever done it, it's never been intentional. I've been stabbed in the back myself and I don't have the heart for that game. I want to do well and I want everyone else to do well too. If I don't like someone, or if things don't work out, I wish them 'away,' but I also wish them well."

"Is it always that easy for you? Poof—and they're gone?"

"No. Not always without sacrifice," Marlena said. "When you work twenty-hour days chasing news you can leave people behind without realizing it until you turn around and find they're not there anymore." She thought of Tom as she spoke, not of Roger. Roger smiled, accepting her statement as a partial answer to his old question.

"Friends, lovers, husbands?"

"All of the above. But you're not playing fair. You're supposed to be telling me about your life."

"Back to 'My Life, by Roger Marley.' There I was the bright and shining star of the prosecutor's office, touting truth and justice for all, ready for the big cases that would become landmarks. And I was getting arsonists and second-story men, hookers and junkies, the small fry. I wanted the big fish, but I knew I had to pay my dues too."

"You didn't get disillusioned by the system?"

"Only a little tarnished. I went in knowing the courts were overcrowded and the system was flawed, but I was playing the game, honing my killer instinct, all but notching my arm every time I sent one away."

"Going for the jugular." She nodded.

"Sometimes I think it's that very gamesmanship in prosecutors' offices that keeps the system from total corrosion. If the law is enforced and justice wins out, it doesn't matter what the motive is."

Marlena thought about the prosecutors she'd known. The good ones, like Will Austin in Philadelphia, had a lust for winning as well as a commitment to serving justice. "The end justifying all."

"The game itself isn't everything."

"So there you were in your nice white armor . . ."

"And my wife had finished law school and was working for legal aid. Public servants with a full-time housekeeper." He slipped off his damp shoes. "Mind?"

"Of course not. Maybe you'd better take off your socks too."

Roger shamelessly peeled off the wet offenders and draped them across his shoes. Gerda stirred and ventured over for a sniff test to determine if they were edible. She gave a sneeze of rejection and padded back to plop down beside her mistress.

"All right." Marlena looked up from Roger's long, slender toes, oddly white and pink, like a small boy's. "When did the idyllic bubble burst?"

"When my father went bust in the early seventies. If mother hadn't had a small income of her own, I don't know what they'd have done. He'd bought into a St. Croix land deal in a big way and when it failed he was left holding worthless paper.

"My wife was working part-time at legal aid while Alison was in Montessori school and we were paying our housekeeper almost as much as her take-home salary at legal aid." He stopped abruptly, then asked, "Do you believe in ERA?"

"What does the ERA have to do with living on fourteen thousand dollars a year?"

"We could have made it by managing carefully if she had stayed home, but she proclaimed her right to work, insisting she hadn't gotten a law degree to drown herself in chocolate milk. She insisted on continuing to work. Baby-sitters, transportation, fast food, and extra dry cleaning cost more than she made. She was exhausted most of the time. I thought it was dumb for her not to quit and stay home with Alison. No dice. I remember pointing out that we were in worse financial straits than her clients. She didn't laugh."

"It's not the funniest thing you've ever said."

"I was angry and frustrated. Looking back, I guess I resented not getting enough sympathy from her. That's human enough. The change in our life-style was radical. There was no money for dinners out, let alone extra baby-sitters for movies or the theater. And although the sex had never been the greatest, it came to a grinding halt." Roger paused in his confession. "Want some more chocolate?"

Marlena inhaled on her cigarette, feeling a mixed reaction. She felt a tinge of satisfaction that sex hadn't always been great for him. She also recognized her strong empathy for Roger's wife. "Go on."

"I got involved with this girl I met at the courthouse. At first I felt sorry for her. She was fighting a drug habit. She'd been thrown out of the house by her father when she was fifteen and picked up by a pimp within a week. When I met her she was eighteen, with the face of an angel, huge dark eyes and long dark hair, the whitest skin I had ever seen—except for the track marks on her arms."

Marlena felt a rising irritation at the sound of infidelity in his voice.

"She thought I was a hero. She'd come to the courthouse with her case officer, who was arguing for a suspended sentence. Teresa was living in a halfway house run by the city, putting up a fight to go straight. I couldn't believe she'd been on the streets for four years. She looked too . . . untouched."

"But not untouchable."

"We were both needy, needy and insecure. I played the big brother at first, taking her to museums and parks, talking to her and helping her with her reading. The poor kid could hardly read. You know what her big goal in life was? She wanted to become a nurse's aide."

"Mmm. Heart of gold. So what happened?"

"I was really feeling guilty about the affair, knowing I was stealing time away from my daughter, not to mention my wife, and giving it to Teresa. But she was warm and funny and eager . . . and sexy. When I got home at night my wife was none of those things. Besides, Alison was already sleeping unless she was sick or screaming.

"I resisted sexual involvement for a few months, rationalizing that I was only being a humanitarian, but I never told my wife about it. I think I knew from the start." He paused. "Then it all started driving me crazy. My wife didn't comment when I came home later and later. She didn't seem to notice that I didn't want to make love to her anymore."

"Maybe she was too overworked herself."

"That turned out to be true, but I didn't know it at the time. Propelled by my own guilt, I projected it on her. I began thinking she was having an affair with her boss, a rich, arrorogant snot from Boston." He shook his head and a curl tumbled down on his intense forehead, removing ten years. "The guy had everything that I'd had before my father went bust. His life-style was that of the man she'd married, not the guy she'd ended up with."

"You were jealous of him for what you had lost."

"Perceptive of you, but I wasn't very perceptive at the time. When my wife's father had a mild heart attack she packed up Alison and drove to Connecticut.

"She left in a rush and asked me to drop some papers off at her office. When I got there I discovered her boss was also out of town. I built it all into a giant conspiracy when I called her and her mother said she was out for dinner with 'friends'—no names given."

"She probably needed the diversion."

"I was a big emotional slob. I moved Teresa into the apartment. She made up an excuse for her case officer and the halfway house people—said she was visiting an aunt or something. I can still remember the perverse pleasure I felt as I showed her around the apartment and made love to her in our bedroom."

Marlena had an uncomfortable mental flash of the bedroom she'd left behind years before.

"But it was a total disaster. Literally. Teresa needed only five minutes in a room before it looked like there'd been an all-night party. Glasses, cigarette butts, bottles, clothes."

"A messy little love nest."

"I turned into a father figure, I guess, nagging her about cleaning up and giving her lists of errands to run while I was at work. But I was still too angry with my wife to kick Teresa out. She was my pay-back.

"Soon we were having daily shouting matches. I think she wanted them. She deliberately did things to infuriate me.

Anger was probably the only emotion that she really understood."

"How long did you put up with it?"

"Until my wife came home early and found her lounging in the middle of the mess—in my wife's own negligee."

"How did she get her out?"

"I never asked for the gory details. That night—I can still picture it so clearly—I opened the door, expecting to see Teresa's inevitable disorder, and was surprised to discover a spotlessly clean apartment."

"Where was your wife?"

"Sitting like an iron statue on the couch. The shouting matches with Teresa turned out to have been the preliminary bouts. We were still at it when the sun came up."

"Who won the bout?"

"Nobody. TKO on both sides. Then came the tears and promises. All the weeks walking around on emotional tiptoe. It was hell."

"Is that when you moved to Connecticut?"

"No." He chuckled. "That's when I sold my soul to the company store. Not having enough money makes it hard to lighten up any relationship. So I left the noble offices of the public prosecutor and joined the real world of Driscoll, Greene and Weinberg. Nice and respectable. Even learned to shine my shoes and stripe my ties."

"A real Republican." She shuddered.

"I didn't go that far, but I learned to keep my political opinions out of boardrooms."

"And bedrooms?" She lifted her eyebrows.

"Yes, most of the time." He laughed. "I stopped bringing my third-world waifs home to haunt me. Not that there aren't always temptations. Chemistry is chemistry." He looked into Marlena's eyes, measuring.

She leaned down to scratch Gerda's nice, safe back. "If I

were your wife, I'd be nervous about the commuting relationship. I know. That's what created the strain with Tom, my
first husband. Without that, we might have made it."

"Was there a second one?" He explained when she hesitated, "You called Tom your first husband."

"I guess hope springs eternal. No, so far, he's been my
only one. I suppose I should say ex-husband."

"Why didn't it work? What went wrong?"

"Now *you* sound like the reporter."

"Does it bother you to talk about it?"

"No. It was just so long ago. Over ten years, now." She
slipped off her shoes, curling her legs on the couch, searching
for a comfortable position. "Tom and I were originally hired
by WIB-TV in Philly as a team, news director and reporter.
My slot opened up first and Tom's kept getting postponed. He
didn't mind. He didn't want to leave Wilkes-Barre in the first
place. We had custody of his son Toby, but Toby's mother was
in Wilkes-Barre. She didn't want him moved to Philly."

"Did you?"

"I loved having Toby with us in Philly. It's a great city
for kids." Her faced brightened at the old memory of the zoo
and paddleboats on the river. "But there were other problems."

"Such as?"

"At WIB Tom would have had to work under a man
he'd trained years before in Chicago. I was too young to understand how hard that would be on a man's ego. I also think
Tom liked being a big fish in a small pond."

"Wilkes-Barre qualifies as that."

"There's nothing wrong with a small pond. It's just that
I was younger and wanted to keep moving and learning. I
wanted newer, bigger stories. Tom was settled."

"You sound almost regretful."

"There were a lot of good things about Tom. And many

moments of regret along the way," she admitted. "But we were out of sync, in different time zones. If I'd been fifteen years older or he'd been younger, we'd have been good for each other. Tom had worked in network management and rejected the power struggles involved. But as a reporter I didn't think I'd be affected, so I wasn't turned off by his war stories. They only whetted my appetite."

"And ambition."

"That too." She uncurled her legs and stood, walking toward the window. "No, I don't regret not staying in Wilkes-Barre. And I don't regret having married Tom." She looked out at the snow, falling across the window like static on a TV screen. "I regret the way it ended. It got messy and everything got twisted for me . . . with the Philadelphia affair . . .

Roger's ears perked up. "Aha! So you had an affair too. You weren't the perfect angel, either."

Hardly, she thought. But she hadn't really lost her wings in Philadelphia, not the way Roger was thinking.

"I want to hear about it."

"I'm ready for a cup of coffee. How about you?" She walked toward the kitchen. She didn't want to talk about her Philadelphia affair. And the word was wrong. *Affair* didn't describe the beginning of a relationship that should have worked.

"Come on, Marlena. I spilled my guts." He followed her to the kitchen and watched as she ground coffee beans and filled the coffee maker.

"It was one of those normal soap-opera affairs," she heard herself lying. "Lonely wife, week nights alone in Philadelphia. Sympathetic boss. Dinners and comfort and too much wine."

"I hope it was tidier than mine," he quipped, watching the coffee begin to drip.

"Hardly. Andy was Tom's old underling and my new

boss. Think about all the guilts that could involve. Besides, he was married."

"So were you, remember?"

As she turned to go into the living room to empty the ashtray while the coffee was dripping, she noticed that he was about to follow her. "Stay, Roger," she said in the tone she normally reserved for Gerda. "I'll be back."

She looked around the impersonal decorator living room for a moment, her thoughts drifting back to Philadelphia. This wasn't the best place she'd ever had, but it sure beat Philadelphia. A picture of her "Victorian museum" flashed into her mind and held.

Philadelphia

Alan settled back uneasily in the velvet Queen Anne chair and accepted the glass of wine. "Thanks." His smile was tired. He was getting lined, a new aging. "This place is like a museum, Lena. How can you breathe?"

Marlena looked around the Victorian parlor with the priceless Chinese vases and carved furniture. The doctor and his wife from whom she had sublet the town house were collectors. "Carefully." She laughed. "It's good for me. It forces me to be neat. Bessie had me spoiled—not that I was ever such great shakes as a housekeeper. But sometimes it does feel like a museum at night."

"Tom doesn't get down much?"

"He was down a lot, almost every other weekend until the news director's job didn't come through on schedule last September. Even though he still had reservations about moving from Wilkes-Barre. I think he would have if things had opened up as scheduled. It wasn't Andy's fault that IBS didn't give Baumgarten the network slot. Baumgarten jinxed that himself by having a mild heart attack."

"So the move is off?"

"Andy keeps telling Tom he'll work something out soon, but Tom's mind is sealed like a coffin on the subject. He wanted me to tell Andy to go fuck himself and come home to Wilkes-Barre last September."

"Wanted?"

"Wanted. Wants. I don't know what he wants right now, Alan. I haven't been home in six weeks. And he finds excuses not to come here.

"I've been putting together a series on slum landlords, covering at least one story a day, sometimes two. This is the first night I've taken off in two weeks." She pushed at the ice cubes in her martini, watching the ice swirl the vermouth like oil against the ice.

"You look tired."

"So do you."

"It's tough climbing the ladder." He laughed. "A lot of people think NET is semiretirement. Christ, back home I had a bigger budget to cover half of what we do in Pittsburgh. I spend as much time fighting for money for repairs and for crew overtime as I do working on news."

"Tom said that would happen."

"He knows the business."

"Yeah. He does know that." She gave her old friend a weak smile. "So how's your social life out in the west?"

"Ha. It makes my life in Wilkes-Barre seem like big stuff in retrospect."

"How's your kitchen?"

His laugh was hearty enough to make the chair creak in objection. "It's in perfect condition because I'm too busy to buy groceries to rot these days."

"I guess that's a perverse kind of progress. Have you seen your family lately?"

"I drove in via Wilkes-Barre." Alan looked away from her. "They're all fine. Ma's bothered by a touch of arthritis, but she'll feel better when the weather gets warm again."

"See any of the old gang at the station?"

"Stopped by and said hello to Anna, Michael, Clarence, Ed, and Millie. That's about all."

"And Tom?"

"Yeah, I saw Tom." Alan cleared his throat. "Millie finally moved out of her parent's house and got her own apartment."

"It's about time." Marlena laughed. "She's been talking about making the big move ever since I can remember. Does she have a new boyfriend?"

"You might say that, or maybe an old boyfriend." His gaze shifted up from the old Oriental to Marlena. He studied her for a long moment. "Are you going out much yourself?"

Marlena's stomach muscles tightened and she felt a fluttering of fear. "What are you trying to tell me, Alan?"

He nervously smoothed his pale hair back from his receding hairline. "Maybe I shouldn't say anything. It looks bad. You know how I feel about you and you know I never wanted you to marry Tom. Half the reason I took the job in Pittsburgh was that I couldn't stand your being with him."

Marlena waited, trying to digest Alan's meaning.

"I just don't want you to get hurt . . . more than you have to. I mean," he stammered, "I don't think they're playing fair—that is if you don't know what's going on. If you do know, it's something else, I guess."

"Are you saying that Tom and Millie are having an affair?" Her tone was brittle, cold. "I don't believe you."

"Why would I lie? I live in Pittsburgh. I won't be around to pick up the pieces even if I wanted to."

"Millie's my friend," she said flatly.

"The way I hear it, things are getting pretty thick between them. If Tom's important to you, well, I think it's better that you know."

She sat frozen, shocked. Her self-imposed work schedule had not included time for questioning Tom's activities back on the home front. She kept telling herself that Andy would work things out for Tom as he had promised. She was doing so well at WIB, getting good reviews from the station's viewer-response polls as well as from Andy and her fellow reporters. There was no question in her mind of turning back.

But she felt a shuddering sense of loss at the thought of being without Tom. Maybe Alan was mistaken, but Tom's attitude had shifted radically in the past couple of months. His negative attitude had been replaced by strong encouragement. She'd been pleased, believing he was finally growing past his macho resentment of her doing well without his supervision.

"I'm sorry. I thought you would have already suspected something . . . a hint." Alan's statement hung in the air.

"Some reporter I am."

"I wouldn't have dropped it like that if I . . ."

"You'd have waited until after dinner so you wouldn't have spoiled my appetite?" Marlena's smile was too bright as she insisted they go out. She had made reservations for them at Bookbinder's.

Marlena introduced Alan to the maître d' by name. The black-tie bowed with the respect wise restaurateurs give local celebrities and led them to a comfortable but visible table. Marlena ordered a double martini, ignoring Alan's protests.

"You are upset. I'm sorry."

"Why should I be upset? Life is 'peachy keen.' Andy is talking about giving me a shot as a weekend anchor. You know how much fun it is to be an anchor when the ship is sinking." She looked around the room at the nautical decor and laughed half an octave higher than usual.

She drank two double martinis like ice water and insisted on a carafe of white wine with her lobster. She left the lobster untouched and called for a second carafe. She refused to discuss Wilkes-Barre or Tom as she pushed Alan to give her a detailed account of his NET operation while she rushed him through the after-dinner coffee he'd ordered for them. She took one sip and waved for the check, insisting on paying for it to spite Alan, at that moment resenting the messenger as well as the message.

She raced out ahead of Alan and flagged a cab, dropped him off at the Ben Franklin Hotel, and directed the cab back uptown to the empty Pine Street sublet. She was lonely, too, she fumed. But she had kept her commitment. When Councilman Morgan had taken her to dinner and wanted more than cherry pie for dessert, she'd been firm. She was a married woman.

Tom said he loved her. If he couldn't handle the Philadelphia problems and the physical separation, he should try harder to work it out with her. Not crawl off to some sordid little apartment with Millie behind her back. Marlena's anger was a cold fire that burned deep.

Inside the warm apartment she moved purposefully to the phone. She had to talk to him.

Tom answered drowsily. "Hi. Just get in? Working late again?"

"No. I was out to dinner with Alan. He's in town for a NET conference." She waited for a rise. None came.

"Oh, yes. He stopped in yesterday and I gave him your number. I thought he might be able to talk you into taking a dinner break for a change."

"Meaning *you* can't?"

Tom's laugh held an edge of strain. "Something like that."

"I miss you."

"Seeing Alan made you miss me?"

"I guess so, but I miss you more than just . . . missing you." She couldn't bring herself to say anything seductive. Just the thought of saying sweet nothings brought nasty images of Millie and Tom to mind.

"So. Alan's doing well in Pittsburgh?"

Marlena's jaw squared. The bastard couldn't even say he missed her too. But she wasn't going to fish for a warmer response, not if she could help it. "Yes, but he's still underpaid. I bought him dinner."

"That was nice."

"Andy's talking about letting me anchor on Saturdays."

"That's great!"

"Is it? It would make it doubly difficult to get home weekends. And it would lock me up down here with a new contract."

"It's what you want, isn't it?"

"There wouldn't be any weekends in Wilkes-Barre, Tom."

Tom was silent.

"What do you want me to do? What do you want, Tom?"

"I want what's best for everyone. I wanted you to come back in September, but you wouldn't even consider it. I thought you'd made your choice then about what's more important to you."

"Andy promises that things will still work out with the news director spot."

"Sure."

"I'd quit and come home right now if I didn't believe that. It's only a question of time before you and Toby will be here too."

The phone was silent against her ear. The cool control cracked and hot tears fell on the receiver.

"Marlena? Marlena!"

Her sobs became audible.

"Listen, love. Decisions are what life is all about. It's not such a terrible thing."

She felt that he was making her choice for her when there were other choices for both of them.

"Oh, Tom, I . . ." She choked, unable to continue.

"Lena, calm dawn. I'll come to Philadelphia this week-end and we'll talk things out."

She couldn't stop crying, afraid Tom only wanted to come to say good-bye when that was the last thing she wanted.

The liquor, which had little effect under the anger of her discovery of betrayal, now swam into her mind. She closed her eyes and grasped the phone like a lifeline.

Tom tried to change the subject. "We gave all the puppies away this week, except one. I think Bessie went directly to church to light a candle in thanks. You wouldn't believe the way Madame is training the puppy we kept to be just as imperious as she is. They sit side by side right next to Toby at the dinner table."

She sniffed, irritated by his obvious attempt to divert her, but she couldn't resist listening.

"Toby has the little one eating from a fork already, just the soft stuff, but Madame barks up a protest if she doesn't get the lion's share."

"What . . . what did Toby name the puppy?"

"Box Car."

"Box Car."

"Bessie said the puppies look like little black boxcars. Toby thought that was hilarious and decided to call his puppy Box Car."

Marlena laughed despite her tears.

"Toby's getting so grown up," he said.

"You act as though I've been away for years. I saw him six weeks ago."

"It seems longer."

Marlena appreciated the poignant tone. Tom did miss her. It was only that Millie was handy—and willing. Irritation at both of them flared in her heart. "Out of sight, out of mind?"

"Do you know what Toby suggested last night? He thinks we should give you Madame. He said you probably get lonely for Madame at night. He was talking about the way Madame used to sleep at your feet."

Marlena bristled at the past tense, but she didn't interrupt.

"And he said that since he has Box Car as his very own dog, you should have Madame with you."

"I don't just get lonely for Madame!"

Tom's sigh was clear. "You only get lonely when you have time for it."

"That holds true for everyone."

"Some folks are just busier than others."

"I still remember the months and months when you were trying to train Rawlings and I was horribly lonely night after night. But *I* waited it out until things got better."

Tom didn't rise to the bait. "You sound tired. Why don't you take a nice hot bath, and then crawl into bed and get a good night's sleep for a change? I'll be there Friday night as early as I can."

"No. I'll come home. I'll even take Thursday off so we can go away for the weekend if you'd like. Somewhere like Vermont?"

"Skiing's your thing, not mine."

"Toby likes to ski too."

"We'll see." He used the phrase he reserved for Toby to postpone a no. "Call me in the morning and we'll coordinate."

Marlena felt deflated, empty, spent. Tom sounded distant, cool. Nothing he had said above or below the lines dispelled the suspicions.

Tom broke the silence. "I've got to go now. Lena . . ."

"Yes?" She asked hopefully.

"Promise you'll go to bed now."

"I will."

"Sleep tight."

"You, too. Bye." She held back her explosion until the connection was severed. "Damn!" Tom was acting like a grown-up hiding something from a child. She wasn't a child. He was. A selfish child who wanted everything his own way. In a way he was as bad as Roger. He was just a little older and more subtle about it.

She opened the window, pulling in the night air. She needed a clear head. What were her options?

She could call Andy first thing in the morning and say she was sick and drive home. Or she could quit. Do what Tom had wanted her to do in September. Come home, play ball with Toby, anchor the news, join the golf club, find the blue-bird of happiness in the bush leagues, wrinkle, grow old and die. No. That wasn't the answer.

With new determination, she walked back to the phone and dialed.

"Hello?" a woman answered sleepily.

"Nancy." Marlena was apologetic. "I'm sorry to call so late, but I have to talk to Andy. Is he there?"

Andy came on quickly. "Hi, kid. What is it? Fire, flood, a cop-killing? What's breaking?" he asked excitedly.

My heart, she thought, but she couldn't say that. "I can't talk over the phone. Can you meet me somewhere? It's an emergency."

"Where are you now?"

"Home." She bit her tongue. Home was the wrong word.

"On my way."

She frowned as he hung up the phone without asking

for the address, but she forgot about it by the time he arrived, half an hour later.

"Sorry it took me so long. Nancy is a pain in the tail sometimes. She wanted to come along."

"That would have been all right. I wouldn't have minded."

Andy, tall and broad, looked like what he was, a bright former athlete who'd become addicted to good food and transportation. He fancied himself a ladies' man and enough ladies agreed for him to continue to cultivate the image. "I would have." He winked.

When she started to speak Andy was irritated that she'd dragged him out so late to discuss Tom. "Look, Marlena, things are changing now. Dave Baumgarten's doctor is recommending that Dave work half days. We can't stay in the game with our general manager on the injured reserve list forever. Thing will break soon. Trust me."

"Soon isn't good enough, Andy. You've got to work something out now."

"Dammit, Marlena. You know I offered Tom the chance to take over my news director slot in all but title. I told him he could call the shots on the news operation. What else can I do right now?" His eyes leveled with hers. "You know what the real problem is?"

"What?"

"I think he'd sooner rot in hell than work under me. And I can understand that. Twenty years from now I wouldn't want to work under Carl." Carl was a pimply faced desk assistant and trainee.

"But what am I supposed to do? Go bury myself in Wilkes-Barre again to protect his precious male ego?" She burst into tears.

"Hey." Andy's strong, former-fullback's arms pulled her close, offering support. "You act as though this is some kind of final hour. Has old Tom given you an ultimatum? Come home or else?"

"Something like that." She sniffled against his imported British raincoat.

"I'm not the one to give you objective advice because I don't want to lose you. I admit I hired you as the bait to get Tom down here, but you've earned a front-line position on the WIB team in your own right. You're a damn good reporter already and I think you will be more than just another pretty face as an anchor. And I'll give you that chance here—because you deserve it."

Andy felt solid as she held on to him, and his positive words helped and hurt in tandem.

"I'm planning to put you on as the Saturday anchor, starting April first. I know we've talked about it, but I hadn't given you a solid date. You're moving up fast in a major market, Marlena. If you go back to Wilkes-Barre, you'll be throwing it all away. There's no guarantee there'll be another chance like this. There are a hell of a lot more bright and eager young reporters than there are chances."

She let go of him and sat down on the Victorian couch, trying to sort out the pieces of her puzzle.

"I think you could become one of the best. I know I'm not a master builder like Tom. I can't make silk purses out of sows' ears. But I can spot the good ones. And you could go all the way. It depends on what you want, what you're willing to work for."

"I guess I want it all." The phrase brushed her with a hollow echo. Roger had said that a lifetime ago.

Andy chuckled sympathetically. "Don't we all? The difference between being a grown-up and being a little kid is recognizing the need to compromise, knowing it's not reasonable to always have everything your own way."

"Then Tom isn't grown up yet," she grumbled.

"Maybe, maybe not. It depends on what goals he's comfortable with. My idea of growing up is learning what works for you and then settling for that."

"But if you marry someone and that someone doesn't want to just settle for that, shouldn't you compromise?"

"I'm glad I don't have to worry about that with Nancy. She has no ambitions other than promoting mine. As long as I keep her charge accounts at Saks and Bonwit current and put my face in at her black-tie benefits, I can be my own man."

"Are you telling me I should go home and be a good little wife for Tom?" she snapped.

"Good God, no." He laughed at the idea that that was what she'd thought he meant. "I was pointing out that you might have to face the fact that Tom may like it where he is. And it doesn't make him less of a grown-up. But if you want to realize your own ambitions, you might have to let go."

"No," she whispered. "There has to be another way." She stared down at the floor, not even looking up as Andy sat beside her and took her hand.

"I know something I want that wouldn't interfere with anyone's ambitions."

Marlena frowned and looked at him. "What?"

"You." Andy put his arms around her. "Marlena." His voice had thickened.

Scared by his sudden intensity, she pushed him away. She wanted a father to hold onto, an anchor in the stormy night. It wasn't a night for romance.

Six

❖

TOM ARRIVED ON FRIDAY night on schedule. Determined to stay calm and cheerful as though nothing were wrong, she fought back tears as Madame bounded out of the old Mercedes, the dog's ample body wriggling in delight at the sight of Marlena. Marlena buried her face in Madame's thick coat. This much is mine. This much is loyal.

Tom acted nervous and tense, ready to ward off any approach, it seemed. She avoided heavy discussions and made painstaking efforts with dinner. Boodles gin for the martinis, miniature croissants with the steak Diable, and the most expensive port the state store had to offer. She was wooing him.

He sat at her table like a hypocrite, she thought, talking about life at the station, congratulating himself because the news director was doing well and the girl he'd hired to fill Marlena's spot was improving quickly.

"Are you showing her all the ropes like you did me? The little blue spruces and everything?"

"Don't be silly, Marlena. She's just a kid."

"So was I."

He was telling the truth about that. She could hear it in his voice. She didn't mention Millie. Neither did Tom.

She urged him to bring Toby down the following weekend to see the Flyers. She made the suggestion hoping it would remind Tom of the hockey stick and skates she'd given Toby for Christmas.

"He'd like that," Tom began, "but I don't know if it's a good idea right now."

She didn't push him. She swung between hating him for not having the courage to be honest and hating him for not accepting and loving her enough to agree to move to Philadelphia—or at least beg, really beg her to come home. But she also felt self-contempt because she herself didn't have the strength to force a confrontation.

She scrubbed at the dinner dishes while Tom sat on the horsehair sofa in the parlor. The typical Victorian couple with a closet full of well-fleshed skeletons.

She joined him for a glass of port. "I'm wiped. How about you? Long day?"

"Long day."

"Ready to go to bed?"

"In a minute. Relax a little. That was a wonderful dinner."

"Thanks. It's been too long since I've put on the dog for you."

"That's because you didn't have the dog here to put on." He smiled sadly and scratched Madame behind the ears.

Marlena sat beside Tom on the green damask, leaning away from him against the arm of the sofa, studying him. "Alan says this place looks like a museum."

Tom sipped his port. "Prince Albert was here, all right. Now there was a smart man. He died in his youth, in full glory."

"What a depressing thought." She suddenly giggled.

"He probably woke up one day, took a good look at Victoria, and died instantly of a heart attack."

"Don't be mean. I think he died of some kind of virus or plague."

Marlena reached for Tom's hand. It was loose and open. "She loved him. Whatever her faults, she loved him."

"I suppose, but it seems to me she kept him at home ready for ceremonial display while she devoted herself to her political ambitions. Made him a bit of a dishrag, I'd say."

"But when he died she spent forty years mourning him. That's sweet and tragic."

"Some people don't recognize what they have until after it dies." Tom's hand closed, warm around her own. "Come on, I'll tuck you in and make you snug as a bug in a rug." Maggie's favorite good night. She shivered. Neither the childhood rhyme nor the thick blanket helped.

The next week she accepted Tom's lame excuse about scheduling problems and gave away the Flyers tickets. She didn't push for a rain date. Calls dwindled. With Madame in Philadelphia, she found fewer and fewer mutual concerns to check about with Tom. Did Toby ask about her.?

Fragments of children's conversations as they bicycled past while she and Madame walked around Rittenhouse Square broke against her like icicles, leaving shattered memories that melted like tears, slow to evaporate.

On good days, when sources answered her calls and the pieces fell into place in the jigsaws of her reports, she felt magnanimous. Millie would be good for Tom and Toby with her good-humored salt-of-the-earth style. On bad days Marlena looked back and the salt was in her own tears.

Andy was a problem. The last thing she wanted was to have an affair with him. Even if he weren't married, she wouldn't have wanted to get involved. Ever since the night she'd called him, he'd been making moves, telling her she had to forget Tom, that he could help her. She begged off, turning down even casual dinners, telling him that as attractive as he was to her, she couldn't let herself even be tempted until things had been worked out with Tom. As it became more obvious that things weren't working out, she switched to religious grounds. She couldn't even look at another man while there was any hope of reconciliation.

"Until I'm a completely free woman, Andy, legally and morally, I can't let any other man near me," she told him late one night when he'd caught her alone in the newsroom.

"But you need someone to be good to you, Marlena," he objected. "I'm a nice, uncomplicated answer for you right now. I not only wouldn't stand in the way of your career, I'd push it even faster." He moved close to her. "It wouldn't be hard for you to convince me to make you a full-time anchor."

That felt crummy to her. "Or just make me?" she snapped.

He refused to take offense, insisting she was making a great mistake, that they could have a terrific relationship.

"I can't argue with that, Andy," she said, soothing his ego. "You're more than attractive, but I've already told you. Not until I'm free." She hated the fact that she was leading him on, letting him think that if Tom were gone he'd be next in line.

It wasn't that she didn't like him at all. She enjoyed brainstorming with him about her stories and she liked listening to his war stories. She just didn't like it when he tried to get physical. There wasn't any chemistry there for her.

She drove herself furiously on the job, working long hours and finding enough good stories to keep the empty hours few. She managed to keep Andy at bay, flirting enough to let him think there might be hope. She didn't like to examine her fear of what could happen to her job if she stopped playing the one-sided game and told him what she really thought of him.

When her father arrived in Philadelphia for a medical convention in May she painted a glowing portrait of her commuters' marriage. She didn't want to admit the emotional failure or tell him that Maggie's warnings had been right.

She and her father wined and dined each other between the pediatric seminars and the newscasts. They ate hot dogs at the zoo and raced each other up the steps of the art museum. For those few weeks in the spring Marlena returned to the spirit of her carefree youth.

As she drove her father to the airport, she told him how sorry Tom was that he'd missed seeing him. She lied, saying that Tom was coming to Philadelphia the next days.

Bill gave his daughter a big bear hug. "Take care of yourself, Marlena Lilli Williams. It's not so bad to make mistakes. It's only bad if you don't deal with them and let them fester."

"Spoken like a doctor." She blinked back tears, feeling like a third-grader hiding a bad report card. "Oh, Daddy . . ."

"Why don't you come home for a visit? Your mother would like to see you. She's a little worried about you."

Marlena swallowed hard. "I will. When I can. Give her my love and give the boys a hug for me."

"It'd be better for you to do that in person."

"I know."

Bill hurried away to the gate as the last call for his flight was announced. She still had a home, she thought. But she couldn't go back to Des Moines. There was nothing there for her now except some love and sympathy, an emotional cushion she was determined not to fall back on out of weakness.

In September the teachers went on strike and Andy pulled Jill Gregson off the story, giving it to Marlena. Jill was a bright, ambitious reporter, five years older than Marlena, who had been covering education and consumer issues for the past four years.

Marlena liked Jill. Her high energy level and bright mind were appealing. Marlena found her a valuable sounding board for ideas, always willing to share her greater knowledge of the ins and outs of Philadelphia. Jill even shared sources, a sign of trust and respect.

Marlena's reaction to Andy's latest sop was pure and simple fury. She stormed into his office, berating him for playing favorites. She wouldn't accept the assignment. It wasn't fair. "If you think you're going to get me to sleep with you by giving me Jill's big story, you're wrong," she shouted.

"You're a fine one to play Miss Virtue. How did you get your start in Wilkes-Barre? Why did Tom make you an anchor so quickly? I thought the only way you knew to do business was horizontally."

She slapped him on the cheek as hard as she could, astonishing herself more than him. She froze, breathing hard, regretting her loss of control. But she had no intention of apologizing.

"All right. It was a lousy joke. I probably deserved that," Andy said easily. "But you're reading me wrong. I didn't pull Jill off the story to bribe you into sleeping with me. I'm not that desperate. I did it because you're a better reporter."

"You're right. It was a lousy joke. You know damn well that I didn't get to be a decent reporter because I slept with Tom. And I damn well don't want you giving me plums because you think I should sleep with you."

"Will you sleep with me if I don't give you plums? If I put Jill back on the story?"

She couldn't help laughing. "No, Andy. But please, just to keep Jill on my side, put her back on the story. She's been good to me. She's the one who taught me the ropes here. I owe her a lot."

"If that's the way you want it."

"Please, Andy."

"You can be nicer to me than that."

"Pretty please, Andy," she crooned. "That's the best I can do right now."

Later the same day, Jill approached Marlena and thanked her. Marlena brushed the thanks aside and suggested they catch a movie together on Sunday, feeling she needed a friend.

Jill and Marlena complemented each other, physically and mentally. Jill was short, dark, and high strung while Marlena's softer image was blond and calm. Fire and ice. They became closer and closer, shopping and lunching together on slow news days, unburdening their souls, and sharing hopes and fears. They even traded notes and edited each other's scripts when the news was breaking. And Marlena discovered that Jill served another purpose. She helped keep Andy in line.

When Andy got high and called her at night it was easy to get him off the phone quickly by saying "Jill and I are . . ." whether Jill was there or not. For all his cavalier airs, Andy liked to keep his affairs behind closed doors. Nancy was too well connected with the IBS brass, socially and financially.

Marlena was well aware that Andy's wife didn't like her. Whenever she stopped by the studio Nancy made a point of asking about Tom. It was obvious to Marlena that Andy hadn't said anything to Nancy to indicate the Wells's marriage was cracking under the commute.

A week after the teacher's strike incident Andy presented Marlena with a diamond pendant cunningly shaped like a bird. "It's an I-am-sorry old bird."

"For what? I slapped you and I'm sorry."

"No. That's not the point. The bird is also sorry that you're still not free. It's supposed to cheer you up and let you know that the bluebird of happiness is out here waiting for you."

Andy was a corny romantic, she decided. She didn't want to accept the present, knowing it would fan false hopes. The whole thing was becoming an ugly tease. Not that old faithless Andy didn't deserve some of it, but he wasn't a complete bastard. He was giving her a chance to grow as a reporter. He deserved better from her, but she didn't know how to change the game without alienating him.

"You're a nice old bird," she said, giving him a circumspect kiss on the cheek.

The next day she gave the pin to her cleaning woman and told her it was costume jewelry, which made Marlena feel both better and worse.

She wanted little more than to tell Andy to take a flying leap, but she had a feeling he had a hidden vindictive streak. She didn't want to test the theory. Her job was all she had.

She poured all her frustrated energy into the Cherry Hill murder trial she was covering, hanging around the courthouse cafeteria both breakfast and lunch, pouncing on defense and prosecution attorneys alike, working hard to get a full picture of the proceedings.

The only one she still hadn't gotten to know yet, that day in December, was the chief prosecuting attorney, a young man in his early thirties, athletic and ivy, with a look that was untouched by failure but devoid of arrogance.

She found him more than attractive, and she'd caught him looking at her more than once. Tingles. Definitely tingles. Perhaps that was why she'd saved getting his side of the story until last. On all levels, she felt a mixture of hope and fear.

She went to the cafeteria for lunch that day, thinking she might look for his assistant and find out more about him before she went in search of him. Disappointed that she didn't see any of his staff in the room, she picked up a tray and silver and went through the cafeteria line, stopping as she passed the cashier to scan the lunchroom.

"We've got to stop meeting like this." A friendly voice spoke from behind her.

She turned her head and was stopped cold by the full force of Will Austin's very blue eyes two feet behind her.

She caught her breath and quipped, "Do you have a better place in mind?"

"I sure do, but these days I never seem to get back to that place until after midnight." Will fell into step with her as she looked for an empty table.

"Yes, let's find a table all to ourselves," he addressed her thoughts easily.

"Midnight doesn't scare me. I'm a night person myself," she said, surprised at her own boldness. She was practically inviting herself over to his place. What was she doing? Wasn't her life messy enough at the moment?

Will sat beside her and removed the tuna salad platter and dish of Jell-O from her cafeteria tray, then put the tray on the side table without asking, as though he always did it for her. It felt simple and natural.

"What does scare you?" Will asked as he began unloading his own tray.

"I don't know. Maybe having Channel 6 or 3 get ahead of me on a story and surprise me."

"You don't like surprises?"

"Not that kind. Of course, I don't mind surprising them with a scoop," she added mischievously, staring at the array of food in front of Will. Pot roast. Side dishes of mashed potatoes, peas, red beets, cole slaw, a hard roll, and cherry pie with whipped cream. "William, do you have a tapeworm?"

"Will. Just Will. And I hope I don't have a tapeworm. I'm not big on cooking for myself late at night. The food here's cheap and healthy, and I'm getting to like bologna."

"I'm a peanut-butter-and-jelly person, myself. You

haven't roped some poor girl into taking care of you yet?"
Again she was amazed at her own audacity.

She followed Will's glance to her left hand and noted,
happily, that last summer's ring line had long faded.

"How about you? It doesn't sound like you have anyone
waiting at home for dinner either."

"But I do."

He tried to keep the disappointment from showing.
"Don't tell me you're one of the ringless marrieds."

"Not quite. My waiting creature is an eighty-pound lap-
dog who eats shoes if I'm late."

The warmth returned to his blue eyes and he looked
into hers for a long moment to share it. The chemistry was
extraordinarily strong. Marlena struggled to remember that
she wanted to talk to him about the case as she felt the back of
her knees go weak, even sitting down.

Will cleared his throat. "Whew." It was obvious that the
vibrations were flowing both ways. "Talk about surprises. I
thought you'd be dynamite up close, but . . ."

She liked the way he acknowledged it. Clean and
straight. The least she could do was reply. "Kaboom."

They both laughed, sealing the mutual attraction.

"Right now, while I have you here, I have to play reporter. I hope you don't mind."

"Yes and no." His meaning was clear. "At the moment
I'd rather you were a hatcheck girl, totally disinterested in the
case at hand."

"Me too, but a woman has to finish the job at hand."

"Okay, Lois Lane, what can I tell you?"

"There's a rumor floating around that you have a surprise up your sleeve. It doesn't seem to bother you that the
defense is doing a pretty good job of establishing reasonable
doubt about your evidence."

There'd been two murders in the same Cherry Hill

neighborhood, days apart. The accused, who worked as a mechanic in a local garage, had known both victims as customers, had no alibi for the crimes, and had admitted having asked one victim for a date and having been unhappy when she'd turned him down. He also had a history of violence when drunk.

The one neighbor who'd run outside at the sound of the shot during the second murder had originally identified the accused from a lineup, but had come across as very uncertain during cross-examination. The rest of Will's evidence was totally circumstantial.

"You're worried because I don't look worried?" He laughed.

"And I want to know why." She dimpled suddenly as she thought of a humorous approach. "When I was little I played a lot of cowboys and Indians with my younger brothers. I was always the Indian."

"What does that have to do with this case?" Will was intrigued.

"No torture known to man could wrench any secret from my lips."

Will shook his head, amused, and took a huge bite of pot roast.

"Now, is there any truth to the rumors that you have a surprise witness up your sleeve?"

Will raised his eyebrows, then his eyes darted to the other tables around them to see who might be listening.

"When should I expect your surprise?"

"I didn't say I had a surprise."

"You didn't?" She tilted her head at him and added a quizzical smile. "My ears must be failing me. I could swear you asked me if I liked surprises."

"But I always played the Indian too," he said.

"Then what we need is a tribal pow-wow," she replied.

She took a breath, gathered her courage, and followed her own lead. "A very private tribal pow-wow?"

"But at the moment we're in different tribes, aren't we?" His eyes turned serious as he looked into hers. The electric currents filled the air between them. "I'd like that . . . if we don't have to discuss business."

She swallowed hard and let herself swim in the currents. "What trial?" she asked softly.

"Dinner tonight?"

"I'm not free until after the news, around midnight."

"That's my normal dinner hour," he said, beginning to frown.

"What's wrong?" she asked anxiously.

"I wish you weren't a reporter. I don't like to mix business with more personal affairs."

She blushed.

"I didn't mean it like that. I know you're not . . . a swinger. At least that's what my dirty young assistant tells me."

She smiled, pleased that he'd been asking about her. "Will, I believe in the same thing, not mixing business with pleasure. But what's a person to do if they . . ." She paused, searching for the right words. ". . . just happen to mix?" She looked at him unhappily. "Maybe we should stay away from each other until the trial is over."

"And maybe I should stop breathing." Will let the words slip out. "Marlena . . . do I have to call you that? It sounds so formal."

"Lena. Just Lena's fine."

"Lena. I like that." He smiled.

"I like you," she replied.

"I'll bet we can do better than that," he said, and then added quickly. "So. How does it sound if I pick you up at midnight and we grab a bite to eat?"

"As long as we walk the dog first."

"Dog lovers are always good people." He moved to give her hand a soft squeeze that turned into a long moment of hand holding. "Honest, loyal, crazy . . ." This time Will was the one who swallowed hard. "If you don't get out of here," he said, noticing that she'd finished her salad and Jell-O, "I could ruin your reputation right here and now."

"I'm going, counselor, I'm going."

"But not too far," he added as she rose.

"Hey, Will!" one of his assistants called from across the row of Formica tables. "Can you come here a minute?"

"See you," Will said as he stuffed the last bite of pot roast into his mouth and got up, chewing.

She watched him stride across the gray and aqua tiles and wondered if that meant they had a date.

Their breath was like frozen smoke as she and Jill traded notes in front of the Broad Street entrance to WIB-TV. She'd avoided updating Andy, but she'd told Jill she was seeing Will after the show.

Jill knew Marlena's marriage was in the last stages of its death rattle, and she'd been encouraging Marlena to date. She already knew who Will was, since Marlena had told Jill the night before about the courthouse rumors.

"Will Austin is attractive?" she asked, as she kept Marlena company while she waited for Will.

"Yes."

"And?"

"And he's attractive." Marlena didn't feel like explaining or sharing the unexpected turn of events.

"Do you think he'll tell you what he has up his sleeve for the trial?"

"I don't know."

"You're being awfully mysterious, Lena. What's the story?"

"No story. I'm just wondering whether he's even going to show up."

"You underestimate yourself."

"Thanks, but he's already ten minutes late."

"Want me to wait awhile longer?"

"No, that's silly. You have your own date waiting. If he doesn't show up in another five minutes, I'll grab a cab and go cry in my pillow."

"Don't do that. Come on over and have pizza with Steve and me."

Marlena shook her head. "Madame still needs a walk, one way or the other."

"Hope he shows soon," Jill said, pecking Marlena good night on the cheek.

Jill's cigarette glowed against the dark walls of the old buildings as she walked away, then disappeared around a corner. Marlena shivered. Her knees below her miniskirt weren't protected from the chill December air.

Across the street, a car engine suddenly came to life, and moments later the car made a U-turn and pulled up beside her.

She started, backing toward the entrance as Will got out, grinning mischievously as he walked around to open the passenger door for her. "Alone at last. I thought she'd never leave."

"Dirty pool! You were waiting across the street the whole time!"

"A good reporter might have noticed."

She threw her notebook at him as she got into the car. He caught it neatly and held onto it as he slid behind the driver's seat. Then he flipped on the overhead light and ruffled through the pages.

"Unfair!" She reached for her notes and a tussle ensued, friendly and warm with young-puppy physical contact.

"Unfair?" Will kept control of the embattled notebook. "You want my secrets and you won't show me yours?"

"Go ahead and look, then." She pushed her curls back into place and smiled. "It won't make sense to you anyway."

The notebook included lists headed FACTS and POS- SIBILITIES, but the lists themselves were her own abbreviations and code names. Some pages were dated and had rough drafts of scripts and stand-ups. One page revealed a short shopping list, a mundane contrast: tin foil, hair spray, dog food, Tampax, and vermouth.

"Aha! You do have a dog, you are a female, and you like martinis."

"Nice going, Sherlock."

He flipped on, stopping at the last page dated December eighth, the previous day. She moved closer to see what he saw.

Cornsilk: Hvd und. Yale law, clk Ill, Hi crt-pere, no marr'd, free.

"No 'marred.' I like that." He moved his finger down the page and looked at her, inches away.

"What are those?"

"Not for translation," she said, aware that the chemistry was as strong as she'd remembered.

"Cornsilk. Why do you call me cornsilk?"

She leaned back to stop herself from moving forward too fast. "How do you know it's you?"

"Harvard, Yale, clerk for the Illinois Supreme Court, and a father who is on the Federal Court of Appeals in Ohio. Who else? But why cornsilk?"

"Your hair."

Will pulled a soft strand down to examine it, cross-eyed. "Hmm. Cornsilk."

"Don't feel bad. I call Tooney for the defense 'Dandruff.'"

Will chuckled and returned the notebook.

"So now you know all my secrets," she said. "Does that mean I get to look at your notebooks too?"

"My mother advocates trusting women when it comes to high-court matters," he said as he restarted the engine of his three-year-old Mustang convertible. "But that's always a matter of debate, according to my father."

"What does your mother do?"

"She's a lawyer."

"I almost went to law school once," Marlena said, brushing against the thought of Roger. "But I didn't think it was right for me."

"Two-lawyer households can be stimulating. Too stimulating, sometimes." Will's grin was engaging. Then he sobered, looking at her silently, affirming the charged air between them. "I don't want to play games, Lena. I'd like to take you home with me right this minute." He paused. "How do you feel about that?"

Talking wasn't easy when all she wanted to do was have him kiss her. She cleared her throat. "I'd like that. But . . ."

"But what?"

"First we have to go to my place and walk the dog, remember?"

They never made it to Will's place that night. And Madame had to wait for her walk until after they'd made love, "in Victorian splendor," as Will joked shakily as they shared a cigarette.

They were left shaken by their lovemaking. Words did not come easily.

Even Madame sensed that this intrusion was different and waited patiently until the passion had stilled before she trotted over to lick the salt on Marlena's shin.

"Careful," Marlena warned as Madame moved closer to Will.

That eased the feeling of overwhelming emotion, although the warmth and closeness remained.

"Poor Madame," Will said as he rubbed the dog's thick coat. "I guess we should get dressed and walk you. When's the last time she was out?" he asked Lena.

"It's not as dire as you think. I hire a teenager to walk her every night at seven."

"You have a good mommy," Will said to Madame.

"And there's a garden for emergency situations like tonight."

"What's the emergency?"

"Do you really want to get dressed right now and walk her?"

"Where's the door to the garden?" He asked.

After Lena let Madame out the speechlessness returned. Will opened his arms and they cuddled in front of the mock fireplace, having no need for any other flames.

Later Lena let Madame back in and walked into the bedroom with Will. Making love with him was as natural as breathing, she thought. Her mind had no wish to wander. "This is new to me," Will whispered against her ear.

"I know," she said softly. All the phrases. It's never been like this. You're wonderful. I think I love you. I do love you. They all felt too trite to her. And to him. She didn't need to say them or hear them. It was enough to feel them right then and there.

They fell asleep easily and slept soundly until the six A.M. alarm. Marlena slid easily back to her old domestic habits and had bacon and eggs waiting as he emerged from the shower.

"And she can cook too," he said happily.

"Comden and Green," she said.

"I know the song." Will sang a few lines in a practiced baritone.

Lena sensed they had a lot in common. Bodies that seemed created for each other and old songs were just the beginning, she thought, completely content.

"Will you live up to your promise to me?" He asked with wide blue eyes, looking across the small kitchen table.

"What are you talking about?"

"You promised you'd come home with me after we walked the dog."

"It's a working day, remember?"

"I'm talking about tonight."

That felt good. She realized that Will had to be feeling the same way she did, wanting to have little time or distance come between them now that they'd found this closeness.

"Madame," Will addressed the dog at his feet as he fed her a piece of bacon. "You'll love my place, really. It doesn't have a garden like your mother's, but it has a great view and a balcony if you get bored."

Lena loved it. Will didn't seem to feel the slightest bit silly about treating Madame like the person Lena knew her to be.

The day in court was a trial for both of them. They struggled not to let their feelings show. It wasn't easy.

Lena almost applauded out loud when the judge recessed early for the day.

Then she returned to the studio and forced herself to concentrate on her script for the eleven o'clock news. She laughed at herself as she recognized that she was feeling lonely, missing Will when she'd seen him only hours ago and would see him, more than see him at midnight.

His high-rise apartment was sparsely furnished with expensive Scandinavian modern. "One good piece at a time," he explained shamelessly.

The view, looking out across the Delaware River toward New Jersey, was spectacular, an eagle's aerie above the surrounding ghettos.

"All right. Tonight it's my turn," he announced, leaving Lena to watch Madame give every object in the hall and living room the sniff test while he retreated to the kitchen.

"You wanted to know about my surprise, right?" he called from the kitchen five minutes later.

"It doesn't matter," she called back.

"Well, here it is. Surprise!" Will returned to the combination living-dining room carrying a lacquered tray replete with frosty martinis, Brie, Carr's crackers, and a perfect bunch of deep purple grapes.

"You hypocrite," she said, applauding nevertheless. "Is this the man who eats bologna sandwiches alone in his bachelor apartment?"

"One and the same." He placed the tray on the coffee table, leaning down to kiss her at the same time.

They couldn't stay apart any longer. Their hands raced to discard the clothes in the way of their need for perfect closeness. The aching and trembling they inspired in each other, the need to melt, to move together, to build and climb with one another into a dizzy sky of simultaneous explosion had to be assauged before they could say another word.

"Madame must think we're complete libertines." Will laughed. Tonight words were easier afterward.

"She'll never tell," Lena said as she handed Madame a piece of Brie. "She's easy to bribe."

Will obliged by cutting off another piece of cheese and handing it to Madame. Then he looked directly at Marlena. "I love you. I'm not just falling in love with you. And all the words sound too used, if you know what I mean."

"I do."

"You do what?" He moved close again, close enough to kiss her lips gently.

"Both. I know what you mean." She swallowed hard. "And I love you."

"So. When do you want to move in."

"Oh, Will. It's not that easy."

"You're right, Lena. I forgot about the 'conflict of interest.' The attorney general would have a heart attack. We'll have to wait until after the trial and see if the idea still appeals to you."

Will had read it wrong, Lena realized. She suddenly thought about her personal conflict of interest, the husband who hadn't officially left her, although she knew, thanks to Alan, that Tom and Millie were now openly living together. She hadn't talked to Tom in weeks. She didn't know if he was ready to talk divorce or not. It hadn't mattered before now.

Her line about it not being easy to just move in was intended to let her slide into the revelation that she was married, not an easy admission at this point. Things felt so good and wholesome, so free and open with Will, she was afraid to introduce complications. But she wanted to be completely honest with him. She trusted her feeling for him and his for her, as new as they were.

"It's funny," Will said. "I don't feel as though we only met yesterday. It seems as though we've made love a thousand times before."

"That's pretty romantic for a prosecutor."

"Who says prosecutors can't get mushy? And can't feel ravenously romantic?" He nibbled her ear. "Hungry?"

"Now that you mention it." He sat up as Madame, drooling beside the remaining Brie, barked sharply. "My women don't have to beg." He laughed. "It's yours for the asking." Will put the Brie on the floor.

"Women?" Lena raised her brows.

"Don't look so concerned. I meant you and Madame. Madame is a woman too," he said.

"And a very loyal one," Lena added. "My father says dogs are like women. Be faithful to them and they'll be faithful to you. Mess around with another dog and they'll bite your head off."

"Is your Dad a lawyer?"

"A pediatrician at his clinic and a vet at home."

"Come on, tell me about your family while we make a salad. The steaks are ready and waiting." He stood, taking her shoulders in his hands and turning her to face him. "How are you on salads?"

"Try me."

"I have. And you inspire seconds." He kissed her gently, softly exploring her lips. "You're probably good at just about everything in the world."

"Will." She put her fingertips to his lips. "I'm not that good. Please." Her voice held an edge of real pleading. "Please allow me some room for error."

The concern became his. "Do you think . . . aren't you sure . . ." His words couldn't keep pace with his tumbling thoughts. "Are you having second thoughts about me?"

Her reassuring hug answered him quickly. "Oh no. Not the tiniest reservation. Nothing's ever felt as right. But I'm not as pure as the driven snow . . . and I wish I were for you. I wish I'd met you when I was nineteen, before I knew anyone else."

"That's biblically, I assume."

She nodded.

"You silly, silly girl." He stroked her cheek gently. "I didn't expect you to be a virgin. These aren't the *eighteen* seventies."

"I know, but . . ."

"But I'm hungry. We can share all our old skeletons later, for dessert." He led the way into his kitchen, which was spotless and well equipped.

"I'm impressed," she said.

"Wait." He held up his hand. "I must first prove to you that I am an honest man." With that, he opened the refrigerator and took out a bologna.

"You've made a believer of me," she hugged him from behind.

As they made the salad together and waited for the steaks to turn medium well, another happily discovered shared taste, she entertained him with tales of Wilkes-Barre and Alan's notorious kitchen, her practical jokes with roaches and rubber insects, and her first story with the wrong mayor.

Will shared in kind, beginning with a disastrous account of his job as a construction worker between freshman and sophomore years in college. "What a blow to my ego at the end of the summer," he said, ending the funny saga, "to be told by a fellow laborer that I wasn't worth four cents an hour, let alone four dollars. There was nothing left for me to do but become a lawyer."

They continued the personal yet impersonal anecdotes that build the fabric of long relationships through dinner.

She liked the way Will explained the merits of the good Bordeaux when he realized she knew little about wine. He did it to teach her, not to impress her.

Finally, with coffee, she bit the bullet. "There's something I have to tell you, Will."

"We don't have to take out the skeletons tonight, Lena." Will started to suggest they save all confessions for another day until he looked at her face. "I'm sorry. Please, go ahead."

"This is hard for me, Will, because I feel . . . I feel like you're the first man I've loved in the right way. Do you know what I mean?"

He nodded.

"I should have told you when you asked the question, but I let it slide and answered the next one. I know I'm speaking in riddles, but it's so hard to say without it coming out all wrong."

"Lena, Lena . . ." He stood and pulled her to her feet, away from the dining-room table. "It can't be that bad. And nothing's that complicated, unless . . ."

"Unless?" She held her breath, terrified he'd say "unless you're already married."

"Unless you're in love with someone else too."

"Oh, no. No one else. Not now. Not ever like this," she protested, sitting on the couch beside him.

"Then what?"

"There are complications. I don't know how else to say it but to say it. I'm separated, physically, but legally, I'm still married to a man in Wilkes-Barre."

"Well." He sat, silent, for a long moment, digesting the information. "I guess we'd better talk about it."

Tears streamed down her face. "I'm sorry, Will. I wish it weren't so."

"Shhh. It's going to be okay. I believe you. And I still want you."

He had answered her questions before she had asked, as her father always had for Maggie, still could after years of marriage.

It was a long night. She talked and talked, explaining why she and Tom hadn't worked out, explaining to herself as much as to Will. Will admitted he found the listening almost as painful as she found the telling. He didn't like to think of her as belonging to anyone else, father figure or not.

By the time they fell asleep their relationship had grown in understanding and shared pain. More than Marlena's marriage had in four and a half years.

They didn't dwell on it the next night as they dined in a cozy French restaurant near the waterfront. It was as though they both understood that the emotional part of Marlena's marriage was past. Marlena reported that she'd sent Tom a letter saying she wanted to move forward, to start divorce proceedings. Will suggested a divorce lawyer he knew.

There was amazingly little negative charge to the subject. The positive charge, the magnetism that made them both want to spend every free moment together wasn't diminished. If anything, the confession had opened another, deeper door to Lena's heart. And Will showed no reluctance to move as deeply inside her as he could.

The openness extended into all areas. By the end of the next weekend they were trading notes on the trial like old friends as well as lovers. Will was sincerely interested in her evaluation of the jury. Marlena complimented him on his objectivity, but sensed how much he wanted to win.

"Farino's guilty, Lena. There's no question in my mind. He's guilty as sin."

"I'm not sure the jury's convinced."

"If we can just find this guy Wald who lived next to Elaine Hanson . . ."

Wald, as Will had told her before, was the next-door neighbor of the first murder victim. He was a salesman who had gone on the road early on the morning before Elaine's body was discovered. But one of the other neighbors had told the detectives that Wald had mentioned seeing Farino coming out of Hanson's house late the night before.

"The neighbor who talked to Wald might have some influence on the jury," Lena suggested.

"That's secondhand knowledge. I need Wald. We have an all-points bulletin out for him now, all over the south. That's his sales region."

"Will the judge grant you a recess to find him?"

"I'm hoping that won't be necessary. I'd like to get this wrapped up before Christmas."

"What happens Christmas?"

"I was getting to that." He smiled. "I'd like to take the women I love skiing in Vermont, if you can take vacation from WIB-TV for a week."

"I'd love that. How did you know I love to ski?"

"I didn't. It's just another one of those happy coincidences." He looked more than pleased. "Can you get away?"

"I have vacation time coming. The only story I'm covering right now is the trial. If you can end it before Christmas, I'm as free as you are."

"Who says man cannot control his destiny?"

"The jury?"

"That's one of your endearing qualities."

"What?"

"You're an irrepressible wiseass."

"But I can cook."

"Mmm. Let's go to my place and 'cook.'"

"Okay, but . . ."

"I know," he interrupted.

They said it together. "First we have to walk the dog."

By the next weekend Will was getting edgy because Wald still hadn't been found. On Friday afternoon he suggested they take a drive to Riegelsville for lunch at an old inn.

"Maybe if we get away, stop watching the pot, Wald will show up," Will said hopefully on Saturday morning as they left the city, heading north toward beautiful Bucks County.

"Look, Will," Lena said. "Madame's smiling." The elkhound's black nose pointed out the window; she was laughing in the wind.

"Sorry," Will said as they approached a gas station ten minutes out of town. "One last check."

Five minutes later they were racing back toward Will's offices. Wald was on his way in. The pot was boiling.

Lena dropped Will off and took his car back home to her place to wait for him. It was midnight before he arrived, still brimming with excitement.

"We have Farino cold," he announced, and the story poured out while she broiled steaks.

"Jonas Wald, the salesman, did see Farino leave the Hanson house close to midnight. Remember, the coroner fixed the time of death as between eleven-thirty P.M. and twelve-thirty that morning. Wald was in his driveway, packing his car for the extended sales trip he was leaving on the next morning. There's no question about Wald's identification of Farino. Farino works on Wald's car regularly."

"Not bad," Lena said. "But where was he during the inquest?"

"On the road. He came back after the inquest and left again days before the trial started. Missed all the publicity."

"Timing. Life is all a question of flukes and timing."

"He'd been down to Miami and all the way back up the coast through the south before they found him north of Baltimore, on his way home."

"I knew there was a reason the union won the war."

"Wait. The story gets better. Wald wondered if Farino had a thing going with Elaine. Wald had been thinking about asking her out for a while. So he walked across the street to talk to Farino, just out of curiosity. Farino acted 'spooky' when Wald asked if he was dating Elaine and denied even knowing her, saying he'd gone to the wrong house, a mix-up with addresses."

"Did Wald know if Farino had been drinking?"

"He said he smelled liquor on Farino's breath, but that that wasn't unusual for Farino. What bothered Wald was the wrong address bit. Wald had been outside arranging samples in his trunk for over twenty minutes with an unobstructed view of Hanson's house. He saw Farino leave, but hadn't seen him enter. That meant Farino had been inside for at least twenty minutes and was lying about the wrong address. It didn't make sense to Wald."

"Why didn't he report it?"

"He left at dawn before anyone other than Farino knew she was dead."

"Oh, Will." The reporter in her came to life. "I'd give my eyeteeth to interview Wald before he testifies in court."

"On camera?"

"When he gets to court the judge will order him not to discuss his testimony until after the verdict, right? So I'll be stuck with courtroom sketches just like the other stations."

"You're cute when you smell a scoop. You look like Madame." He turned serious. "Would you get mad at me if I said no?"

She paused, giving the question honest consideration. "No. I'd understand, but I'd probably wonder why you didn't trust me."

"I'll think about it. We're not going to put him on until the last session before the Christmas recess. I want to surprise the defense counsel and send the jury home for the holidays with Wald's testimony on their minds."

"Dessert?" she asked, changing the subject while mentally filing the schedule.

"Just you," he said.

"Ready to call it a night and make love like regular people do?"

"How's that?"

"Regularly." He grinned. "Night after night."

"I love you." She reinforced the words with a kiss. Suddenly she pulled away.

"What's the matter?" Will's puzzlement turned to

amusement as she explained that she'd left her diaphragm at his place, thinking they'd go there when they got back from the country.

"You don't need protection from me, do you?"

She colored, feeling the full force of their chemistry.

"But what if I got pregnant?"

"We'd speed up the divorce and get out the shotgun, I guess," he said easily. "Lena, I don't believe in abortion. And I don't feel holier than thou about it because I only make love to women I'd be willing to make a commitment to. My modern version of Puritanism, maybe."

Sidestepping her ghost of guilt, she retorded, "It's a miracle you haven't gotten married yet."

"It helps to be a workaholic. My affairs have been few, careful, and far between. The one time I came close, I admit the thought of marriage was frightening, but it was a false alarm."

"I'm glad." She lifted her face to be kissed. He complied quickly.

"With you, for the first time, the thought of marriage isn't scary. It feels inevitable. And, correct me if I'm wrong, you've taken every step forward with me as easily as I have."

"I plead guilty, counselor."

He guided her to the bedroom to close the case for the night.

When she arrived at the station on Monday morning the receptionist said that Andy wanted to see her immediately.

"Where've you been lately?" He didn't look happy. "Even Jill hasn't seen you for days."

She consoled herself that this grimy flirtation was all but over. The day the trial ended she would go public with Will.

"I can't reveal my source, Andy, but I've stumbled on some great inside stuff on the Farino–Cherry Hill murder trial. I've been out checking and double-checking." That was close to the truth.

Skeptical, he pushed her for specifics. Finally, to get him off her back, she said she'd learned about a surprise eyewitness who would clinch the case against Farino. Perry Mason stuff. She added that she had a shot at an exclusive interview on camera before he testified in court.

Andy got excited. For all his faults he recognized a scoop. "What odds do you give your chances for the interview?"

"Sixty-forty."

"That's enough to get started." He'd have new promos produced, hyping her regular trial coverage. He agreed not to even hint at any surprises, only promote the trial in anticipation. He waved with crossed fingers as she left his office.

Later in the afternoon Jill told Marlena why Andy had had such a fit at not being able to reach Marlena on Sunday. "Nancy's out of town. Andy probably had his big move all planned and then he couldn't find you." They shared a laugh and agreed to meet for lunch at one.

By one Lena needed to confide in Jill. She wanted to tell someone, if not the whole world, about Will. She swore Jill to secrecy until after the trial, oblivious to Jill's unhappiness with Andy's raging enthusiasm for his ace reporter. Andy had pulled the artists and producers away from Jill's education report to work on Marlena's promotions.

Lena had no trial piece to cut until Thursday, when she promised Andy she'd have a summary ready.

She told Jill she was going to the courthouse, but instead she went shopping. That night they planned to be at Will's place. She knew she could get a private summary of the day in court.

She surprised him by being home with the veal Milanese waiting when he arrived at nine. And Will surprised her by saying he had arranged for her to interview Wald the next day. "That's provided you have a cameraman we can trust."

"We do."

"You'll have to disguise the equipment so the neighbors don't get suspicious. And I have to have the right to decide if anything he says has to be kept off the air."

The terms were tough, but he'd just handed her a grand slam. "You don't have to do this, Will. You know that."

"I know that. That's why I'm doing it."

She understood.

"The lid has to be absolutely sealed on this, Lena. I don't want the defense to have time to come up with anything cute and I want Wald on that stand right until noon when the judge recesses for Christmas weekend.

"I'm sorry the trial's dragged on this long. No Christmas skiing this year, but we can reschedule for Valentine's Day, okay?"

"It's your schedule on this one, counselor."

"Speaking of schedules, Thursday night after your story has run, divorce or no divorce, conflict of interest or not, I'd like to drive my little Mustang to that Victorian mausoleum you rent and move my women out, take them home. How do you like that schedule?"

"It's okay with me if it's okay with Madame."

They both laughed as they looked at the dog curled up like a huge, fuzzy mealy worm on the white couch.

"Will," she said later as they lay close together in the moist afterglow of good loving, "do you have to wait until Thursday morning to put Wald on the stand?"

"It's the best timing."

"For you." She reached for cigarettes for them both. "But nobody watches TV Christmas Eve. Everybody's in church or at parties."

"Lena." He reached for her hand. "It'll still give you points with WIB-TV."

"You're right, Will. It's your call on the timing. I

wouldn't have a story to time without you." She felt content again. "I wish you could come to the WIB Christmas party Wednesday night," she said with true regret.

"I'll come home to your place after the party and help you pack instead. I shouldn't be there the night before the interview airs. I'll come next year, I promise. Okay?"

"Okay," she said before she stubbed out her cigarette, nuzzled against him, and slept dreamlessly.

The interview with Wald was powerful. Wald came across as articulate, bright, and poignant. His description of Elaine Hanson, the twenty-eight-year-old account executive he'd admired from across the street, was tinged with a would-be lover's despair. It made great television.

Lena carried the cassette back to the station like a holy grail and asked the receptionist to lock it in the safe so no other reporter could look at the tape, even by accident.

She didn't tell Andy she had it. She was nervous about when he'd want to air it, realizing he knew only too well how deadly the Christmas Eve audiences were. She calmed his nervous impatience by saying the odds were now 95–5. The interview was scheduled for Monday. That bought her peace.

That weekend with Will was magic, in a soft, domestic way. They both felt good about their week's work. Will had the defense off guard, he was sure, and Marlena had Wald in the can. They lazed at his place, reading bits of articles to each other from the Sunday paper, walking Madame, and talking about when they'd meet each others parents. Nice and easy.

Monday was calm. She did a one-minute trial piece, nothing fancy, and hurried home to Will's, where he had fettucine waiting.

Tuesday morning was less peaceful. Andy was waiting in her office when she arrived, again furious because he

couldn't find her on off hours. She told him she'd been working on details for the interview, but he kept fishing for more.

His tone was whiny as he said Nancy wouldn't be back
until Wednesday night and finally she exploded. "Andy, this is
dumb. You know my position, so just drop it." She surprised
herself with the outburst, but regretted it as she saw his neck
turn red. "Look. This is the big week. The week that Wald
testifies."

"Wald? That's the guy?" He jumped at the new crumb.

"Jonas Wald. And if it makes you feel better, I've done
the interview already. It's in the can."

He all but salivated. "Let's see it."

Her stomach knotted with apprehension, but she
agreed.

Andy was impressed. "Great. Great television. I love the
look on Wald's face when he says, 'I'll always be grateful they
found me in time to help put Tom Farino where he belongs—
death row,' You can see Wald thinking about pulling the
switch."

"Just stay calm until it airs Thursday night, please."

"Shit!" It hit him. "Not Christmas Eve. We have to run
it Wednesday. Ahead of the news, not behind it."

"Thursday. I gave my word."

"Don't be naive, Marlena. We run it Wednesday night
and beat this whole goddam town by twenty-four hours!"

"Andy, the condition for my getting the interview at all
was that it couldn't run until after Wald testified in court."

"Blame me. I'm the boss," Andy said happily.

"Wednesday or Thursday, it's still a scoop. We have the
only on-camera interview. The other stations will only have
courtroom sketches and shots of Wald walking in and out of
the courthouse, if they're lucky."

"Why settle for half a loaf? The news audience for
Wednesday will be twice what it is for Christmas Eve."

"If I burn my source, I'll never get anymore inside information on any trial in Philadelphia."

"Who cares? I'm planning to have you anchoring full-time and off the streets before you need to worry about that."

"My source will never trust another reporter again."

"Who is this pure and holy source?"

Marlena ignored the question. "If you run that story tomorrow night, I quit."

"You're bluffing."

"Try me." She started to storm out.

"Marlena. Think about it overnight. We'll talk tomorrow. And think about anchoring full-time while you're at it."

A different kind of bribe, she thought, feeling miserable for the first time since the beginning of December.

She got to Will's early and made a simple stew that matched her mood.

Will picked up on her anxiety and asked her to talk about it right before the phone rang. It was one of his assistants needing help on a pretrial motion on another case.

Recognizing that it could be a long conversation, Lena decided to take Madame for a walk to get some air.

When she returned her spirits had revived. She'd decided on a way to stop Andy from double-crossing both Will and herself. First thing in the morning, she'd take the interview tape from the safe. Andy couldn't air the story if he didn't have the tape.

In the shower Will asked what had been bugging her earlier.

She dismissed it lightly. Andy had been giving her problems, but she and Madame had solved it on their walk. She didn't want Will to get nervous before the final day of testimony. Then they got down to more stimulating matters, as they shared soap and passion with equal enthusiasm.

On the way out the door in the morning Will happily

reminded her that he'd arrive at her place at midnight to help her start packing.

Cheerfully, Lena finished dressing and dropped Madame off back at her place, savoring the thought that the shuttle between homes would soon be over.

Life felt straightforward as she asked the receptionist to get her Cherry Hill murder tape from the safe. She put it in her briefcase and walked to her office to check for mail and messages. A call from Tom.

Nothing felt threatening. She called Wilkes-Barre and learned Tom was out at meetings for the rest of the day. She laughed, hoping the meetings weren't in Philadelphia, and left word for him to call her when he could.

It was nearly four o'clock when her intercom rang. It was Andy, asking her to come to Studio A. She glanced at her watch, realizing the moment of truth was approaching.

Andy wanted her to check the lead-in for her interview to make certain there were no factual errors. He'd decided to lead with the interview on the six o'clock news and repeat it again at eleven. "I want every little mile out of your sweet little scoop."

"The story won't run until tomorrow, Andy."

"It's running tonight. As I said before, you can always blame me." He patted her on the back. "I already have the champagne on ice for the Christmas party tonight, for the double celebration—the story and the season. We'll all get very, very merry."

"You can't run it." All statement.

"Watch the news tonight."

"Watch my lips, Andy. You can't run it tonight because I took the tape."

He frowned at her.

"I took it from the safe and that's what it is now, safe from you."

Andy roared with laughter. "Do I look like a total fool? You think I wouldn't have a copy made of anything that important?"

It was Marlena who felt like a total fool. She turned heel and ran back to her office. She had to reach Will. As she reached her doorway the phone rang.

She grabbed it quickly, praying it was Will.

It wasn't her day for timing, she thought as she heard Tom's voice, kind and friendly. He wanted to talk about her letter. He agreed it was time they took legal action.

Her stomach churned. It was important to herself and Will that she get her former life settled, but at the moment she was more worried about messing up the present.

She talked to Tom longer than she wanted to, but it was hard to cut him off abruptly when he was offering to pay her divorce expenses, asking if she needed anything, trying to make it easy.

If she hadn't been so panicked, she might have told Tom about the problem with the interview. If anyone could have interceded with Andy, it was Tom, she realized much later in the day.

The rest of the day and evening were a blur. Cab to the courthouse. The judge had recessed for the day. Call to Will's office. He was out, no one knew where. She left a message. She got frantic. Cab to his place. No sign of him.

She rushed back to the station, praying there'd be a message from him, telling her where to find him. She walked into the newsroom at 6:01, in time to turn her back on the monitor where her interview was playing and walk to her empty message box.

Andy grinned at her from across the newsroom. "We did it, kiddo. We cleaned their slates." He held a bottle of champagne high. "We're starting the party early. Time to celebrate. Studio B. The gang's all there." He dropped the AP and

UPI regional wire stories that quoted Marlena's WIB-TV interview with Wald, his face flushed with pleasure.

"Jill!" Marlena waved her friend over. "Walk me to my office." Quickly, Marlena explained the upset and begged her to tell Andy that she had gotten sick if he noticed she wasn't at the party.

"Marlena, you have to go. He's announced he's making you full-time anchor."

"Even that's not worth having to look at his face tonight."

Jill nodded, hugged Marlena, and wished her luck in finding Will.

Madame leaped with pleasure as Marlena slumped in the door. The big dog's time clock said her mother was early. Marlena followed Madame's happy leaps out into the street. Maybe they could walk it off together. Her mind felt as cold and muddy as the gutters as she and Madame took a lonely turn around Rittenhouse Square.

A block from the house she heard her phone ringing as if to guide them to the correct door. It stopped as they entered, then started ringing again a few seconds later. She raced to answer. She wanted to explain to Will. "Hello?" she spoke breathlessly.

"Marlena, where the fuck are you?"

"Andy." Her voice died. "You made me sick tonight." She didn't give him space to protest as she hung up the phone, realizing she had a new dilemma. If she left the phone on the hook, Andy could call back. If she took it off, Will couldn't get through.

"Watched pots don't boil," she reminded herself. But she dialed his number and let the phone ring twenty times before she took her phone off the hook and submerged herself in a hot bath.

The bath relaxed her and she felt prepared to explain

to Will, and equally prepared to quit or be fired if Andy didn't personally apologize to Will. She had to clear the air with Andy once and for all.

In a peaceful state of mind, she put the phone back on the hook, waiting for the dial tone to return, and tried Will again, her peace becoming more fragile as it rang and rang, unanswered.

Madame suddenly raced for the door, hackles rising as she barked a warning seconds before the loud knock.

Lena's heart jumped into her throat. Will. The knock turned into a pounding. Why would Will pound? He had a key.

"Marlena!" She heard Andy's angry voice clearly. "I know you're in there. Open up."

"Cool it. You'll wake the neighborhood!" She called back, deciding that now was as good a time as any to have it out with the man.

Andy burst in, breathing hard. He took a position in the center of the room, looking like a bull flaring its nostrils at a matador. She half expected him to paw the oriental with one foot. "Wipe that smirk off your face!" he ordered. "You're not funny. In fact you are an ambitious, vicious little tease."

"Andy, sit down before you have a heart attack."

"Don't act pious." He held his ground. "I know all about your little game. 'No man can touch me until I'm a free woman, Andy, all I can do is work, work, work,'" he mocked.

"You don't understand. I wasn't intending . . ."

"Christ!" He threw himself onto the couch. "Get me a scotch," he ordered.

"You've had enough."

"You're damn right. Enough of your hypocrisy. What a fucking fool I was, giving you credit for being a hard-working A-one investigative reporter when you were being spoon-fed by the prosecutor because you were fucking him."

She turned white with fury at his phrasing. He was dumping his filth on a relationship that had been clean, until he fouled it.

"Don't you dare." She held her own ground, still by the door. "Don't you dare talk that way to me."

Andy's anger drained away in the face of hers. "I'm sorry, Marlena. But when Jill told me, I saw red. You can understand that, can't you? Here I've been, waiting in the wings for more than a year . . ."

The man was so blind, Marlena thought sadly. She went into the kitchen to get him some coffee. Then they could talk.

"Where're you going?" he demanded.

"To make us some coffee," she said. The place was small enough that he could easily hear her.

"Marlena, you can understand how it struck me, can't you?"

"I suppose." She stared at the water, wishing it would boil.

"And I can even understand things from your point of view. You want the anchor slot, I know. And you thought this scoop would land it for you. Your thinking was straight there. But to sleep with this guy to get it, that's low, Marlena. Really low." He paused, waiting for a response.

"It wasn't that way at all, Andy."

"Do you know what it made me feel like? This is really bizarre, because you've never let me touch you. I felt like a cuckold. Right out of the nineteenth century. I wanted to shoot this low-life bastard Will Austin and strangle you for betraying me." He paused, then added, "I've never even met the bastard."

Marlena thought it was even more bizarre because Andy was married to Nancy. She quipped, quietly, "How does Nancy feel about it?"

"What? I couldn't hear you."

Boil, dammit, she begged the pot. "I said I love him."

"Get in here. I can't hear you."

She left the pot to boil on its own. "I said it's not like that at all. I love him. For the first time in my life, Andy, it's right. He's not too old, not too young, not married, not secondhand merchandise."

Andy bristled. "Like me, huh? Marlena, you don't know what you're talking about. You're not in love with this guy. You're kidding yourself. It's like Tom. You're in love with what he can give you. And this Austin guy's already given you all you want from him—the best goddamn story of your career so far."

Without holding back, she slapped him as hard as she could. The phone rang on cue.

"Damn you," Andy spat.

She ignored him as she picked up the phone. "Hello?"

"Lena, I've been trying you for hours. *What* happened?

"Will, thank God." She fought back tears of relief and failed.

"Are you all right? I've been trying to call you back for hours."

"I tried to call you when I got home, but"—she choked on the phrase—"first I had to walk the dog."

"Yeah." The pause was heavy.

"But I called you at your place the moment I got in. And I've tried since . . ." She didn't feel she had the right to ask where he'd been.

As usual, he answered her unspoken question. "I've been out drinking. I'm upset, too, Lena. And you know why."

"I know. It was a lousy . . ."

With her back to Andy, she didn't see his expression get ugly as he watched her cradle the receiver and listened to her tone of soft supplication for Will. She wasn't prepared for it when Andy suddenly grabbed the phone from her.

"Austin," Andy said with hearty good humor. "Tom Wells here. My wife tells me you did her quite a favor."

Marlena opened her mouth to scream in protest, but Andy's ham of a hand clamped down on it like a vise, pulling her close to him as he continued. "She's been trying to call you to read you the AP and UPI clippings on it."

Marlena bit down, hard.

Andy winced and dug his fingers into her cheeks as he added, "You both've gotten some great press out of this—you, for finding this Wald character and . . ." Andy released her and smiled. Not a pretty smile. "Dear me. He hung up on me. See? He's not such a nice man at all." He looked at his hand. "No blood. I'm stronger than you think, Marlena."

"Andy. Get out. Now."

In the kitchen the pot boiled dry, then cracked under the heat as Marlena dialed and dialed Will's number until well past dawn.

The next morning Marlena sat at her desk and wrote Will a long letter, analyzing it all for herself as well as for him, begging him to understand, and giving him the telephone number in Des Moines.

On her way out she stopped by the receptionist's desk to drop the letter in the open wooden box for outgoing mail just as Andy emerged from his office.

"Leaving already?" he asked as he stepped beside her and rested his hand on the outgoing mailbox.

"You okayed my request, didn't you?" She'd written an official memo asking for an immediate two weeks' sick leave.

Andy nodded, his expression cool.

"I'm not sure I'll be coming back."

"I'm not sure you should."

Marlena turned to walk down the long hall. Behind her, she heard Andy's voice, talking to the receptionist.

"I'm going out to a meeting. I'll drop these in the mailbox on my way, save you a trip."

"You're such a nice man," Marlena heard the receptionist coo in reply. There were a lot of adjectives that fit Andy, Marlena thought as she stepped outside, but nice wasn't one of them.

"Just you and me for a while, kiddo," she said to Madame as Marlena slid behind the steering wheel to begin the long drive.

She concentrated on the traffic, fighting her own speculations about when Will would get the letter and how he'd react. She ordered herself to relax, but she couldn't help thinking how much Maggie would like Will. He was so . . . decent.

Seven

ROGER WAS LOOKING OUT at the snow still blowing in Central Park as Marlena returned, carrying steaming mugs of coffee.

"What are you thinking about?"

"The letters you never answered," Roger said.

She almost spilled the coffee. Unanswered letters. Was he reading her mind?

"Why? Why didn't you write back to me?" He joined her at the coffee table.

"I don't remember the rationalizations at the time. Looking back, insecurity, perhaps, guilt for being too weak to face things head on." She paused, her mind on the letter she had written to Will, the letter he had never answered. Will's reasons for not replying would have been different—anger, hurt, a feeling of being betrayed, or perhaps disappointment in her weakness.

"How could you write me off that easily?" Roger persisted.

She'd never had the chance to ask Will that question. Suddenly she felt empathy for Roger. "It wasn't 'that easily.'"

"I hate loose strings. No matter how long it takes, I like to get them tied, at least in my mind."

"To make it all nice and neat." The Roger she'd known needed that. "So that's why you called me? To tie your loose string?"

"No. It was Alison." His gray eyes softened. "All right, it was that old dangling string too. I never understood why you ran away so dramatically."

"At twenty life is dramatic."

"And at thirty?"

"At thirty I was plugging away like a news zombie in Baltimore because Philadelphia had gotten *too* dramatic." She chuckled.

"The affair?"

For a second she was puzzled. She hadn't told Roger about Will; then she remembered her lie about Andy and nodded.

"I understand. Sometimes the best thing to do is get out of town. I know. That's how we moved to Connecticut. Dramatically."

"After your affair?"

"No." He looked into her eyes, letting the sadness fill his own. "It was after the tragedy with Jennie. I sublet the Riverside Drive place, holding on to it, because I knew it would go co-op someday. It did," he added with satisfaction. "I sold it a few years back and put the money into expanding the beach house."

"Wait a minute. Back up. You're losing me."

"I don't ever want to do that again," Roger said softly.

Marlena sipped her coffee, disconcerted. Roger was reaching for her on every level. She leaned back against the plump arm of the couch, adding distance. "Who is Jennie? And what was the tragedy?"

Roger stared down for a long moment, smearing a drop

of coffee with his finger, making circles on the glass coffee table. "Jennie was my second daughter, the happy one whose chubby little smile could turn around the darkest day in the world. She died in a tragic accident."

"That's terrible."

"She slipped in the bathtub. Hit her curly little head on the side of the tub. You remember that deep old bathtub with the claw feet, don't you?" He looked at Marlena for reaction.

She nodded, suddenly remembering the thought of drowning in it herself. But that time the baby had died before it could be born. Not by accident. She only felt a small shadow of guilt. Her feeling was more one of regret for the sacrifice necessary at the time.

Roger broke the silence as he continued. "My wife had asked me to give Jennie a bath while she did the laundry. So I filled the tub with toys and left Jennie to her own devices while I proofed a manuscript, a brief, that was due in the morning."

"Most accidents happen in the home. Perhaps because that's where we feel too safe," Marlena commented.

Roger nodded, then he continued, almost reciting, "Alison was lying on the living room rug beside me, crayoning while I read. Soon she became bored, as four-year-olds do every four or five minutes. She hopped up and announced, 'Daddy, I'm going to play with Jennie's rubber duck.'

"I'll always remember the screams, high-pitched and shrill. I ran toward them, my mind trembling for Alison. It was a scream of naked fear.

"Alison stood beside the old tub, the edge level with her heart. Jennie was face down in the water. The water, already growing cold, was only eight inches deep, but deep as death."

Marlena's eyes were moist. "Poor Roger. It's sad, but you tell it so beautifully. You should write." A tear trickled down her cheek.

Roger's mood lifted again. "Maybe you're right. I like to

think I have a feel for words." His smile was gentle and it focused on her as he handed her his handkerchief. "I don't care what the papers say. You're not a cold lady."

"Never believe what you read in the papers or see on TV," she said lightly. "Believe me, it's a mistake."

"Speaking of mistakes, sometimes I think it was a major mistake to move out of New York. I'm not a commuter at heart. Two hours into town and back are a royal pain in the kazoo."

"I thought you said you had a townhouse on the Upper East Side."

"Oh, yes. I do," he said quickly. "And it's been a lot easier since we have both places."

"It sounds ideal. Your wife can come into town for nights out and you don't have to worry about fighting the traffic, night or morning. Does she still work?"

"Yes, but in Connecticut. She doesn't like to come to the city if she can avoid it."

There was an undercurrent to the statement that Marlena couldn't interpret.

"Still, it gives you nice flexibility for togetherness and a place of private time, alone."

"Funny." A light went on behind Roger's eyes. "That's exactly what she says."

Marlena saw the glow. Roger must love her very much, she thought. "I'm green with envy, Roger Marley. Your wife is a lucky lady. It's not easy to find men or women who are willing to compromise and be flexible enough to make life work well."

"How about you? Are you still flexible?"

"I hope so. But I'm less willing to compromise than I was at some points in my life." She heard the irony in that and smiled, more for herself than Roger.

Marlena picked up the empty coffee mugs.

"When are you due at the station?" Roger followed her into the kitchen.

"Ten o'clock tonight. I have to go over the scripts and lineup, and add my personal touches." She winked as she rinsed out the mugs. "Oh, shit. I didn't pick up the newspapers yet."

"Send the doorman," Roger said easily. "Can I come along?"

She turned off the water and dried the mugs. "Where?"

"To the studio. I'd love to watch you tape the show tonight if you wouldn't mind."

"It's not what I'd call comfortable. We don't have a real studio audience, just some folding chairs for friends and family of the guests and staff."

"I hope I qualify," he said.

"If you really want to, sure, why not? But I can't take you along at ten. That's when I do my real work, from ten to one."

"I'll come whenever you're ready for me."

"Show up between twelve-thirty and twelve thirty-five if you're serious."

"Sounds good." He crossed his arms and relaxed, leaning against the doorjamb, blocking the passage.

Her eyes darted from the refrigerator to the cupboard. "I think I could whip something up. I have plenty of steaks in the freezer and . . ."

"No." He laughed. "I'm not lobbying for a free meal. I thought we could go down the street to the Petit Cafe at the Sherry Netherland. Nice piano music. You know the place?"

"Just for drinks."

"The food's fine, and it has the added virtue of being within walking distance, unless you want me to get my car."

"No, I'd much rather walk in the snow. It gets dark early these days, dark enough for the streetlights to do their snow magic."

"I could use a little magic." Roger unlaced his arms and opened them wide in a gesture that could be interpreted as an invitation to walk into them.

Get thee behind me Satan, Marlena told herself as she thought about accepting the unspoken invitation. "Couldn't we all," she agreed as she turned and carefully hung the mugs on brass hooks beneath the cupboard.

Fire was fire. She should stop this disconcerting flirtation, thank him for lunch, tell him to have Alison call her directly, and send him on his way. Good-bye, Roger. Nice seeing you again.

She concluded her silent self-help lecture by turning to Roger with a smile. "I'd better change into my working clothes. There may not be time after dinner."

Still blocking the doorway, Roger didn't move as she stepped closer. She stopped a foot away, question in her eyes.

Roger's arms replied by pulling her closer, ending the physical distance as he kissed her. There was no question that his kiss was intended to reclaim lost territory.

For a long moment she let herself go, let herself feel the maleness of him, let herself think about how long it had been since she'd made love to anyone. Months? A year? It was pathetic that the image of her last brief, unsatisfactory affair was so dim she couldn't even put a face on it. She felt Roger's hands move lower and she backed off abruptly.

"Marlena . . ." He said her name as though it meant "Come back."

"That's not fair, Roger Marley," she sputtered. "You have other commitments."

"What about commitments to strong feelings?"

"Tell me about them after the divorce." She walked out the door he no longer barred.

"All right. Abracadabra. I'm divorced."

"You're impossible!" She tossed the words over her shoulder as she hurried down the hall to her bedroom. Suddenly, she stopped and turned, aware he was behind her. "Roger." She thought quickly. "While I change would you go out and get me copies of *The New York Times,* the *Daily News,* and the *Post?*"

"Always opting for the news over me." Roger grinned. "Okay, I'll be back in ten minutes. If you're not dressed by then, you'll be in trouble."

There was no way to misinterpret what he meant by trouble.

"Could you take Gerda with you? The fat old dear could use an extra walk."

"She's already done her yellow snow for the hour," Roger said. "You're the one I want to walk in the snow." He turned to go. "I'll be back."

"Don't rush," she said as Gerda padded down the hall and sat at her feet, reclaiming Marlena as her personal territory. She scratched Gerda's head and smiled as she moved into action to change her image for the evening.

She scrubbed her flushed face, trying not to think about the embrace that so forcefully reminded her of her nun's existence. She kneaded her upper arms. Still firm. Her body was in peak condition and she missed making love.

It wasn't as though she had lost all sex appeal, she consoled herself as she put on her makeup. But as much as she missed the lovemaking, she'd vowed she wouldn't make love just to fill the emptiness. Better to eat chocolates. Still she hungered for an honest relationship with a man she could openly desire.

"You need a father, Gerda," Marlena said aloud as she stared into her closet, debating what to wear. "At least I'm honest about needing a man."

Gerda rolled over, exposing her white belly as she wiggled and barked for a rub.

Obediently, Marlena knelt and scratched. "I'll tell you,

Gerda, the next time we meet an unmarried man who sets off sparks in your mother's body and soul, we're going to be so goddamn flexible it'll make your head spin."

Marlena rose, wondering if she would give up her TV career at this point if it took that. "Within reason, Gerda. He'd have to love dogs and, if he really loved us, he'd want us to be happy with our work too. Wouldn't he?"

Gerda barked in response. If Marlena was looking at her, Gerda thought she should be scratching.

"No more, Gerda. I have to get dressed." She pulled a high-necked paisley dress in various shades of blue from the closet, rejecting the sexier green silk hanging alongside. Roger had crossed the line back in the kitchen. Why should she encourage invitations she had to refuse? The paisley, elegant and ladylike, was still a bit too soft and sexy in its own way. She added a navy blazer for good measure as she heard the doorbell. Perfect timing.

Grabbing her coat and purse, she ran down the hall to open the door for Roger.

"We humans are contrary creatures," he said as he helped her into the fox coat.

"How so?"

"We shiver in weather like this and wish for summer. And in summer, when the humidity in New York is one hundred fifty percent and you sweat grime, you think about the beautiful, cold snow."

"I love snow." She smiled, feeling a safe social distance from Roger under her layers of clothing. "And the cold doesn't bother me."

Roger held open the door for them to leave. Gerda began to trot toward it. "No, Gerda. You stay." She leaned down to calm the leaping expectations of her pet. "You go out first, Roger, or she'll slip between your legs." After Roger was safely in the hall, door closed, Marlena hugged Gerda quickly. "I'll be back. Alone. Then it's just you and me, kiddo."

"Don't your neighbors object?" Roger asked, the sound of Gerda's protest following them toward the elevator.

"I don't know. I never see them."

"Wish I could say the same." Roger chuckled. "I wish I didn't see mine so often. This year they wanted me to help with the block party by sitting on a platform above a tank of water while kids paid dimes to try to drown me."

"Did you do it?" she asked as they stepped into the elevator.

"I bought them off, calculating the cost of staying dry at twenty-five dollars."

"This was your Upper East Side neighborhood, right? For a moment I wondered. A block party in Greenwich?"

"I don't really have . . ." He stopped and stepped back as the elevator stopped at the fifth floor and a young woman got on, holding a baby with one arm and a two-year-old hand with the other.

"Thank you," she said. Her clothes were expensive, but her smile was tired. "Don't, Henry," she protested as the two-year-old jumped up and down.

Henry responded by letting go of his mother's hand and trying to run. He tripped over Roger's foot and was screaming as the elevator door opened at the lobby.

"Please," the young mother entreated as Marlena helped right the howling Henry, "could your husband push the hold button?"

"I've got it," Roger said easily as Marlena handed Henry back to his father, who'd been waiting in the lobby.

"Thanks," said the woman. "It's the terrible twos."

"More like Henry the terrible," added Henry's father. But they looked happy; even Henry was now smiling.

"Know the age too well." Roger nodded as he casually put his arm around Marlena's waist to usher her outside.

The snow glittered like fine silver dust, haloing the streetlights.

"We look like an old married couple," Roger said as they walked south on Fifth Avenue. "Funny. We could have been."

"I'm not sure it would have been funny," she quipped, determined to keep it light.

"But I'll bet it would have been fun." He gave her a wide, mischievous smile. "We did have fun while it lasted, remember?" He took a few fast steps ahead of her, jumped in the air, and clicked his heels. "Bet you didn't think I could still do that."

"It hadn't occurred to me to wonder," she said. Dear Roger; the world would always be his playground.

Then they were inside the restaurant. The brief, brisk walk had stirred her appetite and she turned her head to see what the other diners were eating as they followed the captain to a corner banquette tucked between mirrored walls.

She saw her reflection with pleasant surprise. Eyes glowing, bright and alive. Curls casual and snow-sparkled. Her appearance, navy blazer not withstanding, was hardly forbidding.

"Am I invited?" Roger smiled down at her.

"Isn't this where we came in before? Please. Sit down, Mr. Marley. You must be exhausted after the long, hard day at the office."

He sat, facing her across the corner of the table, a mirror behind him also. "I've had worse."

"We're like an elegant Quaker Oats box." She laughed. She could see her face and the rear of his head in the mirror behind him. She knew he was seeing his face and the back of her head. "Bouncing images."

"Isn't that what you TV people like to do? Bounce images?"

"And what do lawyers do?"

"Bounce checks, I guess." He reached for her hand.

"But speaking of images, I feel as if I've spent the day with three women. First the lady in silk at lunch. Then the barefoot girl in the glass apartment. And now the glamorous TV reporter out for an elegant dinner."

"Same woman, different facets. Is it my fault I've only seen one of yours?"

"I took off my shoes. Should I have taken off more?"

"Stop flirting, Roger." She retrieved her hand, but she was still smiling.

"You're right. Teasing isn't nice. I may have made the biggest mistake in years by letting you out of the kitchen unravished."

"Roger!" Real indignation colored her voice.

"There's always later tonight," he said.

A reply was delayed as the headwaiter brought the wine list. "Good evening, Mr. Marley," he said.

"Thank you, Manuel." Roger turned to Marlena. "I hope you don't mind. I always skip the before-dinner drinks and go directly to wine. Then I make up for it with lots of fine old cognac afterward, right, Manuel?"

"Yes, sir," Manuel said patiently.

"I'm afraid it's Perrier on the rocks with a twist of lime for me, Roger. Remember, I still have to work later."

"Right. So we should order everything at the same time." He glanced at his watch. "Seven-thirty. We have to get out of here by nine-thirty, right? How about if I order for both of us. This is one of my haunts."

"Fine. I'd like that." Tonight she'd forget the debate of fattening and delicious versus healthy and palatable. She watched Roger discuss the specials and order quickly. "No soufflés tonight, Manuel. The lady's working later."

Manuel bowed slightly. "I recognized Miss Williams, sir. It's my pleasure to serve you both."

As Manuel hurried away to take their order to the

kitchen, Marlena stared at Roger. "Oops. Will this get you in trouble?"

"Trouble?"

"With your wife. If they know you here."

"I'm a big boy," Roger said, laughing. "And, unfortunately, I haven't been compromised by you yet." He laughed as a look of discomfiture shadowed her face. "Does kidnapping sound appealing? You'd love my beach house on the point at Cape May. Stereo speakers in every room, even the bathrooms. Two wet bars, a soda fountain, a Jacuzzi, and a heated swimming pool. I've even jerry-rigged an old Lionel train set to choo-choo drinks from the beach to the house."

"Like Dudley Moore in *Arthur*?"

"You caught me. I admit I got the idea from seeing the movie. But I don't have a butler," he added with an engaging grin.

"And you never will grow up, will you?"

"I hope not. But I'm not finished telling you about my beach house."

She only half listened as she picked up the *Post,* thinking it was a good time to scan the headlines.

Roger stopped midsentence. "You're not paying attention."

"I'm sorry, Roger, I don't mean to be rude, but I've got to take a look at these before I get to the station." Her eyes caught on the second headline: PIZZA PARLOR CONNECTION BUSTED SICILIAN EXTRADITIONS TO FOLLOW. Her attention jumped from Roger's Cape May beach house to the headline and flashed back as her mental connection went from Cape May to Sicily . . . to Albie. As she stared blindly at the newsprint, her memory tape sped backward to the pivotal point where that connection had begun.

Eight

Annapolis, Maryland

"WAIT HERE. He'll be ready for you directly."

She stood in the inner room and focused on the walnut-stained pine paneling on the walls, a knotty background for the awards and photos. State Senator Albert S. Comparo. Appreciation from Maryland's Boy Scouts, Junior Achievement, Junior League, Sons of Italy, Daughters of the Revolution, marches for Dimes, Cancer, and Hearts. And, of course, the "photos with": Kennedy, LBJ, Nixon, Ford, the Queen of England, Mayor Rizzo of Philadelphia, the Pope.

"Miss Williams."

She turned at the sound of her name. Her first thought as she saw him was that Albie Comparo didn't photograph well. The cameras didn't catch the clear blue thrust of his eyes. For a second her mind blanked as she felt the almost physical impact of his eyes.

Then her mind went racing. It doesn't happen like this.

Not across the room with politician who had three children and a wife who chaired benefits for the White House.

No, she protested as electricity raced between them, not with the man she'd been sent to "nail to the wall," the man her source, Spadoro, postulated could be the hidden *capo di tuti capi,* head of all heads of the organized crime families.

"Miss Williams?" His eyebrows lifted in inquiry and amusement.

She stepped back and cleared her throat, if not her mind. "Yes, Senator Comparo. First, thank you for taking time to see me this morning. I know you're busy, but we're running a series of profiles on the legislators we believe are the most influential." The words rattled out, seemingly senseless, and she felt her skin tingle as he looked at her steadily.

"And you'd like to do me?" His eyes relayed a different meaning. "I saw the piece you did on my friend Senator Gibbons. *Profile* is a very polite term for what you did to him."

Her professional pride took precedence over the personal chemistry that had rattled her. "That was a straight news story. It wasn't part of the profile series. It was all documented fact."

"Facts, perhaps, but was it the truth?"

"Gibbons is a public official. Public officials can't afford to abuse power and manipulate state finances."

His gaze didn't falter. "I agree with you wholeheartedly, but you damned him without showing any of the good he's done."

"We said some of the ghost employees were sick relatives who couldn't get jobs."

"No, I'm not defending his ghosts. Putting family on the public payroll is a sleazy way to help them. But poor Gibbons isn't the villain you portrayed. He co-sponsored the Harbor Renovation Bill and stays on top of the little things in his constituency."

"A thief is a thief, even if he's also the pope."

Comparo chuckled, warming again. "He's been called worse."

"Why did you agree to this interview if you think my reporting is so biased?"

"I thought . . ." He paused, deliberately letting the air get heavy between them. "It was time to start helping the press get a better perspective. I know you're always hungry for good stories, but I get tired of you people going after guppies with elephant guns." He took a step, pushing the thick air toward her.

"I see." She closed her eyes against him for a second, fighting the images flashing in her mind. She wanted this total stranger to take her into his arms. It was irrational.

"Sit," he ordered softly.

The aide pushed a green-and-white-striped chair behind her and she perched, struggling to remain cool and professional.

"Coffee, Jack." The Senator nodded at his aide. "Miss Williams?"

"Please," she said as she reached into her pouch for pen and notebook.

He didn't retreat behind his desk as she'd hoped, but moved beside her, looking down at her, aware of his own magnetism.

He probably plays his sex appeal for all it's worth, she thought, irritation rising. He probably oozes it over secretaries and chambermaids alike. A reporter is just so much the better.

"Tyler Gibbons is a friend of yours," she stated, taking the offensive. Gibbons, a state senator whose district abutted Comparo's had been indicted on thirty-one counts of conspiracy to defraud. "I hear he's pleading guilty, nolo contendre, despite a very attractive offer to turn state's evidence."

"Yes, I've heard that Justice was hoping Gibbons would

turn into some kind of turnkey for busting open organized crime."

"What do you think?" she asked.

He gave Marlena a long, level look, which she felt like a touch. "I don't think Gibbons has any inside information that would help them," he smiled. "Jack!" Comparo looked past her at his aide. "The coffee?"

Her head swung around in time to catch Jack's air of disapproval as he slowly walked toward the door. Instinctively, she picked up her notebook, which had fallen unheeded on the floor.

The Senator caught both gestures and deliberately placed his hand on her shoulder as he stood beside her, creating an nineteenth-century tintype pose. "Miss Williams, being sweet enough, will have hers black. Bring extra sugar for mine. I need all the help I can get."

He was corny. And pompous. He was an amoral, conniving, self-serving bastard.

But her feeling self was centered on the pressure of his hand on her shoulder. She fought the mental picture of being in bed with him. If his hand through the wool of her jacket and the silk of her blouse had such profound physical impact . . . she shuddered.

Jack returned bearing coffee. The senator gave her shoulder a fleeting squeeze of approval and moved toward the tray Jack was placing on the desk. "It seems Miss Williams is interested in my opinions, Jack." Albie smiled and handed her a Wedgwood cup with deep orange clipper ships adorning the sloping side.

"Wedgwood? For the office?"

"Don't worry. It wasn't bought with taxpayers' dollars."

He tossed his head back with a deep laugh. "See, Jack? I told you she was interested in issues." Albie gracefully circled from behind his large desk and filled a soft leather chair.

"Speaking of issues," Marlena said, on the offensive. "Why are you such a strong proponent of gambling? Is it family preoccupation?"

"My, my. We have a feisty one here. How shall I answer that? Okay, I'll give you my philosophy on gambling.

"Gambling fascinates me. I think it appeals to the child in us, the child who has the simple belief that good things do fall from the sky, that there is fate or luck or a God or wishes-come-true. You name it. And the adult in us likes to think that random chance might hand us something we don't have to struggle for, unlike most things in this life.

"Every time most people throw the dice, they kid themselves that their chances are getting better, that they're getting closer to that stroke of luck. The big score. Of course the odds always remain the same."

"But different games have different odds," Marlena objected.

"True. But the odds, once established, are arbitrary for that game."

"So the only way to change the odds is to change the game?"

"Or change games." He smiled, enjoying the repartee. "But to get back to my reasons for supporting legalized gambling, I think those childlike and adult motivations are intrinsic to humankind. They're not going to be legislated away any more than you could or should pass laws against making love. They're a lot alike. People don't do it twenty-four hours a day, unless they're compulsive gamblers or nymphomaniacs, but now and then they get the urge."

She willed herself not to allow her eyes to be held by his.

"Of course, poets and ordinary folk like to compare love itself to gambling, taking risks, rolling the dice, et cetera, but what I'm getting at is that gambling is as old as history.

Anyway, to get to my most important point, gambling with dice or games or numbers or wheels gives people hope, which is more than the government does these days. But if we legalize gambling so government gets a cut of the house, we'll have more money to give real hope to people."

"Well." She wondered if he expected her to applaud. "Do you give speeches on gambling often?"

"I co-sponsored the bill to create the State Lottery to open the door. I want legalized gambling in Ocean City. Maryland took it on the chin when we were out-maneuvered by New Jersey. But we'll bounce back. You'll see."

"Why's it so important to you? Hidden interests?"

"Sure, I sit on the boards of some companies that have beach property, but that's not the issue. The why is that the antigambling laws are like prohibition. You don't stop people from drinking and gambling by making laws. It's the same with drugs. Puritanical laws feed the underworld's bank accounts. Surpressive piety that runs against human nature breeds corruption."

Marlena's eyes widened at the phrasing. The man was amazing—from Wedgewood to social philosophy in two minutes.

"Getting back to the 1970s," she said. "Do you have any projections on how wide-open, legalized gambling would affect the bookies, numbers, and other illegal gambling operations?" Her smile was saccharin. "Nothing personal."

He grinned in response. His watch suddenly pinged with electronic insistence. "Time for a committee meeting. Sorry. I haven't given you much time." He turned to Jack. "How does this afternoon look, my boy?"

"Teamsters at one. Malpractice hearings at three. A couple of appointments in between. The hearings will last until five-thirty at least."

Comparo directed his solid blue gaze on Marlena. "How

about five-thirty? I'm clear tonight." He looked at Jack for a confirming nod. "Yes. Tonight I am speechless for a change."

Marlena swallowed. It was she who was speechless.

"Call Klein and tell him I'm on my way."

Jack nodded and left, leaving the door ajar.

Marlena cleared her throat, searching for her voice. "Five . . . five-thirty here?"

"For openers. Maybe we can grab a bite while we discuss issues." He leaned back in his soft chair, making no effort to dispel the weighted silence.

What should she do? She could beg off, but she had no studio commitments. She'd taken the week off from anchoring for research. And Albie was certainly research. "Fine. That would be fine."

"Good. We can meet and take it from . . . here." Efficiently, he tucked his reading glasses into his tailored pocket, picked up a folder, slid it into a leather briefcase and moved toward the door, stopping inches short as she spoke.

"One last question."

"Yes?"

"Do you have a phone I can use?" A pause. "And do you mind if I look around and ask your staff some questions?"

"My office is yours. Feel free." He gestured at the bank of phones on his desk.

The man seemed fearless as he walked out without looking back.

First she called Pat Spadoro, her friendly source at the DEA, the Federal Drug Enforcement Agency. He'd asked her to tell him how she read Comparo. It amused her to call Pat from Comparo's office and entertain him with anecdotes, including "guppies with an elephant gun." Then, realizing Pat would not be amused by where she was calling from, she cut the call short. She phoned Paul at the station and give him an abbreviated version.

Paul was delighted with the start. When she said Comparo would see her again at five-thirty, Paul told her to stay over in Annapolis for the night so she could keep digging.

She looked up to see Jack still waiting like a shadow. "May I ask you a question? Is there a typewriter I can use?"

Jack looked relieved. "No problem. In the outer offices."

The intercom buzzed on the senator's desk before Jack could usher her out. He answered quickly.

"Jack?" questioned the mechanical voice. "The senator is already on his way to the hearing?"

"Just left. What's up?"

"It's Mrs. Ranelli. She says the senator is expecting her call."

"Oh, yeah. I'll take it." Jack jabbed out a blinking light on the large phone console. "Mrs. Ranelli. Jack Turchio. We talked yesterday. I did tell the senator about your son's interest in Annapolis. No. No problem. The senator talked to Congressman Wade this morning. They're good friends and Wade is a former navy man. Don't worry about a thing. Wade's word is golden—especially to the senator. No, no. It's all part of our job. It's what we're here for." Jack hung up the phone and smiled at Marlena.

A nice little scenario of the helpful senator's office. Had Jack set up the call to impress her? "Doesn't Wade sit on the Naval Appropriations house subcommittee? It must be nice to have him as a friend when your district includes the Baltimore harbor."

"Of course he's a friend of the senator's. That's part of the job." Jack bristled at the implied criticism. "Follow me. I'll find you a typewriter."

She wasn't ready to leave that quickly. She looked at the photos on Comparo's desk. "Does he spend time with his family?"

"As much as a dedicated politician can." Jack followed

her focus. "But he's dedicated to those kids. He takes the boys to baseball games and to political rallies, everywhere he can. And Georgio, the oldest, he thinks the sun rises and falls with that kid." Jack warmed to his subject. It was obvious his own sun rose and fell with his boss.

"Both boys are good-looking," she agreed.

"And his daughter's a knockout." Jack looked at the picture of a dark-haired teenager.

Pretty, but not beautiful, Marlena thought.

"Smart too," Jack added. "Pre-law at Cornell. Helena. Has a classic sound to it, don't you think?"

Marlena felt a burst of sympathy for Jack as she suddenly saw the prince charming hidden inside the unattractive man, staring blindly at the photo of the princess. She looked back at the young boys in the photo. The younger one reminded her of Toby. Dear Toby. She had missed seeing him grow up. She brushed the thought away like a spiderweb in her mind.

"Nice family," Marlena commented. "How does Mrs. Camparo enjoy the political life? Can you arrange an interview with her for me?"

Jack's voice acquired a barely perceptible edge of strain. "She's in Baltimore most of the time, with the boys. But I can check with her secretary if you'd like."

"No photo?" Marlena asked casually.

"She didn't like the old one we had. We're waiting for her to give us a new one." Jack turned abruptly. "You still want a typewriter to use?"

"Lead the way." She didn't like the way her heart had lightened when she'd noticed what wasn't there. But she didn't want Jack to get the wrong idea about her interest in his senator, so she threw him a curve.

"How close is the senator to Fred Brader?"

Jack's face closed. "Ask the senator."

"The senator recommended Mr. Brader for the post of Cigarette Commissioner. Were you aware of his criminal record at the time?"

"You'll have to ask the senator. I never dealt with Brader."

Spadoro had tipped her off about Brader. His name had come up in an investigation of a cigarette-smuggling operation that was a cover for drug distribution. They didn't have enough to indict Brader yet. Only an allegation that Brader was getting a cut.

Paul, her news director, had gotten excited. "Brader could be the connection, the missing link to Comparo and organized crime." Paul had a kind of obsession about Comparo. Like Spadoro, Paul believed the vague rumors that Comparo was connected with organized crime. Unlike Spadoro, Paul claimed he would give a year's salary for hard proof. Every year for the past ten he had sent a new reporter out to follow the scent Paul smelled in his gut. So far they had come up empty.

Paul had been good for her in the last few years. He was the first boss who treated her as a reporter and colleague, period.

Although Paul could be demanding, she thought as she followed Jack down a long narrow hallway, all his reporters respected his news judgment and fairness. Single, in his late thirties, Paul was tall, slender, attractive, and gay. She had liked him on sight at the interview arranged by Tom after she'd told him about the situation with Andy at WIB-TV. "A divorce present," he'd called it. First Paul had put her on general assignment for a year. Next he'd moved her to the court-and-cops beat. Now she was the main weekend anchor and did special reports during the week.

Yesterday, when Marlena had told Paul about the allegations about Brader, he'd pulled her off everything else she was working on and, in the spirit of a nineteenth-century spymaster sending yet another assassin to kill the king, told her she was now ready for her "shot at Comparo." She flushed to remember that Paul had told her she had a better chance than the others because "Comparo has a weakness for beautiful women." She'd forgotten to tell Paul she had a weakness for bright, confident men with blue eyes.

"Well. Here it is." Jack stared at her strangely. She wondered how long she'd been lost in thought.

"Jack, I'm sorry to put you to all this trouble, but I really don't think I'll need the typewriter after all."

She tucked her notebook into her purse. "Thanks anyway." She smiled. "I'll be back."

After batting .500 on a coffee shop with decent food and indecent service, she struck out with Brader's office.

Brader didn't even have a PR flack or information officer on his staff to dish out political pap. Maybe he's a smart man, she thought. Maybe the safest information is no information.

Patiently, she waited in Brader's outer office for a "word with his secretary." Finally a narrow-faced woman in her late forties came out to inform her that the commissioner had nothing to say to the press.

"It's the taxpayers' money he's dealing with. They have a right to hear from the commissioner."

"Unless you have an appointment you'll have to leave." The stoneface blinked.

"Then please make an appointment with the commissioner for me."

"We're very busy right now. He won't have time."

"Would you please ask him?"

"Write him a letter and we'll get back to you."

There was no point in pressing the issue, Marlena

thought as the woman turned her back and marched into the inner offices.

Outside again, away from government corridors, Marlena lost her sense of urgency. The spring wind ruffled her short curls.

For the first time in weeks she did more than look at the sky. She saw it. As though a screen lifted from in front of her eyes, she found herself in an unclouded world and felt the warm sun on her skin.

What a day for a picnic. A loaf of bread, a jug of wine, and the company of a man whose eyes were a harder version of the soft spring sky. Not that Comparo looked the picnic type. He was too tailored. He probably had an Abercrombie matched picnic set, complete with houseboy. But he'd look wonderful in white duck pants and a blue turtleneck, she fantasized.

For a hard second the heart went out of her day as she thought about Will, whose eyes were bluer and whose life had to be less clouded than the mysterious senator's.

She couldn't help comparing the physical impact and attraction of the two men. Just catching Will's eye from across the room hit her right in the solar plexus. Closer than that and her knees went weak. Why? she asked herself, how could he just close the door on her, never answer, never ask?

A tern flew across her path, followed by another. Two by two. As nature intended.

But how did she know Will was still free? She didn't. And if he were to walk across the street right this second and tell her he was married, what would she do? She stopped to consider her own question. It would depend. If he didn't want her, she would turn away before it hurt again. But if he wanted her? She'd fight to keep him, married or unmarried, because they'd been right together, body, mind, and soul.

In a perverse way the mental debate made her feel even

more eager to test the strong chemistry with Albie Comparo. She decided to forget about checking land records on Brader. She was more interested in getting ready for five-thirty.

When in doubt, shop. She didn't want to make a radical change lest he think she was trying to seduce him. She settled for a soft cotton blouse with a deep inset of fine lace on the bodice.

Soft and Victorian. As the summer sun sank lower toward Annapolis' harbor, she retrenched, now hoping she could come on straitlaced.

She wanted to be neither early nor late. She targeted her arrival for five thirty-five, but she couldn't control her stride, which seemed to cover ground involuntarily. She entered his offices at 5:17.

"Ah. Right on time." Comparo smiled and rose from behind the now unmanned receptionist's desk. He reached out and took Marlena's hands in his. She felt as if some pact had been sealed.

"Jack will be back to close up. The rest are gone," he said, not letting go of her hand. "I'm afraid I can't tell you much about today's hearings," he said. "I thought about you all afternoon." He pulled her toward him, enclosing her in his arms. His mouth met hers and felt in its proper place, at home, as though it had been there a thousand times before.

Shaken, Marlena stepped back, away from the embrace.

He didn't try to stop her.

"I came back . . . as a reporter . . . to interview you."

The voice of Senator Albie Comparo was not steady as he said, "I'm glad. I'm very, very glad."

She tried to hold her distance.

"Well. Fire away." He opened his arms wide. "I'm all yours."

As if drawn by a magnet, she moved toward him.

The door burst open. Jack entered, saw them, and

stopped short, looking from Marlena to Albie, feeling the charge in the air.

"Uh . . . sorry I'm late, Senator. Traffic's bad."

"No problem, Jack. If anything, you're early."

Jack smiled, always happy if his boss was happy. "You leaving for the night, or do you want to go over your questions for the Teamsters' hearing later?"

So smooth, thought Marlena, giving Albie the opportunity to cue him without being obvious. She held her breath, as if waiting for her own cue.

"We can run through that in the morning. Thanks, Jack." The dismissal was in his voice.

"Right." Jack's head bobbed at Marlena, and the thaw was obvious in his voice. "Nice meeting you, Miss Williams."

Albie's arm repossessed Marlena's shoulder as he guided her out of the offices. She liked the strength of the motion.

"Jack likes you," he said, stopping at the elevator.

"Jack likes everybody who he thinks you like," she echoed.

"A man of sense," Albie said dryly. Then he reached up, pushed back her curls, and kissed her forehead softly.

She hadn't known a kiss on the forehead could be sensual.

"Let's go and discuss issues," he said as the elevator arrived. Inside the empty enclosure he kissed her again with a strong, sudden passion, bruising her lips against his before quickly backing away, breathing hard. He pushed the down button.

Their priorities coupled well. Dinner would come later. There was no hesitation, no fumbling, no nervous hedging. Clothing slipped away, allowing them brief and satisfying moments to appreciate each other's bodies before they came home to each other, feeling, tasting, wanting, in building rhythms until they were one. Exploding. Filling. Holding.

Right as rain, she thought as she lay moist and warm beside him in the king-size bed. Almost. He stayed close inside her, holding her gently for a long, silent time as they floated together on the edge of sleep.

Then Marlena felt him stir inside her with slow, rising passion, and she ached with burning pleasure as he moved faster and harder for a longer, deeper time until the walls inside her shuddered and they screamed with one voice. "Yes!"

"No." Marlena sat up, tears streaming down her face.

"Hey . . ." Albie's hand caressed her cheek. "What's this?" He held her in close comfort.

It was as if a band around her heart had broken. She wished she had the courage to tell him that feeling full and warm and coupled again made her cry for the loneliness of the busy single life she led, getting famous in Baltimore.

"It's strong for me too," he whispered.

The tears kept flowing, tears for Will whom she'd lost so long ago and tears for Albie, the man she was assigned to expose, the man who was making her realize she still could feel and want and love. It didn't seem fair.

He held her through her tears until they both fell asleep.

A phone was ringing somewhere. Marlena jolted awake and reached out to answer. It wasn't there. Where was she?

Then she focused and saw Albie sitting beside the bed, talking on the phone.

"No other way. We have to cut him loose." Albie saw she was awake and smiled at her. "Can't get into it now, but the decision is final. We'll discuss the 'how' in the morning, but the 'who' is firm."

She reached up for him. Even a bed apart he seemed too far away.

"Hungry?" he whispered against her ear.

"Famished." She laughed softly. "We've been working hard."

"All those issues," he agreed, pulling her up.

Nimbly, she ran into the bathroom.

"There's a bathrobe on the door," he called after her.

She mapped the fine lines beside her eyes, surveying her face in the mirror. Tired but happy, flushed from satisfaction.

What was she getting herself into? Was it all pro forma with Albie? Did he put his mark on every woman he wanted, notch his belt and ride off into the sunrise, untouched? Not a nice thought.

But a relationship between them could get as messy for him as for her. A married man, a public person, an election coming up the next year—with or without the rumored "family" connection.

"Hey!" Albie's deep, warm voice resonated through the door. "There's a line out here." He opened the door and entered freely.

She turned from the mirror to see his firm, athletic body, feeling her own nakedness more acutely than she had in the dim bedroom. Instinctively, she reached for a towel.

Albie grabbed it first and dropped it on the floor. "There is absolutely nothing for you to hide." He gently ran his strong hand from her hips to her rib cage. "A perfect specimen."

"That sounds clinical, Senator."

He tossed her a terry robe. "Now cover up so I'm not distracted while we think about dinner."

"Aha! And you pretend to know nothing about cover-ups." She laughed while he only smiled.

The warmth and privacy of Albie's Annapolis town house felt too precious to abandon. They scavenged in the kitchen and emerged with frozen manicotti and anchovies and greens for a Caesar salad.

"Leftovers from a committee luncheon," Albie said as he put the pasta in the microwave. "I have the cook go Italian all the way for my official luncheons, in case they make the papers. I actually prefer nouvelle cuisine, but I have to keep up my image."

He watched her toss the salad and cube the bread for croutons with a practiced hand. "I didn't know modern women cooked."

"One of my hidden talents." Then her voice became more serious. "What do you hide?"

He answered equally seriously. "My domestic discontent. A wife who doesn't like to cook for me."

Marlena didn't want to hear about his wife and what she did or didn't do. "That's not the area I'm talking about at the moment."

"What are you talking about?"

"You're awfully young and good looking to be a godfather."

Clearly the question startled him, but he replied easily, not committing himself. "Not so young. And where did you get that crazy idea?"

"Rumors."

He laughed. "There are always rumors about Italian politicians. I am what you see," he spoke softly, giving her a light kiss on the lips with each comma, "an aging, overworked, underappreciated, harassed, plagued, and occasionally respected legislator who is very content at the moment." He released her and looked at the untossed Caesar salad. "Also very hungry."

She laughed and got back to the job.

"Speaking of records," he said as he checked the manicotti, "I may know about some you might find interesting.

Records that could kiss Brader good-bye for a long, long time."

"I thought Brader was a friend of yours." She glanced at his back as she carefully dried the individual lettuce leaves.

"It's the age-old ethical dilemma. When friends get dumb and greedy should you cover for them or help uncover them?"

"What's wrong? Didn't Brader follow your orders?"

"Now why would I tell Brader what to do? I'm not on his oversight committee. I just play golf with him now and then."

"So how would you know about any damaging records?" She squeezed lemon into the oil.

"I bump into people. That's what politicians do, spend their lives bumping into people, you know. But a friend told me there's a guy inside Brader's office who's pretty unhappy, a guy who might like to talk to a reporter if you're interested."

"If!" She dropped a lettuce leaf on the tile floor. "What's in them, Albie? I'm dying to know."

His blue eyes clouded for a fleeting second. Then they cleared with his smile. "I wouldn't have the slightest idea in the world."

"Albie, you can tell me. I always protect my sources." She ignored an uncomfortable flashback to Will, who could give lie to that protest.

"I'm not a source on this and I don't ever want you to protect me. I'm the protector around here, Lady reporter," he said as he picked up the fallen lettuce leaf and tossed it into the disposal.

"But who do I call?"

"Isn't it whom?" he joked pedantically. "I'll tell my friend to pass the word along. Don't be surprised if you get a call from a poor worried accountant who's about to turn state's evidence."

Marlena dropped an anchovy into the olive oil. It slid to the bottom of the bowl without a sound. "I see. You want Brader 'cut loose.'"

Albie looked at her, irony in his eyes. "Only the truth can set the man free."

Rinsing the oil from her slender hands, she clutched the Irish linen towel. She found this oblique offer to help confusing. She didn't want to be part of Albie's setups. But if Brader was genuinely corrupt and was going to the prosecutor anyway . . .

"You look bewildered."

"Dammit, Albie." Without forethought, she called him by his first name for the first time. "You make me wish I were a . . . a waitress at the Brass Elephant."

The thought amused him. "You wouldn't last two hours as a waitress. You'd be caught ferreting through pockets and briefcases, looking for secret evidence."

"Wiseass." She threw the towel at him.

"You don't want the Brader documents?"

"How can I say no?"

"Just say 'no,' and my friend will call Jack Steppe on the *Baltimore Sun.*"

"No." She paused. "Don't have him call Steppe."

"Don't you want to be a socialist?"

"I don't get it."

He moved close and took her hands, facing her. "If we're going to play together, we might as well work together."

Her laughter caught in her throat. He was making it clear that he wanted much more than a one-night stand. But it was equally clear that he was both willing and able to use her as a reporter. The "able" part scared her.

Silently, Albie rubbed his knuckles on her smooth cheek, looking into her eyes for the answer to a question of his own. Then she saw a softening glimmer in his eyes as he lowered his head to whisper before he kissed her. "We can be good for each other."

"God." She broke for air. "I could hate you."

"It cuts both ways," he said as he lowered his arms, "but better you should love me."

Nine

THE OTHER SIDE of love was not necessarily hate, Marlena thought as she looked across her Perrier at Roger. It could be regret or loss or old wishes gone dry. The other side of love could be emptiness.

But Roger wasn't talking about love or hate, he was painting a seascape, describing the joys of walking on the beach at dusk. She remembered the covert weekends in Cape May as quiet, emotionally charged escapes, her body turning a golden tan while her prayers reached up beyond the blue sky in a plea for change. "It must be nice." She smiled at Roger, returning from her old shadows.

"Understatement."

"It must be nice," she thought aloud, "to have a beach house where you can invite friends. Barefoot elegance, cocktails under the stars. Does your wife like to entertain?"

Roger nodded.

Beach buffets, seafood and salads, onion rolls and raspberry ice, she imaged. "Roger." She frowned at him. "What's your wife's name?"

Roger studied her a minute. "Why?"

"Why? Why not?"

He tapped his left hand on the table and looked at the ring. Lea." He smiled. "Her name is Lea, Lea like a meadow with the same sound as lee like shelter from a storm."

Marlena looked at him curiously. She must have been mistaken in thinking the relationship was rocky.

"Is she as dramatic and whimsical as you?"

"Of course. Would I marry any other kind of woman?"

"I don't know. People do strange things when it comes to marriage. Tell me more about Lea." She used the name deliberately to give added reality to the thought of Roger's wife, using it as a shield against the currents Roger was sending in her direction.

"I'm not sure how well I know her after all these years."

"After all these years?" she repeated.

"How well do we ever know anyone?" He answered with a question. "She's done a good job juggling her career and family."

"And putting up with your strange and sundry assortment of friends too?"

"With wit, charm, and a delightful degree of native sarcasm." He smiled at her.

"You don't deserve it. You're still an SOB."

"And my mother always said you were such a nice girl." He shook his head and sipped his Chardonnay.

"I thought your mother didn't approve of me, that my social-register rating didn't meet her standards."

"Nonsense. She thinks you're the greatest thing since sliced bread. She's never forgiven me for letting you get away. She's one of your greatest fans. Never misses the show."

Marlena couldn't help feeling flattered, but she'd never met Roger's mother and she could still remember the sizzling phone call to Roger when his sister had squealed on Roger's love nest.

"It's strange how we can misread things." The diamond on her finger caught the candlelight, reminding her of Roger's family diamond, still in her purse. Was this the time to give it back? "If we could apply the same test for truth to our personal lives that we do professionally, we might know more," she said.

"You mean with interrogatives and corroboration? With everyone entitled to the best defense and a second source?" He laughed.

"It would make for a hell of a first date, wouldn't it?"

Resting his elbows on the white linen, Roger leaned toward her. "Funny. Today's almost like a first date. All the background stuff. The what-have-you-done-with-your-life, all the things people say while they're testing the gut reaction. That's where it's at, Marlena. Your basic gut reaction." He parodied a leer. "Not to mention other organs."

"Cut the shit, Roger," she snapped. It was unfair and adolescent for him to play his shadowy mating game when he was already mated. She was glad to see their waiter approaching.

As the gold-rimmed soup plates were placed before them, Marlena stubbed out her cigarette and decided to talk about Roger's family. "So your family is just Lea and Alison. That means you and Lea will have more freedom soon."

"What do you mean?"

"When Alison goes off to college."

"Columbia," Roger stated. "Our school." He inhaled deeply, then discarded his cigarette and picked up a spoon to stir the creamy soup. "But . . ." He looked up, catching her eyes. "We still have little Johnny, the two-year-old. He's the apple of our eye. You'd love him, I know it. His hair is pale and fine, cut in a Dutch boy bang. And he has the most curious hazel eyes. A lot like yours."

She found the subject irritating suddenly. She didn't like Roger comparing his two-year-old's eyes to hers. Roger was attractive, but there was something bizarre about hearing him describe himself as a doting father and his wife as a Roman goddess while he kept reaching for her on every level, including the physical.

The blond image of Sophia swept into her mind. She didn't need another man equipped with a beautiful wife.

Baltimore

Teetering on five-inch silver sandals, Marlena turned to survey the crowd.

Marilyn Gibbs, her favorite neighbor on Charles Street, waved conspiratorily from across the room, grinning at their unaccustomed elegance.

A mass metamorphosis, Marlena thought, wondering how many other housewives had dropped their jeans and gardening gloves for sequins and diamonds. The crowd looked like extras in a Cadillac ad. The patrons of the historical society were doing well by the centennial event.

The assignment, to cover the benefit for the dedication of Baltimore's renovated City Hall, was not her usual beat, but when autumn flue had strained the reporters' pool, Marlena was turned back into a general assignment reporter for the night.

"Some fairy godmother you turn out to be," she complained to Paul. "Didn't Cinderella get upgraded?"

Paul laughed, but he didn't let her off. He told her to go get dressed up like Cinderella and the fairy godmother would give her a day of comp time.

"Be a good little street reporter and maybe you'll find your prince at the ball," Paul retorted, tapping her head with his pen turned into a magic wand.

But that was why she didn't want the assignment. Albie was on the Historical Society board. She hated being "not with him" at public events. Especially now, when Pat Spadoro had shown her the new . . .

She heard his voice, then his laugh as he grabbed her arm to steady her, and looked down at her sparkling feet. "Spare me the elegance. You look beautiful," he said softly, quickly releasing her arm as her name was called from behind.

"Marlena!" The call was repeated, closer.

She turned to see Don, her favorite young cameraman, dressed in a tuxedo, lugging his bulky equipment through the crowd.

"Want to interview me?" Albie asked.

"You're such a ham."

"I was instrumental in getting the federal grant for the renovations."

"What did you trade off for it, Senator?"

"A barrel of pork rind and Earl Weaver's soul," he grinned.

"Start rolling, Don." She nodded at her cameraman. "The senator has been strong-armed into a few comments."

"Yes, Miss Williams," Albie said smoothly. "Returning City Hall to its nineteenth-century splendor is but one more sign that Baltimore is coming back. Center Stage is going strong again, the harbor is coming alive, and we're on the upswing. In too many cities people ask what their government is doing. Here, we have only to look around at the visible progress."

"What did the renovation cost?"

"Close to 6.5 million dollars, a small price to pay for municipal pride."

"Is that why you voted for the increased cigarette tax?"

"No." His look was level. "That money goes into a different pot, for subsidized housing programs. Our difficulty with those programs, however, is getting our constituents to understand how the programs work and how to apply."

"Thank you, Senator," she said, nodding to Don to stop taping. "We'll have to look into that in greater depth."

"Thank you, Miss Williams. It always makes me happy when reporters follow positive issues as well as nitpick in people's dirty laundry."

"I've heard that the governor's wife is sending his shirts out to the Chinese laundry because she's unhappy with the domestic staff at the governor's mansion. Can you comment on that?"

"Check with the *Baltimore Sun*," Albie quipped. "You TV people always get your news from them, anyway."

"Don." Marlena smiled at her cameraman, full of saccharin. "Let's go in search of some intelligent comments. Something less long-winded, perhaps."

"Nice talking to you, Miss Williams," Albie said pleasantly.

"My pleasure, Senator Comparo."

She stepped away from Albie.

"Are you two having some kind of a feud?" Don raised an eyebrow. "Your nails were out."

"Reporters always have adversarial relationships with politicians," she said piously.

Albie had insisted on giving her the down payment for her ground-floor luxury garden apartment on Charles Street, insisting that he should contribute even more, considering the amount of time he spent there.

She had enough trouble rationalizing her acceptance of anything of material value from him. Now, with the DEA report etched in her mind, she wasn't sure she could take anything from him again if she wanted to salvage her own self-respect.

Trailing Don through the crowd, she picked out famil-

iar faces to ask for comments—the mayor, the project architect, secretaries with offices in the hall. With everyone dressed
to the nines, it would be a colorful spot for the eleven o'clock
news.

A small orchestra played, grouped around a large column. She recognized "Bird in a Gilded Cage." Did Albie recognize it too? Did he consider her his "kept woman?" The
thought was disastrous to her self-image. The condo and the
emerald ring, suddenly seemed tainted.

But they were symbols to her, more straw's to clutch as
signs that he loved her, even if he couldn't say the words. "I
adore your laugh," "Love that dress." The only time he'd said
"I love you," she'd almost missed it. He'd sat on the edge of
the bed, in silent meditation, staring at the shoes he was about
to slip into before he rushed out to a late-night meeting. He'd
whispered it toward the shoes, without looking up at her.

His actions spoke louder. When he was away from her
even for a few days he returned hungry, caressing and loving.

She had fantasies of standing beside him in a crowd,
shouting "I love you." But she hadn't tried saying it to him.
His silence muted her own words. She told her pillow and her
percolator and the seascapes on the wall while she waited for
him to say it first.

The glitter of the crowd swam back into focus. A group
of state politicians and their wives clustered together like a
football team moments before the huddle. She saw Albie stride
toward the group, the quarterback returning to call the play.

Lovely and elegant in a shimmering white silk gown, a
woman stepped away from a tall blond man in the group and
moved to welcome Albie.

"Darling, there you are." Her voice was low and warm,
her smile soft. A diamond band sparkled cunningly amid the
artfully arranged tendrils, a modern version of classic Roman
curls. Marlena froze. She was lovely. Albie's wife.

"Caesar's wife," Don quipped, following Marlena's focus as they saw Albie take Sophia by both hands. Was this the empty marriage?

Blinking back tears, Marlena turned from a scene too clearly etched to ever forget, suddenly dreading Albie's return "home" after the news. But how could she accuse him of unfaithfulness with his wife? She almost laughed at the thought.

She wandered after Don and the camera, her mind no longer focused on the local color.

Which part of us chooses our loves? She hadn't wanted to love this man, whose warm smile revealed so little of the power web he wove with dark delicacy. She had fought against her own feelings through the long summer, concentrating on the Brader trial.

Paul Humphries pushed her to follow up on the Comparo leads, and she kept Paul happy and diverted as she broke a string of exclusive stories, making Paul and IBS look good.

Albie's gifts were double-edged, cutting into her conscience while bringing obvious rewards. She had a direct line to the grand jury meeting on the governor's alleged involvement with some funny bond deals relating to racetracks. The source was the secretary of one of the defense lawyers who introduced herself to Marlena at her hairdresser's as a "friend of Jack's," as she suggested they have a quiet drink later.

Never look a gift horse in the mouth, Marlena rationalized.

Marlena sensed, from a few comments Albie had dropped, that he had warned the governor not to get mixed up with the two-bit pony pushers. Since his advice had been ignored, Albie felt no responsibility to make an effort to save any part of him.

Albie was not easy. Too many questions couldn't be asked or even implied without the walls closing down in his eyes. She tried not to examine the depths to which she was compromising, at the very least, her professional self.

Even as he covertly arranged for sources to deliver inside information, she recognized that he was handing her the discards while she played into unseen cards he held close to his chest.

"Don." She smiled too brightly. "Let's do the stand-up with the orchestra for a background." She led the way back to the grand lobby. For the first time in her life she felt like the "other" woman, as the self-created fiction of Albie's witchy wife peeled from her mind like sunburned skin. She felt raw and angular as she compared herself to Sophia.

"You look terrific tonight," Don said as she posed herself beside a column, the orchestra in the background.

"Thanks." She wished she could believe it. She smoothed the skirt of her soft print gown, looking at the pattern. Sea foam, the designer had called it. Inspired by the ocean with pale sea colors of waves on the edge of breaking or tears waiting to fall.

She cleared her voice and widened her eyes for the lens. "Take one. Five, four, three, two, one." She paused a beat.

"In 1875 Baltimore celebrated the completion of its magnificent new City Hall, worthy of her flounders . . . oops."

"Crabs, Marlena." Don laughed. "Baltimore's famous for crabs, not flounders."

"I'm the one that's floundering." She shook her head. "Okay. Keep rolling. Take two. Take two." She began again from the tops, keeping her founders separate from the crabs and flounders straight through to the concluding lines.

"Tonight the grand old hall glitters again, gold restored to her cornices and pride returned to those to whom she belongs—the people of Baltimore." She paused and tagged. "This is Marlena Williams, WIMD-TV, from the century-young City Hall in Baltimore." She looked at Don for reaction.

"Looks great to me."

Call it a wrap and let's get back to the station."

"But aren't we supposed to go live at eleven?" Don asked. "The new microwave truck is waiting outside."

"Don," she said patiently. "Why would I have to tape the stand-up closer if I planned to be live? There's no advantage to going live from here. No one's being held hostage. Paul just wants to play with his new toy this week."

"But won't Paul get mad if . . ."

"Look, Don," she interrupted. "Yours is not to question why. Yours is only to do what I say. Got it?"

"Yes, Mother, but you better call Paul."

Playfully, she thumped Don on the head with her beaded purse. With tight bronze curls and big blue eyes, Don looked like a cherub grown. Fresh out of college, with only six months on the job, he was already as good as any other WIMD cameraman and getting better. Still, he was naive in station politics and pecking orders. How could he know that she had paid enough dues in the past five years to pull a change on Paul? "Mother." She smiled at his phrase. Sometimes she felt like his mother, when he looked so earnest, so serious.

When he looked like that, he reminded her of Toby. It was hard to believe that Toby was well into his teens. The years had skipped by on a thousand stories, special reports, potential relationships, and casual dates that got lost in the news shuffle. And now Albie. And Sophia. It was more than time to leave.

She gave Don a hug, camera and all. "Be a good boy and tell the guys in the truck to head back in. I'll call Paul and clear it—by the book." She grinned.

"Fine with me. I'm not big on this bird suit, anyway." Don pulled at the rented tuxedo tie.

"It does wonderful things for you. Makes you look at least twenty."

"Thanks a lot."

"Here's my coat." She gave the girl a dollar and slipped into the soft white fur, reddening as she saw Don obviously admiring it. If he knew, she thought, cringing as she fumbled with the snap hooks. The fur itself should be pink with shame, she thought, fighting the urge to peek into the coat room to see if Sophia had one too. "Meet me in the newsroom with the tape," she said in her professional voice.

"Right. Want to race? A dollar says I can get there first."

"I'll give you a dollar not to get another speeding ticket," she said, laughing.

"If I get there first, without getting a ticket, can I buy you a drink?"

Marlena was startled, recognizing that Don did not think of her as a mother. Puppy love, a crush, she thought fondly. She smiled her regret even as she felt the force of his young desire. She caught a glimpse of the chemistry that could be possible between women and much younger men, but she wasn't interested in experimenting. Her preferred catalysts were more mature. "Have a cup of coffee waiting for me, and you'll be my hero."

"Thanks, Mom."

"It's okay, son."

Back at WIMD she went directly into Paul Humphries's office. Disregarding her formal attire, she pushed a straight-back chair toward Paul's desk and straddled it, tomboy fashion.

"I thought you were going to hold the fort at the big party. Hors d'oeuvres that bad?"

"I wasn't meant for these fancy shoes," she said kicking them off.

Paul eyed the silver straps speculatively. "No. Not my type either." He winked, at ease. Marlena was one of the few privy to Paul's private truth. Paul and his friend Bernie had long dropped the pretense with Marlena that they were only roommates, rather than lovers. She liked cooking for them and going out as a threesome. It always reminded her of growing up with her brothers.

"No." She smiled. "You're more the golden slipper kind." There was another advantage to Paul's homosexuality. Paul would never be a threat. All he asked from her was good work and an open level of friendship. That had been easy. Until Albie.

But Paul waxed enthusiastic about her work in the past six months. Since Albie. Paul frequently congratulated her on developing the source network that was keeping her days ahead of the competition. He loved discoursing on his theory of sources, using Marlena as an example to all the younger reporters.

"Cultivate the little people," Paul had said. "The secretaries, the neighbors, the relatives, and the cleaning ladies. It's rare that the kingpins show off their own secrets. It takes more digging, but little people can have big ears."

Marlena always squirmed, knowing her "little people" were hand-picked by the kingpin, but Paul's pontificating amused her. She could see him making mental notes for the seminars he willingly gave at the University of Baltimore.

"What Paul doesn't know can't hurt him," Albie had said. But if Paul did find out, it would hurt him. And would more than hurt her.

On this night she missed the open and honest camaraderie she'd once had with Paul. She found it even more painful that Paul believed their communications were still that way.

If Paul knew, he'd have little sympathy. His was the wrong shoulder to cry on. Paul intensely disliked Albie. It seemed almost personal, although Paul never explained. He constantly encouraged her to dig for something conclusively damaging about her covert lover. Albie was the prime quarry in a large corner of Paul's news mind.

"It's still early," Paul noted. "Want to anchor tonight after all?"

"No, let Babs get the experience. I'd like more time off from anchoring this fall—maybe even use up some of the enormous leave I've amassed working for a certain Simon Legree." She grinned. "That's Simon, Paul; not Simon, Peter."

"Getting biblical on me. You never cease to amaze me." He ran his fingers through his curly dark hair.

Marlena frowned, noticing a touch of gray for the first time. "Paul? There's something I've never asked you, something personal."

"I thought you knew all my skeletons. Well, let's see. You've been here almost five years. I guess that's long enough for you to ask a personal question."

"How old are you?"

"That's personal?" Paul cackled.

"Your personal age," she persisted.

"I never reveal my age," he said archly. "No woman worth her salt ever does." He grinned boyishly. "And I've been meaning to suggest you do some revising yourself. You're getting a bit long in the tooth."

"I'm only thirty, you bastard. All right. Thirty-one next month."

He calculated for a moment. "Born in 1944. It would be easy to make the four a nine. 1949. Woosh. Poppa Paul, your fairy godfather, has just granted you an extra five years before you push forty."

"Where is your lust for facts, truth in reporting?"

"In this business youth is money. A year saved is a year to earn. Especially for women. Trust me." He shared his mug of milky coffee with her. "For your birthday I will personally have your file updated."

"You are something else."

"That's what my shrink tells me." Paul's mouth lifted wryly. "But why this sudden interest in my age? Thinking about having a baby?"

"Paul, you're crazy! I'm not even married."

"I know. But I thought you might be proposing to have a cover. I might be interested—for a price."

"I'm not that liberal."

"Just as well. Bernie would never understand."

"He'd be right in line with my mother. What ever made you think of that?"

"You're getting on, you know." He grinned. "Babs is getting that lust for maternity and she's three years younger than you."

"And married."

"For this month. Maybe not by next month." Paul took a perverse delight in divorce. He claimed it proved his belief that men and women were constitutionally unfit for cohabitation.

"You're avoiding my question."

"I'm older than you—and younger than Cronkite."

"Old enough to know better and young enough to do it anyway." She smiled. "We're the same age."

"And too dedicated to our careers to have the time to do it is closer to the truth." Paul looked at the news photos on his wall. "When I think of those poor bastards like Bob and Marty juggling news beats with mortgages, cub scout meetings, and church dinners, I shudder."

"It's not so bad. There are other rewards."

"How would you know?"

"I had a family once, when I was married to Tom Wells. He had a little boy and . . ."

"Don't go getting sentimental on me. We still have a show to do. Have you and Babs been reading *Man and Super-*

man or something? What's with this sudden urge for motherhood?"

"Not me. There are plenty of mothers' around here for me to worry about. Including you."

"Whew." Paul wiped his forehead in mock relief. "Better to be a mother than a father, that's what I always say."

"Me too," she said, but she was touched that he would consider marrying her so she could have a child.

"You're doing too much good for our ratings to contemplate maternity leave. And," his tone elevated, "you don't even have a man around the house to do the job. Who am I worried about covering for?"

"Damned if I know."

"First you have to find the man before I worry about it."

"Yeah. That's the tough part."

Paul laughed. "I know. It took me years to find a good one."

Marlena stretched, rose, and leaned down to kiss Paul's forehead. "Savage."

A sigh rewarded her. "Sometimes you make me wish I were straight again."

"A perfect way to end a beautiful friendship."

She picked up her sandals. "I'm going home. My feet hurt." She turned at the door. "I've left production notes with the editor. You can call me at home if there's a problem."

"Drive carefully."

"You always say that. It's only fifteen minutes without traffic."

"More accidents happen within two miles of peoples' homes than anywhere else."

"Thanks, Mom."

"And remember to brush your teeth and say your prayers."

Don was waiting by her desk with a cup of now lukewarm coffee. Devotion always seemed to be found in the wrong places. She took the coffee "to go."

"Messages?" She stopped by the front desk. The girl on duty unpinned two from a cork board behind the desk. "Thanks." Marlena glanced at them. The Highway Commission investigator had returned her call. Alan Cameron had called from Pittsburgh. It made her feel stronger, more wanted, as she headed home to Albie.

Albie was already in the bedroom, starting to undress. She stepped into the room without saying hello, just walked three steps in and halted, trying to find words worth saying.

He looked up, feeling her presence. "Hi. You're back early."

So familiar and domestic, she thought, like a husband. But he wasn't—at least not hers. Her eyes dampened and salty tears spotted the frozen waves of her gown. "Am I so politically useful in helping you get rid of your enemies that you throw me crumbs, a few hours here and there, in gratitude?"

Albie's shoe echoed as he dropped it, startled. "What in God's name has gotten into you?"

She stepped back, leaning on the doorframe, confused. Despite the warmth she thought she'd perceived between Albie and his wife, Albie wasn't with Sophia tonight in their luxurious estate south of the city. And he didn't need her to leak information. Dozens of other reporters in town would kill to know her cued informers. But the image of Sophia hurt.

"Lena, I have an early meeting at the capitol tomorrow and I have to drive down tonight. So get whatever's really bothering you off your chest so I can spend time working on something other than your mental state." He smiled.

"I really don't understand you."

"I've never asked you to understand me, only to love me."

"I thought they went together. Love and understanding."

"For someone who's supposed to be an expert in communications you're doing a lousy job, kiddo. What's wrong?"

"Kiddo. That's what I felt like tonight, an awkward kid, the outsider at a grown-up ball."

Albie scratched behind his ear and his blue eyes looked puzzled. "You're a reporter, right? That's always being the outsider, looking in. I thought that's the role you like."

"I do, but . . ."

"But what?"

"She . . . your wife . . . is so lovely." Her voice caught. "You make such a beautiful couple."

"Goddamn." He guffawed. "I should have known. Women. Yes, she's a beauty, all right. Just loves to have her picture in *Town and Country* and *Racing News*. And she's the most admirably civic-minded person in Maryland, not to mention an exemplary mother who's never missed a PTA meeting or a game. She's one hundred percent organized one hundred percent of the time. If she'd been in Hitler's High Command, we'd have been doomed."

"I thought you admired efficiency. And I couldn't help see the way you held her hands."

"So I admire her. I'll admit it. I also admire works of art and fine machines. She's perfect for the social side of politics. And, oh how she'd love to be Maryland's first lady."

"I think you'd make a terrific governor if you went straight."

"Very funny. Both of you better get rid of that idea. I'm supposed to go make myself a target like a clay pigeon when I own the pond?"

"You're pretty good at carving decoys," she said dryly.

"Nobody's perfect." He wiggled his dark brows, trying to be funny.

He didn't get a smile in return. "It must be nice."

"What?" he asked as he started to tug at the other black patent-leather shoe.

"To be in a position to make neat little game plans for your life."

The one shoe still on, Albie hobbled across the room to hug her hard. "Nobody makes plans for my life but me. And my own plans aren't always so little or so neat. You, for instance, have a nasty habit of making me come unglued."

"Do I, really?"

"You know what you do to my pulse," he whispered against her ear.

"Not really. Your heart is a mystery to me."

"Shouldn't be. It's all yours." His kiss was long and sure.

Stopping to breathe, she rested her palm against his cheek and searched his eyes with her own. "How much is all mine?"

"As much as you can handle."

"And if I can handle more than I get of it, of you?"

"Are you sure, really sure about that?" He reached behind her to unzip her gown.

"Really sure." She stepped over the pool of silk and led the way naked; to the king-size bed.

"You could get in too deep."

"Never." She opened her arms to him. "I can't ever get too deep. And I want you in so deep, you can't ever get out."

"God, I want you." His voice was harsh. And then they were together, struggling to get inside each other, body, soul, and heart.

"Albie," she whispered as he rested his head on her damp shoulder afterward. "Sleep here tonight. Go to Annapolis in the morning. I promise I'll get you up in time."

He chuckled, a lazy, naughty sound. "You'll get me up, all right. That's always a sure bet."

She reached for the cigarettes and silently offered him
one. "You only like sure things, don't you?"

"Who doesn't?"

She inhaled deeply, then breathed out, watching the
smoke rise to meet the dark ceiling.

"What's bugging you tonight?"

"Nothing original, but then being the 'other woman'
hasn't been original for a long time, has it?"

He caught the drift. "Sorry. I'd have warned you Sophia
would be there if I'd have known you were coming." He toyed
with the short, unruly curls at her temple. "Nobody hates
being blind-sided any worse than I do. But I swear to the God
I'd like to believe in, Marlena, that I think of Sophia the way I
think of a tie—a social custom, something I wear for the sake
of form."

"I suppose you could call it a marriage of convenience,
since you find power so convenient."

Albie looked at her sharply. She returned the look
steadily, wisely. Then he reached for their robes on the chair
beside the bed. "Maybe we should talk."

"Maybe we should."

Albie mixed drinks while she began. "They've made an
interesting connection, Albie. Some people are calling it the
missing link. I thought you'd appreciate that as a trustee of the
Historical Society."

"Go on." He didn't need to ask what she was talking
about.

"Anna Maria, Sophia's mother, was Sicilian, despite the
carefully laundered name, deGenore. Washed by marriage? Is
that what you call it? Despite the Baird and Wellesley and the
debut at the President's Ball, Sophia is the granddaughter of
Don Scaffaro. Bingo." She paused, waiting for a response.

Albie's jaw was set. He opened his mouth only to sip his
scotch.

"Sophia's father, the Count DeGenore, was a milksop aristocrat who died in a car crash. An accident?"

"An accident," Albie clarified.

"And poor Don Scaffaro, there he was, a widower with only a daughter, Anna Maria who was now a widow. No heir for his organized crime family. So what was more natural than for Scaffaro to introduce his young, polished but tough *consigliere* to his granddaughter, the only child of his only child? Like my story so far?"

"It's an interesting little fairy tale. Go on."

"I think your fairy goddaughter, Sophia, is more than a social custom like a tie." Her tone was sardonic. "More like a tie that binds. Hardly optional for a man who loves power."

Unexpectedly, Albie threw back his head, and his deep, rich laughter echoed against the windows.

"Would you tell me what is so goddamn funny?" She was furious that his response was laughter rather than shock.

"How and why do I let myself forget that you're a reporter and a damn good one at that? Grandfather would turn purple if he could hear you."

"How do you know I'm not wired?"

"Do you really need an answer for that?"

"No." She couldn't help laughing. "But I could have the place bugged."

"Not with my cleaning woman around three days a week."

"Doesn't it make you nervous that they've dug up your direct family connection?"

"A little. But not very."

"Because you have it all structured like behind the lines army intelligence operations? Dead drops. Cut-outs. Compartmentalized information. Not to mention misinformation," she continued. "False trails that lead back to their own beginnings?"

"So you know I was in army intelligence. That's public record. It's part of my standard campaign pap. You've put an interesting little twist to it. Or somebody did."

The somebody was Pat Spadoro. Pat had been fascinated by the Scaffaro family operation for a long time. Listening to him, it was evident that he grudgingly admired it, called it the best run family operation in the country.

From the moment he started probing into the Scaffaro operation in Maryland his gut had been telling him that Comparo was connected somehow. The junior partners of Comparo's former law partners, had formed their own firms when Comparo left law for politics, but they kept showing up as the attorneys of record when the small fish, the "family guppies" as Pat called them, made careless mistakes. But that was the most, he could get on Comparo, until he'd found a friendly Interpol agent with good Italian sources.

"Poor Don Scaffaro. Classic irony. He had to stay away from his only grandchild's wedding and keep her mother away, too, so that he could give you his greatest wedding present, covert control of the family operations. But I'm sure he and Anna Maria saw the home movies later." She looked at him, then buried her face in her hands. "Goddammit, Albie. I'm so tired of all this crap. I just want life to be clean and simple, without all the double-talk."

"Or double cross?"

She froze, wishing she could edit her conversation like a news spot. Cut out the parts that didn't play. He stood, looking out the window. "Are you leaving?" she whispered.

"Maybe I should." His voice was too soft, but not soft with the quiet ice of controlled anger. The modulation held a dissonant harmonic. The soft sound of pain. "I've never liked that word."

The scene had played too well. She'd wanted to goad him into seeing a need for positive action, not hurt him and have him withdraw. "No." She went to him, putting her arms around him from behind. "Never, never, never." She pulled at his clenched hand and pried open his finger to mesh them with hers. Their hands joined, becoming a shared fist.

His eyes clouded with caution, he turned his face to her.

She kissed him softly, caressing his lips with hers. "Never," she whispered against his mouth. "Only a single cross." She stepped back and crossed two fingers carefully for him. "Like two fingers on one hand. Like two people with one heart."

"One heart and two minds. That could be tough." His eyes held hers. "Who's your source?"

She knew she had only two options. Neither felt right. To tell him some was to tell him all. To tell him nothing was to lose him.

"It's your choice," he said simply.

"It's not easy for me."

"Or me," he echoed.

"I love you. Do you believe that?"

"Yes. But it's all in or all out."

"A family proverb?" She tried to slide by the hard choice.

"The source, Lena?"

"The Drug Enforcement Agency here has gotten a good link with an Italian Interpol agent. He's been pulling documents, birth and property records, putting together a more complete family tree for Scaffaro. He says he's suspected you were behind the Scaffaro operations for a long time, but he had no evidence before."

"Now he has proof?"

"Only the proof of relationships. And evidence of who was and wasn't in places that fit into his premise."

"Such as?"

"Scaffaro and Anna Maria not coming to the wedding

when you married Sophia. If you were clean, why wouldn't they come?"

"Scaffaro was deported in 1962. He couldn't have come. That's all they have?"

"Yes. And he says he doesn't want it leaked that Sophia is Scaffaro's granddaughter."

"Why not?"

"He doesn't care about the society page, he says. He's waiting until he gets you nailed to the wall, until he can prove the big picture. He's a dedicated investigator. Blue collar, true-blue Fed. You know the kind."

"Irish?"

She paused, recognizing the moment of truth and betrayal, which were twisting together.

"Yes."

Albie took her hand and kissed the inside of the palm, not wanting to look at her face as she said the name.

She swallowed hard. "Pat Spadoro, half Irish, half Italian-American. It's a tenacious combination."

"Bet he has a great sense of humor," Albie said easily, the tension gone from his voice.

"He calls you the Elephant and the investigation's code name is 'Safari.' He must have heard your speech to the press club about not going after guppies with an elephant gun."

"But why's he sharing his confidential files with you?"

"You'll love it." Her smile was ironic. "Pat's been a source of mine for years. When I first came to WIMD and had the cops-and-crime beat, we traded information on a couple of cases. Anyway, Pat gave me enough information to whet my appetite. He wanted me to do a double-team effort to get hard evidence on you.

"He said you used to be a real womanizer until a year or so ago, but he thought I could break the ice and get close to you if I tried."

Albie was thoughtful. "I don't love it. He may know more than he's saying. Stay away from him, Lena. He could hurt us."

"He's already hurt us." The dream of Marlena Williams Comparo, anchorperson-wife-and-mother, emerged stillborn as she'd read the Safari file. "It was like pouring acid on my dreams," she said sadly.

Albie nodded, understanding too well. "We should get away for a while. Paris. Copenhagen."

"We can't set foot in Europe together. Pat has you on the Interpol list now."

Her thirty-first/twenty-sixth birthday was spent at the quaint old Riegelsville hotel in Bucks County, Pennsylvania. It sounded familiar. When she remembered why, she vowed not to lose another chance for happiness. But she pushed the thought of Will into a small, sad corner of her mind lest Albie suffer in contrast.

Soon after they arrived at the hotel, while they were walking beside the Delaware tow path, Marlena found the moment she'd been waiting for. She skipped along beside him, giving him a humorous rendition of the birthday call from her mother. "Maggie said it's high time I was thinking about children and I promised her I'd think about doing a series on juvenile crime."

Albie looked startled, caught off guard.

"What do you think? Do you think she's right? I love children."

"I think you'd make a terrific mother." He smiled warmly. "It would be interesting to see what kind of a child we could produce."

She waited for him to say more, to fill in the brush strokes to show her how it could work. But she didn't push him. She tried to believe time was on her side, that every day and night he spent with her would weight the balance in her favor.

Christmas in Des Moines was brief. She felt optimistic because Sophia had taken the children to Italy while Albie stayed at home, working and waiting for Lena to come back from Des Moines, like a good mate.

Her hopes were high for the new year. But as the months passed, things moved at a slow and plodding pace.

Without acknowledging that Pat Spadoro had been correct in his assessment of the Scaffaro clan, Albie was becoming more open in his conversations with Marlena, although he was careful not to name names. He'd also stopped planting stories with her.

But she clung to the small changes and signs of an increased level of trust, catching straws in the wind to add to the nest she was building in her mind.

The last Sunday in May Albie stormed in late. "That bitch!" he spat as he headed for the liquor cabinet to fill a highball glass with undiluted Scotch. "I should have her committed. She may look sane, but she's nuttier than her whacko mother, who needs a full-time nurse!"

Marlena tossed her book aside to deal with Albie's rage. "Who? What? Where? When? Why?" She mockingly played the reporter.

"It's not funny." He paced the floor between her and the window. "Sophia's been running around drumming up support for my gubernatorial campaign. A lot of heavy people think I'm playing bait and switch. I may have to send her to some Mediterranean beach to have some sense knocked into whatever lives under that hairspray." He winked at Marlena. "Hey."

"Hey what?"

"You know I'm happy with you."

She didn't comment, too aware of where he was coming from.

"Let's get away for a long weekend. How does the honeymoon suite at the MGM Grand sound?"

"Fine, if there's a real honeymoon to go with it."

There was a pause. "We could get there yet, lady."

The phone interrupted before she could open the floor for a real discussion. "Hello?"

"If it's Jack, tell him I'm at the North Pole, anything."

"Alan." Marlena's voice was without enthusiasm. Alan Cameron was planning to be in Baltimore June seventh and eighth for a PBS conference. "Dinner Tuesday night, June eighth." She looked at Albie for guidance, but he was studiously engrossed in *Newsweek*.

"I'll have to check my calendar at the station. Can you call me in the morning? Fine. Talk to you then. Bye."

Albie looked up from the magazine as she crawled back into bed beside him. "Who's Alan?"

"An old friend from Wilkes-Barre. Jealous?"

"Violently," he said lightly.

"Don't worry. He's like a little brother."

"Mmm." He didn't sound convinced. "I'll get home Tuesday night from Annapolis by midnight, I promise."

"I'd like that." She nestled against him.

"I love you."

"What?"

"I said I love you."

"Just like that. You're going to say it out loud?"

"You want it louder? *I love you*! Well?" He waited.

"I love you," she said and proceeded to prove it.

That night she slept soundly on a pillow of straw.

The next week was calm. Carter had lost the Maryland primary to Jerry Brown, but he won the June first primary in

South Dakota. Then he lost to Brown in Rhode Island and to Church in Montana. But his percentages were growing. The unknown was gaining momentum.

Albie was full of I-told-you-sos. Not that he liked Carter, but he was predicting his win. "Udall is too clever and craggy, Brown is too flaky, and Church is too smart and honest for his own good. Carter's appealing to middle America and unknown enough to swing it."

"I hope you're wrong. His smile is too wide and his ideas far wider. Everything to everybody," she said. "A classic campaign chameleon. I've been reading his speeches on the wires. He'll promise higher wages when talking to workers and lower if he's in management's corner."

"If television dug deeper than smiles and close-ups of people applauding, Udall might have a shot," Albie retorted. "All I can say is that my folks and I put our money on the Carter campaign months ago. I can always smell a winner."

"Even if he's an ultimate loser for the country?"

"As long as we can influence a few key appointments, we win."

"Is that we the people or we the Family?"

"I don't like to think that there's a difference."

"I don't like to think that either, but . . ." She didn't finish.

"So what *do* you think?"

"I think it would make a great news story if I could document the money that organized crime is putting into Carter's campaign."

"You plan to quote me on that?"

"That's not fair."

"Whoever said the world was fair?"

"Not you, mister, that's for sure."

Ten

❖

FAIR, MARLENA THOUGHT as the waiter placed a delectable platter of succulent oysters in front of her. Life wasn't fair. People were starving in upper Manhattan.

Roger waved his glass to toast. "To old friends and new times."

"I'll drink to that." Marlena sipped the wine. Light, crisp, and tart, she decided, the way she felt when her interviews were working.

"California," Roger said, holding the goblet closer to the candle to examine the pale color. "A quiet little vineyard, Chateau St. Jean."

"Very nice."

"It's a perfect complement for the oysters. You'll love it."

Did Roger always tell people how they would feel? she wondered. Although she had to agree, as she took a bite of the oysters and followed with a sip of the wine.

"I get wonderful oysters at the beach." Roger spoke between bites. "Great clams and mussels too. Those are local. My favorite fish market also specializes in fresh lobster, flown down daily from Maine."

"I love seafood. And wherever these oysters come from, they're delicious."

"Chesapeake. The prime ones all come from there. Oysters could be my favorite food. If there's a heaven, the gates are pearly because the celestial chef has a staff shucking oysters."

"You're a silly man." Marlena smiled between bites. "I don't know if I'm that fond of oysters."

"Do you know where I tasted the best oysters I've ever had? This will sound crazy, I know, but it's true. In the dining room of a hotel in Las Vegas, probably flown in for somebody's godfather." Roger grinned, winking at her. "You've probably been in Vegas hundreds of times."

Marlena laughed. Roger's vision of her glamorous life was amusing. "Hardly. I've only been there once. Back in 1976. It was tackier than I'd expected. One of my network producers once called Las Vegas an entire city with the ambience of an adult bookstore."

It was hard to keep her mind on Roger. Why did he have to mention Las Vegas?

Las Vegas

"Not quite the peaceful little inn in Virginia, is it?" Albie's mood was buoyant.

People were milling about in the huge lobby, a potpourri of humanity. Never had Marlena seen such extremes of dress in one room. Tennis shoes and shorts, blue jeans and T-shirts oblivious to the sequined jackets, furs, and brocade skirts.

"A trifle busier," Marlena understated, smiling to hide
her pique that Albie was once again registering them as "Mr.
and Mrs. Horn." Now she would have to keep checking in with
her Baltimore answering service to stay on top of any WIMD
crisis. But she held her comments determined to make this a
magical weekend.

Although she savored the freedom of being with him
without wigs or caution, she hated the glitter of the casinos.
Neon and plush were the trappings of shallow affairs. She
knew her relationship with Albie went deeper than that, but
the tawdry showgirls and people on the prowl reminded Marlena that her own love was hardly aboveboard.

A half life, she thought. Or a half death.

Albie seemed oblivious to her disquiet as he held her hand
for luck at the crap table. He couldn't stop winning. It seemed
the more she willed the die to roll against him so they could leave
the casino to the garish strangers, the more he won.

"Albie, baby!" A bear of a man waddled over to them,
ignoring Marlena and encompassing Albie in an appropriate
hug. He eyed the pile. "Not bad, baby, not bad." His dark little
eyes, half concealed by drooping, puffy eyelids, slid across
Marlena like a snake. "You're doing real well," he said, equat-
ing her with the pile of chips as his eyes slid back to the table
to calculate their worth. "Some people are just born lucky."

"Some of us work real hard for our luck."

"And some just seem to inherit it."

Albie tossed the man a pile of chips. "I think I'll call it a
night. Enjoy a round on me."

"Not even an introduction, Albie?" The reptilian eyes
fastened on Marlena.

"Lee Wells, Baby Morris." Albie nodded from one to the
other and quickly guided Marlena away from the table, tossing
"Nice seeing you, Baby" over his shoulder.

"You're a liar," she said the moment they were out of Baby's earshot. "You weren't happy to see him. Who is he?"

"A big bookie."

"Big is no lie."

"Nor is the bookie part. His territory is almost as big as his appetites. A man to be real careful around."

"I don't think I'd have liked him, anyway." Marlena stopped short as she entered their suite, trying to swallow her revulsion for the bordello trappings. Red flocked-velvet wallpaper, four-inch-thick carpeting, and a heart-shaped bed. For a honeymoon it would be a wonderful giggle. But it wasn't a honeymoon.

"Tomorrow we'll cash in our chips and I'll take you shopping."

"Tomorrow I'm flying home."

"Huh? Just because I introduced you as Lee Wells?"

"No, because I'm not very good at playing a mobster's moll."

"Lena, Lena. This isn't 1930 and I'm not that kind of mobster. I pay taxes. I own legal corporations. I don't make profits off drugs or prostitution. I don't order hits."

"Listen to yourself. You don't personally order hits. What a perverse rationalization! You don't profit from drugs? Maybe, but can you say you don't have a say in who does? And from the way sweet little Baby Morris talked, I'll bet you have a hidden interest in this casino."

"Not personally." He responded to her raised brows and added, "I'm guardian for a trust that owns a piece of this casino."

"Who's the beneficiary? Sophia and the children?"

He nodded unhappily.

Her hands flew over her ears. "I don't want to know this much. And I sure as hell don't want a souvenir to remind me of another weekend as Mr. and Mrs. Horn." She glared at him as he mixed drinks for them at the Naugahyde-padded bar. "Don't you care? Don't you care that it hurts?"

He carefully placed her martini in front of her. "I care," he said softly. His voice was hoarse as he added, "You make it damn hard for a man to live with himself sometimes."

"But I'm not worth damn much when it comes to motivating you to stop rationalizing."

"Things can take time."

"And time can run out."

"I'm sorry. Vegas was a lousy idea on my part."

She sat on the scarlet couch beside him. She placed a hand on each side of his face and softly kissed him, while her fingertips moved against his temples, touching, feeling.

"What are you doing?"

"Feeling your pulse, maybe trying to get a line on your heart, wondering if we can ever do better than this . . . this charade. Maybe hoping I'm not alone in my struggle for answers."

She saw respect in his eyes as well as understanding. "No, you're not alone. I do love you, Lena, and I'm trying."

"And I'll try too, try to be kinder."

"But you are," he objected.

"No, I have to work at it until you're free to love me in public."

In the morning they flew home. Sunday they went to an Orioles game, sitting in the upper decks, disguised only by sunglasses. She sensed that Albie was getting bolder, but it made her nervous to think that rumors could reach Paul or Spadoro. The tangled web wasn't all of Albie's weaving.

On Monday morning Albie left for Annapolis and Marlena went to the station prepared to tackle a mounting pile of calls and correspondence. She worked late to clear her slate for an early dinner with Alan on Tuesday night.

Alan's appearance was a pleasant surprise. Although

they'd stayed in touch by phone and holiday letters, she hadn't seen him for more than two years. Gone was the gaunt pallor, which always reminded her that his ancestors had been Welsh coal miners. He'd filled out. "A Bordeaux type," she teased him. "You improve with age."

"Then let's order Bordeaux," he said with new smoothness. The gleam in Alan's eyes behind the new complimentary tortoise shell frames of his glasses made it clear his feelings for Marlena still flickered.

Long before the Black Forest cake arrived in ultimate temptation, Alan had made it clear that before he made a decision about whether to take an offer from CBS to become assistant bureau chief in Washington, he wanted a measure of her present interest in him.

"I can't believe you haven't remarried, Lena. You're not a loner. Aren't there any good men in Baltimore?"

"Who has time to get serious when you're working eighteen hours a day? And anchoring the eleven P.M. news doesn't do much for the old social life," she said dryly.

"But there are always early dinners, like tonight." He smiled. "And drinks, and things after." He paused, gathering courage. "And if you don't like Baltimore, I know I can get you a job in Pittsburgh or Washington."

She sidestepped the direction in which he was pointing her. "Alan, you're misreading me. I love Baltimore and I love my job. I even love my boss."

"Oh, no," Alan groaned. "Welcome to Wilkes-Barre."

"No way. You'll see when you meet Paul. You're the one he'd fall in love with that way, not me."

Marlena returned to her safe topic, life in Baltimore, concluding with, "There's only one thing that I don't have here that I had in Wilkes-Barre and Philadelphia that I miss—and that's Madame."

"Whatever happened to Madame?"

"Dognapped by my own father. When I left Philadelphia under my black cloud I drove to Des Moines with Madame. Then, when I took this job, I left Madame at home until I was settled. By then my dad and Madame had fallen in love. It's a cruel person who stands in the way of true love. But I do miss her."

"Whatever happened to that lawyer you were so hot on?"

"When?"

"You know, the source that Andy burned on that Cherry Hill murder thing."

"Will." For a moment Marlena forgot she'd unburdened her soul to Alan about the disaster. Then it all came back and she smiled. "I remember your offering to go punch Andy out for being such a bastard. You wanted to defend my honor. The mission I should have sent you on, speaking of 'that lawyer,' was to go to Will and find out why he never answered my letter."

She reached out to push some soft wax closer to the candle's flame. "It never should have ended the way it did." She shook off the old sadness and quipped, "He doesn't write, he doesn't call, he doesn't send flowers."

"Wrong joke," Alan said. "And if you'd have asked me to play go-between, I'd have been a John Alden." He turned the conversation around again. "Lena, I can speak for myself now. I'm not in my hungry twenties anymore. Neither of us is getting any younger."

"But I am. I'm only twenty-six. Paul doctored my official IBS records as a birthday present."

"Tell that to your obstetrician. It's dangerous to put off having kids. We did a special on birth defects last fall. The longer you wait, the higher the risk."

"Alan, I'm sorry. I should have told you that I'm in love with someone else here, but I can't talk about it."

He stared at her, looking like a wise young owl. "I hope you're not mixed up in another lousy situation. I'd hate to see you get hurt again."

"That's not the worst thing that can happen to a person, Alan. I look at other women who hide behind scars from bad relationships, walls around their hearts so they can't ever be hurt again. But they'll never be able to feel real joy either. I'd rather take the chance of getting hurt than take the chance of getting numb."

"He must be some guy," Alan said, not hiding his disappointment.

"I think this time there's a real chance that it could work, but things have to change first."

"It sounds like he's married."

She chewed on her lower lip, looking away from Alan. "That can be messy."

"You're telling me?" She lifted her head and smiled.

"Lena, if it doesn't work out, call me. Don't wait until I call you."

"Come on, I've got to get to work tonight."

She kept Alan busy talking about the people he worked with as they turned onto the overpass above downtown Baltimore and headed to the hills beyond the bay where the TV towers stood in electronic vigil.

Alan had matured a lot, Marlena thought as she introduced him to Paul and Babs and the WIMD-TV family. The awkwardness of old was gone. He was more comfortable with himself, more willing to let his quick mind show.

"Nice guy." Paul winked as he left for the controlroom. She took it as a compliment to herself as well as to Alan. She'd almost forgotten how pleasant it was to be able to share a man with friends. Maybe Alan wasn't such a bad ace in the hole.

The show ran smoothly until Marlena had to introduce a piece about a breakout from the Baltimore county jail. As she finished the lead-in, indicating the three escapees were still at large, she finished: "Here with more on what happened at the jail today is Ellen Considine."

Two seconds later the jingle "You deserve a break today" echoed in the studio, as the trainee engineer rolled the McDonald's commercial instead of the cut piece Ellen had put together earlier.

Marlena didn't dare look at anyone else's face in the studio until the "on air" light blinked off and the whole place exploded with laughter.

"What a lead-in for McDonald's!"

"You deserve a break today, from the jailhouse." Paul sang his version of the McDonald's jingle as he danced out of the controlroom.

"Live television." He wiped away his tears of laughter. "There's nothing like it."

"It's never as funny in the retelling," Alan agreed. "You have to be there to see the horror on the director's face."

"How about the obscenities in your ear?" She winked at Paul. "I'm taking my friend out of this place of ill repute."

"Want to join me for drinks?" asked Paul. "Bernie's already at the pub."

"Oh, Paul, sorry, I've got to get home," she said with double regret. Why did she have to fall in love with a man she had to keep under a rock?

They crossed the dark lawn to the parking lot and Marlena returned to her safest topic with Alan, baseball.

"I have a confession to make, Alan. I'm now a complete convert to the Orioles. I bought three orange outfits last year, just for the Birds."

"I can't hold it against you for deserting the Boston Red Sox. That was your team, wasn't it? The one that Cincinnati chewed up and spit out in the World Series?"

"It was a freak series. How many times has a sixth game

been postponed three times because of rain? Anyway, we won that game on Carlton Fisk's homer in the twelfth. So we lost it in the seventh game. That's not chewed up, that's squeaked out."

"Sure you're not still a Sox fan?"

"Not until the Orioles are out of the race."

"I never did know why you were such an avid Red Sox fan. You're not from Boston."

"My dad is. He tells a story about when he was a little boy in Boston. His father used to take him into the cathedral to light votive candles for the Red Sox before every home game. And they weren't even Catholic."

"Sounds apocryphal to me." Alan laughed as he watched Marlena maneuver her navy Mercedes down the long, curved drive to swing out onto the main road.

"Nice car," he said.

She cut off the main road onto a narrow side street that wound down a hill. "Doesn't have the same character as the old one."

"You were quite a sight driving around Wilkes-Barre with Toby hanging out of one side and Madame the other," he said. "You really should have a kid of your own, you know."

As they approached a sharp corner, headlights glared in the rear window, coming too fast. She stopped listening to Alan as the lights swung left as though to pass them, then swerved right, toward Marlena's side. It was a big, dark car.

"Look out!" she shouted, veering right toward the embankment as she felt the impact and fought to control the wheel as they went into a spin. Her foot jammed on the brake in a reflexive action. She felt herself being thrown forward.

"Lena! Lena!" Alan's voice sounded distant, urgent, as if from a thousand miles away. "Lena!" She felt him shaking her and she forced her eyes to focus on his face. He looked stunned, white with fear.

"What's wrong?"

"Blood. On your face," he gasped. Her fingers moved up, reaching the source of the stickiness, a gash on her forehead. "Nothing serious." She accepted Alan's handkerchief and dabbed at the blood.

"We better get you to a hospital."

"No, I'll be all right, but what about the car?" She stared out the windshield at the dark bank beyond the reach of the headlights. They were angled pointing down.

"We'll see," Alan said grimly. "Be careful getting out. We're near the edge."

She shivered. "Another couple of feet and . . ."

"You'd better forget about this short cut. Let's see if this buggy will still run. All right if I drive?"

"Mmm." She'd taken this back road hundreds of times. No one used it except locals. No one ever sped. It was too winding. Her car was unique in the area, easy to follow. She didn't want to think further.

"Drunken drivers," Alan muttered as he inched the car back, away from the precipice. The engine purred, seeming no worse for the trauma. "I've been thinking about doing a series on drunken drivers. Now I'm going to get cracking on it."

"Good idea," she said, not moving her eyes from the road as Alan navigated the bridge intersection. Thanks to Albie, she had added a lot of fuel to the fires that had burned a big handful of local politicians. Had it been a drunken driver?

When they reached the main highway Alan wanted to take her to the emergency room. She refused, insisting that he take her home. But she carefully debriefed him on every detail he remembered about the incident.

He volunteered to sleep on her couch, play guardian angel, but she'd have none of it. Despite the horrible headache now throbbing behind her left eye, she packed him off with a promise that if she started feeling worse, she'd call him. And she agreed to have breakfast with him in the morning, since he was being such a worrywart.

With Alan gone, she relaxed enough to feel the full force of the pain building behind her forehead. Aspirin. The bright kitchen light glared at her as she fumbled, knocking down tins of tarragon and rosemary in her search.

The phone rang, hurting her head with it's loud insistence.

"You're home!" Albie sounded relieved.

"Sure. I'm alone, if that's what's worrying you."

"No, it's not that. I just wanted to check and see if you were okay."

"Not entirely. I have a beast of a headache." She was about to explain when she realized he might be of more immediate help. "Did you move the aspirin from the kitchen?"

"No, but there are some in my navy blazer, the inside pocket," he said. "I'll be home in fifteen minutes, okay?"

"Okay." She hung up the phone, found the aspirin, and returned to the kitchen.

Everything felt like slow motion, soft and blurred, except the pain in her head. She sat down at the kitchen table, fighting nausea. Long moments later her stomach calmed enough for her to try taking the aspirin. Milk. Milk might help. It was hard to swallow. She choked and coughed while she fought another wave of nausea.

"Hello! I'm home!" Albie called from the hall, like Dagwood in a TV sitcom.

"Albie . . ." A weak cry for help.

As she turned, she saw his face go pale with concern. Then she crumpled to the floor.

Albie carried her to the bedroom. Still in his tie and jacket, he sat beside her, holding a cool, wet towel to her head. "Hi," she whispered.

His eyes narrowed in concern. "Lena, tell me what happened. The gash on your head . . ."

"It was an accident . . . I think. Alan thought . . . drunk drivers . . . crazy . . . at the turn."

"When did it happen? You sounded all right when I called from the road."

"Mmm. I wasn't so dizzy yet. But it was before . . . on the way home from the station. I didn't think it was so bad."

"Try to tell me exactly what happened. Where and when."

"You forgot who," she murmured.

"Lena, it's important. Start from the moment you left the station."

Pushing for alertness, she stumbled through, describing the back route and the turn, the glaring headlights bearing down and swinging left as though to pass, then veering right, forcing her off the road.

"Did you get a look at who was in the car?"

"No, I was fighting to stay on the road. The car was big and dark. Alan's guess was a late-model Lincoln. He saw two men in the front seat. The driver was big, young, and blond. He thought the other guy was short and dark, but it happened so fast. He couldn't get the license."

The puzzlement in Albie's eyes was swept away by a sudden dark anger. "Damn," he hissed as his hand formed a hard fist and clutched the towel he'd used to bathe her head.

"Who is it? You know. I can see it. Was it deliberate? Tell me!" Tears dimmed her already blurred vision as she reached for his hand. "Please, Albie, I need to know."

"I'll take care of it," he said tersely.

Her mind reeled as she tried to think, to stay above the rising pain and bile. Brader? With Albie's help she'd burned at least a half dozen others. But hurting her couldn't stop stories that had run months and months before. Unless, of course, the motive was vengence.

The doorbell rang. A shadow of apprehension passed from him to her. "Let's hope it's the doctor."

"The doctor?" She hadn't called any doctor.

"I called him while you were out. Out cold, that is."

Dr. Salvatore Marone strode in on short legs with a bantam cock's assurance. His very roundness seemed tidy and reassuring. "Caught me on the way home from the hospital, Senator," he greeted them cheerfully. "I knew I was in trouble the moment you gave me that car phone for Christmas." He chuckled.

The round pink face looked familiar to Marlena. As Albie introduced doctor and patient, she realized he was chief of staff at St. Elizabeth's Hospital, the old-guard society institution. Was he safe for Albie? But she knew he wouldn't have been called otherwise. They had to be friends. Marone? It could be Italian. Where did the doctor fit on Albie's family tree?

The portly doctor interrupted her thoughts to ask the medical questions and check her pupils, pulse, and temperature. "Shock," he reported to Albie. "And at the very least a concussion."

"The bastards," Albie hissed.

Marone ignored Albie's response and patted Marlena's hand. "Young lady, we have to get you to the hospital tonight to find out how hard that pretty little head really is."

Albie nodded. "Best room. Best everything. Take care of it, Sal."

Marone reached for the telephone. "Don't worry. I'm a great fan of Miss Williams'."

Replacing Marone by her bedside, Albie stroked her cheek. "If you file a police report on this, it'll be headline time. There'd be an investigation that could get messy depending on who handles it."

"What do I say?" She frowned, then winced as the frown irritated the gash on her forehead. "Slipped and fell in the bathroom?"

"Good a story as any."

"What about Alan?"

"Would he raise a stink if you told him you didn't want the publicity?"

"No." Albie was asking if Alan would lie for her. Dear, faithful Alan. The tangled web was reaching into the last clean corners of her world.

"Hey. It's going to be all right. I promise." Albie leaned down to kiss away her tears.

She looked past the blur of Albie's shoulders at Dr. Marone, patiently waiting beside the phone. "Who was it, Albie?" she whispered with a cold shiver of fear.

"I think it was just meant to be a scare. I'll know soon, but in the meantime I promise you'll be safe."

Marone cleared his throat behind them. "Albie, the ambulance will be here in about five minutes. It could be sooner."

"Still taking care of me, Sal." Albie stood and put his hands on his old friend's shoulders. "Right now I want you to worry about taking care of Marlena. I wish I could stay," he said softly, to both of them and to himself.

Then he was gone and Dr. Salvatore Marone played ladies' maid, helping Marlena pack and chatting about growing up with Albie in the slums of Baltimore as he pulled things out of drawers. "We started out breaking bones and disrupting neighborhoods." He chuckled. "Now I fix bones and he organizes neighborhoods." He glanced at the ceiling. "Maybe there is ultimate justice out there."

"You're nice," she said drowsily. Marone looked like a series of zeros from her blurred perspective. His open-mouthed smile formed an 0 below his round eyes behind his round glasses, all circled by his round face.

When they heard the ambulance approach Marone stopped and turned to Marlena, speaking deliberately. "You must be more careful, Miss Williams. Slipping on a bar of soap like that is very dangerous. I think you have a concussion from hitting your head on the side of the tub. You're lucky you came to and called me." He paused, giving her time to absorb it. "Got it?"

She nodded, thinking the little round doctor who didn't miss a beat must be Albie's "family" doctor.

"They're here," he announced as the doorbell rang.

For a long second she felt very alone.

A week later she was still in the hospital. "I'm going buggy," she complained to Paul. "I don't feel that bad anymore. I don't see why I can't come home and go back to work." She scowled at the phone, listening to Paul chirp like a mother, telling her to obey the doctors and be a good girl.

She listened with half an ear, fiddling with a long-stemmed rose on her tray, one of the dozens of mounting blossoms that were threatening to take over the hospital room.

"Oh, no!" She interrupted Paul midlecture. "More flowers. I've already sent two loads over to the children's ward. I've got to go do something about this new delivery. Love you too." She made three short kissing noises at the phone and hung up.

"Who were you kissing?" asked the deliveryman, who was hidden behind a massive floral arrangement in the shape of a horseshoe, with only a green hat with BLACKIE'S FLORISTS showing above the foliage.

She would recognize that voice anywhere. "You're a crazy man." She laughed.

Albie dropped the horseshoe bouquet on the floor and closed the door. "That's better." He sat beside her on the narrow hospital bed and kissed her for one long, breathless minute, then sat up and grinned. "Can't stay long."

"Not even long enough for a fast 'nap'?"

"Can't get caught napping. I could lose my job. Blackie's a tough man to work for."

"What did you have to pay him to get hired for the day?"

"Very funny." He stepped away to view her critically. "Not bad. Still a very, very pretty lady. You don't look the worse for wear. In fact, you look more rested than you've been in months."

"A hell of a way to take a rest cure."

He stepped closer again and brushed the hair back from her forehead. "Not even much of a battle scar."

"Ah, shit. Does that mean I don't get my Purple Heart?"

"We'll have to check that with Corporal Marone."

"I'm a healer, he says. That should look good on my military record."

"And does the good doctor say I'm a heel?" Albie asked the question seriously.

"No. He doesn't discuss you."

He picked up a rose and sniffed it as he looked around. "Nice enough room."

"Not acceptable as a topic. Your cryptic reports—it won't happen again and it's under control—aren't good enough. I'm not a cub reporter."

"It's a long story and I can only stay a few minutes."

She sank back on her pillow, distancing herself. Times like this hurt the most. "The flowers are lovely. At least they don't have to be hidden."

"The flowers are only a sign of all the good things to come."

"How? Where? In dark corners with phony names? It's getting old, Albie. Maybe we're taking the wrong things from each other. Things like respect. You don't even respect me enough to tell me why I'm here."

Wordlessly, he bent to kiss her hand.

"Are you listening to me?"

He lifted his head and looked at her, his gaze reaching deep into her eyes to touch her dark thoughts without revealing his own. "I hear you."

"But do you understand me?"

She let her hand lie limp in his firm grasp, trying not to admit to her own anger. Not so much at being exposed to danger because of him, but anger that he held back so much.

She shut her eyes, not wanting to see anything less than complete candor in his.

"Tired?" he asked softly.

Her eyelids flew open, flashing cold sparks. "I'm tired of your keeping me in the dark, tired of waiting for your calls, tired of disguises, and sick and tired of mystery games."

"Poor Lena." Albie's voice caressed her. "You've every right to be angry. I'm sorry. It's my fault you got squeezed in the middle of all this."

"All what?" Tears of frustration splashed down her cheeks.

"Shhh." His embrace was warm, protective. "I won't let anything bad happen to you. I'm not sure if it's a blessing or a curse"—he punctuated his words with a soft kiss—"but I love you very much."

Her surprise stopped the tears. "Right out loud. Just like that," she said softly. "So where do we go from here?"

"Home soon, I hope."

"Will you drive me home?" she asked pointedly.

He shook his head. "But I'll be there waiting for you." His lips met hers again as the door opened and a young floor nurse entered, bearing the afternoon's apple juice and cookies.

"Hi." Marlena's cheeks turned rosy. "I was just thanking the deliveryman for all the wonderful flowers."

"I'll put this on your bed table for when you're ready." The nurse abandoned the tray with an embarrassed clatter and fled.

Albie's laugh rolled after her. "Wait until greater Baltimore learns how their number-one rated anchorwoman thanks deliverymen. You'll be swamped with flowers." He grinned.

He leaned down to resume kissing her.

"First the nurse, then the doctor," Marlena announced.

Albie shook his head in warning, grabbed the florist's clipboard, and lowered his head. "Please sign here, ma'am," he drawled in a phony Southern accent, his back to the door.

Marlena waved. "Doctor, would you please sign for me? Just in case there's a bomb hidden in the roses?"

Marone stared at Albie's back for a moment and shook his head. "I thought you were better, Miss Williams, but it appears you're becoming paranoid."

Albie turn to Marone with a shit-eating grin.

"You're a crazy man." Marone chuckled. Then he sobered, and looked from Albie to Marlena and back. "You're also playing with fire."

Albie shrugged. "So I'll wear rubber pants to bed. The alert's off, Sal. Tony's back in Italy. Nobody's going to get hurt anymore."

Marlena frowned. "Tony? Who's Tony?"

Both men ignored her.

"There are a lot of ways people can get hurt, Albie. And a lot of people."

"Lena, have you met my conscience?" Albie's laugh was defensive. "Completely self-appointed, I might add."

"Without me," said Marone, "the senator wouldn't have lived to see his sixteenth birthday."

"I can't ever forget that." Albie winked at his old friend. "This bastard won't let me."

"And now, Senator Deliveryman, I strongly suggest you get the hell out of here so I can examine my patient."

"A born bully. People never change." Albie donned the green Blackie's hat and added cheap dark glasses to complete the disguise.

"It's my hospital, remember?" Marone folded his arms across his round stomach like an impatient Buddha.

"All yours, Sal?" Albie winked at Marlena. "Then I should forget about donating the new scanner you want?"

"Albie, get out of here before you do something dumb, or should I say dumber?" Marone said cheerfully.

Albie walked back to Marlena, leaned down and kissed her, a soft, lingering kiss without embarrassment at Marone's presence. A husband's kiss, Marlena thought with a twinge of loss as he straightened and asked Marone when she could go home.

"Medically, she can leave now. You can call the shots from here, Senator."

"Then tomorrow it is." Albie smiled brightly, waved, and left.

"Dr. Marone," Marlena spoke as the doctor approached, "What's going on? Why ten days one second and tomorrow the next? And who's Tony?"

"There's nothing wrong with your ears." He pulled out his stethoscope, looking at her. His round eyes were so dark a brown that the pupils and iris blended, making them impossible to fathom. "You might as well call me Sal," he said with a sigh, "since it's all in the family."

"I won't ask if that's a pun."

He chuckled and picked up her wrist.

"So, Sal. You haven't answered my questions."

Marone counted her pulse beats before replying. "Let the senator explain it his own way, Marlena."

Albie might call Salvatore Marone his conscience, Marlena thought, but he was obviously Albie's man.

He released her wrist and leaned inches above her to beam a narrow light into the back of her eyes.

"You love him?" He asked matter-of-factly.

"Yes. I love him." It felt good to say it aloud.

He snapped off the light. Backlit by the window, his round shape took on a mysterious air with his head haloed by sunlight, his expression unreadable. "I'm afraid he loves you too."

"Afraid?"

"For you. For him. Loving you puts him at risk."

"What do you mean by risk?"

"Albie made a hard choice a long time ago. And you aren't part of that. You're from a different world, and that's dangerous for him. It should also be obvious by now to a bright young lady like yourself that it's risky for you too."

"You mean I could end up in a hospital," she said dryly.

"Love is such a strange, selfish emotion. People have lost kingdoms for it, even died for it. And what good does that do?" He pulled a red rose from the vase. "Maybe it does some good. Keeps florists in business."

He handed her the rose. "But then, so do funerals, don't they?"

Her blond curls tumbled across her cheeks as she leaned down to sniff the dark red flower. "Achew!" She dropped the rose on the white bedspread. "You're quite the Pollyanna, aren't you, Dr. Sal? Why are you trying to scare me off?"

He sat heavily on the chair beside the bed. "Maybe I'm getting old, suffering from the urge to meddle while I call it advice, or God forbid, wisdom." He paused to light her cigarette. "To me, love means having a deep concern for the well-being of the person you love. Sometimes it takes more love and strength to let go than it does to hold on—once you recognize that you're bad for the one you love."

She held tight to the rose stem without thorns. "What kind of a conscience are you for him?" She needed to strike back for the unwanted advice. "How can you preach about good and bad? Doesn't it bother you to buy equipment with family money? Why don't you open a drug clinic and really cash in?"

"You're really something." He spoke with mixed admiration. "There's a perverse humor to the thought." He chuckled, rising.

"It's not funny. It's sick."

"Sick. Well. Good. Bad. It's not simple and it really can't be summed up in a minute and ten seconds as you TV people might like. Albie's a good man who's needed right where he is, the way he is, whether you accept that or not." He tucked his equipment in his pockets and took her hand, like an uncle. "It isn't easy for him, Marlena. He has a lot on his shoulders, too much. But he's human. And I look at you and I worry about him."

"My mother would look at him and worry about me," she replied, fighting back tears at his sympathetic rejection.

"I'm worried about you too." He patted her hand. "And all the rest of us. Nobody ever guaranteed that love—or life— would always be easy."

At three o'clock the next afternoon Marlena, still feeling a little wobbly, followed Mario the doorman and her suitcase to the door of her apartment.

Albie stepped out into the hallway, arms wide open. "Welcome home!"

"Aren't you taking a risk?" Marlena asked as Albie closed the door with a wave to Mario.

"There are limits even to my cowardice." He grinned. "Mario's on our team."

Payoffs everywhere. Her jaded thoughts were pushed back as his arms closed around her and she held tight, wanting all distance to end.

"Poor baby." He kissed her forehead. "How about my tucking you in bed for a *backrub*?"

"First we have to talk." She headed for the kitchen. The living room was too dim and formal. She wanted the cherry sunlight and openness of the kitchen, with its hanging baskets of begonias and spider plants.

"Hungry?" he asked, following her into the kitchen.

"Starved. The hospital food was dreadful." She looked at him, testing. "Let's go out for steamers and crabs."

"Aren't you supposed to be lying low?"

"I'm tired of lying low," she said pointedly.

"I'm talking medically."

"I'm not." The silence thickened when he didn't respond. She sat down at the butcher-block table and stared out at the walled garden. Walls and more walls.

"I made fresh coffee. Would you like a cup?"

"Please." She turned a pale face to him as he poured the coffee and sat down across from her. "Albie, who ran me down and why?"

"It's not a pleasant story."

"It wasn't a pleasant accident. Who?"

"My brother-in-law Tony, Sophia's brother."

"But I thought . . . she . . . was an only child." Marlena hated giving Sophia substance by saying the name aloud.

"He's a half brother, Anna Maria's second marriage."

Marlena frowned. "But Spadoro said Anna Maria only had one child, Sophia. That you were the only available heir."

Albie frowned. "Hasn't Spadoro's promotion come through yet? I thought he'd be in Los Angles by now."

She didn't like the insight his words gave her. Pat had mentioned he'd turned down an offer. "But, Albie"—her pulse quickened as her mind raced—"do you realize what you say means there's a real grandson who could take over the business?"

Albie coughed, choking on his coffee.

She held her breath, waiting for him to catch his while her old dreams threatened to take on new life.

"Lena, Tony's crazy, seriously crazy. He's living out

some kind of fantasy. He watches *The Godfather* movies on his Betamax over and over, and plays the score for background music in Sicily."

"He lives in Sicily? With Scaffaro? What does he do? Is he involved? Why's he such a mystery man?"

"This won't work piecemeal. Let me back it up a little so you can understand. When DeGenore, Sophia's father, died Anna Maria was independent for the first time in her life. She discovered a wild streak and became a very merry widow, too merry for Grandfather's tastes. So he took little Sophia away to America with him to shelter her from Anna Maria's *La Dolce Vita* scenarios. He put her in exclusive boarding schools, spent vacations with her, sparing no love or money. She became . . ."

Marlena couldn't help feeling sympathy for Sophia, who'd probably been given no say in the arrangements. She interrupted, not wanting to hear more. "So where does Tony come in?"

"I'm getting to that. Meanwhile, Anna Maria fell for a gigolo named Antonio Verdi. Grandfather found out and bought Verdi off the day after the wedding, but by then Tony was already on the way. Obviously, they couldn't use the name DeGenore, and Grandfather didn't want young Tony called Verdi, so he chose Cadonne, in honor of his favorite dead cousin."

"Cadonne. The unconnected name. That's why we missed him on the family tree."

"Nice to know we did something right. We work hard to keep him off it." Albie grimaced.

"Tony argues for his blood rights," he continued, "but he's unstable. He's gotten mixed up with some young renegades in Sicily who are trying to restage *The Godfather* with coke as well as heroin."

She frowned. It sounded nasty.

"We're looking for a legitimate business for Tony. I told

Grandfather the kid would be better off running pizza parlors, anything to keep him busy and out of Sicily. He's the kind who acts before he thinks, the kind who gets blown away."

"I'm more worried about his blowing someone else away—like me or you." Marlena wasn't smiling. "Why did he try to run me off the road?"

"It started last summer when a friend of Sophia's saw us together at the track in Charles Town. Of course she told Sophia, who started adding things together—my coming home fewer weeknights, all the weekends away—and suddenly her neat little world felt threatened."

"Last August." Marlena nodded. "I felt so safe and anonymous in West Virginia. I remember taking off my scarf to cheer when our horse won."

"Shiloh's Revenge. Some horse," Albie agreed. "Anyway, soon after that Grandfather sent Tony to visit us to get him away from the crowd in Sicily for a while. Tony adores his half sister. He'd do anything for her, including spy on me. I have to admit the kid has nerve, more nerve than brains."

"Did *she* tell him to run me off the road?"

"No, but she inspired it. The idea to run you down on the shortcut was all his. He swears he only meant to scare you, not hurt you. That part could be true. He's as lousy at driving as he is at everything else.

"It all started getting crazy following the City Hall dedication, when Sophia threw a tantrum because she thought you looked even lovelier in person than you do on television. Tony added fuel by reporting that I hadn't gone to Annapolis as I'd said."

"You were with me," Marlena finished, remembering her own reaction to Sophia's beauty that night. She fought feeling empathy.

"That night Tony swore he'd 'talk to me' for Sophia, to defend her honor. I should've smelled the rat Tuesday morning when Tony came to my office and demanded that I stop seeing you, or else . . ."

"What did you do?"

"I told him to keep his snotty little nose out of my business and sent him packing like a schoolboy. It got him crazier, because I didn't take him seriously. I won't make that mistake twice." Albie's eyes turned the color of dusk. "He'll never come near you again. If he even thinks about it, he's looking at his own funeral."

The words grated in her mind, a phrase from a B movie.

"There won't be any more problems," Albie added.

"No more problems?" She blazed with anger. "We live like goddamn moles stealing little rays of sunlight from your unreal gangster world and you say no problems? What kind of a life can we have this way?"

"Things will be different. Tony's taken care of and Sophia won't cause any more trouble."

"No more trouble? Our whole relationship is a walking time bomb for both of us as long as you're what you are." She closed her eyes, half praying. "You say you love me."

"I love you." All statement.

"Then why won't you divorce the whole Scaffaro connection?"

"Oh, Dorothy, you can't go back to Oz."

"We could live like real people, walk into movies together, have friends over for dinner. We could even have a baby."

He paused unhappily, watching a tear slide down her cheek. "You think I wouldn't like that?"

"Is it the money?"

"No. Maybe in the beginning. Not now. How can you understand? You're from such a different world."

"Try. And I'll try."

"Some pledges are sacred. If I broke my word to Grand-father, I'd be a Brutus, the worst kind of Brutus."

"And if Caesar were gone?"

"I'll forget you said that." His voice was icy. "I owe him more than respect, Lena. He's the reason I'm where I am. Without him who knows where I'd have ended up. Or Sal Marone, for that matter. Grandfather knocked our heads together as young punks and kept us out of jail. And after Korea he sent Sal to medical school and me to law school."

"Whatever happened to the GI bill?"

"I told you you wouldn't understand."

"I'm sorry." She sighed. "I didn't mean to interrupt."

"When I graduated from law school," he continued to plead his case, "Grandfather was prouder than my own father. He gave me his trust, his respect, an important role in his affairs, and eventually his most precious gift . . . his only grand-daughter."

Marlena couldn't help wondering if the young woman who'd been "given" had been given any say in the matter. "Did she love you? Did you love her?"

"It wasn't a question of love. It was a question of respect."

"Albie, listen to yourself, how twisted the reasoning is."

Silently, Albie rose to refill his coffee cup. Without asking, he filled hers too. She accepted the cup and took a black sip, feeling emotionally battered.

"Looking back, I don't think I was in love with her." He looked at Marlena across his cup, eyes narrowed. "I'd fallen in love with power."

"A dark, dirty power."

"Lena, it's not that bad. Sure, Scafarro started out rough in Prohibition days, like a lot of families. Booze, numbers, prostitution, all the classic stuff. When Prohibition ended he set up a liquor distributorship and half his business became legal."

"And half didn't."

"One of the reasons Grandfather sent me to law school was to learn how to put the family profits into legitimate businesses, but the old guard didn't want to let go of the rackets. That's when we tightened the organizational structure and developed security." He grinned at her. "Our security's the best. I don't think you could document what I'm telling you."

"The bright young lawyer applies the techniques of modern management and military intelligence to the rackets."

"Don't get cute. It cleaned it up. The old guard respect me and, knock on wood, except for Tony, I can control the young mavericks. I'm the bridge, in a way."

"How noble you make it sound. It's bullshit, Albie. I've read the files. The Scaffaro family isn't laundering money with Ivory Snow, and Annapolis isn't called the Marseille of Maryland because of the French cafés!"

"Do you know what it'd be like without agreements and controls?"

"So you admit you control it."

"Dammit, that's not the issue."

"No?"

"There's control, but not like you think. We don't run drugs or deal or profit from them. We do what the cops can't—control the families that do. Lena, you don't know the hell that can break loose if control is dropped the wrong way."

"Bullets fly in family wars in New York and Philadelphia, but not in Baltimore or Annapolis," she protested.

"Maybe that's because Maryland is run better."

She slapped her hands over her ears. "No, it's all wrong for you. You're better than that. You're a good senator, Albie. Isn't that enough? Let Scaffaro find another bloody bridge for his slimy organization."

"What if it's been mine for over fifteen years?"

She lowered her face into her hands.

"Lena, you have the wrong idea of what it means to head family interests. It's like being chairman of a corporate board."

She looked up, pale. "It's frightening to think you really believe that."

"Remember that first night?" Albie measured her steadily.

"Every moment."

"You said that you could learn to hate me and I answered, 'Better you should learn to love me.' Maybe I was wrong."

Her fingertips stretched across the butcher-block table to touch his lips and silence. "It's too late for that. I love you, but I don't know what that means right now." Suddenly she needed air, fresh air. She stood and slid open the garden door.

Before she could step outside he stopped her, turning her around to face him. "I know it isn't fair, but I love you and I need you."

He was right. It wasn't fair.

As Albie carried her into their bedroom, she remembered a conversation with her mother. "Nobody ever said loving is easy," Maggie had said. "Both of you have to compromise sixty percent of the time to make it work." Maggie had been talking about Tom at the time. Marlena wondered what Maggie would say about Albie. Maggie might not approve of both needing to compromise a hundred percent all the time.

Flowers and a huge WELCOME BACK sign greeted her in the WIMD office a week later. They made her feel more unworthy. If Paul knew the truth—the whole truth—behind the accident, would he have responded with roses and welcomes?

Paul's welcoming hug was warm. He was bubbling with good news. In her absence he had persuaded the general manager to approve the request for money to buy computer time. Her proposal for an in-depth statistical investigation of Maryland's judicial system had been approved by all.

"Good news directors, like good reporters," Paul preened as he spoke, "never give up. I know it's been eighteen months since you drafted the proposal, but I told you I'd get it through and I did."

"That's wonderful, Paul." She forced enthusiasm.

"Take it at your own pace. I don't want you pushing yourself until you feel a hundred percent."

"I'll have to read it again," she said. "I thought it had been lost and forgotten—at least I had forgotten."

"Then it's time to remember. It's a damn good proposal." Paul sounded almost miffed at her admission. "And it's your reward. Since you've taken over as co-anchor for the evening news, we've become unbeatable. Number one. And the ratings have made money for WIMD, so it's only fair that you should get some spent where you want it."

"What's the timetable?"

"Early fall, in time for ratings. Can you do it by then?"

"If you want it by then, I'll get it done."

"Marlena, see how it goes. I don't want you to push yourself." Paul was being more accommodating than she'd ever seen him before. It made her feel even more like a rat.

She skimmed the ten-page proposal she'd written almost two years before to see if it still made sense. She'd proposed a three-part series, entitled "Questions of Justice, An In-Depth Analysis of Maryland's Courts."

"Segment I: Is Justice Fair?" Here she'd planned to study the Criminal Court's sentencing patterns statistically. First she'd get the average time of sentence for a specific crime for each of the judges, using all relevant cases for the past two years.

After that was fed into the computer she'd use the judges' averages to compare sentencing patterns for various crimes. She gave an example: If Judge X gave an average sentence of two to five years for breaking and entering and Judge Y's average was ten to fifteen years, it would show the system as unfair. She'd added that bail, pretrial motions, and appeals could be compared the same way.

Segment I was straightforward enough.

"Segment II: Is Justice Equal?" This was her brainstorm for seeing if an old-boy network existed and if, as rumored, it did have an effect on justice. First all available information on every judge, prosecutor, and defense attorney involved in the sample cases would be fed into the computer for cross-referencing, starting with their family trees, and going on to hobbies, clubs, schools, churches, military service, children, divorces, property, and any unusual information about relatives and associates.

Then she would look for patterns in trials, much as she would with sentencing. If lawyer X tried cases before Judge Y, did he win more often, or were the sentences softer?

Ouch, she thought. She must have been full of energy when she'd dreamed that one up. She vaguely remembered what followed.

"Segment III: Is Justice Clean?" The other sections were really background research for this final one. Here, she'd proposed drawing up a vulnerability profile: debts, divorce, problem children or relatives, problems with drugs, alcohol, promiscuity or homosexuality, illness, expensive habits, any present or previous connections with organized crime through family, friends, et cetera.

The vulnerability categories would be weighted and tabulated for each judge and prosecutor. Then trials and legal actions in which the "vulnerable" were involved would be scrutinized.

If the statistical analysis proved worthwhile, they could repeat the process in the civil courts.

"Whew." She dropped the proposal. It was more ambitious than she'd remembered. Albie could help, but she couldn't ask, not with a clear conscience. Suddenly she realized she couldn't touch this project, not until her own relationship with Albie was clear, one way or the other. Unless she wanted to become a total hypocrite.

She marched into Paul's office and laid the proposal on his desk. "I can't do it, Paul. It's too much."

He looked as if he was about to cry. "Marlena darling, I fought to get it funded for you. I love it. I want it done. If you don't do it, I'll assign it to somebody else."

"That's like taking a baby away from a welfare mother and putting it up for adoption."

"Your baby has good bones. It needs a good mother. I can understand if you don't feel up to it, darling, but you can see my side, can't you? You know how the budget people are. If they give you money for something and you don't spend it, they take it away."

Her fingertips touched the slim folder now on Paul's desk. "Paul, it's overwhelming. It's a twenty-eight-hour-a-day proposal. I can't do it on top of anchoring five days a week."

"Tell you what I'll do. I'll give you two reporters who will work on it full-time and you'll supervise. That'll cut your work load on it by at least seventy-five percent. Is that a deal?"

She nodded, not feeling good about it. Was it possible to be only twenty-five percent hypocritical?

Late that afternoon she went over the project with the young reporters Paul had assigned to her. "If you make a mistake with the facts you feed into the computer, we'll be wrong, dead wrong on the final analyses. Accuracy, my dear young friends, is the greatest antidote to potential libel." She listened to herself and found it funny that she sounded like Tom.

Segment I was scheduled to run the second week in September. To her surprise Albie found the project both fascinating and worthwhile. "There are too many judges who are hard-nosed just to create some macho images they'd like to have." She didn't describe the segments they were planning for the next year. She was hoping things would be different by then.

Following the "accident" Albie spent less time with her on Charles Street, but they spent most weekends at a small, private cottage on a remote beach near Cape May. The summer was uneventful. Albie seemed relaxed and attentive most of the time, but even as they walked barefoot along the night surf, she felt as if they were walking on spring ice. Something had to give.

Segment I of her project turned out to be a ten-part series, which they ran the last week in August and the first week in September. Paul was delighted with it, but saw red when Senator Albie Comparo introduced a bill into the Maryland Senate proposing specific guidelines for bail and sentencing, narrowing the discretionary parameters for judges.

"Trust that scumbag to cash in on other people's work. God, he moved fast. He must've had his aides working night and day to put that piece of legislation together. Marlena, have you fed all the information on Comparo into the computer yet?"

"We're working on all of it, Paul."

"I've half a notion to use my vacation to study every file I can find on him."

Marlena shuddered. That could crack the ice.

Freak circumstances rather than calculated planning are more apt to uncover things that are hidden. Things as simple as a warm night in September striking too many people as a perfect night for a ball game.

In the mid-afternoon Albie called Marlena to see if she

could get away to catch the game. She loved the spontaneity of it all and talked Babs into subbing for her without Paul's authorization, since Paul had gone to New York for meetings with the brass.

It was the bottom of the third inning, score tied one to one, when she glanced at the row behind them, turned to be certain, and struck out. There, staring at Albie's back, was Paul.

Marlena turned to Albie, "Please," she spoke with soft urgency, "let's go out and get some crab cakes."

"Not now. Wait until the inning's over."

She stared straight ahead, trying to watch the game, not noticing that the inning had ended, score still tied. She was startled to feel Albie's lips nuzzle her ear. "I love baseball games with you. But then, I love everything with you, around you, about you, in you . . ." he teased.

She could sense Paul leaning forward, ears tuned. As far as she knew, he'd never met Albie face to face. Maybe she could bludgeon her way through. She looked behind her again, pretending surprise as she looked first at Bernie and then at Paul.

"Paul! Bernie!" she exclaimed as she made a mess out of the introduction to George Horn.

Paul, with the pained look of a betrayed lover hardening his eyes, knowingly punished her by switching from George to Albert to George while discussing Palmer's chances for the Cy Young Award.

Bernie, unconscious as ever, gushed that he loved Marlena's series. "The title, 'Is Justice Fair in Maryland,' I love it. Of course, I've told Paul for ages and ages that everything's fixed in Maryland. It's about time you people looked into it."

"Maybe Mr. *Horn* could put a word in with his representative in the state legislature, Bernie," Paul said.

"Oh." Bernie looked at Albie and then back at Paul, frowning. "How do you know he can do that?"

"Everyone in Maryland's supposed to have a representative."

Bernie looked puzzled. "You're in a weird mood again, Paul."

"Why don't you run get us all crab cakes, Bernie? My treat." Paul handed Bernie money.

"No, you won't." Marlena dug in her pocket for loose bills. "We'll pay." But Bernie was already gone.

"Well, senator," Paul said. "I must say this is a surprise."

"It's been a long time, Paul. I'm glad to see that you're looking so well."

"I didn't think you cared."

Now it was Marlena's turn to be puzzled. "I didn't think you two knew each other."

"Paul used to be a press aide for a friend of mine, way back when in my first term as a representative."

Paul didn't comment.

"Paul?" She frowned.

"I'm sure you'll hear about it later," Paul said.

Albie smiled at her and patted her hand, one of his it's-all-right pats. "Watch the game," he said easily.

Bernie returned with the crab cakes, and Paul focused his attention on the game, not saying another word to Marlena or Albie.

Marlena barely noticed when Reggie Jackson blasted a homer in the fifth inning. Paul had bought the crab cake now churning in her stomach, but she knew she would pay for it in the morning.

On the way home Albie told her about his run-in with Paul. Paul had made a pass at one of Albie's assistants. The young man had politely said no and Paul hadn't pressed him, but Albie decided Paul was the wrong kind of person for the legislature and had convinced his colleague to fire Paul.

"What ever happened to freedom of speech?" She objected, defending Paul.

"What about the younger, less experienced pages?"

"But Paul didn't *do* anything. It wasn't ethical to have him fired just for asking."

"It was a question of morals, not ethics."

"I didn't know you knew the difference."

"Hey, Lena." He gave her a big hug. "Don't take it out on me because you're afraid of that aging fag. If Humphries tries to take it out on you, I can prove he does more than just ask."

"I couldn't do that, Albie. You don't understand. Paul's the most ethical newsman I know."

"If you say so, but if you need help, whistle."

She wasn't whistling as she met with Paul the next morning. It was painful for both of them. More was left unsaid than was said. He offered her the chance to fabricate an excuse. "Have you been seducing him to get inside information?"

She couldn't lie to him. She was terse but honest. Yes, Albie had been a source for a long time, but she wasn't out to burn him. She loved him. Seriously, irrevocably.

Paul didn't demand the hard choice—her job or her relationship. In light of the ratings she'd brought WIMD and the stories she'd broken, she could remain as anchor. Period.

She received an Emmy for the series on Justice, and Albie's standard sentencing bill passed before Christmas. It didn't help. She and Paul worked together as strangers. It put a pall on the entire WIMD-TV family. Marlena lost weight without dieting for the first time in her life. She had to be the one to make a move, since Paul's position was frozen.

She walked into his office right after the New Year and handed him the golden statue. "This is yours. I can't keep it."

His eyes, despite the wall, were sad as he touched the

cold metal. "I'll give it to the promotion department. They can add it to the trophy case."

"Paul. I've found another job."

He became very still. "Where?"

"Chicago."

"Is it over with him?"

"It's getting harder."

"It never was easy, was it?"

She blinked back tears.

"Maybe Chicago will help," Paul's voice softened.

"Maybe. Paul?" She took a deep breath. "Don't go gunning for him after I'm gone. Please."

"I dropped the project already, Lena." He paused thoughtfully. "Not for his sake. He's still a bastard. But for yours."

"I love you, Paul." The tears were silent and honest.

"Oh, you say that to all the girls." He stood to hug her hard. "Come back to see me. The crab cakes are lousy in Chicago."

Eleven

HANDS REACHED IN FRONT of her and removed the empty plate. Wordlessly, Manuel, the head waiter, whisked away invisible crumbs from the white linen.

"Did you enjoy the crab?" Roger asked.

"Wonderful! Your selections were superb." She hadn't the slightest idea what it had tasted like. She had been lost in her old time warp, losing the pleasure of the present. She could have been eating diet Jell-O as her mind masticated the age-old dish of rue.

"Hi!" Roger winked at her, pulling her more solidly into the present. "You went away. What were you thinking of?"

"Old trophies and awards." That much was true. "But as I tell the young reporters, you're only as good as your last story and you're always best remembered for your worst story."

Roger turned to wave at the waiter. "That's enough to make a person stop telling stories."

"I'm sorry, I didn't hear you. Come again?"

"I can't remember coming the first time today."

She listened to his laugh, deep and masculine. It was too nice, too practiced. Ever confident, he ordered black coffee for both of them.

He didn't give her time to drift back into her thoughts as he ran his finger lightly from her wrist to her shoulder, making the soft, fine hairs stand on end. The tiny goose bumps rising on the soft skin inside her upper arm belied her cool expression. She chided herself for taking off her jacket.

"You shouldn't talk about young reporters that way."

He leaned away to make room for the busboy to pour coffee.

"How should I talk about them?" she asked.

"When you say 'young reporter' like that, it sounds like you think of yourself as an 'old' reporter."

"What should I say? 'Short-in-tooth' reporter?"

"How about inexperienced?"

"Making me old and experienced," she retorted.

"There's nothing wrong with experience. I'm all for having lots of experiences." Roger paused a second, then chuckled at the expression on her face. "I said experiences, not affairs. It would be like living a thousand extra lives. You get a chance to look inside other life-styles, places, issues."

"For brief moments and usually on the outside. Sometimes I think reporters are emotional parasites, feeding off other people's tragedies. We're the modern version of the old maiden aunt telling other people how to raise children."

She didn't see the emotional curve coming as Roger said easily, "Don't you miss having children?"

She wasn't prepared. She cleared her throat, taking time to form an answer. What would he do if she said, "Not since the abortion I had before taking the job in Wilkes-Barre." But that wasn't true. She'd missed children ever since she'd left Toby behind. So she answered honestly. "Yes. I do, but the circumstances were never right. When the man was right the timing was wrong, and vice versa."

Roger looked serious. She wasn't sure she liked that, so she pulled out her favorite anecdote on the subject of having children, a nice, safe Alan story.

"What are you smiling at?" Roger asked.

"I was thinking about the time, a couple of years ago, when I decided I needed a baby. Prince Charming hadn't shown up yet on the Loop in Chicago, so I approached it logically."

"Ran an ad?" Roger joined in the lighter mood.

"Not quite. You've known the kind of guy who always comes in second, the male version of the girl who's always the bridesmaid."

"The guy who's always the usher, you could say. They always wore glasses." He winked. "Now I guess they're the guys who are always under tables at parties, looking for a contact lens."

"You've got the picture. Mine was Alan, dear, sweet Alan, who'd been the bright young news director at WWKB-TV way back when. And no matter where I moved he always stayed in touch, always let me know he was still on hold."

"So you called this Alan and said you wanted to have a baby?"

"I wasn't quite that cold about it." She smiled. "But I did call and ask him to come to Chicago for the weekend. I told him it was important, but I didn't tell him what was on my mind. I guess I wanted to see if I'd get cold feet face to face."

"Did you?"

"A red face is more like it. But you'll ruin my punch line." She waited a beat and went on. "Alan loves practical jokes and I was feeling reckless, probably nervous about the decision I'd made. When Alan called and told me what plane he was taking from Pittsburgh to Chicago, I got a really dumb idea for a joke. I decided to fly to Pittsburgh and really surprise him at the gate, then fly back with him to Chicago."

"That's not so dumb. I'd like to be surprised that way, by you."

"Not the way I surprised Alan—and myself. There I was, positioned right by the security check Alan would have to pass through on the way to the gate."

"What did he say?"

"The scene never played. Alan arrived with a sweet young thing in her midtwenties. And the good-bye kiss he gave her was definitely not brotherly."

"Terrific," Roger said.

"It got worse. Before I could turn away, Alan saw me. I don't know who was more embarrassed. I muttered something and ran."

"Did the girl notice?"

"I didn't stick around to find out. I disappeared, then had Alan paged and told the Chicago meeting had been canceled. I was totally humiliated. I flew home and went on a shopping spree to convince myself I didn't need a man to supply diamonds and furs." She remembered the feeling of perverse satisfaction at writing a $7800 check for the diamond now glittering on her left hand.

"So, thanks to Alan, you gave up men in Chicago?"

"Or vice versa," she retorted airily. "Chicago can be cold and lonely in winter, and hot and lonely in summer, but it's not bad if you're working thirty-hour days." She fingered her diamond.

"All I know about Chicago is what the song says," Roger began to sing.

Marlena's thoughts slipped back to the city that had been both a personal and professional crossroad.

Chicago

Marlena had gone to Chicago hoping for a fresh, clean start as a reporter. But in the beginning there was little opportunity for real reporting. "Eyes on Chicago," the local talk show she hosted, required long hours skimming books written by touring chefs, animal trainers, how-to experts, and how-not-to confessors.

She scripted questions for her own interviews and wrote lead-ins to introduce other reporters' stories as co-anchor of the weekend news. Her work had all the depth of a water lily.

The schedule made a new social life difficult. Starting at six A.M. Monday, she taped two half-hour interview shows. Tuesday and Wednesday she was technically off, reviewing a pile of books and bios. Thursday she taped two more shows. Then on Friday morning she did a live fifteen-minute news interview in the middle of an hour show, "Cooking in Chicago." Weekends, she co-anchored.

Her second hope, that the distance would pressure Albie to either commit or let her go, was equally frustrated that first year in Chicago. Albie loved the new arrangement. He flew out frequently and called her luxury apartment overlooking the lake the safe house.

But there were good times for them in Chicago. Albie's midweek visits were the best, when she wasn't on call.

Albie valued Marlena's thoughts on policy. At her urging, he became an advocate for children's rights, softened his antiabortion position, and sponsored a bill for heavier sentences to discourage drug dealers peddling to children.

She appreciated his spending hours critiquing "Eyes on Chicago" with her, brainstorming on program ideas.

Although he no longer hid his role in the underworld, he no longer used her to plant stories. He openly regretted the personal and professional conflicts he'd caused her in Baltimore. She forgave him more easily than she forgave herself.

Still, it was clear to her that their goals were as far apart as their cities. Marlena wanted Albie as a full-time husband, while he was content with the weekend romance. It wasn't all bad, but it wasn't enough for her.

"We finish each other's sentences, like an old married couple," Albie remarked one early autumn Wednesday in Chicago.

"Just a few documents missing," Marlena said dryly.

He turned her hand over to kiss the palm. "I feel more married to you than any paper has ever made me feel."

They sat on her terrace, looking out on the lake. Her eyes reflected mists although the sky and lake were clear and blue.

"I'm working on things, Lena, but it's a tangled mess."

"How old is Don Scaffaro?" she asked, looking at a cloud.

"He admits to seventy-five." Albie chuckled. "But that could be his TV age." He tweaked her nose in passing as he went for more ice.

"His mother's ninety-nine, alive and kicking," Albie tossed over his shoulder. "That's why 'seventy-five' is suspect. Italians married young and wasted no time in those days."

"Unlike childless WASPS pushing forty?" She couldn't help sniping at him, although every cutting word and sarcastic comment created another bittersweet good-bye, corroding her good memories.

In mid-November Albie announced he couldn't get back to Chicago until the Maryland Senate broke for the holidays.

Isolation set in. She read in a TV column that Andy Froelich had been named general manager of WIB-TV and Jill Gregson, now WIB's talk-show host, had given birth to twin boys in October. A double insult. Happy Holidays, Marlena told herself, go buy a rocking horse for your ratings.

She Christmas shopped with a vengeance. At least her family and friends could enjoy her success even if she couldn't.

On camera she managed to convey an image of high spirits and professionalism as she faked interest in her guests. It wasn't easy or fun.

During Christmas in Des Moines, Marlena was amused and touched as Maggie dragged her to a marriage encounter session, where Maggie lectured on "Loneliness," the consequences of living life alone. Trust Maggie to tuck advice for her single daughter into the middle of a talk to troubled married couples.

Bill was easier. As she drove with her father to the local kennel, the discussion centered on dogs. Only when he presented her with Gerda, a cunning three-month-old elkhound he had bred for her, did she realize he shared Maggie's concerns.

"Gerda is a sure cure for loneliness," he said. "And I've already called your apartment building in Chicago to find out if dogs are allowed. You're not the only good investigator in this family."

Nestling Gerda in her arms, Marlena kissed her family good-bye with a strange new surge of loss.

As she turned east toward Chicago on I-80, she wondered if she had turned in the right direction years before.

Staying in Des Moines had never seemed remotely reasonable, but she suddenly saw her family in a new light. They lived an emotionally secure life, open and free. How often did she hold her breath, wondering if Albie had caught the plane or if they'd been seen by the wrong people?

The small, rough tongue licked the salt from her arm where a tear had fallen. Small comfort.

A telegram from Albie was waiting at the desk for her. "Unexpected delay. More later. Always."

And less now. Always. The thought sent her stoically to paper the kitchen floor with the *Sun-Times* for her almost-trained puppy, whose nose was pressed to the glass terrace door, mesmerized by the night lights of the city.

Marlena crouched beside Gerda and followed her view, past the dark skyline to the darkness beyond that she knew to be the lake. "I agree, baby dog. This is a dumb place for a person who likes to plant seeds and bulbs. I used to have a garden, but it's gone. I'm sorry."

Liking the soft sound of Marlena's voice, Gerda licked at the salt on Marlena's cheek and nestled down beside her.

The phone rang. She didn't move, debating. Only Albie expected her tonight. How long would he persist? Her own patience ran out on the seventeenth ring.

Albie's certainty that she was home irritated her. "Lena, I'm truly sorry, but a problem came up."

"There's a problem here too," she interrupted, not wanting to hear another excuse.

"What? What's wrong?" Concern filled his voice.

"What's wrong is that I spend too much of my life alone."

"You don't know how complicated it is for me here."

"But I do and that's a problem too." She held her voice steady, but the phone was wet with tears.

"Lena, I'm as upset about the delay as you are. Just give me two days and I'll be there so we can talk things out."

"We've been talking things out for too long. We . . . I need . . ."

"Time. A little more time. Lena, just don't crowd me and I'll make it all work for us."

"Crowd you!" Her trigger fired. "God forbid I should crowd you. Look, don't hurry out here. Stay, take your time, because I don't want you to fly out. Not soon. Maybe not ever."

"Lena, you're tired and upset. You had a long drive. Get a good night's sleep and I'll call you in the morning."

"No!" she snapped. "I don't want to wait for another thing from you—not even a call. No more waiting!" she slammed the phone down, determined to cut the connection.

Door-to-door in five hours. Albie set a record, thanks to a new pilot at the Lear charter service.

As he entered the apartment, using his own key, Gerda uncurled herself from the couch, tail wagging in welcome.

"Hey, who's this?" He leaned down and picked up the wriggling but willing puppy. "You're a big girl."

Wearing a pink-flowered flannel nightie, Lena walked into the room, trying to focus. "Albie?" she gasped, incredulous.

"Introduce me," Albie demanded as Gerda licked his chin.

"Gerda the guard dog. Some guard dog," Marlena added. "A mobster bursts in and she makes a fool of herself. She's worse than her mother."

Albie chuckled and gently put Gerda down. "Where's my welcome from that mother?" He opened his arms, ignoring Gerda's yaps for more petting.

"You're insane, Albie. What time is it? How did you get here so soon?"

"I couldn't get here soon enough. I want you to believe that nothing in the world is more important to me than you. What more could you ask for?"

In slow motion she walked into his hug. "I could ask for a situation where you didn't need to get here because we were together."

There was no bravado in his response. "I love you, Lena. That doesn't change for me."

"And I love you." Her voice cracked. "But I don't see an end to this tunnel because you're not doing anything to get out."

"It's delicate. You know how long I've been involved. You think I like having to keep you hidden?"

"You know what I think? I think you want it all—the family, Sophia, the children, the State Senate, me—all of it. And you rationalize that you're a good public servant, a good public husband, a good private lover, a good father, a good godfather. It must be exhausting, being that good."

"Don't be brutal. I'm not above pain." His expression confirmed the words.

"I'm scared, Albie. I'm afraid to be honest, to show you how angry I feel, afraid I'll lose you. So I hold back and lose myself. I'm beginning to feel numb and that scares me too."

"You're nerves are stretched. What we need is some beach. The Senate is out until early February. How's your schedule?"

Beach. The thought had appeal. Maybe she could deliver the ultimatum more easily on neutral sands. "Let me think. The last two weeks in January are clear, but not before."

His face darkened. "Shit. I promised to take my children to visit Grandfather then."

"Your plans can change. You do it all the time to me."

"Can't you shift your schedule, trade vacation time?"

"Come here, Gerda," she coaxed the puppy to come away from Albie. "Here, baby dog." Gerda didn't budge from Albie's side.

"See? Gerda trusts me. She knows I'll always be back."

"It's impossible to win with you. We don't play by the same rules."

"Try a little compassion. Grandfather's getting old. He wants to see the children. Besides, you know I owe it to him."

"You owe him the way Faust owed Mephistopheles." Her eyes clouded with suspicion. "Who's going on this 'family' outing?"

His silence made it clear.

She lit a cigarette and blew smoke at him, studying him.

"You're never going to get out, Albie. She and Scafarro know every trick to twist your sense of honor to keep you right where they want you—right where you are."

Albie pulled out a cigarette, too, not looking at her.

"The last time you mentioned divorce she threatened suicide. Next time she'll swallow ten aspirin, just enough to keep you there another ten years." Marlena's voice softened with genuine surprise. "I'm beginning to believe you really aren't aware who's controlling the game."

"You may not believe me, Lena, but I feel as loyal toward you as to any of the family. I left last night, upsetting a lot of people and plans, because I knew you needed me now."

A year earlier she would have railed at his twisted logic, but now the scars added distance. "I believe you feel loyal to me in your own way, but loyalty can be divided. What I want from you can't be split as easily. I want faithfulness and commitment."

He was silent.

"Albie, if you go to Italy with her, I want you to remember one thing. I loved you. And I mean it exactly that way. It will be past tense. Loved."

"It'll work out, I promise."

Her lovemaking that night was halfhearted. Accustomed to his, her body responded while her mind churned with ultimatums. Her worst fear was that he would go and come back, as always. Old habits, and loves, were hard to break.

Fears are often self-fulfilling. But Albie returned from Italy on a cold February night to fulfill hers with a twist she hadn't anticipated.

As he recounted it to her, he had taken Georgio, his oldest son, to Italy by himself, technically living up to Marlena's ultimatum. He had convinced Sophia that she and their son needed time together.

"It was like an underwater bomb, Lena. Georgio and I had a delightful dinner with Grandfather, talking about the Sicilian underground in World War II. I could see Georgio was intrigued, but I didn't see it coming.

"After dinner we took a moonlight walk on the beach. I was only half listening to him because my thoughts were on you.

"I was thinking about how much I wanted you that moment, right there in the moonlight on the warm sand.

"I remember looking from the beach at the villa on the cliffs, thinking that Grandfather had found his peace and was denying me mine. I was building strength to confront him, to tell him I had to get out and go my own way. And then . . ."

"Then?"

"This isn't easy to tell you, Lena, because the fallout will affect 'us' as well as me."

"Don't play mystery games."

"There's no game. I'm working up to it because it changes things. But not everything, at least not easily or quickly."

She squeezed his hand hard, aware that his struggle was genuine. She willed herself to be patient, to give him the space to be honest.

"At that moment," Albie continued, "while I was thinking of you, Georgio announced he'd decided what he wanted to be when he grew up. I expected to hear lawyer, race car driver, doctor, I don't know what." Albie's face paled as he paused, the image etched in his mind. "And you know what he said?"

She shook her head, afraid to guess.

"He said he wanted to be like me and Grandfather. *Capo de tutti capi.* He said he'd analyzed it and thought he had the leadership and brains to handle the responsibility."

"Oh, my lord," she whispered. She knew too well how Albie felt about his children. I'm the first and last Comparo in the Scaffaro Family, he had said firmly.

"My son stood there, tall and proud on his grandfather's land, and pledged he would work with all his heart and soul to become 'worthy' of taking over the family when his time came."

"How did Georgio find out? You'd worked so hard to shelter him."

"Tony, that bastard Tony." Albie's outrage exploded. "Tony had filled Georgio's head with romantic images of the family business. I'd made it clear from day one that my children had to stay clean. It was part of my deal with Grandfather."

Looking into his eyes as he shared his profound distress, Marlena understood when Albie said the only way he could keep his son out of organized crime was to get out himself. This time she believed him when he said he was getting out.

She'd been right. It was possible for him to get out, but this wasn't the way she'd envisioned it. The irony confirmed her decision that the affair had to end. Not that she didn't love Albie, not that she wasn't deeply glad he was getting out. She did and she was.

"You can only give me one of two things, if you love me. Total commitment or complete freedom. It's real black or white, just like family business. All in or all out."

He protested, but he didn't offer immediate commitment.

"Albie, there's only one choice for a man who would give up control of a powerful family for the sake of his children. A man like that wouldn't give up his children for another woman."

"You're not 'another woman,' Lena. That's not fair to yourself."

But she knew she was. All that was left was to say good-bye.

That night they both laughed through the last shared passion and tears, because at the end it still sounded too much like an old Bogart movie.

"If you ever need anything, Lena, I'll be there for you."

The next morning she left for the studio before Albie had packed to catch his plane. Marlena knew he had to leave, but she didn't want to watch him go. She faced the cold winds of the gray morning and determined to turn "Eyes on Chicago" into the best talk show in the country. She refused to let Chicago be all bad for her.

Twelve

"THEY DO THINGS they don't do on Broadway . . ." Roger finished singing the line.

Marlena returned to present-time New York with a smile. "Ever dance with your wife in Chicago?"

"Not me. I wouldn't spend my hard-stolen money in Chicago."

"Chicago's not all bad. I learned to like it a lot. I did some of my best, solid reporting in Chicago, once I'd turned my lollypop talk show around." She'd almost phrased it, "Once I'd dumped my mobster boyfriend and gone straight again." She didn't feel like a long, public postmortem on Albie.

"Yes, but it's in the Midwest."

"You easterners are myopic. You think the United States is all coasts, east and west, with some kind of cultural DMZ zone in between. Did you know that more national newspeople come from the Midwest than both coasts combined?"

"That's a strange little fact. Why do you think that's so?"

"Maybe we're less jaded. Maybe it's because the American dream is still alive and well in the open spaces."

"Dreams in the cornfields." He listened to the phrase. "No, it'll never sell in Peoria." He laughed lightly. "But all right, I'm convinced. You can take me to visit Chicago to see all the generations of achievers."

"I don't know about generations of achievers. Few of the achievers I know do much real parenting even if they physically have children. Maybe it's more fair to let those who have the time have the children—people like you and Lea."

"Whoa. I don't consider myself a nonachiever. That sounds pretty defensive."

"I'm sorry. I didn't mean to say you weren't an achiever, I meant the compulsive workaholic achievers, like me."

Marlena, you're rationalizing. You've always adored children. I'm surprised you don't have any."

"You're right. I'm rationalizing. I know I could juggle babies and nursemaids and the show. I did it in Wilkes-Barre with a lot less money. But I have this talent for relationships where if the man is right, the situation is wrong."

"Maybe you deliberately pick impossible situations to avoid commitment."

"No, I don't think so. I think I've wanted commitment, but I have a lot of stubborn and romantic Irish in my soul. It makes me think I can change situations or people. And I haven't always been fast at distinguishing between real possibilities and false hopes. It's a Gaelic disease called eternal optimism."

She took a sip of coffee, thinking she could call her past relationships with Tom and Albie "taking the cure."

"Yeah. I've been there. Hoping, in the face of fact, that things will get better, work themselves out somehow if I just hang in, being my own sweet self."

"If you really love someone, and you aren't good for each other, it can take more love, and certainly more strength,

to let go before you hurt each other so much you're left holding nothing but scars."

"Even if you don't love someone it can be hard to let go
if you don't have a new nest feathered and waiting."

"I guess men feel that way too," she thought aloud.

"The irony is that when you finally get up the courage
to end a bad relationship it's never as traumatic as the images
you've built in your mind. It's so anticlimactic that afterward
you beat yourself over the head for waiting too long."

She was getting the sense that Roger's marriage was less
than perfect. Her reaction was unsettling. Roger was still attractive, but she had little heart for the prospect of waiting for
Roger, or anyone else, to make it through a nasty divorce.

"Maybe the hardest part," he continued, "is recognizing
the inevitable." He picked up her hand to study her palm.

There was still a hint of chemistry between them, but
there was no point testing it without full freedom. Burned and
learned, she hoped. Besides, there was a two-year-old boy, another potential heartbreak like Toby.

"Relationships are like good news stories," she said as
she broke contact to reach for a cigarette. "You have to distin-
guish between what you think, or would like to think, and
what you know. Good reporters never assume anything."

She accepted a light from Roger, well aware that he was
acting like more than an old friend as he steadied her hand.

"Thanks." She inhaled and smiled at him. "Perceptions
are dangerous. I'm always twice as careful in covering anything I have strong feelings about. You can't help seeing things
in your own shadow."

"Or not seeing things because of it."

"Touché."

"Do you still really care about the issues involved in
your interviews and specials?"

"I hope so, but I also hope I never turn into a crusader

who gets so caught up in the crusade that she loses sight of the facts—and fairness."

"You do mostly consumer stuff and social issues, don't you? Ever cover political scandal?"

"Some." She exchanged her cigarette for her coffee cup. There was more than enough in Chicago to pass around the bureau." She laughed. "But by the time I got to Chicago I was doing a talk show and co-anchoring. It's easier on the nerves when you're just another pretty face."

"Balderdash! I love that word, don't you? I read about the Peabody you won for the network special you did out of Chicago a couple of years ago. Reporter, writer, co-producer. Not bad for a pretty face."

She smiled, appreciating the approval. She'd been proud of that special. It had taken long months to do the re-search and find the abused children who could or would talk about their feelings. That had been harder than finding abusers in or out of prison who would talk on camera. As one psychiatrist had explained to her, the abusers are trying to overcome feelings of rejection by adults. The camera gives them acceptance and recognition.

"Lena. Your eyes glazed for a moment. What were you thinking about?"

That special. It was very important to me."

"I'd love to see it sometime. You must have it on tape. I'm sorry I missed it. I was out of the country," he said, "but the reviews I read were terrific."

She questioned his sincerity, wondering if he even knew what the subject had been, then chided herself for getting jaded. "Sometimes I think I've seen and heard too much— even when I'm only sitting behind the desk, reading the day's news. Everything gets boiled down into a few brief minutes neatly packaged for twenty-one-inch color TVs that give bombings in Beirut a sameness with late-night war movies. We show ninety seconds of peoples' tragedies and go away. I can't help wondering if that doesn't mislead people into thinking the problems of the real world will always go away in a minute and a half."

"That's a heavy perspective."

"I think an informed public is important, but some things are too complicated to explain well that quickly."

Roger nodded. "Like my life."

"Maybe. Most TV news stories are a fast emotional injection. The message is fear, sympathy, outrage, anger, amusement, pleasure. There isn't time to digest much information."

"That's not bad. Emotions inspire action."

"Even if it's fleeting emotions, one right up against another?"

"Are you burning out on TV news?"

"Not a bit. Our network news has merit. Busy people can get a wide range of what's current and then read in depth about issues that pique their interest. I have the best of all worlds on my new show. I start with the in-depth interview on a serious subject, have a consumer-information segment, a five-minute news roundup, and finish with a celebrity guest, to end the evening the way I like best, upbeat with a smile."

"Amen." Roger grinned, lifting his wineglass. "I'll drink to that."

She raised her coffee cup to click it against the glass.

"And what happens after the show?"

"I usually grab a drink with one of my staff or a guest, depending on who's on the show. It takes me about an hour to unwind."

"Perfect. Then we'll have a drink afterward and I'll let you know if I think you picked the right career."

She laughed. Same old Roger. "Speaking of careers, you haven't said one word about yours. Do you still like the law?"

"Haven't been a lawyer in years," he said in a W. C. Fields voice. "Can't stand the things, myself."

"So what do you do?"

"What do I look like I do?"

"Hmm." She tilted her head, analyzing the good bones and long lashes above the laughing gray eyes. "You're a soap-opera idol."

"You're getting warmer. I don't have to worry about facts getting in the way of my tall tales anymore."

"I give up. What do you do to pay the rent?"

"Here's a clue. I don't pay my rent. It's paid by folks like Barnaby L. Brown, John Clancy Rutherford VII, Xavier Marshall, Victoria S. Queensberry . . ."

"Who are they?" She frowned. "They sound familiar, but . . . unreal."

"Ever hear of Roger Blough?"

"Of course. The mystery writer." She stopped cold. "Roger, are you that Roger?"

"That Roger and this Roger. Blough was Mother's maiden name. I wrote both Barnaby I and II while I was with the staid old law firm of Driscoll, Greene and Weinberg. I kind of expected Driscoll, the head of the firm, to laugh me out of the office when I announced I was quitting to write full-time. You could have bowled me over with a feather when he said he was a dedicated Roger Blough fan and he thought I was a better writer than I was a lawyer."

"You phony! You acted like *I* was the celebrity. You're famous. You've even done an American Express commercial, but I didn't recognize you. You should never have worn the fedora and trench coat."

That broke him up. "How quickly they forget," he said when he finally stopped laughing. "She didn't even remember my voice."

Marlena tried to think if she'd ever read any of his books. She'd almost bought Barnaby II when it was a best-seller. Almost.

"So." She grinned. "Here we are, fact and fiction."

"And how much of our lives is fact—and how much is fiction?"

"These days people use fiction to get at the facts." She explained when Roger frowned, "I'm thinking of the stings like Abscam."

"Ah yes, the old it-takes-a-thief-to-catch-a-thief routine." Roger winked.

Why did Albie keep resurfacing in her mind like a winter corpse floating to the surface after the spring thaw? Maybe it was Roger's smile, a little crooked and roguish. An Albie kind of smile. She refined the comparison. Like Albie's public smile, charismatic and self-aware.

Roger raised his left hand to his mouth to inhale his cigarette. His wedding ring winked at her, a tangible reminder that Roger was like Albie that way too.

Their silence was interrupted as the Oriental busboy moved next to Marlena and whispered, "I like your show every night." He glanced over his shoulder, hoping no one would see him violate the speak-when-spoken-to rule.

Her smile was reassuring. "Thank you very much. That's wonderful."

"You are wonderful." He flashed a smile and bobbed away as Manuel's head swiveled in their direction.

"That's my audience, Roger, the night people—busboys and waiters, cabbies and junkies, insomniacs and mothers with croupy babies." She spoke warmly.

"Sounds like you need a vacation from the vampire world."

"I like my vampires," she said.

"But picture this. A winter scene. Snug and cozy by the fire, looking out at a snowy beach, going out for a gourmet dinner at Maureen's in Victorian splendor."

"You won't stop, will you?"

"I'll never stop singing the praises of Cape May. It's like

Key West before the drug money moved in. When I'm in a
swinging mood I can buzz up to Atlantic City for clubbing and
action, and then drive home and step back a century."

Marlena still didn't mention she knew the town, from
the ice-cream parlors to the old-fashioned band shell where
American Legion bands played on Saturday nights.

"Have you gotten the image yet? It's still a town as well
as a resort. I'll take you there anytime you'd like to go."

"I'd like that, on one condition."

"Anything. Name it."

"You bring your wife along."

Roger barely covered his shock. "The articles about you
didn't say you were a Victorian."

"You're the Victorian if it's true that they were only concerned with the appearance of fidelity, not the reality."

He became strangely silent, then lifted his coffee cup to
toast. "To the Victorians in all their horsehair splendor. You
know, my grandmother had a horsehair settee. It was covered
in brocade and I couldn't see anything horsehair about it. I
remember thinking I'd learned the secrets of the universe
when Father explained the horsehair was inside.

"Then I demanded he cut it open so I could be sure he
was right and that it wasn't stuffed with goose feathers."

"I guess a person has to have some faith somewhere,"
Marlena said. "It'd be disaster to go around slitting every sofa
in the world."

"I'd think it wouldn't be necessary to slit them all, that
after awhile you'd learn by the seat of your pants to tell the
difference between goose feathers and horsehair."

Marlena shook her head. "Enough."

"Lena," Roger said with a grin, "how could we forget
about horse feathers?"

Obviously, he was referring to something she'd forgotten, but it couldn't be important. "Roger, please relax. My

poor brain can't take any more let's-remember games for a while. I still have to work tonight."

"Don't underrate your brain. It's one of the best I've met."

"It's not as smart as it used to think it was. It's especially bad at games, especially those with fuzzy rules."

She let her eyes fall and hold on his ring finger. "Good, honest, and open fun and games, yes. Games played in the dark, no." She didn't add "Not any more." She was ready to stand or fall on her own terms in present time.

Roger's eyes avoided her as he lit a cigarette deliberately and stared at himself in the mirror behind her.

She resisted the urge to turn and look at his reflection, to see if the image he was seeing was somehow different from her unreflected view of him. "Roger? What are you thinking about?"

"Games. You're right about games." He slipped off the wedding ring and laid it on the table between them. "I feel like a real shit."

She frowned at the gold circle, trying to read the puzzle. "Why? For feeling tempted? You should feel noble, not guilty," she spoke dramatically, trying to make him smile. "You resisted temptation. You can return to your wife with honor intact."

"If I had a wife."

The five syllables dropped like a bomb. She was speechless.

"If," he sighed, "but I don't, not since 1978."

Marlena's hand slapped down on the table as she leaned forward, the accusor. "Then why the ring? Why the big pretense? Is this some stupid game you dreamed up to get a reaction for one of your cheap thrillers?" She raged on, forcing herself to speak low, knowing a temper tantrum reported in the gossip columns wouldn't win her points with IBS.

Head hung low, Roger listened in silence.

"You're crazy, really crazy. I've met men who pretend to be single, but to pretend to be married and make a pass is psychotic." She picked up the gold circle lying between them on the white linen and threw it at him.

His reaction was quick. Making a neat catch, he slipped the ring into his shirt pocket and waited for her to calm down.

She avoided looking at him as she took out a cigarette. He held out his lighter as a peace offering. She used the candle to light the cigarette herself, not wanting to take another thing from him.

"Sorry, I didn't mean to go this far with it."

Take a deep breath, she ordered herself to relax as she leaned back against the padded banquette.

"Feel better?"

"No." Her eyes were ice. "I feel had, emotionally had." If the marriage he'd been discussing all day was fiction, then all the emotions she'd felt, the envy, regret, sympathy, warmth, became equally false. Then another horrible possibility hit her.

"Roger, how do I know you're telling the truth now? For all I know the divorce could be your wishful fiction and your marriage to Lea the fact."

"Will the story stand the test of time? Where is the fictional Lea Marley at this very moment?"

"No games, Roger, or I walk out this minute. What does that mean?"

He dropped the bantering tone. "My ex-wife's name is Jennifer. Lea was my flash of 'what-if,' my diminutive for Lena."

Her mind caught on the name Jennifer. "Jennifer? I thought that was the name of your daughter who died tragically."

His nod was chastened. "That scene took place in Barnaby II. It kind of fit with the story I was telling."

"Roger! Why?"

"I was testing to see if you'd read the book," he admitted.

"Why the whole charade to begin with?"

Despite herself, she didn't resist as he took her hand. She watched him unclench her fingers one by one as he spoke. "Maybe I was reversing the old Hindu adage, 'Only by acceptance of the past can you alter its meaning.' I simply turned it around: Only by altering the past can you accept its meaning."

"That's called running away. And running away doesn't work."

"But that's what you did. You ran away. Can you blame me for wondering what might have happened if we'd stayed together?"

She had run away. That was a truth she could accept. Not approve, but understand and accept. But Roger had played a nastier game. "My being young and awful twenty years ago doesn't make you less of a bastard right now." A laugh of dark humor bubbled up of its own volition. "Maybe I should have stayed, as a gesture of humanity, to save you from drowning in fiction."

"Then help me, before I go down for the last time."

"You want to know what I think would have happened if I hadn't taken the job in Wilkes-Barre?"

He nodded soberly.

"If my memory isn't failing me, we were both long on ideas, short on maturity, and not big on compromise. But you were stronger, surer. You'd have bullied me into going to law school and I'd have hated it. And you." She paused.

"And I thought you were the strong one. I didn't think I could get through law school without you. I needed you."

Surprise softened her sardonic anger. "You felt that way?" She considered the possibility. "But why the marriage charade?"

"If you were a man who still had a tender spot in his

heart for a famous woman who'd rejected you twenty years before and you got roped into calling her for lunch . . ."

"Roped? Who roped you?"

"I'll get to that."

"Explain it now."

"My ex-wife Jennifer knows we were an item in college. When Alison got interested in journalism Jennifer pressured me to get in touch with you to see if you could help."

"You asked me to lunch because your ex-wife pressured you." Marlena couldn't help laughing.

"I'm trying to be honest."

"I believe you. Nobody, not even you, could make that up."

"You'd rejected me before and I didn't want to give you the chance to reject me again. So I thought I'd play it safe. Call it protective coloration."

Marlena reddened.

Roger noticed and lifted her left hand. "Is this protection or is it real?"

"It's real," she laughed at herself. "I should know. I bought it in Chicago."

It was romantic, seen from another table, as Roger turned over Marlena's hand to expose her empty palm and planted a soft kiss. "I'm available to be a lot more than your escort. Honest."

"Honest! You don't even know how to spell the word."

"H-o-n-e-s-t. See, I can learn. There's hope for me." His look was a plea for pardon.

"I don't know. You've left me shell-shocked."

"Lena, you can't imagine how rotten I feel about getting carried away with my fantasy. And I'm not sure why I kept up with it. My own perverse ego, I guess. Maybe I wanted the force of irresistible attractions to make all barriers meaningless. Maybe I was just insecure."

The last two words finally had an honest ring to them. Maybe there was hope for Roger to grow up.

"I'm glad you resisted me this afternoon. I'm ready for a wife with old-fashioned principals."

"Not so fast, old friend." She retrieved her hand, pulled off the diamond, and dropped it in her purse. "Let's start clean." Then she remembered and took out the small, worn velvet box.

"My mother plagued me about that ring for years," Roger said as he flipped open the lid. "Guess it's come full circle."

She felt detached as she watched him slip it on her finger.

"Will you marry me, Marlena Williams, will you make me an honest man? Yesterday would not be too soon."

So romantic, so scripted, and so irritating. She pulled off the ring and put it back in the box. "Roger, take it back. I want to be able to say I finally had the guts to do the right thing and return it."

"All right. It'll give me time to have it cut down while I'm redeeming myself with you. Then you'll see that we can all fit perfectly."

"You're incorrigible."

"That's half my charm." He beamed. "But just answer one question. Can you see yourself even considering marrying me? The anchor and the author, not a bad combination. Do you need a second source at this point?"

"Maybe I have one, a figment of your imagination named Lea."

His chuckle was pleased. "I know she supports my case."

"She's only an example of why anyone, including me, should take some time to ferret out the whole truth where you're concerned." She glanced at her watch. "It's late. I've got to get to the studio."

"Call in sick. Half of New York is down with the flu."

"But I'm not." She slid from behind the table and waited for Roger to follow.

Roger smiled broadly at Manuel as they walked toward the door, stopped, took out a fifty dollar bill with a flourish, and tucked it in Manuel's pocket. "May you share our happiness," he said as he winked at Marlena.

The contrast with Albie's smooth and gracious palming of generous tips hit her hard, like a fighter unprepared. Not that she wanted Albie. But at that moment she hated him wherever he was, hated him for letting her suspect what whole might feel like. That made it tough to consider settling for half a happiness.

"M'lady." Roger gallantly held her fur.

Manuel hurried toward them, velvet box in hand. "Mr. Marley, I believe you forgot this."

"That's not mine, Manuel," Roger announced. "That belongs to the lady, my fiancée." Roger took the box and dropped it in her pocket.

"Roger!" she protested.

"I'm being premature," Roger confided to Manuel. "It hasn't been publicly announced."

Manuel smiled, unconcerned one way or the other. He was content and happy that Mr. Marley, ordinarily a two-dollar tipper, was so happy.

Marlena thought about decking Roger then and there, but he was already outside, holding the door for her.

"I know, I know," he said contritely as the door closed. "But I couldn't resist seeing how it sounded."

He looked at her angry face, then appeared to deflate and genuinely struggle for words. "Lena, please, don't write me off so easily. It's been a crazy day for me. Somehow seeing you again, facing all my mistakes . . . I got a little crazy."

"More than a little," she said, waiting for the upswing, which didn't come.

"What I'd like to do," he said, "is go home, clean up, then come to the studio to watch the show, if I'm still invited. Afterward, we'll have a quiet drink somewhere. I won't even try to get you alone. No pressure, no proposals, just some time to unwind. Then I'll take you home. How does that sound?"

Nice, if it worked out that way, she thought. She was emotionally exhausted, too tired to argue. Besides, fair was fair. She hadn't been completely candid all day herself. Maybe there could be a new start in the morning.

"Sure you can't call in sick?" Roger tagged as she stepped into a cab.

And maybe not, she sighed as the taxi drove south. She turned her head in time to see him giving her a high, wide wave, standing beside the big old clock.

Had time passed for him? Despite the difficulties he'd experienced, real or imagined, she wondered if he'd ever loved hard enough, if there was any chance for him to grow up.

"Hurry, please," she spoke to the cab driver.

"Running late, Miss Williams?"

"Not yet, but I could be if we hit traffic." She felt a surge of good energy; it was nice to meet a friendly viewer on the way to the show. She read the name on the cab license. Tonight she would talk to Sammy McAllister when she looked at the camera. She told him so, then regretted it as he ran three red lights so she wouldn't be too late.

Thirteen

❖

SHE HURRIED into the newsroom, brushing off snow as she headed for the coffeepot.

Cup in hand, she stuck her head in the office door of Evan Morrow, the producer. "Hi, all calm and bright?"

"Don't panic, Lena, but tonight we're shooting from the hip. The whole format's changed. We've built the show around the big drug busts today."

"Saw the headlines. I love it. 'The Pizza Parlor Connection.'" She stepped into his office and held out her hand. "Okay, let's see the new lineup and draft script. Looks like I got lucky."

"How so?"

"I played hooky. I asked Lennie to do the draft script for me today so I wouldn't have to come in at three."

"You're a tough lady," Evan joked. "Making poor Lennie do your work twice."

"I'd rather think of it as my lucky day."

Evan glanced at the clock. "Bet they want you in makeup."

331

"Not as much as I want them." She winked. "Even with luck, I need all the help I can get today."

Peter-John, the staff hairstylist, wagged his finger at her in mock despair. "Darling, whatever are we going to do with you? You're a disaster area. And we don't have time for a wash and set. I'll simply have to make do with the curling iron. The situation is desperate."

"Never desperate," she said, laughing. "Only critical, like my love life."

Eddie, the floor director, looked in, making sure Marlena was there on schedule. "What's critical about it?" he asked. "Yesterday you were complaining about a dry spell."

"Eddie, you're too nosy," scolded Peter-John. "What do you know about man trouble?"

"A lot. You think it's easy being a man?" Eddie quipped. "Guests should start arriving in half an hour, Lena," he tossed over his shoulder as he hurried off to complete his checks.

"Damn," she frowned. "I don't even know who the guests are going to be."

"So you'll have mystery guests," Peter-John shrugged, adding a touch of rouge to complete the rosy image he was creating for her. "You've got to get some sun, darling. You'd make my life so much easier if you'd get a little tan for me."

"Sun and sand sound wonderful," she agreed, "and if I manage to get there this winter, I'll be doing it just for you."

"Smartass." Peter-John chuckled. "But I love you anyway."

"Just the way I am?"

"No, just the way I make you. Look!" He turned her toward the mirror. "A miracle!"

Her curls fell softly, artfully framing her face. Gone were the dark circles, and her eyes sparkled, dusted with soft green powder.

"Farewell to the image of the poor little match girl who

straggled in here." He kissed the top of her head. "I'm such a genius."

"Better than that." She added a parting hug. "You're really worth more than a hundred dollars an hour."

"Tell that to the brass." He grinned as she ran out in the direction of the green room.

"Sorry, I'm running late," she breathed to Eddie, as she narrowly avoided crashing into him in the hall.

"At least you're running," he called after her. "One of your guests has arrived."

That stopped her, but only for a moment.

"He's waiting for you in the studio."

"Shit. I mean good. Eddie, I'm crunched. I haven't even looked at the lineup or the script yet. Could you show him the control room and get him settled for me? I'll owe you one."

"New romance?" asked Eddie, ever curious. "What happened to the dry spell?"

"Who knows," she shot back, "I don't have time to worry about it right now."

At the door to the green room the intern, Robin Morrow, niece of the producer, waited eagerly, the lineup and draft script in hand.

"Thanks, Robin." Marlena grabbed the papers and began to scan. "Robin." She looked up, pale. "Will Austin, our first guest, is he here?" Were all her old ghosts coming back to haunt her like a scene from *A Christmas Carol*?

"Not yet. He said he'd be a little late. Something about a basketball game and his daughter. He sounds real nice on the phone."

All the old ghosts seemed to come equipped with families.

"His life would make a great TV sitcom, Marlena. Imagine this. A divorcé with custody of four daughters, eight to fourteen, with an ex-wife who ran off with the pediatrician years ago." Robin didn't pause for breath as she lowered her voice dramatically.

"By day," Robin continued, too intent on the scenario to notice Marlena was fast losing patience, "he's the tough public prosecutor going out after the mob, ordering cops and detectives around. But at night he's a pussycat, bullied by his teen-aged daughters, who keep trying to fix him up with their teachers so he doesn't 'hover over them' as they put it."

"Robin," Marlena was seething. "Do you get the life history of everyone you talk to? You're not supposed to interrogate guests if they call in about schedules. You're supposed to take messages."

"Yes, Miss Williams," she said, chastened. "I got carried away."

"That's an understatement."

"I better tell you that I invented some of that. He doesn't have four daughters, just one thirteen-year-old and an eight-year-old son, and only for the holidays. And I don't know a thing about his ex-wife, except that she's 'ex.' I was just giving you an *imaginary* plot for a TV sitcom."

"Dammit, Robin," Marlena exploded. Courtesy of Roger, Marlena had more than reached her day's threshold for illusions.

"The first half of this show is a *news* show and we don't invent things about our guests," Marlena lectured, "not even as a joke. What if I'd asked Mr. Austin about his four daughters on the air?" Robin could be dangerous, she thought, especially tonight. She had enough problems with the real scenario.

"I'm sorry. I won't do it again."

"You'd better not. Meanwhile, just take messages. Period."

"Do famous anchors personally answer messages?" a male voice queried from behind.

Marlena swung around, fearing the best. "You're early!" The blue eyes hit her squarely.

Will held her eyes. "Right on time, but that's earlier than I'd said," He paused, smiling warmly. "Let me look at you. Yes, it is you, Lena."

Nervously, she cleared her throat. "Is that good or bad?"

"Good. Absolutely nothing but good."

"Robin," Marlena turned to the young lady frozen with interest beside them with a look that precluded comment. "Would you please get some coffee for me and Mr. Austin?" She looked at Will. "Just black," she added, half statement, half question.

Will nodded. "You remembered." The tone was pleased.

There was no point in avoiding the past, good or bad, "Coffee's the easy part. I also remember the stunt I pulled."

Will laughed easily. "I accepted that long ago as part of the game, and it was mild compared to what's been done to me since."

Accepted it that easily? It hardly seemed fair. As much as she'd wanted to see him again, she'd frozen at the thought, tied in knots by embarrassment. "Hmph. Well, I never did that to a source again. That one haunted me for years."

"Really?" Will looked at her, his smile rising in Fahrenheit degrees as he recognized her sincerity. "That's a shame." He paused, flashing through his images of those December weeks nearly fifteen years before. "A damn shame."

She nodded, sharing a smile of regret.

"Especially since I've been a good friend of the press for years. I learned the game has two sides. My staff calls me the promoter instead of prosecutor behind my back."

"I just discovered you were on the show when I walked in. Did you call us," she dimpled, "and bump our scheduled guest as the public promoter?"

He was amused. "I might have if I'd thought of it. But when I heard it was your show, I agreed to make it an exclusive."

"I'd have thought that would have inspired you to call NBC and offer them the exclusive."

"Why would you think that? You're the one that wouldn't return my calls, remember?"

"But I wrote you that long, agonizing letter. And I never heard a word . . ."

Will looked blank. "I never got a letter. If I . . ." He stopped upon Robin's approach.

"Here's the coffee, Miss Williams. Mr. Morganblum, the economist who's your last guest, is already here, with Eddie. And I took a message for you from William Morris. Mr. Fresca's running late."

"Did he say how late?"

"I didn't ask. I just took the message," Robin said piously.

Patience, Lena, she counseled herself. "Robin, take Mr. Austin into the studio so Eddie can show him the ropes while I say hello to Mr. Morganblum. Then call Bobby Fresca's manager back and find out exactly how late he'll be and tell your father. Then bring Mr. Austin back here so we can discuss the questions for the opening interview. Do you think you can remember all that?"

"Yes, Miss Williams."

Will smiled at Robin. "So you're Robin. We talked on the phone."

"Yes, sir." Robin fought for formality.

"Robin likes to talk," Marlena said dryly. "She probably gave you my life story."

"Not quite." Will's smile was all for Marlena. "I suspect she doesn't know everything."

Marlena felt the warmth rising in her face as Will's blue

gaze threatened the backs of her knees. She shook it off and laughed. "Go see Eddie. We have to get serious around here."

Across the room she saw the producer talking to a man who looked like a banker. It had to be Morganblum. She hoped he wouldn't be as dull and serious on camera as he looked in person.

There wasn't a lot of time to worry about it. She spent a few minutes with the man, revising the questions and trying to put him at ease.

Then Robin returned with Will and the news that the celebrity guest, comedian-singer Bobby Fresca, would be the last guest, rather than follow Will as originally scheduled.

"Hope it's not going to be one of those nights." She forced herself to concentrate as she quickly ran through the interview format with Will, discussing the suggested questions and adding a few new ones. She wanted to do a solid interview, in part to prove to him that she'd become a real professional. The thought that Roger was in the studio was also on her mind. She wanted to impress him, too, but she wasn't sure how.

Then they were on the air.

"Tonight, we've been fortunate enough to arrange an exclusive interview with William Austin, U.S. Attorney for New York, who's in charge of the case that headlined today's papers, the case that's being called the 'Pizza Parlor Connection.'"

She thanked Will for coming on such short notice and noted that they'd both started out in Philadelphia at the same time.

"Too many years ago to count," Will answered easily. "On some of us, like you, it doesn't show," he added graciously.

She slid by the compliment and quickly dug into the meat of the interview.

"Do you think these arrests will have a real impact on mob activities? As I understand, the crime family organizations are like worms; you chop off the head and the tails take over."

Will smiled at the comparison. "That was true in the old days, before we had sophisticated surveillance techniques. Now we're looking at rounding up whole networks on both sides of the Atlantic and shutting down the illegal activities as well as the men who run them."

"How's that different?"

"Since the days of Capone and Luciano, the Justice Department has known who headed the crime families, but they couldn't get proof that would hold up in court.

"But didn't Dewey send Luciano and others to jail back in the late thirties and early forties?"

"Not for running organized crime. Until recently, prosecutors could only get crime family leaders on other charges, like mail fraud and tax evasion. That way, they would go to jail for a while, but it wouldn't shut down the operation. Your worm theory."

"And those white-collar crime convictions would give them sentences in minimum-security facilities, the so-called country club prisons?"

Will nodded, adding dryly, "Which explains why Allenwood Federal Correctional Institution has a boccie ball court."

She smiled to show she'd appreciated the joke and waited half a beat to ask the follow-up question. "And you think it's different now, that despite high-priced attorneys, these pizza-parlor drug-runners won't end up in country club prisons?"

"We're talking a new ball game. Murder and extortion, and peddling hard drugs. That spells hard time."

"Hard time means maximum-security facilities?"

"The Leavenworths rather than the Allenwoods." Will nodded. "There's another factor that's changed. In the old days the crime families controlled the prisons. If somebody didn't talk and went to jail, he knew he'd be taken care of inside."

"How's that changed?"

"First the wardens and staffs are more professional. Fewer take bribes and, more important, the blacks now control the jails on the inside and they don't give a . . . hoot . . . about family codes. These days the second or third offenders facing hard time are doing handstands to turn state's evidence rather than face cellblocks controlled by the blacks."

"You're saying hard time has gotten harder?" Quickly, she glanced down to see where they were going next. She'd gotten too absorbed in Will's answer. *The new generation,* her note read. She tried to think of a good transition to that question as Will gave his first short answer.

"A lot harder."

She had no choice but to ask the next question abruptly. "What about the present generation of the old families, Gambino, Lucchese, Genovese, Profacio . . ."

"That's another problem for the families. We're talking about second-or third-generation Americans. And the ones who've inherited the ambition and brains of their fathers and grandfathers who created the family organizations aren't staying in. They're going to good schools and getting their MBAs. The ones smart enough to run an underworld organization are also smart enough to get out and make it legally in the real world."

"Your description makes it sound like the mob should be falling apart, but obviously it isn't. Why not?"

"Sicily. A new breed from Sicily, but just as hungry and greedy as Capone or Luciano were in the thirties. They've carved deals with the old guard here, but they've sent their own people over from Sicily to run it."

"The nice young men with Italian accents who work in the pizza parlors?"

"They aren't all so nice, but I don't want you or your viewers to panic. Not every pizza parlor in the country is a front for drug operations. Most of them are exactly what they seem, nice, neighborhood fast-food places."

"That's a relief."

"Pizza parlors aren't the only covers used. They just happen to be involved in this big case."

"What other businesses do they use?"

"I'll let you know *after* all the arrests are made."

Marlena smiled, trying not to wonder if he was thinking about the time he hadn't waited to give her inside information. If so, he didn't show any signs of bearing a grudge.

"Isn't it dangerous going after the mob? Don't you ever get nervous that they might come after you?"

"I'm hoping they've learned a lesson from what happened in Italy not long ago, when they shot down an honest chief advocate who was making serious inroads against family operations."

"What happened?" Although she knew, they'd agreed she'd ask the question that way, to break up the answer.

"For the first time Italian law enforcement is working with us closely, cooperating fully, sharing files, making deals for extradition."

"Will you be extradicting anyone from Sicily to testify on the Pizza Parlor Connection?"

"We already have a tight case, but it looks like we're going to get the godfather, Bonalucci, and a young turk named Tony Cadonne brought over to testify, which will make it airtight."

Marlena swallowed her surprise, trying to frame her

next question. From the corner of her eye she saw the floor
director waving furiously, signaling for a commercial break.

She smiled into the camera. "We'll be back in a minute
to hear more about the war on the mob from U.S. Chief Prosecutor Will Austin."

She relaxed, looking at Will. "Very nice, counselor."

"The butterflies don't show?"

"No time for butterflies on camera. I save mine for before and after," she said quickly, looking at her notes. "Okay to
talk about wiretaps next?"

"You're the boss."

She glanced at the small studio audience. Roger caught
her eye, grinned, and blew her a kiss. She smiled and quickly
looked back at Will, hoping he hadn't noticed. Then Eddie
started the countdown and Marlena positioned herself again.

"Will," she said rapidly, "cheat your head a little more
toward the camera when you talk. Don't look directly at me."

"But I like looking directly at you."

"Shh. Ten seconds," she said. The blush added a flattering color to her face as she welcomed the viewers back.

"Earlier you mentioned modern surveillance equipment. How important is it in going after the mob?"

"It's the difference between suspecting and knowing.
Plus, with proper court orders for wiretaps and careful pro-
cedures on the investigation, it's admissable in court. There's
poetic justice in a man being damned by his own words."

"And with the tapes they can't plead the fifth amend-
ment?"

"It's like having your own witness in the room."

"Impressive."

"Some of it gets pretty funny. For instance, we have
tapes of phone conversations where they're pretty sure they're
being bugged. So what do they do? They whisper." Will dra-
matized in a hoarse stage whisper. "'Hey, Lena, we gotta be

real careful. I think this line's bugged.' They act as if a tape recorder can't pick up a whisper."

"But you can't convict people for being dumb."

"Depends on how dumb. Here's another one. They use code words for drugs. A kilo of marijuana is a refrigerator. An ounce of heroin is a shirt. So, on the phone, they'll say they're placing an order for half a refrigerator or three and a half shirts. Imagine trying to convince a jury your client's an ordinary appliance or shirt salesman."

Her memory was absolutely right, Marlena decided. Will did have the bluest eyes she'd ever seen. Absolutely true blue. Marlena almost missed seeing Eddie's hand rolling in the air, signaling her to speed it up. She recovered quickly. "How soon do you estimate this case will go to trial?"

"A couple of months. It depends whether or not the judge will agree to a delay for us to arrange the extraditions."

"Will there be more arrests?"

Will glanced left for a second, distracted as Eddie's wave became more frantic. "I hope so," he said quickly, getting Eddie's message.

"Well, I wish you luck with your present and future cases. Thank you for joining us tonight." She turned from Will, full face to the camera. "We'll be right back with investment counselor Dr. Irwin R. Morganblum with some year-end tax tips."

"Marlena, don't do that to me." Eddie wiped sweat from his forehead as he walked toward them to take Will's mike and give it to Dr. Morganblum.

"But we got out in time?"

Eddie nodded. "God knows how."

"Mind if I stay and watch the rest of the show?" Will asked. "Maybe we could grab a drink after? Tomorrow's Saturday, you know."

"I'd love it," Marlena said quickly, aware of the time

clock. Then she realized she'd forgotten about Roger for a second. "Oh, Will," she began.

"Don't mean to rush you, Mr. Austin," Eddie interrupted as he clipped the lavaliere mike on Morganblum's tie, "but we're live in thirty seconds. You can sit anywhere." He glanced toward Roger, who was smiling at Marlena. "Here's good." Eddie indicated a seat right out of camera range, putting Will's back to Roger.

As Will quickly sat, Eddie leaned close to Marlena for a quick mike check. "What's with the men?" he mouthed.

Then Eddie shouted "Fifteen seconds" as he backed away.

Marlena answered with a shrug. How was she supposed to answer that in the middle of the show?

Usually, in live television, time seems to fly by. Tonight, in this second segment, it dragged. She kept resisting the urge to stare at the side of the set where Will and Roger sat off camera, ten feet apart. She knew she wasn't doing her best job of turning a dull subject and guest into a sparkling interview for her TV audience. It was tough to care at the moment.

"Mr. Morganblatt," she asked, after he'd finished a dreary recommended checklist for end-of-the-year tax planning, "would you recommend tax-free municipals for middle-income people after retirement?"

Mr. Morgan*blum,* the investment expert, answered unhappily, his ego wounded.

Realizing her faux pas, she gave Eddie a self-depracating grimace while the camera focused on Morganblum's charts. She forced herself to focus on the interview. She breathed a prayer of thanks when it was over and her next guest, the well-known Vegas headliner, Bobby Fresca, came on.

They'd had Bobby on the show before, and he was a

funny, easy interview. Besides, he was scheduled to sing. She could relax while he sang.

"I don't know if it's safe to plug the show I'm rehearsing or not. The U.S. Attorney hasn't gone home yet, has he? Before we mention my new show, I just want to go on record as saying I have not sent out for pizza once during rehearsals."

It was suddenly obvious to Marlena why Bobby had been booked on the show that night. She looked into the camera.

"Bobby's talking about his starring role in the Broadway revival of *Guys and Dolls* that officially opens Christmas Eve." She looked back at Bobby. "You're playing the lead, right?"

"The romantic lead, no less." He beamed. "Guy Masterson, a combination of Bat Masterson and a wise guy. It's a great role. I'm having a lot of fun with it. I get to wear black shirts and white ties."

"White shoes and a black hat?"

"Bad guys can be fun . . . on stage. Right, Mr. Prosecutor?"

Looking at the monitor, Marlena saw Will nod with a gracious smile as Evan Morrow, in the control room, took the shot from the B camera turned on Will. Obviously Morrow liked Bobby's shtick.

Marlena laughed. "Revivals are big these days. Is it the economic factor?"

"It costs double-digit millions to stage a Broadway musical today. That's why producers are bringing back things that have worked before."

"It's a comeback to New York for you, too, isn't it?"

"Like I said, the producers want to bring back things that have worked before." He laughed. "Yeah, after the big Broadway hit I did in the late sixties, I caught the gravy train to Vegas and Hollywood."

"What brought you back?"

"My mother. My mother made me do it."

"Your mother?"

"Yeah. She told me she was embarrassed by having a son who couldn't hold down a steady job. So now I'm working six days a week instead of six weeks a year, at ten percent of the money and one hundred ten percent of the work. Anything to keep my mother happy."

Marlena laughed easily. Bobby made it fun. She let him take over the conversation and fed him straight lines. They both enjoyed it.

"All right, lady," Bobby jumped up when they returned from the commercial break. "Do you want to hear me sing or do you want to hear me sing?"

"Both. A song from the show?"

"I've gotta rehearse somewhere," he grinned, perching on the corner of her desk. "Here's a sleeper, one of my favorites that never made it as a hit. I don't get to do it in the show, so I'm going to do it for you."

With that, he picked up the hand mike while the five piece orchestra that had come with Bobby started playing the lead-in for "More I Cannot Wish You."

Bobby stayed sitting on the desk, like a Vegas stool, singing the song half to Marlena and half to the camera.

He's better than good, Marlena thought, as she found herself listening to the lyrics. Bobby ranked right up there with Sinatra when it came to phrasing. He sang the song like he really meant it. And the lyrics hit so close enough to home as to be disconcerting.

"Wonderful!" she said as he leaned down and kissed the tip of her nose. "I want to hear more."

"I knew you would. That's why we prepared another song. This one I do sing in the show." He hopped down from the desk as the band played up tempo, struck an angular pose, and started snapping his fingers as he sang "Luck, Be a Lady" directly for the camera to finish the show on an up-beat note. As she watched, Marlena silently echoed the sentiment.

Eddie raised his right hand to give them a big okay sign as the song ended, then raised two fingers on his left hand, signaling two minutes.

Marlena thanked Bobby and promised to attend the opening-night performance and bring her whole family from Des Moines. Then she wrapped up the show and quickly promo-ed the guests for Monday.

She stood and talked with Bobby, mikes off, while the credits rolled over the shot of the set.

While looking at Bobby for the benefit of the camera, she smiled and spoke to Eddie, just out of camera range. "Sorry about the Morgan*blatt*, Eddie."

"So was Morganblum. He didn't stick around to see the rest of the show." Eddie motioned to Will, waving him to come back on the set. "Shake hands and smile while the credits roll."

Bobby laughed. "I wouldn't worry about Morganblatt. The part of his interview I watched backstage was so dull I almost booked a flight to Havana rather than stick around to do the show."

Bobby continued, for Will's benefit as well as Marlena's, "Then I remembered. They don't run red-eyes to Havana like they did when I lived here before. Some guy with an Italian-sounding name took over from the families. Castro, that was the guy." Bobbie winked at Will. "Is he connected?"

"I'd have to check my files. I've heard of him some-where before," Will parried.

"Yeah, well, let me know."

"Ten seconds," Eddie called as Roger decided to join the on-camera farewell.

Eddie, looking at his watch, didn't notice. Marlena did, but it was too late to do anything about it as Roger pumped Bobby Fresca's hand, complimenting him on his performance.

"And to black," Eddie announced. "Party's over, folks. Time for beddie-by." He walked on the set. "When it rains it pours," he muttered to Marlena. She glared at him.

Will stepped close and took her hand. "Ready for that drink and maybe a little peanut butter and jelly? Or have your tastes changed?"

"Not where it counts." The firm feel of his hand was good as she returned the squeeze, suddenly remembering Roger.

Before she could figure out a good way to handle the situation, Roger was beside them.

"Ready, darling?"

A disappointed Will dropped her hand.

"You do a mean interview, Austin," Roger said. "I'd love to get my hands on the transcripts to use in one of my books."

She couldn't avoid the introduction. "Will Austin, Roger Marley."

"That's Roger Blough to the reading public," Roger added.

"Yes." Will forced his face to brighten. "I've read some of your books. I like the way your plots twist around, but I'd hate to have to prosecute any of your cases."

"After tonight I'm a fan of yours too," Roger said. "I take it you two know each other from Philadelphia."

"Everyone has to start somewhere," Will quipped.

Roger put his arm around Marlena and smiled. "We'll have to have you over for dinner soon. It was great meeting you, but we've got to run. I've a car waiting for us outside." Firmly, hand on her back, he guided Marlena out of the studio.

"But . . ." Marlena didn't have time to object without creating a major scene.

"Tell you what, Mr. Prosecutor." She could hear Bobby's deep voice follow them from the set. "I'll buy you a drink and you can tell me about the real mob. Maybe you can give me some tips for my role."

The sound of Will's voice faded as they reached the elevator.

"I have to go back for my coat." Marlena turned.

"I have it with me. I thought ahead and asked Robin."

"You really like to take over, don't you? I noticed that little number where you walked on the set."

"I knew it wouldn't matter with only ten seconds left." He grinned. "I'd told my friends to watch tonight."

Her anger rose as the elevator dropped. Roger certainly had shut off the evening's options arbitrarily. She thought about how much fun it would have been to have drinks with Will and Bobby. She liked to relax after the show, share a few laughs.

"And another thing. What was with the *'we* must have you over for dinner'?"

"I want you all to myself for a while," Roger said.

"At this point I'm so tired, I think I'd prefer a ride home, a quick walk for Gerda, and a good night's sleep."

"Then I'm at your service, m'lady. Your car awaits."

Car was an understatement. Waiting in front of the studio lobby was a sleek black limousine with a license plate that read BARNABY I. She couldn't help being amused, but she still debated on calling it a night and taking a cab home. Fatigue and confusion were crowding her mind.

Her debate ended as a lanky young man leaped from the limousine, grinning broadly. "You must be Marlena." He hurried toward her. His whiskey vapors reached her first.

She amended the adjective "young." Up close he looked and smelled like a runaway from a twenty-five-year Princeton reunion.

"Just call me Claude." He stuck out his hand. "I'm driving for Roger tonight." He opened the door for her. "I'm a sculptor who Roger rescued from artistic starvation in Soho."

Once a rich liberal, always a rich liberal, Marlena thought as she remembered their Columbia days, when Roger had promoted and subsidized artist classmates who had more hope than talent.

Roger's enthusiasm and ability to buy the booze and bail them out when landlords got impatient had made him the student patron of the arts. A nice ego kick, then and now, it seemed.

Claude drove uptown and east with the precision of a man aware that his blood level wouldn't pass the test. "You should see my stuff." Claude spoke louder than necessary. "Hey, maybe I could design something for the set of your TV show."

She hated being promoted. She felt a headache coming on.

As Claude eased to a stop beside a substantial 1920s' vintage brownstone, Marlena realized she didn't know what street they were on. The number was 417, somewhere in the east eighties, she guessed. "Where are we?" She could hear the jazz pouring from the house.

"Home sweet home," Roger replied, leading the way through wrought-iron gates and a well-manicured garden to the unlocked door. Inside, a cast of dozens was making merry.

Roger hollered from the doorway to a colorful group of arty-looking people, "Hello! Here she is, everyone, my beautiful Marlena!"

All she could do was turn 180 degrees to leave.

Roger caught up with her in the garden. "Lena, what's wrong? This party's for you."

"Oh, Roger, why?"

In the shadow of the garden Roger couldn't read her angry eyes. "You should see what the streetlight does to your hair. You're so beautiful."

"Roger, it's been a long day. I'm simply not up to all the people."

"Come on inside and let me share you with my friends just for a few minutes. Then I'll kick them out. I promise. A quick introduction and they're gone."

"I'm sorry, Roger, but I can't."

His voice turned petulant. "You have to. I woke up all my friends and bullied them into coming over to celebrate our reunion."

"Roger, while Bobby was on the set tonight, he said something about Broadway revivals that made me think. They're only bringing back shows that have worked before. It makes sense. It also makes sense not to revive things that didn't play well the first time."

"Shit, Lena, that only proves my point. We were in love before and can be again."

"Oh, Roger, I'm sorry. I'm sorry you see it that way." Quickly, she remembered what she still hadn't done. She opened her purse and pulled out the velvet box and handed him the ring for a final time. "I should have given this back earlier."

"You can't do that, not like this. You owe me more than that."

For so many years she had felt guilty because she had never explained things to Roger. The guilt disappeared. Roger was incapable of seeing any perspective other than his own. "You're quite a person, Roger. I'd like you to be happy, but I'm not the one who can make that happen for you."

"Now I know why you're called the ice princess," he lashed out. "The original Miss Fridgedaire, the worst kind of tease."

It felt good to have him angry with her and know he couldn't make her feel guilty anymore. Maybe the day hadn't been wasted. "Good-bye, Roger." She turned to leave.

"If you walk away like this, it's the end."

She almost laughed. It was impossible for him to accept rejection. He had to turn it around. Some egos never changed.

"Lena, call me when you get home and we'll talk."

She kept walking, without reply. Grateful for the open gates, she left quickly, not looking back. She pictured Roger walking back inside with a "You aren't going to believe this, folks, but . . ." She had confidence in his inventive mind. The story was sure to be dramatic. In a way she'd handed him a consolation prize, a good story for cocktail parties.

Without an adrenaline charge from either love or hate to warm her, she shivered in the cold December morning, walking west. She reached Second Avenue and saw the sign saying 89th Street. And not a cab in sight. She laughed out loud. Fifteen minutes ago she'd had two men vying to be at her beck and call. In a way, she'd walked out on both of them.

Did people freeze to death from stupidity, alone with frozen feet and unyielding independence, out in the cold, thirty blocks from their apartments?

Trudge, trudge. Oh what a glamorous life.

A cab sped past as she reached the corner of Lexington Avenue. By the time she screamed "Cab!" it was a block away. Others mocked her with their OFF DUTY and RADIO CALL signs.

The bars were closed and it was too cold to stand on the corner like a rejected hooker. She took a deep, cold breath and headed for Madison Avenue.

There was more traffic on Madison. That was encouraging, but the stream of bread trucks and unmarked vans was not. A battered yellow van slowed as it approached her. The young Latino driver flashed white teeth and honked, offering a ride.

She turned her back to signal "no sale" and spied a phone booth on the corner. She could call for a news courier, but she'd get teased for months—with or without explaining. Was the rescue worth the embarrassment? Normal people didn't get caught like this. Normal people had husbands or lovers to play the white knight on snowy, white nights.

Inside the phone booth she paused, trying to think rationally. If she had her druthers, she'd call Will, but Will was probably still out drinking with Bobby and the band.

Maybe she'd been rash to walk away from Roger in a huff. It wouldn't kill her just to say hello to his friends for a minute, then insist he have Claude drive her home. But she'd have to call and apologize first.

Outside the phone booth a patrol car slowed down at the corner and stopped for a red light. Marlena didn't notice as she dug among the keys and lipstick and scraps of paper in the bottom of her purse, looking for loose change.

A young black patrolman got out to remove a broken bottle from the street.

Inside the telephone booth Marlena spilled her purse and burst into tears of frustration as she knelt to feel for coins like a blind woman.

Outside, the patrolman picked up the jagged pieces of glass, inspecting carefully to be certain he'd gotten them all. Then, as he walked back to the trash beside the phone booth, he noticed Marlena talking on the phone, tears glistening on her cheeks. He stopped, concerned, watching as she hung up the phone and leaned her head against the cold glass.

"Miss? Miss?" He rapped sharply on the glass.

Marlena swung around, startled. With relief, she identified the rapper as a policeman.

"Are you all right?" he called.

"Yes," she sniffed, emerging onto the sidewalk. "I'm fine, now. My . . . my husband will be here to get me soon." The spontaneous white lie made her feel more respectable for the moment.

"You seem upset," he said uncertainly.

"I was working the late sh . . ." She bit off *show* and substituted *shift*, not wanting to explain. "I got upset when I couldn't find a cab, but I'm okay now."

"It's quiet tonight. Not much happening. I can wait with you if you'd like."

"I'd appreciate that."

Two cabs, empty and available, chased each other down Madison Avenue. "It figures." She chuckled, her spirits reviving.

"What figures, ma'am?" The patrolman was young and polite.

"It figures there'd be cabs after I'd broken down and hollered for help. I'm not supposed to do that. I'm supposed to be a strong, liberated woman."

"Yeah? That's not liberation. Liberation's when you're strong enough to call a spade a spade." His grin was wide and streetwise. "You're in a jam? You call your man. That's liberation."

"Officer Cady." She read his name below his badge. "You're a philosopher."

"I'm a cop who knows these streets aren't safe at night. Next time you're working late, call a radio cab and wait inside until it comes. I don't like people hurt on my beat. Blood ruins my evening." He checked his watch. "How far are you going?"

"Sixty-first and the Park."

His look turned scrutinizing. It was nice to know there were curious, concerned young cops around in the dead of night.

"If your 'husband' isn't here in five minutes, my partner and I can drop you off on the way to our coffee break."

Marlena didn't like the way he said "husband." Obviously Cady had put two and two together and gotten five.

"Thanks, but . . ." She started to segue into an explanation that would allow her to reveal she was a TV personality, but she lost the chance.

Cady's head swung around as a cab squealed toward them in a mighty U-turn.

"I don't believe my eyes." Cady's eyes were wide. "Right in front of a police car." He marched toward the cab, waving the driver to get out. "All right, buddy, let's see your license."

The passenger door burst open. "Officer, I ordered the driver to do that." He pulled out credentials. "Will Austin. U.S. Attorney, southern district of New York. It's an emergency situation."

Cady stopped short, looked at the credentials, and then looked from Will to Marlena, standing by his side.

Will put an arm around Marlena protectively, "You okay?"

"Now I am," she murmured.

Cady grinned. "Mr. Austin. Next time tell your wife to let New York's finest know who she is. We can call you on the police radio and we'll be happy to drive her home."

Will looked at Marlena, startled. She grinned sheepishly.

"It's okay, buddy," Cady said to the cabby, waiting nervously behind the wheel. "You're free to go."

The driver, whose English was a lot newer than the cab, took the phrase "free to go" as an instruction and pulled out quickly.

"Shit," Cady said. "That's not quite what I meant."

"It's been one of those nights all night long," Marlena said wryly.

"Mr. Austin, I'll be happy to drive you and Mrs. Austin home."

"Thanks, officer, but I don't like to abuse privilege." Hatless, wearing a navy sports jacket turning tweed with snowflakes, he managed to look completely at ease as he squeezed Marlena's shoulders. "The emergency's over."

"It's up to you, sir."

"But Will . . ." Marlena started to object, then caught the look on Will's face.

"Thanks just the same," Will said easily.

"I don't understand," Marlena said as Cady pulled away in the squad car. "Why didn't you accept the ride?"

"I was avoiding embarrassment for both of us, not being sure where 'home' was, *Mrs.* Austin." His blue eyes were shadowed, puzzled. "What kind of game is it now, Lena?"

At the sound of the word *game* she burst into tears, letting loose all the frustration and recollection that she'd held back all day.

"Hey . . ." Will pulled her close, comforting, holding, trying to calm her.

She held tighter, wanting to pull in strength from him.

"Lena, come on." He tried to think of something to say that would stop the flow. "A big strong TV woman like you shouldn't cry in the street," he said with his head bent close to her ear. "You'll ruin your image."

She raised her face to his, gulping, blinking against the threat of more tears. She hadn't let herself cry for so long, it was hard to stop. She looked into his eyes as her own focused, so honestly concerned, truly puzzled, nothing hidden.

"I'm sorry," he said softly. "I didn't mean to push the wrong button. But can you understand that the cop's statement startled me? I still don't understand."

"It was a white lie," she sniffed. "I felt totally disreputable standing on the corner. I didn't want the cop to think I was a streetwalker, so I said I was waiting for my husband. I didn't use your name. All I said was husband."

Will's laugh was easy. The sequence made sense to him. He pulled out his handkerchief to wipe her tears. "But it's funny, not sad. Why the tears?"

"You're going to ruin your handkerchief," she warned him. "I didn't take time to clean off the TV makeup."

He ignored her warning, continuing to carefully remove the smudges, doing it firmly and well, like a practiced parent. "You haven't answered my question."

"I'd spent the afternoon with the famous Mr. Blough, who'd played nothing but mind games, one lie after the other. And somehow when you accused me of playing a game, as though that's how you remembered me . . ." Her voice choked.

"I wasn't referring to any games of the past. I was talking strictly about tonight. First it felt like old times, only better, especially when you agreed to drinks after the show. Then you do an about-face and disappear with that self-appointed Rudyard Kipling. The next thing I know is you call for help, promising to explain when I arrive, and when I get here I discover that the cop thinks you're Mrs. Austin."

Her lips smiled of their own volition. Put that way, it sounded terrible.

"Now how would you read that if you were me? What would've been the first words out of your mouth."

"Next stop, Bellevue, maybe." She laughed, feeling safe as the threatening clouds rose higher, beginning to blow past. "But you see that it was an honest misunderstanding, don't you?"

"Not candid, but honest?" He shook his head. "Lena, there's a lot I'd like you to explain to me, but first I have to deliver on what I promised—a rescue from the lonely corner of Eighty-ninth and Madison."

He scanned Madison Avenue for an empty cab. "Hope one shows up soon. Life's tough for us white knights these days. Just not enough steeds to go around."

The snow began again, lightly, sparkling the night and dusting Will's navy ski jacket. "I'm prepared." He glanced at the sky and put his arm around her. "Cold?"

"I'm fine." Her smile meant it.

"While we're waiting, do you want to tell me how you landed up on this corner alone at three in the morning?"

"Do you want the long version or a one-liner?"

"I assume this Roger fellow was the game player you referred to, the one you spent all afternoon with."

She nodded. "It's not like it sounds."

"I'll grant that possibility," he said sincerely, "but I want to know what happened after you let him whisk you away."

"It was awful, wasn't it?"

"I thought so, but you went along with it . . . with him," Will clarified.

"It's not that simple."

"And probably not that complicated. Bet you can give it to me in two minutes and twenty seconds."

Her face lightened. "I'll take the bet. Start clocking me." She paused, mentally editing. "Take one," she began. "Roger Marley, an old college boyfriend of IBS's Marlena Williams, appeared at noon today for the first time in twenty years. Unfortunately, Mr. Marley remains as rich, spoiled, and delusional as he was known to have been in the 1960s.

"After bull-shitting Miss Williams at both lunch and dinner, Marley, alias Blough, attended the live broadcast of her night-owl show. Immediately following the broadcast, he railroaded Miss Williams away from her heart's desire, promising her a ride home. He took Williams, under protest, to his Upper East Side home where a middle-aged version of a fraternity bash was already in swing.

"Miss Williams, having retained her sanity against great odds, got the hell out of there." She paused, smiling into the blue eyes of her audience, and tagged "and called the first man she thought of . . . and hadn't stopped thinking of since another December a long, long time ago."

Will was silent as he took a deep breath and put his hands in his pockets. Marlena picked up her imaginary microphone again to tag the story. "This is Marlena Williams, IBS, New Y . . . oops, sorry. I have a cleaner closer. Tag, take two.

Take Two: This is Lena Williams, stranded on Madison Avenue, New York."

"Not true." Will closed the distance between them and took both her hands in his to warm them. "You're not stranded."

"It is true," she protested. "We're both stranded."

He didn't back off as she looked at him, letting the full force of his blue eyes set off the old, unforgotten trembling, reaching from her mind to the back of her knees and returning to him with double the impact.

He watched a snowflake catch in her eyelash and fought off an urge to melt it with a kiss. He wanted to hear the rest of the story. "So you called for a ride home or a drink or what?"

She swallowed hard. If she didn't keep talking, she'd turn into a complete fool and put her arms around him right then and there. "I called because I had to try, even though I was sure you'd be unlisted. And after I got the number I was sure you wouldn't answer, that you would still be out with Bobby."

"There's nothing like a sure thing." He grinned and succumbed to the urge to kiss away the snowflake before he stepped closer to kiss her properly.

All Marlena's old images that Will had written her off forever melted away. She felt his hand lift her chin so she could share his smile. "I didn't want to have a drink alone with Bobby. I wanted to have a drink with you."

"I wanted that too." She looked into his clear eyes and knew he believed her. "It's all . . ."

"Hold on!" he interrupted, lifting his arm to flag down an approaching cab. "One rescue coming up!"

He held the cab door open for her and slid in beside her. "Where do we go from here? It's your choice. The Brasserie? The all-night diner on Eighth Avenue?" He cleared his throat, trying to sound casual. "Even the old 'your place or mine?' You name it."

"What's the address?" grumbled the cab driver. "I don't have all day."

"But we do." He looked at Marlena for confirmation.

She nodded, relaxed for the first time since noon, happier than she'd been for a much longer time than that.

"Just turn on the meter while we decide," Will said.

"It'll cost you double," the driver announced.

"That's all right." He returned his full focus to Lena. "The woman's worth it."

She smiled and reached for his hand. "I like you."

"I'll bet we can do better than that."

She blushed freely, letting the blood flow. It felt good not to wonder if she should hold back or be afraid that she, or he, was moving too fast. She took his hand and held on. "They say it's like riding a bike."

Will's own face flushed with a warm happiness. "All right, ladies and gentlemen, we must come to a decision here. What's it to be? Steak *au poivre* or peanut butter and jelly?"

"Will, you're not going to believe this, but . . ."

"Tonight I'll believe anything. Go ahead."

"First we have to walk the dog."